BY HER SWORD

Aoibh Wood ~ Jules Revel
Rose Goodwin ~ Erin Branch ~ Gwenhyver
Cassidy Percoco ~ Selina Rossman ~ Erin Casey
Susanne Salehi ~ Alyssa Jensen
Evelyn Shine ~ Anna Burke

Ishin-denshin x Yōkai
以心伝心 x 妖怪
Aoibh Wood

(Japanese Translations: Geo Kinebuchi)

NOTE: This story contains passages in native Japanese. Please know that this is an intentional choice, and you are not expected to understand these sections. The inclusion of Japanese is meant to create an immersive experience, allowing you to share in Yasmin's sense of being truly alone in an alien land. We hope this enhances your connection to her journey and deepens your understanding of her feelings.

YASMIN COULDN'T DENY THE NATURAL SPLENDOR OF this place. Tall peaks wedged high into the clouds surrounded by forested ridges with winding rivers and streams snaking between, down through rugged valleys, but —blessed be Allah—it was freezing here. She stamped her feet to help her circulation as she scanned the path ahead.

She tucked a stray lock of hair back under her hijab and pulled the niqab around her mouth and nose more tightly to ward off the biting wintry winds this far north. What had the locals called this region? Ezo? It didn't matter. She only wanted to kill the monster and return south, perhaps catching a Dutch vessel bound for Al-Qatai from the port city of Nagasaki. From there, she could certainly find a caravan westward toward her beloved desert if such was in the cards for her. Only Allah knew where the winds would blow her next.

She'd been on the trail of this particular Jinn for months. Through seventeen villages and four cities, she'd tracked the creature into the wilderness, following the trail of murders. Yasmin's odd appearance was a constant hindrance in this accursed land where everyone looked the same and instantly recognized her as an outsider, with her large golden eyes and long wavy hair, not to mention her manner of dress and her now somewhat rusting chain shirt.

This would be the twentieth Jinn she'd killed. The memory of each one sat in her stomach like a rock, weighing heavier and heavier. To kill the Jinn was to kill its host. It was bloody and disgusting work, but she never felt satisfied that she'd done enough to stop those monsters. Now, she'd found her way to Nihon, the islands to the east.

Yasmin noticed stray prints in the snow, ice, and mud and stopped to examine them. One set, bare and small, suggested a child. This realization filled Yasmin with fury. The Jinn had found a new host, an innocent child, consuming its soul and leaving behind a mere walking corpse. It was a sight Yasmin dreaded, but she knew there was no other choice. She had to find it before more died.

The second set of footprints was larger, but Yasmin could tell by the narrowness of the print and the sandal length, about ten iisbae, that an adult woman had made them. The stride length of about one and a half dhira indicated the woman was perhaps five feet tall. Just as important, the water in the prints hadn't fully frozen yet, a sign that the woman was not far ahead. Whoever she was, she trailed the Jinn closely.

Pulling her muddy cloak around her and wrangling away the images of her daughter lying face-down in the blood-soaked sand, Yasmin pushed onward into the denser portion of the highland forest. Somewhere among the fir, spruce, and larch ahead lay her quarry, perhaps her last, given how cunning this creature had turned out to be.

Another mile ahead, the path grew extremely narrow and winding, and Yasmin followed it for some time until it opened into a wide clearing. Before her, back turned, stood the woman who had made the second set of tracks. She seemed to be considering a small cave set into the ridge.

"As-salamu alaykum," Yasmin ventured.

The woman spun, and her blade was three fingers out of her scabbard before Yasmin could blink. Yasmin's hands flashed to her sword and dagger, drawing them fully. She didn't want to fight the woman unless necessary—she didn't get to finish that thought, though, as the woman drew her blade and took two steps backward.

"Shit," Yasmin muttered, dropping into a stance of her own. Yasmin expected the woman to charge in, but she didn't move. Their stony gazes locked, and Yasmin spotted the fierce warrior's commitment in those thin, brown eyes. Beneath the robe and wide-legged pants, Yasmin knew she'd find scars, probably many.

Yasmin moved to her right, circling. The woman stayed put, only shifting slightly to follow her. She was sizing Yasmin up, examining her footwork and stance, playing out the fight in her mind. Her hesitation revealed something to Yasmin, though. This woman had never fought against someone like her, practiced in a dual-bladed style. The warrior was unsure of how best to counter Yasmin's technique. Yasmin could see it in her eyes, the slight adjustment of her grip, and the tension in her legs. She donned a crooked smile. The other warrior had already lost. All that remained was to play it out.

Of course, as the woman charged and both weapons caught nothing but air, Yasmin thought perhaps she might have misjudged. The curved blade slapped against Yasmin's chainmail, rending it effortlessly and biting into her flesh. The cut wasn't deep, but it hurt, and if she hadn't been armored, Yasmin would surely have been gutted. As it was, the smile was certainly wiped from her face.

"Well, then," Yasmin muttered somberly. "I'll have to put some effort into this."

The woman darted in again. She was insanely quick, but Yasmin had more of a measure of her. She countered the swing of the other woman's weapon with her own. As expected, the woman spun and shifted her grip, coming in toward Yasmin's neck. Yasmin's dagger was there, though, and the blade skidded off harmlessly. Yasmin didn't wait for her to reset her footing. Instead, she kicked out toward the woman's leg. The other warrior lifted her foot, easily avoiding the sweep. But that was a feint. Yasmin spun with her momentum, stomped forward, and thrust out with her dagger and sword simultaneously. The warrior blocked the sword; the dagger, not so much, and it cut deeply into the woman's outer thigh, missing any vital blood vessels but damaging the muscle. Crying out, the Nihonese woman staggered back.

Yasmin backed off. She didn't want to kill her if she could help it.

With a scream, the demon in a child's body charged from the cave and off to the west around the ridge side on which they fought. Yasmin found her opponent momentarily distracted, and that was all she needed. She charged in and whacked the woman on the head, knocking her cold.

"Damn, you're good," Yasmin wheezed, catching her breath. She glanced after the demon in irritation. "You, on the other hand, I'll catch soon enough."

"THE STARS AROUND THE BEAUTIFUL MOON, HIDING their glittering forms whenever she shines full on earth..." Yasmin quoted in a whisper absently as she pressed the cold rag to the young warrior's brow.

Looking down on the captivating face of the young Nihonese woman had brought the words to mind unbidden, wrested from the depths of her memory. It was a trinket from the time before Aswad had taken her family and the life she'd had.

Fatima, her sometime neighbor within the tribe, had given her the book of poetry, translated from its blocky Greek script into beautiful, flowing Arabic. Yasmin hadn't thought of the book or Fatima in a very long time, and the reminiscence ached in her chest. She missed Fatima's quick smile and easy manner. Most of all, she missed the nights they'd spent together when Hasan and Amir were off falconing for hares. Both had been good men, but Yasmin had never loved Hasan, not really, not in the way a wife should. And though Fatima had truly loved Amir in all ways, she always found her way to Yasmin's bed. Neither husband would ever know the separate and precious thing that the two women shared. Perhaps it was wrong. The scripture never explicitly forbade such relationships, in women at least, but still.

She didn't know why she thought of Fatima at that moment or the poem. This woman before her was certainly nothing like the Arab she'd loved. This woman was truly foreign, with a pale complexion, triangular face, and the same strange eyes that everyone here had. And yet, she was a lovely thing to behold in her own right, stunning with her well-toned muscles and long, luxuriously straight black hair.

Pulling herself from her admiration, Yasmin stoked the fire a bit more with the wood she found in the cave mouth, probably left there by some hunting party for lean times, and placed the weasel she'd caught on a spit of wood to roast. As the sun slipped down to the horizon, Yasmin drew out her prayer rug, matted, worn, and dirty. She placed it as neatly as she could on the ground and tended to the Maghrib, the evening prayers. With that completed, she returned the rug to its place in her pack, doing her best to clean off the dirt and mud.

"It's all but ruined," she muttered, but there was nothing for it. She would have to replace it when she returned home—if she ever returned home.

While the meat sizzled and the smokey aroma made her mouth water, Yasmin bound the woman's shapely leg, stymying the bleeding with a linen cloth and myrrh poultice from her pack. Now she waited for her to stir, watching silently and tracing the contours of her face, over and over.

The moon was high, showing the passage of time, but Yasmin had no clue how to use it, or the stars for that matter, to track the time with any accuracy. She was no astronomer and really had no interest in the discipline. The stars were beautiful, as was the moon in all its phases. That was enough for her. Normally, her intuition guided her, telling her when dawn was approaching, but at these northern latitudes, the days were much shorter and the nights far longer.

Drawing out her pipe, Yasmin loaded it with some of her remaining tobacco. She tried to be sparing, as she had little left, but she felt she needed something to take the edge off.

"You should kill her," Aswad breathed in her ear.

Blinking in exasperation, Yasmin took a deep, cleansing breath and then a long drag from the pipe. "And why would I do that?"

"I should think that obvious," the Jinn responded, a bit of pique in his tone. "She kills our kind."

"There is no *our kind*, demon. One day, I'll rid myself of your intrusions and kill you myself."

"Now, that isn't very nice. I keep you healthy and alive when you might otherwise die. If I leave, those wounds will return, you know."

"So you say," Yasmin countered blithely. "Now leave me be." Yasmin's eyes drifted back to the woman, who moved slightly but didn't wake.

"If you're so squeamish, let me do it," Aswad murmured. "I'll make it quick. I promise I'll even return your body to you when I'm done."

"No," Yasmin said firmly.

Dark, deliciously malignant laughter filled Yasmin's ears. "A woman besotted with her enemy dies quickly."

Yasmin snorted a laugh of her own. "I'm not besotted."

"A hearty protest to hide the lie," the demon retorted, an oily drip entering his voice. "I feel the flutter in your chest when you look at her."

She rolled her eyes. "Oh, go away."

"Would that I could," Aswad said and was silent once more.

Now, what did that mean? Yasmin wondered, but the demon didn't elaborate.

A groan caught Yasmin's attention, and while the demon had been somewhat correct—Yasmin did find the woman attractive—she still touched the dagger at her waist for comfort. Pretty as she was, the woman was still a threat. The last thing that Yasmin wanted was to find herself at the woman's mercy, but she couldn't bring herself to bind her or kill her. She probably should have. It wouldn't have been the first time she'd killed a fellow demon hunter to save her own skin, but it had been the look in the woman's eyes when they'd taken their measure of each other. There was deep feeling there, a passion that felt like kinship.

「え？ ええ？ 」 the woman moaned, holding her forehead and gripping the oozing wound in her leg, which she then examined in the firelight, touching the binding. She looked at Yasmin. 「どうして？ 」

Yasmin raised an eyebrow, completely befuddled by the native language. Normally, she was a quick study, but some words seemed to have many meanings, and the writing was completely baffling. However, she did catch the woman's tone. The Nihonese warrior was definitely asking her a question, an angry one if she didn't miss her guess.

Hard eyes confronted Yasmin from the other side of the firelight when the woman sat up. Their darkness was only eclipsed by the forest around them. Yasmin's heart pumped a little harder, but with the adrenaline of knowing she might have to restrain the woman or something else, she wasn't sure. She couldn't deny the woman was truly beautiful and brought a welling of heat to her cheeks. Then again, Yasmin decided, that was probably the fire. Sure, the fire was hot, right?

Yasmin took a drink from her water flask and then held it out. "Here," she said. "Drink."

The woman looked confused, likely not accustomed to being aided by an enemy. But then again, as far as Yasmin was concerned, they weren't enemies. It had been a misunderstanding. She watched as the other woman tried to rise and then sat back down, cringing. *Good,* Yasmin thought, *you'll stay put.*

「自らの刀剣？」 the woman said. Yasmin just shrugged and offered the flask again. The woman repeated the words, more angrily this time and making a swiping gesture with her arms. Yasmin understood then and held up the two swords she had taken from the woman. "They're right here, and they're staying right here until we can come to some kind of agreement."

The woman scowled but took the flask anyway, sniffed at it, and then drank her fill. She returned the flask to Yasmin and reached for the weasel, but Yasmin slapped her hand away from the meat. "No. It's not ready yet."

The woman was on her feet in a flash, her hands going to her waist for swords that weren't there.

"Sit down," Yasmin grunted. "It'll be ready soon. No need to kill me over your bad manners."

The woman dropped then to her knees and bowed her head, hissing out a string of words that Yasmin couldn't follow. 「大変申し訳ございません。自らの不名誉をぜひお許しいただけますと幸いです。」

Yasmin shook her head. "I don't understand." Frustrated, she stood, walked over to the Nihonese woman, and bent down. "Hey, it's alright. We just need to learn to—"

The woman shot up, shoving Yasmin onto her back, snatching her dagger, and pressing it to her throat. Yasmin put her hands up. She had no desire to die, but neither was she afraid of it. Years of torment by Aswad as he'd tried to break her spirit and force her to take her own life had seen to that. So she just met the hard eyes of the woman on her chest with a fierce gaze of her own. All the while, Yasmin's heart hammered, and she had no delusions as to why.

「どうして？！」 the woman growled.

Yasmin did her best to shrug. "I don't speak your language," she replied to what she assumed was a question. Then she patted her chest. "Yasmin. I am Yasmin."

The woman narrowed her eyes, but she lifted off Yasmin and limped back to the fire, dropping the dagger and swiping up her own weapons before returning to her seat. Yasmin rolled up and pursed her lips, unsure how to proceed.

She tried again as she returned to the makeshift camp. "My name is Yasmin. Name. Yasmin."

「お名前ですね！」 Abruptly, the woman stopped scowling, and some kind of realization crossed her face. She said something else very quickly. 「苗字は武田と申します。」 At Yasmin's obvious confusion, she patted her chest. "Ta-kay-dah."

Yasmin nodded. "Takeda. Okay, that's good."

"Takeda-san," Takeda insisted. And Yasmin cocked her head, bemused. She pointed at Yasmin. "Yasu-men-san." Then she pointed at herself. "Takeda-san."

"Ahh," Yasmin said. "It's an honorific. Okay, Takeda-san." With her dagger, Yasmin cut the weasel's flesh; it appeared to be cooked through. "Eat?" she asked, motioning the act with her fingers.

「お水、頂けますでしょうか？」 Takeda said in answer, and Yasmin shook her head in confusion. Takeda pointed to the flask. "Meeee-zuuuu," she repeated as if speaking to a rather mentally challenged child.

"Ah." Yasmin reached into Takeda's pack and found a small stoppered bottle that looked too small to be for water, but she passed it over anyway.

Takeda gave Yasmin an irritated look. 「これ、違います。お酒です。」

Thoroughly frustrated, Yasmin frowned. "Well, I have no idea what in hell you want." She dug into the pack again and, a little further down, found a fat gourd. She pulled it out. The end had been hacked off and stoppered. Takeda nodded with a smirk. Yasmin tossed her the gourd in irritation. "Here."

The woman used the water not to drink but to wash her hands. Yasmin had done the same before she'd eaten. It seemed that the people here understood the concept of cleanliness, something the Europeans lacked.

"Tabete, kudasai?" Takeda-san said and reached out a hand toward the meat. "Onegaishimasu."

Yasmin nodded, and Takeda took a tiny strip of the weasel. Gingerly, she tested the meat in her mouth, nodded, and then tore some off.

Yasmin made the eating gesture with her hand. "Tabete?"

Takeda tilted her head, and then she smiled broadly before hiding it behind her hand. She pointed at herself. "Watakushi wa Takeda desu." Then she pointed at Yasmin. "Anata wa Yasmin-san desu."

Yasmin repeated the phrases, swapping the names and honorifics. "Watakushi wa Yasmin desu. Anata wa Takeda-san desu."

"Hai!" Takeda said with a grin. Then she pointed at Yasmin, made a stern face, and said, "Tabete," like a command. Yasmin narrowed her eyes as Takeda patted her chest again and said, "Watakushi wa tabemasu." She nodded to Yasmin.

Yasmin looked at her, pointed to Takeda-san, and said, "Anata wa tabemasu." Takeda clapped her hands and looked about to dance. The glee with which this woman seemed to enjoy teaching was infectious, and Yasmin couldn't help but grin. One simple lesson and she had learned the basic words to eat, you, and me. She had also learned the word for water, mizu.

Takeda pointed toward the cave and spoke one more. 「先程の子供は妖怪でした。」She slowed down and, using hand gestures, finally got her point across.

Yasmin nodded gravely. "The child was Yōkai. We call them Jinn."

It was Takeda's turn to nod as she ate more of the meat, washing it down with the water. Then she said, 「やすみんさんはわたくしの味方ですか？」

Yasmin shrugged, again confused. She thought she understood part of it—some variation on watakushi—but the rest was a jumble, except for the ending question word, 'desuka.'

"Watakushi to annata wa," Takeda said, then she put her hands together and locked them tight.

"Allies?" Yasmin replied, patting her chest and pointing at Takeda. "Yes, allies." She made a slashing gesture while saying the word "Yōkai."

Despite their scuffle, Takeda seemed to understand they were both here to kill the Jinn, and she nodded, giving an almost imperceptible smile. Yasmin realized she'd made a friend of sorts, and she knew that this woman was honorable.

"For now," Aswad whispered in her ear cruelly. "For now."

THE MORNING DAWNED LATE, AND WHILE ASWAD HAD bitched and complained that Yasmin was being reckless by sleeping next to such an obvious enemy, nothing untoward happened. Takeda had allowed Yasmin to stitch her wound and rebind it, though it had taken the last of Yasmin's myrrh to reapply a new poultice. Takeda still limped heavily, but they set off in search of the jinn—the yōkai. The two women easily followed the tracks, and the creature made no attempt to hide itself; Jinn rarely did once they possessed human form. Only Aswad had ever bothered to be so clever. Though it had occurred to Yasmin that cleverness might not be the reason. Aswad seemed unable to possess her again as he had those years ago. Perhaps he was weaker than she thought, or she stronger.

The going was treacherous, and they had to stop several times, much to Takeda's apparent irritation, but Yasmin was patient. She had her entire life to find this creature and kill it, as far as she was concerned. A day, a week, a year, she would track it down, and it would inevitably die. She would like to do so before it killed again. Ezo was an island, after all. And, as she'd understood from the Portuguese traders, neither the Cathayans nor the Koreans would be kind to a child arriving on their shores. And it had to eat. That would limit its options. Yasmin's biggest concern was that the creature would take on a new host before it died, as it had done several times since arriving in Nihon.

All the while, Takeda spoke to her, not so much teaching her Nihongo, as Yasmin had come to understand the language was called, but saying things with gestures and expressions that allowed Yasmin to follow along, at least somewhat. Yasmin paid as close attention as she could without losing the trail. Periodically, Yasmin would repeat words, and Takeda would help her understand them. It was a complex language and very contextual, but not impossible to learn.

On the second day of travel, Takeda tugged Yasmin away from the trail, and a bit of an argument ensued. Yasmin found she could neither understand nor get through to Takeda about the importance of staying the course. Eventually, the stubborn Nihonese woman won out, and Yasmin followed her to a small village on the far side of the ridge, nestled in a steeply sloped valley next to a shallow portion of a narrow, winding river.

It was beautiful in a sparse way, not as pleasant as the open skies and expanse of her dunes and deserts of Arabia, but still quite pretty. The small homes were immaculately kept, and many had small gardens enclosed by tall fences. Here and there, torches lit several of the gates.

The people, on the other hand, were less than welcoming. They nodded and bowed to Takeda, but to Yasmin, they offered only suspicious glares. Of course, that was par for the course. Takeda ignored them all for the most part, guiding Yasmin down into the village proper, where they wound their way among the tight byways and then up the ridge on the far side. They arrived at a pair of tall gates, no more ornate than the others, but somehow nicer. It took a moment for Yasmin to realize that the boards that made up the gate and fence were of alternating lengths measured precisely, creating two perfect lines that drew the eye.

Takeda didn't knock. She simply opened the door and strode inside, offering the way to Yasmin with a quick "dozo," which Yasmin had learned meant 'please,' but only when offering something. 'Kudasai' was used to ask for something, or 'onegaishimasu' when asking for a favor, or forgiveness, or about a hundred other things that made no sense to her mind.

"Tadaima!" Takeda called, and a woman, very old and very stooped, appeared on the wrap-around porch of the low home within the wooden fence line.

「お帰りなさい！」 the old woman said as they approached and bowed low. Takeda bowed back, as did Yasmin. No need to be rude. Takeda then rattled off a bunch of Nihongo. Yasmin couldn't follow it, but the woman took off, stopping briefly to remove her shoes, another indication of how civilized the people were. Her own family removed their shoes before entering their tent to avoid tracking sand and dirt onto the rugs.

Yasmin and Takeda followed, stopping to remove their shoes and socks as well. It took a moment for Yasmin to realize that this was Takeda's home. She was mistress here. Suddenly, it all made sense. Why stay on the path and be miserable when her home was just a qama or two away?

"Well, this is convenient," Yasmin muttered, thinking of sleeping on something other than her bedroll and stones. Takeda turned back to look at her with a questioning gaze, but Yasmin begged her off with a wave.

Inside, Takeda drew them into a back room where sat a large bucket, a smaller bucket with a handle, a bamboo seat, a large stone bath of hot water, and washing cloths. There, she proceeded to undress. Yasmin blinked, then blushed, then began to stutter, finally turning her back.

"Uh...What are you doing?" she asked. "Dou shimashita?"

A soft hand landed on her shoulder. 「お風呂に入りましょう。」

"Huh?" Yasmin responded, still not looking at the naked woman.

"Ofuro ni harimashou," Takeda insisted, tugging at Yasmin's shoulder, pointing to the bath, and holding her nose. She wasn't wrong; Yasmin did stink, but still.

Yasmin finally turned around, trying desperately to look anywhere but at Takeda. "Um. . .Takeda-san. . ." Crimson bloomed in her cheeks despite the fact that it wasn't unusual for the women of her tribe to bathe together, but then again, she'd never felt her heart rabbit away like this with any of them, either, not even with Fatima. Yasmin's breath turned short and labored as she tried to figure a way out of this. "Maybe I should do it later."

Takeda narrowed her eyes. Then she laughed, covering her mouth with her hand in that shy way she had that threw Yasmin for a loop every time she did it. Yasmin scratched a slight itch under her hijab. *Well,* she thought, *there are no men here. And it would be rude to ask them to reheat water just for me.*

"Rationalizing a bit hard, aren't we?" Aswad murmured.

Yasmin ignored him and relented, doing her best to look at the floor as she undressed. Still, though, she felt thoroughly embarrassed.

Takeda led Yasmin to the small bamboo stool and offered it to her. "Dozo."

She sat quietly, her arms gathered around herself to protect her modesty. Slowly, Takeda knelt behind her and took up the tiny bucket.

"Oke," Takeda whispered, and Yasmin felt a slight shiver at the word. Even for such a simple item as a bucket, Takeda seemed to be able to make it sound incredibly sensual, and Yasmin felt herself coming undone inside.

Takeda scooped hot water from the larger wooden bucket. "Ofuro," she whispered, placing a hand on it before slowly ladling the hot water across Yasmin's shoulders and, eventually, over her head. Yasmin moaned slightly, then put a hand to her mouth, mortified. *What is wrong with me?* She asked herself for probably the thirtieth time since meeting Takeda.

"Besotted," rang a familiar, if unwelcome, voice in her ears.

"Oh, shut up," Yasmin muttered under her breath. But Aswad wasn't wrong. She was floating right off course, and she didn't know how it could be so easy. For years, she'd burned for vengeance against the jinn. Battling them time and time again to avenge her husband and daughter, even though the one Jinn she couldn't kill was the one responsible. But this woman had distracted her effortlessly, yanking her away from her path of vengeance in a matter of two days.

After she was quite thoroughly wet—in so many ways— Yasmin felt Takeda take to her back with a soapy cloth. She gasped as Takeda found her shoulders and spine, but Takeda continued as if she hadn't noticed. The woman was thorough as well, scrubbing her backside until her rear probably shined. Yasmin wondered if this shouldn't be servant's work. Bathing someone seemed beneath Takeda's station, but she couldn't bring herself to protest or even to try asking about it. Instead, she just sat there, letting Takeda do as she pleased. And it was nice. For the first time since Hasan and Noura had been murdered by her hand, she felt the hole inside herself begin to fill with something other than blood.

Takeda stood a little ungracefully, clearly feeling her injury. First, one leg, and then the other, moved under her as she rose and then knelt in front of Yasmin. Yasmin looked up. She couldn't help it. Her eyes drifted over the taut muscles and long scars that covered Takeda. Her gaze drifted slowly up Takeda's thighs, pausing briefly on the bandage before continuing on to her arms and across her small breasts, then up to those beautiful eyes, the color of polished walnut. They no longer held the hard gaze they had on the trail. They were soft and glittering in the torch-light. Yasmin swallowed hard, her vision darting across Takeda's face.

"You're beautiful," Yasmin whispered softly, unable to contain herself at such a sight, scars and all. And Takeda had a lot of them. They ran all up both arms, some long, some short. Even her hands were scarred.

A corner of Takeda's mouth twitched, and she licked her lips as she washed Yasmin's front, the washcloth trav-eling first between her breasts, then over and around them. Yasmin pulled her lips between her teeth to keep from making any noise. She wanted to moan. Takeda had to know what this was doing to her: the blush, the slight shake in Yasmin's legs, the lust that likely filled her eyes. And yet, she just continued the pleasurable activity in silence. It was all Yasmin could do not to reach out and touch her.

Finally, Takeda slid the washcloth down each leg, pausing briefly at Yasmin's knees and then again at her feet, taking gentle but extra care. Yasmin giggled slightly when Takeda reached the bottoms of her feet, and the slight smile she'd seen earlier on Takeda's features blossomed across her face in a thin line. Takeda turned her face away, hiding the smile, but it was there. Yasmin had seen it.

Scooping out more water, she rinsed off the soap from Yasmin's body before taking another small bucket of luke-warm, cloudy water that smelled of rice and using it to wash

Yasmin's hair. Finally, the Nihonese warrior stood with a grimace and pointed her toward the large stone bath.

"But," Yasmin said, her voice hoarse with want. "What about you? Um. . . Anata wa?"

Takeda only giggled. Then she bowed her head slightly. 「光栄でした。」

Yasmin shook her head and shrugged. "You know, it's not accepted in my culture. For women to be, well, intimate."

Takeda gave her a puzzled look as she bathed herself, but her gaze didn't linger long, and she returned to washing while Yasmin watched, enraptured and more than a little bemused by the whole affair. She didn't understand Takeda at all. Her eyes held such deep emotions, and yet she never seemed to express them, not in words at least. And this entire event, bringing her here, what had it been for? The bath, the way she'd taken great care to wash Yasmin's body, it had been sensual and expressed a need that Yasmin could easily see in the woman's eyes. Despite her stoic nature and her quiet discipline, she was lonely. And where was the man of the house? Where were the children? Yasmin had noted a few birthing marks on Takeda's belly. She'd born children, but there were none here.

By the time Takeda entered the bath with Yasmin, the Arab woman was fed up with her own ignorance. "Where is your husband?"

Takeda tilted her head and gave her a puzzled look.

"Husband, your man," Yasmin said, pantomiming a burly man walking.

"Shinda," Takeda said simply, drawing her finger across her neck and sticking out her tongue.

Yasmin was a little surprised at the response. It was so

abrupt and informal as if Takeda didn't care at all that her husband had died.

"Yōkai?" Yasmin asked.

Takeda nodded solemnly, then said, "Ima watakushi no ban desu." She lifted a finger to her eye.

Yasmin gaped in horror at the unspoken question, lowering her gaze and letting her hair drape around her face, hiding it.

The water rippled as Takeda moved closer. "Me o awasete kudasai." A slender finger crooked under Yasmin's face and drew it upward. Takeda tapped her eye again "Ki-me."

Yasmin couldn't speak as fear gripped her, squeezing at her chest.

"Kill her, now," Aswad hissed. "Before she kills you."

"Yōkai," Yasmin murmured softly, the word colored with shame as she tapped her breast and pulled her chin from Takeda's fingers to look away.

「妖怪にも天命がある。」 Takeda whispered, and even though Yasmin could not understand the words, the meaning was clear. Acceptance.

"Well, I'll be damned," Aswad said in what sounded like both disappointment and surprise.

"You already are," Yasmin replied under her breath, a morose, mirthless joke among the tears that filled her eyes. "As am I."

"Me o awasete kudasai," Takeda repeated, and Yasmin looked up once more. Takeda moved back and made a few gestures, indicating a small child in her arms. She said a few words, some of which Yasmin recognized, like shinda and yōkai. Slowly, Yasmin comprehended Takeda's story.

Takeda didn't cry, but the pain in her eyes was

heartwrenching. She had been married and had had two children, one girl, and one boy, both very young, the boy but a babe. One night, a stranger came to call at the gate. The gardener had answered. Before anyone could do anything, the stranger had slaughtered her entire family and all the servants save the old woman who had greeted Takeda she and Yasmin entered the garden. And while there was clearly no love lost between Takeda and her dead husband, her children, she missed terribly. When describing them, she used a different word from shinda, 'nakunatte,' and she spoke it with more deference.

Yasmin swallowed hard, blinking back her own tears. While some details may have escaped Yasmin's understanding, she knew all too well the yawning gulf that reflected in the other woman's face. Losing Hasan hadn't hurt Yasmin like losing Noura. That had been devastating. That had been what had set her on the path she now trod.

Takeda had hidden somewhere; Yasmin couldn't glean where, but she had survived. Since then, Takeda had trained mercilessly and hunted what she considered the 'bad yōkai.' Not that Yasmin had ever considered any Jinn good, but then again, the scriptures and stories of her youth suggested they existed.

Afterword, Yasmin had tried to apologize for misleading her, but Takeda had simply pressed a finger to Yasmin's lips and drawn her from the cooling bathwater. Takeda ran oils through her own hair and put it up, and then she did the same for Yasmin, though she left Yasmin's hair down, apparently deciding it was best that way. Then Takeda took Yasmin into her room.

Yasmin was in a daze, unable to speak or to truly comprehend what was happening. But with all of the kindness Takeda had shown her, Yasmin wondered absently if perhaps this was some elaborate ritual before killing her. Show good manners to the guest, then kill her and the Jinn within as a mercy. She could understand why Takeda might want to do it, and for the first time, Yasmin cared whether she lived or died. She hoped that Takeda was simply being a good host according to whatever customs she followed. But Yasmin didn't let herself dwell on it, fully expecting everything to fall apart soon.

Of course, the last thing Yasmin had expected was for Takeda to roll out her futon mattress and pull Yasmin to it. Yasmin didn't know what to do. She felt lost. Her sense of purpose had foundered on the rocks of a chance meeting. And though she found Takeda attractive, she suddenly felt shy and very vulnerable. Takeda doused the lantern, draping the house in absolute darkness, and Yasmin began to shake uncontrollably.

That is until Takeda kissed her. Yasmin's breath seemed to leave her body all at once as Takeda's gentle yet calloused hands pushed her down to the mattress. Takeda filled Yasmin's lungs with her hot breath, tasting of tea and mint and a flavor that was uniquely her.

As Takeda straddled Yasmin and bent low, Yasmin wrapped her arms around the woman. Yasmin didn't protest or argue. Instead, so lost was she in the strange turmoil of emotions that she threw herself into the lovemaking, letting it carry her away from the pain and misery that had harried her for years.

Takeda was extremely experienced in the arts of sex, and they spent several hours exploring each other's body, bringing each other the crest of pleasure and then over. Even Aswad was silent, and Yasmin was thankful that the Jinn kept his peace and let her have this one night where a kindred spirit and stranger had taken her to the shores of oblivion.

And not once did Yasmin feel pain, or loneliness, or shame, but she did cry. She cried for Noura and even for Hasan, despite the fact that she'd never really loved him; he had been a good man. She cried for Takeda and all that she had lost. But most of all, Yasmin cried for the relief that the night brought from the years-long agony she had suffered at the hands of the demon that lay within her.

WHEN YASMIN AWOKE, THE SUN WAS ALREADY HIGH IN the sky. The rice paper doors around the room were closed, but a small tray sat to her left holding a bowl of rice, a small bit of raw fish, and a pot containing tea, complete with a small round cup. She blinked and wiped the sleep from her eyes.

"Takeda-san?" she called, but there was no answer. She picked up the small sticks, hashi they were called, that much she knew, and did her best to eat with them, using them to scoop the rice straight into her mouth as she'd seen the Nihonese do it. The fish she ate without much gusto. It wasn't bad, but she preferred her food with more flavor. The tea, she decided, was exquisite. She put a finger to her bottom lip and tugged at it a little as she thought about the night before.

"It can't last, you know," Aswad said, his voice full of grim satisfaction. "She'll abandon you, or worse, she'll try to kill you."

Yasmin gave a deep, heaving sigh of despair and pawed at the burgeoning tears in her eyes. "Can't you leave me be? Just go somewhere else."

"Why would I do that when I'm having so much fun here? And, let's be honest, your misery is your own doing, is it not?"

Rubbing the bridge of her nose, Yasmin tried to banish the memories, but Aswad was relentless.

"You should have never opened the box."

"I know," Yasmin said bitterly.

"And then I killed them all. It was easy, too. You have always had a capable body, even before you started this futile quest to eradicate us. Of course, then, I'd had to creep through the house like some common cutthroat."

"Stop," Yasmin muttered, gorge rising in her throat from the meager breakfast and Aswad's prodding.

"And there was nothing you could do. Now, all I have to do is wait."

"Don't even think it," Yasmin growled.

"Oh, not yet, I don't think. I'll let you have your fun for a bit. Go, catch this creature you chase. Kill it. But I'll warn you now, you should move on after that, don't you think?"

Yasmin shook her head, trying to banish Aswad's voice, but it was no use. He was inside her, taken up residence like some unwanted vagrant lodger, squatting in her thoughts. But there was something in his words. He'd tormented her time and time again. But he'd never pushed her to move on or stay or taken any real interest in anything she did that didn't involve violence.

Pushing that thought deep down, Yasmin took a breath and steeled her mind. "You don't own me," she whispered. Strangely, the Jinn lay quiet, which was unlike him. His usual fair would be to make some snide or wry comment that would be timed to irritate her, but this time, nothing. Something was up. Yasmin was sure of it. He didn't like being here. She stuffed that away as well and focused on other things.

Abruptly, the rice-paper door slid back, and the old servant, the one who had greeted them when they'd first arrived, knelt in front of it. She carefully set a bundle of fabric on the floor and closed the door without a word. Yasmin hadn't even had time to cover herself.

She examined the bundle briefly but dove back under the covers when the door opened once more, revealing Takeda on the other side. She bowed, stood, much more capably than the night before, Yasmin noted, and stepped inside. Then she knelt again and closed the door.

Picking up the bundle, Takeda set it on the bed, drew Yasmin up, and guided her to a corner of the room where sat a small box. Yasmin kneeled quietly as Takeda combed out her waves. The oil from the night before had left a bit of a sheen to it, and the rice-starched water had made it soft. Yasmin expected Takeda to fix it into a bun as she wore, but she left the waves falling over Yasmin's shoulders. Standing once more, Takeda slowly and deliberately pulled Yasmin up, positioning her with her arms wide.

「着せてあげてください。」

Yasmin hadn't understood the words, but when Takeda lifted the short robe and guided her arms into the sleeves, she comprehended.

"Shitagi," Takeda said softly as she slid the white under-garment onto Yasmin's arms, and Yasmin nodded, repeating the word.

With deft hands and precise movements that had a feeling of both perfunctory purpose and tender care, Takeda closed the robe, flattened it against Yasmin's skin, and tied the belt. Standing transfixed, Yasmin watched as Takeda glided around her, naming each piece of clothing as she helped Yasmin into it: hakama, kimono, tabi, obi. If her leg was giving her further trouble, Takeda hid it well.

Ensuring that every fold and surface was flat and neat, Takeda finished off the outfit with a heavy silk jacket called a haori. Every movement seemed to Yasmin as if Takeda had done this a thousand times just for this very moment. The worshipful and delicate way that Takeda had touched her throughout the process brought a flare of heat to her breast and cheeks. She couldn't help it.

"Besotted," she murmured wryly.

"Besotted," Aswad affirmed with a touch of malicious laughter.

When Takeda was done, Yasmin bowed with a quiet "Domo."

Takeda gave Yasmin a polite smile, bowed, and left the room.

Yasmin was flummoxed. The entire affair was intimate in a way that she scarcely understood, but it reminded her of nothing so much as when she would set out Hasan's clothing for the day. Something about Takeda fascinated Yasmin; perhaps it was her quiet and reserved nature, or maybe it was the way that everything she did seemed steeped in precision and ritual that bordered on an obsession with perfection: the way she fought, the way she had dressed Yasmin, the way she had made love, giving entirely of herself without reservation, loudly and passionately.

Yasmin found her hijab and niqab still neatly folded on the bed. As she scooped them up, Aswad spoke to her again. "Aren't we forgetting something?"

"What?"

"Fajr prayers?" he replied with a touch of amusement. "Mustn't keep the almighty waiting."

"Now, why would you remind me to be pious?" Yasmin

asked, her hands on her hips as if she were confronting him physically.

"All things in the heavens and on earth prostrate themselves before Allah, including moving creatures and angels," Aswad quoted cheekily.

"Surah 16, Ayah 9," Yasmin said automatically before facing her best guess of West and performing her morning prayers. Far be it from her to ignore assistance from the murderous thug in her head. Once completed, Yasmin folded the coverlet of the bed carefully and rolled up the futon mattress, orienting it so it didn't suddenly unroll, as she could find nothing to tie it with. Satisfied with the state of the room, she left in search of Takeda.

She found Takeda sitting quietly, eyes closed, in an adjoining room before a low table. As Yasmin entered, Takeda gestured to a seat across from her. "Dozo," she said.

Once she sat, the old servant woman appeared with tea, which Takeda poured. Each took a drink, and then Takeda proceeded to teach, or well, try to teach Yasmin more Nihongo. Slowly, over a few hours, Takeda managed to teach Yasmin a few basic phrases, which Yasmin did her best to commit to memory, including the word "furusato," meaning "home."

"Sorosoro mairimashou," Takeda said after they had finished. "Yōkai o koroshini. Ryokai desuka?"

Yasmin grinned and nodded, and for the first time in a very long time, her pulse quickened as the excitement of the hunt sent a shiver up her spine. "Hai! Let's kill the monster."

"Yes, let's," Aswad whispered in her ear cryptically.

THE TRAIL WAS STILL VISIBLE WHEN THEY RETURNED to the path above the village. The weather had begun to warm, making the ground soft and slick in places, but Yasmin and Takeda made excellent time in their chase. The demon wasn't prone to long periods of inactivity, but it had to feed. Without humans to kill for its food, it left a bloody trail of small and large game. Yasmin shook her head at the waste as they passed a good-sized dear carcass. Scavengers, of course, would make a fine meal of the remains, but it could have fed a family of four for several days, even if meat wasn't a common menu item here. *Strange behavior for a Jinn,* she thought. Jinn could be murderous, certainly, but this seemed more like mindless slaughter.

Takeda said little and gave away even less in her expression. The intense emotions of the night before were now caged beneath the mantle of decorum that all Nihonjin wore publicly, Nihonjin being the locals. Yasmin's people would be called Arabujin, Takeda had said, and Yasmin decided she kind of liked the appellation. It was even written in a special script for foreign words, which Yasmin found fascinating.

"Yasu!" Takeda hissed as they rounded a bend in the trail and found a large, wide clearing in the shadow of a tall mountain. Yasmin ducked down into a tight thicket with Takeda and peaked through the leaves at where she was pointing.

"Why is she just standing there?" Yasmin asked.

The Jinn-possessed little girl stood in a grubby, ratty blue kimono with her back to them in the center of the round clearing, too round. Now that Yasmin was really paying attention, she could see a circle of stone figures. They looked in some ways like the Buddhist statues she'd seen in her travels, but the faces on these stone effigies were horribly misshapen. Some had long noses or massive tusks. One was even a beautiful woman with fangs.

Yasmin and Takeda waited for what seemed a long time for the child to move, but she was stock still, much like the statues that surrounded her. Sick of waiting and realizing that the child was alone, Yasmin launched from the thicket, drawing her weapons. "Now you die, Jinn!"

Takeda called for her in a panic. "Yasu! Yamete!"

"It's a trap, my dear," Aswad said as she tore across the clearing.

Yasmin skidded to a halt in horror as the thing turned. It was no child. Sharp fangs protruded from its mouth, and long, thick claws of sickly yellow curved in place of fingernails. This was like nothing she'd ever seen. This wasn't the Jinn of her homeland—this creature was something else. "Yōkai," she whispered, realizing that the demons of Nihon were not Jinn. She was out of her element.

From around the sides of the statues, more of the small creatures emerged, many looking like small children with horrid deformities: horns, fangs, tusks; one even had a long trunk-like protrusion that waved about. Worst of all was the tentacle-faced monstrosity with massive arms and legs that seemed to materialize from nowhere. Imposing and terrible at almost seven feet tall, it wore black lacquered armor and carried a great curved sword on the end of a pole.

"Blessed Allah, protect me," Yasmin cried as the little ones charged forward.

From her left, steel flashed, cutting down the first childlike creature and jerking Yasmin from her stupified terror.

"Semero!!!" Takeda shouted as she moved back to back with Yasmin and pulled her short-bladed wakizashi into her off hand.

Yasmin muscled her face into a determined grimace and

began the fight of her life. The small creatures were fast, darting this way and that. The long hakama seemed to make it hard for them to gauge where Yasmin's legs were as they struck, mostly catching only the snapping silk. Some blows, though, met their mark, and within a few seconds, both of Yasmin's legs were bleeding from a half-dozen wounds.

Takeda was having a great deal more success. She fought like the demons that faced her, with furiously quick strikes and parries, keeping the claws away as she beheaded two of the short beasts, their remains vanishing in puffs of oily black smoke that quickly dissipated.

Yasmin had never found herself so overmatched before. She'd trained and fought for the last seven years, and she was nothing compared to the warrior at her back. Finally, however, perseverance paid off, and she managed to cut through an ugly fish-headed thing. But even as she did so, she felt the heat of Takeda's body vanish as the woman was knocked across the bespoke battle ring by the massive squid-headed ogre.

Yasmin immediately spun away, guarding Takeda's limp form. "Get up!" she called, and Takeda stirred, trying to rise. One of the swift little ghūls, for that was the only word Yasmin had for them, tried to dart in and strike Takeda, but Yasmin threw her dagger, embedding it in the back of the hideous thing's neck. She hadn't even looked. Despite her lesser skill, Yasmin was a battle-hardened fighter, and she wasn't going to let anything happen to Takeda.

"Besotted," Aswad laughed, sounding somewhere behind her.

"Fuck your father!" she shot back as she grabbed one of the ghūls and ran it through.

"Such language," Aswad chuckled.

The ogre, however, continued forward in his slow,

ponderous gait. Bearing down on the two women. She couldn't kill it with her sword, but her pack held something she'd found in Al-Qatai that would certainly do the job. To use it, though, she needed Takeda to get up. She needed a distraction.

"TAKEDA!" she cried at the top of her lungs.

The woman finally drew herself up and shook her head just as Yasmin missed the last of the little goblin creatures, allowing it to jump on Takeda's back and rake her with its claws.

The silk fabric of Takeda's kimono split wide as the nails carved bloody rents in her flesh.

"No," Yasmin cried, but the ogre was on her, swinging his polearm at her head. Distracted as she was, Yasmin barely blocked the blow on the flat of her sword. The maneuver kept her alive, but her weapon shattered with the impact, sending half the blade off into the trees and several shards of metal skittering across the ground. A kick from the ogre knocked her sprawling, breathless. She turned to see the ogre's weapon dropping toward her.

It stopped cold. Takeda was there, her katana mere inches from Yasmin, holding back the ogre's swing. Buoyed by her lover's recovery, Yasmin screamed and drove the jagged remains of her sword into the ogre's thigh, drawing a bellow of pain as it staggered backward.

Takeda was on it in an instant, slashing and fighting, cutting into any exposed flesh she could find. Yasmin took the moment of distraction to dig into her pouch and found what she was looking for: a small metal sphere, smaller than her closed fist. She lit the fuse on the end of it with a bit of flint and a shard of her sword that lay on the ground. It caught just as Takeda moved around, showing Yasmin the ogre's backside.

Yasmin charged across the clearing and leaped as high as she could, wrapping her legs around the ogre's body, pulling back the rear lacquer plates of its armor with a scream of effort, and stuffing the grenade inside. She dropped off and dove for Takeda. The two rolled behind one of the statues as the grenade exploded with a thunderous crack that shook the trees.

Looking back, they saw a bit of turned-up dirt where the ogre had stood, but the beast was gone. The only indication it had ever been was the oily smoke and bits of lacquer plating left behind by its demise. Takeda and Yasmin heaved for breath for long minutes. Their eyes met, and the depth of longing and affection there shocked Yasmin to her core. She wanted to stay here forever.

Yasmin stood and helped Takeda up, noting the grimace of pain on her face. Quickly, she turned her around and examined the blood-soaked furrows in her back. They were deep, not fatal. Still, they would need treatment soon.

"Uchi no wakizashi. Doko itta?" Takeda asked, glancing around as she swiped her katana down, ridding it of bits of black ichor before sheathing it.

"It's here," Yasmin called, spotting the smaller blade not far from where they'd landed along with the scabbard. Yasmin sheathed the blade and held it out with both hands.

"Time to go," Aswad said flatly. "You've done what you came for."

"No. I don't think I will," Yasmin replied in a whisper. "I'm staying here, you wretch."

Takeda came forward and grasped the blade. Yasmin found she couldn't let go.

"It's time to go!" Aswad growled in her ear, more firmly this time, demanding and threatening in his tone.

Yasmin couldn't move. Her hands were clamped around

the weapon and wouldn't release it. Her feet wouldn't answer her either. She was stuck, helpless. Her eyes widened as she realized what was happening. "No."

Takeda tugged at the blade again and gave her a questioning gaze. 「どうしたの？」

"Yōkai," she whispered in horror as tears rolled down her face. "Koroshite." It was a plea. She begged Takeda to end her life.

「だめ。」 Takeda replied flatly. No.

"If you want her to live, you will leave. Now!" Aswad said.

Yasmin nodded, and the pain in her heart squeezed her chest so hard that she thought it would crack in upon itself. "I'm sorry," Yasmin whispered, her fingers finally releasing the weapon. Takeda didn't shed a single tear. Instead, she dug into her kimono and produced a small bamboo scroll tube, which she pushed into Yasmin's obi.

「長崎に着いたら、これを誰かに読んでもらってください。」 Takeda said, and then she stood on her tiptoes and pressed her lips to Yasmin's in a soft but passionate kiss before starting back down the path. Her head low, Yasmin followed.

When the path split away toward the village, Takeda gave Yasmin one last glance and a thin smile. "Mata ne, genkide ne."

Yasmin nodded at the farewell and waved, her throat too constricted with grief to speak. Perhaps, she thought, Takeda wasn't as interested in me as I was in her.

Hoisting her pack and desperate to put this entire affair behind her, Yasmin turned her back on the little village and headed south, returning the way she'd come. Try as she might, she couldn't shake her memories. Tears periodically stained her cheeks and burned her eyes as she made the long journey southward.

She used the few words that Takeda had taught her to arrange for sleeping quarters in various villages until she reached Edo. With her limited Nihongo and her local dress, most people didn't look at her too closely, though she had to hide several times as she was reported as a foreigner. Nihon was forbidden to outsiders, after all. And trucking with the locals had just as many risks as avoiding them. She wasted no time in booking passage on a small ship bound for Nagasaki. The captain liked silver, and so his silence was easy to buy. Clearly, he felt no compunction to turn her in.

On the second day of the trip, she leaned against the railing and pulled forth the small bamboo tube from her obi. She thought to hurl it into the sea and try to forget this place, but she couldn't bring herself to do so. This was the last thing that Takeda had given her, and her fingers wouldn't let it go. Finally, she opened it and looked at the parchment inside.

It was written in Nihongo, of course, but the words were so beautiful, like the hand that wrote them. It was like looking at a piece of artwork that had dripped in ink from the fingers of a great poet. For all she knew, though, it could be a recipe for proper ocha. But that didn't make it any less special.

"What are you reading?" the captain said in Portuguese as he toddled up to her.

Yasmin swallowed hard and dried her eyes. "I don't know. It's a note from a friend, but I can't read it."

The captain leaned forward and perused the note, then held out his hand for it. Yasmin gave it to him, and he read it again, then he rolled it up and passed it back. "When we reach shore, I have a friend I'd like you to meet. Can I borrow that note from you? I promise to bring it back."

Yasmin sniffed and wiped her nose, replacing the note in the tube and handing it to the captain.

On arrival in Nagasaki, the captain spirited Yasmin away in the dark, taking her to a small home not far from the dock. Yasmin waited outside while the captain went in.

"Taking the scenic route?"

Aswad's very presence sickened her, and she retorted hotly. "No ships are leaving this late at night, so what do you care?" The Jinn didn't respond.

The door opened, and Yasmin was confronted by a man incredibly advanced in years with graven wrinkles, a curved back, and white, unseeing eyes.

"Hairinasai, hairinasai," he beckoned, leading her inside and hobbling ahead into a small common room with a tiny low table. The captain stood in the corner, a hand on the small knife stuffed into his obi.

She expected the place, so small and dark, to stink of the old man's sweat and whatever food he ate, as well as mildew and mold, but the air was clean, even in the humid night. Fresh tatami mats covered the immaculate floor, and the rice-paper door, a shoji, sat open at the rear of the home.

"Sit," the captain said dispassionately, eyes watching her like the proverbial hawk's.

Yasmin sat. She thought she should be nervous or worried, but she was beyond that now. Whatever became of her wasn't important anymore. Aswad had won. Her life would be forever spent killing Jinn until she died or he finally took her completely.

On the table, she noted a bottle of ink, a brush, and some rice paper. To one side lay the note, curled over from weeks in the tube, and, of course, the tube itself. The old man took the brush and wrote several characters. Then he looked at her and spoke as the captain translated.

"I understand you have a demon."

Yasmin's hands began to shake of their own accord, and her body jerked slightly. "Hai," Yasmin ground out through clenched teeth, fighting to stay still.

"And you want it gone?"

With a jerk, Yasmin flung herself backward involuntarily as Aswad tried to take control. She convulsed wildly as she battled with the thing that had her. Her head banged against the floor as Yasmin tried desperately to knock herself cold before the creature could fully possess her. Blackness swirled at the edge of her vision, and spots lit in her eyes, but she remained conscious.

A heavy weight landed on her chest as the captain jumped down on her and pinned her arms to the floor. The demon had her arms and legs now, and it fought with a strength that Yasmin had never known. The captain was more skilled, though, turning her over and locking her arm behind her back as he wrapped his own thickly corded arm around her neck and tangled her legs.

The old man tottered over to the struggling pair. "Do you want it gone?" he asked again, and again the captain translated, though his words were strained from holding her in place. "Then you must ask."

She couldn't move her body, but she fought the demon long enough to speak. "Yoroshiku... onegaishimasu," she squeezed out before her mouth clamped closed, and the blackness began spiraling down through her vision again.

The old man licked the back of the sheet of characters and slapped it onto her forehead.

"No!" came Aswad's agonized scream, ripped from Yasmin's throat as her vision cleared and her muscles responded to her thoughts.

Yasmin coughed and grabbed her neck. *What now?* She thought in a panic. *Is he going to choke me to death?*

Her mouth tasted of burning ash and cinders. She leaned forward as thick, viscous smoke and burning embers plummeted to the floor like syrup, gorged up from within her. She heaved with it like a sickness she'd never known. Her body burned as cuts and rents appeared on her flesh in every place she'd ever been wounded. Three of her ribs cracked painfully, as did her arm, revealing just how much damage big Yōkai had done during their fight. Blood flowed onto the floor as the last of the black taint spilled from her mouth and nose, and she coughed once more.

"And now you die with me," Aswad whispered, his final words.

"At least I die free, you bastard," Yasmin breathed before all went black.

YASMIN MADE HER WAY DOWN THE PATH TOWARD THE small village by the river with a slightly limping gait. The scent of flowers, especially the cherry blossoms, hung in the air like spring perfume. She followed the alleyways and streets to the far side, bowing to each person she passed as was polite. They looked at her strangely, likely because her face was hidden by a bright yellow niqab that complemented her pretty brown eyes. Beneath the layers of silk, Yasmin's skin was a maze of scars, though not so bad as she would have expected. The surgeons of Nagasaki were adept in their skills and had methods her own people had yet to discover. Her left leg, they told her, would never be quite the same, but she could walk without too much of a hobble. And she'd lost two fingers of her right hand, the pinky and the ring finger, but that was the price of freedom and a small one to Yasmin's mind.

She carried with her a chit, requiring a massive sum for Yasmin's safe return, as well as the letter that had saved her. She pulled it out and read the scrawled translation she kept with it.

"The woman who carries this is possessed by a yōkai. It seems neither good nor evil, but I do not believe it allows her happiness. Whoever may read this for her, do not disclose its contents to the bearer. Instead, take her to Moriyama Yoshihide in Nagasaki. I believe he can help her. If you can promise her a safe return to my home in Ezo, I will provide you with two hundred koku. She will know where to go. Please, be kind and show good manners toward the afflicted."

Yasmin smiled. Two hundred koku, she had learned, was a small fortune and far more than the village produced in a year and likely a large portion or all of what Takeda owned.

With as much spring in her step as she could muster, she trod the road to Takeda's. And as she closed in, her smile grew beaming. "Furusato," she whispered to herself at the entrance gate. She had come to learn that the word meant more than home. It was a place one felt most loved, a place one longed to be.

Adjusting her kimono and hakama as best she could,

she licked her lips to ease their dryness, and, as Takeda's voice drifted over the high wall, Yasmin rang the bell. Moments later, the door opened, and Takeda's bright brown eyes met her own.

"Tadaima," Yasmin whispered, the word thick with emotion.

"Okaerinasai, Yasu-san," Takeda answered with a wide smile and sparkling eyes before pulling her inside and wrapping her in a tight embrace.

完

About the Author

After 35 years wrangling corporate drones and government operatives, Aoibh Wood finally traded in the chaos of Cybersecurity for something truly terrifying: becoming a full-time author. With over seventeen years in infosec and a knack for surviving meetings that could kill a lesser soul, she published her debut novel, *Blood Rituals: A Cait Reagan Novel*, in 2022. That kicked off a genre-blending series that now spans three sequels: *Black Mirror*, *Green Rath*, and *Dark Sisters* (Winter 2024). Somewhere along the way, she also dropped the bestselling lesbian romantic thriller, *The Senator's Widow*, proving she's just as dangerous with a love story as she is with a zero-day.

Her latest? *But I'm Not a Supervillain!!!* — a superhero romantic comedy about a bumbling art thief with a flair for the dramatic and a very inconvenient crush on her arch-nemesis. Because why not? The audiobook debuted at #1 on Amazon's Superhero Fantasy new release chart.

Her current project: *Shadow Veil*, Book 5 of the Cait Reagan series, due in late 2025.

Aoibh lives in New England with her wife and their stunningly attractive, perpetually disappointed cat. When she's not writing emotionally devastating fiction, she's probably scuba diving, rock climbing, exploring ancient ruins, or eating something that might technically still be moving. She lifts heavy things for fun and to counteract her writer's posture, which is somewhere between "noodle" and "gargoyle."

Follow her misadventures on BlueSky, Instagram, and Facebook—or join the chaos on Patreon at patreon.com/AoibhWood for exclusive stories, sneak peeks, and entirely too much sarcasm.

Geo Kinebuchi was raised in Japan and works as a literary translator in the Southeastern United States.

Make Me a Sword
Jules Revel

IT WASN'T MY FINEST HOUR, ACCEPTING AN INVITATION from Melly, but boredom prompts poor choices. I fiddle with my ticket stub. The Nine Oakes Night Faire promises an evening of enchantment and delight, it says so in bold print, but with Melly I expect it'll be more like bewilderment and misplaced arousal.

Music, a decent rendition of a lute song played on the wrong instrument, floats over the field. I haven't heard that tune in ages. Maybe this will be fun, if only for nostalgia's sake. I am enjoying the chaos of so many eras being mimicked and mocked. There are dancing girls, too, that's never a bad thing. Although Melly blends seamlessly with the crowd, I spot her immediately, smelling her from a long way off, like a forest floor in the heat of noon. A shocking scent in the middle of a cool autumn night.

Beside me, two poets challenge each other to recite passages of *Sir Gawain and the Green Knight*. Their Middle English is awful. I'm sympathetic—it takes time for the tongue to shape those sounds.

"No, here, like this, more in the throat on that line," I say to one and speak the passage more accurately.

He smiles and gamely repeats my pronunciation. Sometimes the young are so charming. He thanks me.

Melly is watching, though when I look up she seems still engaged with her coterie of admirers. Like most of her kind, she is many. In herself, Melly, but also in the forest all around us. She can watch without looking.

"You came," she trills in my ear a short while later.

I look away from the aerialists, and the flash of their silks as they spin and fall. "Hungry?" Melly inquires.

I close my eyes, vexed.

"Oh, I'm joking. And look, you don't have to hide here. They won't even notice you, and if they do, they'll think it's the most amazing costume." Her voice is laced with the flutter of wings, iridescent and fine over a forest pool. The sound soothes, though I know it shouldn't. She leans toward me and smiles. "Even the ones who suspect the truth aren't frightened. They love it."

"Hmm."

"Oh, it's a nice change of pace, why not enjoy yourself?" She tips her golden head ever so subtly in the direction of the weapons tent.

Long swords, falchions, a few axes, none older than fifty years. The allure is real; she knows it, too. I shake my head and smirk. Whatever she's trying to get me wrapped up in, I want no part of it. I have enough problems of my own, and enough experience to know better than to listen to Melly's advice.

"Really? Come on Nik, for old time's sake. Let's just take a look."

"It's not like your folk to want to play with metal."

"Hmm, but we like to watch." She winks.

I feel it in my body, an unasked-for attraction. No regular person could resist Melly if she wanted to woo them. Fortunately, I am no regular person. "Don't flirt. It doesn't work on me."

"Oh? It does a little," she sings and now it's the hum of bees I hear in the undertones of her voice. She is honey spilling from the split in an oak. If I am old, she is always. She doesn't explicitly remind me of this, but I know it in the deepest parts of myself. *Fucking Melly.*

She's a tactician, but so am I. Perhaps that's the kernel of the genuine respect I have for her. Together we're playing the long game.

"Why not just tell me what you want, Mel?"

"I have a gift for you."

"Just what I need."

My sarcasm doesn't stop her from veritably twinkling with amusement. Still, she manages to pout. "You don't want my gift?"

"Too many strings attached." I smile.

"Let's go look, at least."

Begrudgingly, I give in and follow her past the drum circle and the puppeteers, past the alcove where revelers drink mead from hollow horns. Torches staked into the ground light the path. Beyond a tight circle of tents reminding me of a military encampment is a patch of hard-packed dirt ringed with a chest-high perimeter. The metal smell is stronger here. Iron, steel, bronze, and blood.

My nostrils flare and Melly casts a knowing look. She can be so smug at times.

"Touchy," Melly chides in a whisper.

I don't think she can read minds exactly, but she often knows more than I expect. I make a conscious effort to shut her out of my thoughts and she shrugs.

At the edge of the combat square, lounging under the awning of a tent more like one from Gettysburg than Agincourt, two would-be knights adjust their armor. A man in green and purple silks takes a headset microphone and urges those assembled to pay attention to him. I keep my eyes on the combatants. There are more than I first noticed. At least eight fully-clad in a mix of armor types.

The fighting starts with three on three. For a moment I miss the feeling of a sword. It's been a while since I've held one, though my muscles recall the sensation. We watch together, and soon it's obvious what Melly is up to. The melee victor raises their weapon, basking in the applause before pulling off their helm.

"She's half fae," Melly whispers.

I can't quite fathom it. The woman is tall and although I know they seem to gain a few inches with every passing generation, Melly's people, even their halflings, are usually slight.

"Half," I mumble, looking at the woman, now surrounded by her teammates.

"I know you have a taste for them."

"I do not."

"Nik. Nik, it's just us here. It's nothing to be ashamed of."

"I'm not ashamed of anything." That's not strictly true, but I won't be hashing out the particulars with the likes of Melly.

"I thought you'd like her. You do like her." Honey in the comb, wax split and running with its own fullness, the hum of bees surrounds me.

"She needs training and her sword is shit," I reply.

"You know that's not what I mean, though you could fix all of that, couldn't you?" Melly knows damn well I could.

"Appealing to my vanity?"

"You? Never. Well, if you don't want her, I could always find some other use for her."

Use. No. I don't like the sound of that. It's not like I care about an overgrown halfling, but when Melly starts sounding utilitarian, I get nervous. "Or you could leave her alone."

The fighters in the ring clash and rattle once more. A man falls and the other is declared the winner. It goes on. None of them are especially skilled, but why would they be? It's not the kind of thing you can perfect on the weekend. Still, a few show promise. The announcer calls for a new match, swords and shields.

"This is her best event. I really thought you'd like her. So tough and pretty all at the same time," Melly taunts.

I watch the girl heft the shield. The style is older than that of her armor, but it suits her. Someone with talent has painted it, a tangle of roses atop a deep green field. I wonder what she knows of her parentage, her connections, the thing in her that has marked her for Melly, or for me. "Does she know?"

Melly's brow twitches up, but she offers only silence.

Infuriating. Maybe even Melly isn't sure, though I doubt that very much.

"Look at her, Nik." As she speaks, the world slows. I'm in Melly's grip. Seeing as she sees. I'm allowing this, I tell myself. I could stop it at any moment, but I don't, because I want to look. I want to see the fight with this much clarity, a level surpassing even my own. All of the angles, all of the possibilities, everything glimpsed in a moment. I see not only the fight itself, her blocks and blows, but her whole future, her many futures.

I see her turned strange, a being bound to darkness or

else to a form I cannot fathom, but Melly would know what to call it. I see her unchanged too, as she is now, only with the sun on her shield and roses worked in silk across her gambeson.

"See, you do like her," Melly says and time flows normally once more. The girl lifts her shield up beneath her opponent's chin and thrusts until he falls under the blow.

I do like her. I like her as she is, pulling off her helm and gloves, waving to the crowd, helping her friend to his feet. They are friends. The man claps her on the back and laughs. There are so many reasons I shouldn't be here.

I think about walking away, but the words *another use for her* give me pause. Perhaps the snare has already been tripped and I'm dangling in mid-air without realizing it. Thankfully, I'm the sort to chew off my own leg to get free. I see the girl walking toward us, all well-polished, poorly fitted steel, and a smile. Melly laughs and something in the sound says I had better start chewing.

"Melly! Is this the sword smith?"

I'm struck by how young she sounds. Although maybe it is her fae side that threads her voice with the newness of spring.

Melly gestures toward me with a smile. "Yes. Let me introduce you. Ro, this is Nik."

I tilt my chin up in acknowledgment, but keep my hands in my pockets; even on a cool night I know my skin would feel unusually chilled. "Roe? Like the deer?"

She shakes her head; short dark waves just long enough to be tousled catch the light of the nearby torches. She'd have chestnut highlights in full sun. "It's short for Róisín."

"Little Rose. Explains the shield."

"You speak Irish?" Her playfully incredulous tone delights me. I can't resist showing off a little. It's amusing to watch them react to the catalog of skills one accumulates over many lifetimes.

"Tá beagán Gaeilge agam."

"It sounds like you know more than me, much to my Nan's dismay." Ro's smile brightens, impressed and pleased. Her heartbeat, already elevated from combat, thrums faster.

"There's still plenty of time to learn." Melly's probably on the cusp of volunteering my services for language lessons when Ro goes on talking.

"Maybe I'll pick up a little next summer. I've been invited to train with the women's team in Dublin. That's why I wanted to meet you. I'm really glad you came. Melly says you're one of the best." Her words run together.

I often make people nervous, sometimes downright frightened, but this is different. It's giddy admiration, and I wonder what kind of tales Melly has been spinning about me and why. "Did she?"

"Yeah. She said you're the stuff of legend."

I almost laugh. Thankfully, Ro goes on without noticing. I decide then and there she doesn't know a thing. She can't hear the way her own words vibrate at the frequency of new leaves unfurling. I might not have noticed it myself had I not been taught how to listen.

She looks down at the plain black hilt of her sword. "I don't have the best gear, as I'm sure you can tell, but I'm in the market for a serious upgrade."

Melly turns to me, her face beautiful and golden. "You can make anything, can't you Nik?"

I can. I'm sure I've seen my own craftsmanship in one of those possible futures. "What are you looking for?"

"Honestly, everything, armor, sword. My shield is sentimental but—"

"May I?" I gesture toward her weapon. She hands it to

me without hesitation. It's trash. I don't know how it hasn't already broken with the way she wields it. Part of me wonders if her own power has been holding it together without her realizing. Despite being out of practice, I'm sure I could make her something to rival even the best sword here.

"That gear looks warm," Melly observes and though the words seem banal, I feel the force of suggestion glinting within them. Ro excuses herself to get changed, leaving Melly and me face to face, the girl's sword still in my hand.

"So, what do you think? Do you want her?"

"What's the catch, Melly?"

"No catch."

"I don't believe you."

Melly's amusement rings around us, a pebble dropped in a pond. "She'll keep you company. You're lonely."

I laugh, hard and ragged. What I am missing has no replacement.

"And, a gift strengthens an alliance. Does it not?"

That gets my attention. "An alliance? I wasn't aware we had one."

"But we do." Melly assures me.

I sense no effort to compel my agreement, so when her words feel right, I don't ignore them. An alliance. There is a battle coming. The players and the stakes are only shadows and suspicions, but I'm with Melly. Or she's with me. And the girl? I don't get headaches anymore but if I did this would certainly bring one on. I pinch the back of my neck with one hand and feel the weight of Ro's sword in the other.

"It's a limited time offer."

I don't have a chance to respond when Ro rejoins us, dressed in a linen undershirt and padded chausses. An adorable squire. "So, what do you think? Would you make me a sword?"

Melly watches me watch Ro.

A limited time offer.

I don't prefer a rushed decision, but I nod. It's only a small motion, but Ro catches it and her pulse hums.

"Really? That's so cool! I'm, I'm sorry," she apologizes through a self-deprecating laugh. "I'm just really excited. I didn't want to get my hopes up but, you know, of course I did."

"It takes a long time to make a sword the right way," I caution. I could make a good sword rather quickly if I brought all of my unusual talents to bear, but I won't. I need time to understand the game we're playing.

"Of course."

"It's a lot of work and I'd want you involved in the process."

"Wow, I'd love that." Her eyes are bright, her voice a fresh green rustle, catkins between new leaves.

"Great. I forge at night. It's cooler that way. Come over next Thursday, around seven-thirty. Wear natural fibers, though I suppose I don't need to tell you that."

"Seven thirty, wear wool not spandex. Got it."

I give her the address to a shack in the woods I haven't used in ages. She jots it on her arm. The faint odor of a newly scabbed wound lifts and drifts by me as she pushes up her sleeve. Melly observes the exchange. What is she intuiting? What is she interjecting? Even after so many encounters, I don't understand what Melly's capable of, but I put nothing past her.

"Hey, Ro, are you gonna help us or what?" a man calls from the camp. The other fighters lug armor and weapons away from the field.

"Sorry. I'd better go help. Thank you so much. I really can't wait. Thank you!" She shouts the last over her shoulder as she jogs toward her teammates, bare feet through dark grass.

"You'll thank me later," Melly whispers in my ear. The game has begun and she sounds so sure of victory.

Boredom is no longer a problem. Rising with the next sunset, I realize I have been in a rut for months. Too much comfort and ease. The irritations too fleeting and predictable. Now, puzzling over Melly and planning for Ro's visit, my patterns are ruptured. I need supplies and a functional workshop and I need them quickly.

In the old days I would have gathered iron ore myself, or gone to the pit and traded for it; now, it's a different world. Online shopping to the rescue, and the bulk of the ore will appear like magic in two days' time on the stoop of the house I've been staying in. With that detail attended to, I hop in my truck and drive north under a hazy purple-gray sky.

The forge at Pierce Brook, a busy place in the days of revolution, slumps quietly in a meadow, unvisited except by myself in rare moments. The road in is a single track of neglected pavement that turns onto a gravel path which itself is being reclaimed by weeds and bramble. I mend the roof and clean the chimney; all the while, Melly and Ro infiltrate my thoughts.

I scrub the wide pine boards until they're smooth, thinking, *why give a halfling to someone like me?* Two obvious answers present themselves. One, you want them dead.

Two, you'd like them to live forever. As of yet, I can see no reason this particular girl would need to be assassinated, nor can I imagine I'm the most efficient choice of killers. Melly could do it herself or, easier, she could convince the girl with sweet whispers to shuffle off this mortal coil. A clean and flawless option if death were the only goal. No, it's not that.

Too many years spent mired in political intrigue cause me to wonder if there'd be some benefit to having me do the dirty work. Making me a killer hardly seems an interesting third option. By every measure, I'm already a murderer. In the old days and now. If killing her would trigger some kind of event, perhaps, but she doesn't seem important enough. There's the issue. I know Melly pretty well, and I know myself, but Ro is a mystery.

What makes her so special? Halflings aren't as rare as one might expect: the fae are irresistible and humans are happy to be charmed. A fae vampire, well, those are less common, but what's the point?

I mull all of this over for a few nights. I pick up my packages and drive them to the forge. Every ordinary thing is ready. The chimney cleaned, the bellows replaced, a new handle of hickory is secured to a very old hammer head. I could forge the blade now if I wanted and be done with it. But I am too curious by far.

On the fourth night, I start poking around. There are, in this world, so many kinds of creatures it's almost impossible to keep track, and each type spawns, in time, subspecies who take on their own characteristics. Witches are no different, and while Salem is renowned as the witch city, I' have found my favorite mortal mage prefers to stick to the 24-hour Donut Hole just off Highway 3. It's convenient; she has a sweet tooth and at two in the morning, no one really expects "normal," allowing her and her clientele to flow seamlessly among the regular folk.

When it comes to magic, I don't know much about her skills, but when it comes to fringe society gossip, she can't be beat. Information is power. We have an arrangement and when she sees me coming, her face registers a kind of subtle alert interest that lets me know she's been hoping I'd stop in.

I've already done my due diligence. Database searches, even a foraging trip into the dark web, have turned up nothing remarkable. Róisin Hunter, on paper the daughter of an Irish woman from Sligo and a doctor born in York. The family moved to the States when Ro was a baby. That explains the lack of accent, though she has two passports, one Irish and one American. She's young enough that her whole life is transparent if you know where to look. High school sports accomplishments, graduation photos, college transcripts, a long-neglected Facebook account, and a current, though not much used, Instagram. None of it is interesting. The only potential blip is a car accident which claimed the lives of her parents seven years ago, but even that doesn't raise any alarm. Icy remote roads outside of a ski resort, blood alcohol of the other driver well above the legal limit. It happens. I can't see what it has to do with Melly or with me.

"You're early," the witch says around a mouthful of honey-dipped dough.

"I was passing through." Not a lie, the drive to the forge takes me by this place.

"So, a social call then?"

She wants me to seduce her. That much has been obvious ever since the day we met. Some people get addicted to the feeling of losing control. I am hungry.

Maybe later. "Perhaps. Anything interesting I should know about?"

She tells me all of the sordid stories she's caught wind of in the three weeks since last we met. While interesting in some respects, none of them are relevant to my problem. I jot a few words in my notebook and gaze down at the letters of a language so utterly extinguished only a fool would bother learning it.

"Not what you were hoping for?"

I shrug.

"You're worried. What's bothering you?"

"It's nothing." I'm not about to explain my thoughts to an asset.

She digs around in the giant purse beside her and pulls out a black charm bag. "Here, take this, for protection."

I'm about to refuse the offer when I see the perfectly wrought chrysanthemum embroidered on the sachet. "Who made this?"

"Me. Don't worry. It's the real deal," she assures me.

I don't know if I believe her, but the needlework is gorgeous. "I didn't know you did this kind of thing. Do you ever work on larger projects?"

"Sure, sometimes. Have you got something in mind?"

"I might."

"Well you just let me know. Keep that, it'll help, whatever the problem is." She leans close, pushing my hands closed over the bundle. I don't bother avoiding her touch. She knows who she's dealing with.

I shift the conversation to ordinary things. A half-hour later, I leave her in the parking lot looking a shade paler but feeling on top of the world. I don't bother compelling her to forget. She wants to remember, and it serves my interests to let her.

THE NIGHT RO COMES TO MEET ME, APPLES AND lilacs, fruit and flower side by side, perfume the air. It is the scent of a diabolical summer turned cool and livable at last. The phenomenon is familiar, and it never bodes well. In the deepening dusk I am still considering her question. *Would you make me a sword?*

From a long way off, I hear her approach and eventually glimpse headlights flickering in the gaps between the trees. She stops where the weed-choked road ends and hops down from her Jeep. She's dressed in work wear, a pair of thick canvas overalls and a t-shirt that hugs her biceps.

Little Rose.

I see her for a moment as the ordinary world must— well-muscled, tall, rippling with power and presence. I could break her so easily and Melly, I don't know by what means, but Melly could destroy her.

"Hey! You're really in the sticks out here." Ro smiles and surveys the area, her eyes squinting in the indigo dusk. I've hung lanterns around the shop and the outdoor work area. At the end of the path, they glow.

"Yeah, it's out of the way, but it's got history."

"I'll bet." She follows me, talking about competition regulations, sword styles and weights.

The thought of this blade yet to come being left unsharpened for use in a game troubles me, though Ro speaks of her tournaments with cheerful intensity, lightening the mood.

We'll be outside most of the night. I show her around. The clay furnace, the charcoal, and the ore. I light the fire and work the bellows until it blazes.

"I can't believe we're doing this," she whispers to herself

as I pour in a ladle of ore sand. At my instruction, she feeds the fire. When the iron runs molten from a hole punched in the clay, she marvels at it and asks me if I've ever seen an active volcano. I lie and tell her no. Together we pull the bloom from the ground. She holds the tongs as I hammer.

It's hot work. I should pretend to sweat or think of some excuse for not sweating. The truth is I'm hardly exerting myself. I let her have a go at the hammer. Her aim is true. Interest and good conditioning make her a fine assistant. If she had the time, I'm sure she could become skilled at many things. Perhaps her potential is what Melly wants me to see. It is in my power to give Ro all the time in the world.

I make a show of wiping my face with a rag and try to look exhausted. We've been working for hours. It's well past midnight, well past the time any ordinary person would quit. "Let's call it a night."

"You're probably right." With deliberate care, she sets down the tongs though she clearly wants to keep going. I remember what it was like to be so intensely at work I would forget everything and push on. I haven't had my limits tested in quite some time, save for my capacity to endure loss. That boundary I am always pushing.

"Come next Thursday," I tell her. "Bring all of your tournament gear."

In the intervening days, I busy myself with the usual—managing my maker's affairs and her expectations. She is abroad, busy with something I prefer not to know about. I make the rounds. Collect on debts. Check in on my sisters and the estate. In the empty hours, I think about the halfling. There is no way to shake her from my thoughts. It might be easier were the estate not filled with roses, easier if the same cruel heat that forced the lilacs hadn't also pressed these canes to bloom out of season.

Next Thursday, by lantern light, I examine Ro's armor. She arranges the pieces on a sheet of canvas, like the flap of a tent. Somewhere, a memory of wind whipping such a door surges and retreats. Ro stands across from me, arms folded over her chest, a finger absentmindedly tracing a scar on her forearm. The firelight dances in the metal.

Endless years make many lives. I have dressed a knight before and been dressed in return. I know how, if needed, to bend my knee and show my willingness to aid. I can't help but wonder what Little Rose would make of the gesture.

Regrettably, I do want her.

Perhaps Melly knows me too well. It's a sobering thought.

"I know, it's poor quality."

The note of apology surprises me and I look up at her.

"I plan to get something better eventually. Which reminds me, we should talk cost. I didn't realize, I mean, Melly said you were the best, but smelting the ore? Doing everything by hand? This is way more than I expected. It's amazing. Don't get me wrong. You're amazing. I should've asked about this the last time we met, but I was so into, well, everything, I— I'm sorry. I should've asked, but how much does a sword like this cost?" she rambles, face pinking lightly, the blush spreading down her neck. I watch it reach the edge of her bright white tank top then look away for a moment to refocus my thoughts.

"Do you still want me to make you a sword?"

"Yeah, yes, of course, but I might need to pay in install-ments, I think."

"We'll work something out."

She nods. She doesn't want to talk herself out of this.

"Come on, let's put your armor on, I'd like to check a few things."

She puts on her doublet. I hand her the sabatons. Mentally, I am still considering scenarios, conceivable futures, reasons I might be allied with Melly, reasons this particular halfling might matter. There are too many possibilities and too few elegant solutions.

Ro affixes the plates on her lower limbs. It's difficult—nearly impossible—to armor oneself fully. Without making her ask, I step closer and help her dress. Her chest and back plates are both too stiff. I would add articulation. I make a mental note and cinch the ties, then move on. The shoulder coverings she uses are too wide. She lifts her arm as I tighten the buckle. In the quiet between this plate and the next, I hear a car on the road. Unusual, but I ignore it.

My fingers brush the warm canvas of her doublet and I see again, like a flash of real memory, the rose worked gambeson Róisín might one day wear. The silk stitching of the flowers bright in the sun. The needlework impeccable, the kind made for nobility. Everything smells of green growth and blossoms.

"Is that a car?" Ro squints into the darkness.

A few moments later an impeccably kept droptop '79 Beetle bounces along the drive. Downtempo electronica spills out, disrupting the usual night song of insects and leaves.

Melly.

Uninvited and definitely unwelcome, but her kind go where they will, there's no point in fighting it. "It's just Melly," I say.

Ro has no reason to think anything of it. Maybe Melly and I are great friends who visit each other at all hours. As I secure the final ties on Ro's armor, she waves at Melly.

"Well, don't you look ready for a battle?" Her tone is breezy, but there is a glint of irritation in her eyes reserved only for me.

I allow myself no visible reaction. "We're taking some measurements." I hand Ro her sword and say, "Be right back." On the seat of my pickup, wrapped in a work shirt, rests my most recent blade. It's already a hundred years old, though made in an older style. It hasn't been sharpened in ages, but isn't exactly blunt either. Still, I won't hurt her. We aren't fighting, not even sparring. I'm just curious.

"Come on, let's see how you move." I gesture to the sandy spot where we smelted iron last week. I've since raked it in preparation for tonight.

Ro's eyes go wide when she sees the weapon in my hand. "Holy shit. Did you make that?"

"I did." I assume a stance indicating readiness to spar.

She shakes her head. "You don't have armor."

"No. So don't hit me."

She refuses to raise her weapon. *How noble.* I consider poking her with the tip of my blade to see how she responds, but such a gesture would amuse Melly far too much. "We'll move in slow motion. I just want to get a sense of your patterns. No strikes. I promise."

"Ok."

Like practicing a dance, we go through the motions. A left-handed attack. A parry. Her lips curve as I flick her blade away. I manage to keep my attention on her hands, her wrists, the way she wields her weapon. Too much experience tells me how an alteration in the sword's balance would improve her swing, how better fitting armor would make it even harder for her enemies to overcome her.

"Ok, I've seen what I need to."

Ro almost hesitates, not wanting to stop now that we've

started. How good it would be to really test her. Perhaps one day.

"We should spar sometime," she says as if giving voice to my thoughts.

"Indeed. But first, let's get this lump of metal roughed out into a blade. Sorry, Melly, I can't hang out tonight, we need to get some things done. Maybe tomorrow?"

"Of course," she says and with only a few parting words, hops back in her car and goes. That was entirely too easy. I know there will be hell to pay, but for now, I want to lose myself in the task at hand.

Róisin and I manage a few hours of quiet concentrated work. She turns the metal as I strike and shape it. This blade will be strong, balanced, beautiful, fit for one much more skilled than the girl who will wield it; even so, it delights me to think of her hand on the hilt.

"Hey, there's a faire this weekend if you're interested."

"A night faire?"

"Oh, no. Those are pretty rare. You work weekends?"

There's a hint of disappointment and, in spite of myself, I am flattered. "It's a demanding day job."

"Sure, I get it. Well, the talent and crew all camp out overnight. It's pretty nice. No organized fights or anything, but we all have a good time. It'd be cool to have you, I mean, if you wanted to stop by. It's not too far from here. Maybe forty minutes."

"Give me the details. I'll swing by if I can." I take a notebook from my back pocket and hand it to her. If I know Melly, she'll be planning something. Not for the first time, I curse the disadvantage of my condition. What happens to Ro in the daylight is something I can't control. I curse Melly then for putting her in my path, and curse myself for caring. That's too many curses for one night.

Ro hands back my notebook.

Watch Ro swing metal this Saturday night - Merrimack Faire. 1221 Pine Crest Blvd. A sketch of a sword and smiley face accompany the words.

"Watch Ro swing metal, huh? I though there were no fights, just camping."

"No *organized* fights. We're idiots with swords. Who knows what we'll get up to. I bet we have gear to fit you if you want to spar for real."

It is a very tempting offer.

Ro leaves with no promise of my attending, but happy to know I'm considering it. I watch her Jeep's red lights fade into pinpricks and then darkness. I feel the forest around me, sense it watching me in return, not the usual watching of so many night creatures, but something more. Leaning in the doorway of the shop I oil my old blade, waiting and not for long.

"Why is she still breathing?" Melly's voice carries on the wind.

"Hello, Melly, back so soon?" I don't look up. My hands keep polishing.

She emerges from the trees at the meadow's edge, her dress wet with dew, her waves of golden hair bejeweled with a few early red maple leaves. She looks remarkably like herself, unguarded, pure. It is a gorgeous and terrible sight. "Nik? Why does the halfling breathe?"

"It's complicated." I sheathe my blade. It is complicated. Turning a fae can be done, but even if I wanted to, I'm not exactly sure how. The only people I've met who would know never told me, not even when I was in their good graces, which I haven't been for quite some time. I can't divulge this to Melly, so I feint. "I need time."

"I thought you wanted her. I saw you watching her go.

Take her Nik, why deprive yourself? It would be easy. I've seen the way she looks at you. It would be a kindness. Give her what she wants."

So, Melly has been watching us. I suspected as much, but the confirmation is helpful. "What does it matter to you?"

Youthful amusement shapes her features. "I ship it. Butch for butch little soldiers. Classic. And she's so tall, I think you'll like being her little spoon."

"Melly, I don't need relationship advice."

The glib expression fades, replaced with the stony intensity of a cliff. Melly leans toward me and whispers, "You are a general without an army, Nik."

I meet her eyes. "And what? She is an army? A girl with a tin sword and a scrap of fae blood. She's not even a soldier. She needs training."

"Then turn her, and shape her to our purpose, Nik."

"It takes time. Besides, I thought she was a gift? Why are you telling me what to do with what's already mine?" The use of mine here feels wholly disingenuous, but Melly doesn't push back on that particular claim.

She lets out a long-suffering sigh. "You should be more careful with your things Nik. Especially fragile things."

I manage to stay calm. "Threats are no way to seal an alliance with me."

"Threats? I wouldn't dream of it."

I DON'T LIKE TO IMAGINE WHAT MELLY DREAMS OF, BUT her thoughts, or what I guess them to be, eat at my mind. A general without an army, she says, though I have many soldiers. Does she foresee a mutiny? Or is she trying to get under my skin and make me doubt my own reserves? Perhaps this particular fight can't be won with the kind of loyalties I claim.

Why a halfling and why me? If Melly wants to turn someone, there are plenty of others she might have gone to. Melly and I have a complicated relationship. Why would I ever be her first choice? But maybe I'm not. My thoughts spin. I take comfort in the fact that Melly shows herself in increments. She watches us too closely. She is invested. She is annoyed. Even if I did know how to turn Ro, I don't feel inclined to. I ought to make it unlikely that anyone else will try. If Melly wants an alliance, fine, but she cannot dictate the terms.

I'm glad when the weekend comes and I can see Ro for myself. Like Nine Oakes, the faire at Merrimack draws creatures of many kinds, and has no fealty to either time or place. Italian sixteenth century shoes and a Tudor cap, why not? Fae and witch and human mingle freely, though how openly, it's difficult to judge. My appearance at the gate raises no alarm. A bored security guard in a bright orange vest takes one look at my sword and lets me through. Just another weirdo with a weapon.

I scan the camp, mentally playing zatrikion. If I am one side and Melly the other, who are her pieces? How are they arranged? And if we are on the same side, as she seems to want me to believe, who is arrayed against us? I have many enemies, but those I'm unaware of concern me most.

In all directions, camp assaults the senses, still I find the fighters with ease. Loud squabbling and bets bandy across the perimeter. A bell rings, followed by the clash of steel on steel. I join the audience and watch a stout fellow with an axe fend off an onslaught of two smaller men with swords.

Soon enough, Melly sidles up beside me.

"Oh, you came after all," she titters, then glances scornfully at the chrysanthemum charm I've tied to my belt. I don't know why I brought it, except I did. I suppose I thought it might help me blend. A few satchels from the belt never seem amiss at the faire. Melly shakes her head. "Oh, Nik. I do hope you aren't getting strung along by some little enchantress."

I make a face wordlessly conveying how unlikely that would be. But I realize there must be something to the charm if Melly's marked it out for ridicule. Maybe my friend at the Donut Hole has some power after all.

Melly laughs. "I'd hate to see you get your heart broken."

"Un-fucking-likely"

"Hmm. Speaking of romance, are you here for our little soldier?"

"Yes. You're getting what you want, so don't gloat."

Melly smirks but says nothing. She isn't getting quite what she wants, but I am taking her advice. I should be more careful. I walk away and she lets me go.

In one of the canvas tents, I find Ro cleaning her equipment. She jumps to her feet when she sees me. I feel as if I'm about to be saluted, but instead she smiles; the dimple in her left cheek deepens. She wants to spar and in a matter of minutes she assembles her teammates, one who presents me with a waiver and another with an offer of his armor.

"Your sword isn't regulation," he says. I feel his envy as he inspects my weapon.

"I can fight with anything," I assure him.

"This?" He holds up an unsharpened falchion and I nod.

Two burly guys, lively with mead, join us. They're

already placing bets even as they help me and Ro into our armor.

"She's got a way better reach," the man dressing me observes in hushed tones.

"I'm putting ten dollars on Ro," says the other.

"Twenty on the newbie. She looks crazy as fuck," my dresser boasts, then whispers in my ear, "She's tired from earlier. She won five matches today."

I nod in silent acknowledgement and cast a sidelong glance at my opponent, my gift. Ro looks back at me, face bright with anticipation.

In so many ways, it is not a fair fight, but I control myself, allow myself to issue a few strikes at partial strength. Ferocious and patient in turns, she charges, and our blades glide along each other. The more force I slowly apply, the more she matches with returning pressure. Through the slit of her helm, I stare into her eyes, gray-green as the underbelly of new leaves. All over me a ripple, cool creek water laps against my mind. The surge of new sap reaching up from deep within the earth moves through me.

Shaking myself loose from the feeling of her gaze, I push her off of me and dodge left. The crowd cheers as Ro swings at my retreating shoulder and lands a blow. I catch her by the ankle with a swipe. She wobbles but rights herself. I try the move again and this time she launches her body at me. She is going down, but I am going with her. I stay upright just long enough to land a few more strikes, then let myself fall into the grass beside her with a clatter and thud.

"Good fight," Ro laughs through heavy gulps of air.

My dresser hauls me off the ground and raises my hand in triumph. "The newbie!"

"Newbie! Newbie!" The crowd cheers.

Ro drapes her arm around my shoulder and gives my helm a friendly tap. "Come on, let's get out of these."

We walk together toward Ro's tent and are just getting free of our chest plates when Melly arrives.

"Well, that was lovely," she says.

Everything about her presence right now irritates me.

"What, watching me eat shit?" Ro jokes as she undoes the armor covering her hips.

"Oh you almost had her. Besides, she was fresh to the fight."

"And I had better gear."

"Well, yeah. You had Mike's stuff. He's got a sponsorship deal. IronCore, it's pretty sweet. I mean, he still has to work, it's not like going pro, but it's a big help," Ro explains.

Melly looks down at Ro, who is laying out her armor beside what looks like a second-hand hockey bag. "You need a patron."

"A patron? I wish."

"Do you?" Melly's eyes sparkle—dust and pollen stirring in the deep gold rays of late afternoon sun. It's unnerving.

No amount of calming tricks can ease the fury I feel toward her. I hazard a quick glare fit to immolate, but Melly just winks and wrinkles her nose at me. Ro sees nothing.

"Sure, I mean if this really were the fifteenth or sixteenth century, I'd have one. Well, no, I wouldn't have one. I'd probably have been killed long ago for being a witch or something. A girl with short hair and swords," Ro jokes.

"Don't be so sure," I say without thinking.

Ro and Melly look at me, waiting for more. Melly absolutely glows with amusement at my lapse.

"There were female smiths and probably more than a few women who served as squires or even knights in the smaller kingdoms. Look it up," I say with a shrug. My confident indifference seems to do the trick.

"Well, if you want a sponsor, I'm sure I could find someone for you. I'm very well connected," Melly offers.

"Really? Well, if you find some random rich person who wants to help me out, let me know."

"I will." She spins on her heel and leaves us. No doubt off to cultivate a new asset in a bid to forge a different alliance altogether. I won't be so easy to replace, but desperation can lower one's standards, and Melly seems desperate.

Ro shakes her head. "She's kind of crazy."

"Patrons are a real thing."

"Sure, but I'm not holding my breath. I don't think there'll be any mysterious rich benefactors coming along anytime soon."

I wouldn't bet on that.

How does one say I have more resources than god because I'm almost as old? Or older in some cases. There's no way to do so casually. I try to pivot the conversation. "Don't bother with Melly. You don't need a sponsorship. You need a smith, and maybe a little fighting advice."

She wipes down her helm and gives me a teasing look. "Oh is that right?"

"Yes, it is."

Ro hops to her feet, clearly pretending to be defensive. "You didn't win by much."

"No, but I'm out of practice."

"Yeah, well, you pack a punch. I thought you might knock my arm off. Must be all the hammering." She walks toward me and slips her finger into the leather thong securing the plates over my hips. I let her undo them and pull them off. I hear her heart racing. The heat of her body seeps through my clothes. Melly's right about this. Having little Rose would be easy, and it would be something we'd both enjoy.

"Do you want to take a walk?" I ask, eager to get away from the camp and from Melly. More than I care to admit, eager to be alone with this girl.

"Sure, we can hang Mike's armor here for now, he won't need it tonight."

Beyond the encampment, moonlight bathes the field in a blue-white sheen. Paths of trampled grass and a cool wet fragrance guide me east. She follows behind with exceptionally quiet footsteps for someone half human. Midway to the water, a herd of white-tailed deer startles at our approach and crashes through the brush, raising a cloud of crushed camphor weed and sweet fern to scent their wake. At the river, sleeping mallards seem undisturbed by our presence and bob in the water between the rushes.

"Have you been here before?" Ro asks as we scramble out on a rocky overhang. She sits beside a young blueberry bush that pushes its way through a crack in the granite.

"No, but I saw the map and figured it might be nice."

"It is nice. It's probably beautiful at sunrise. Are you staying tonight? We could hike—"

I shake my head. "No, sorry, work."

"Of course. Well, I'm glad you came."

"Me too." Not least of all because Melly is here, working on a back-up plan. Trying to force my hand.

"I have a down payment for you, by the way."

I look up. "Huh?"

"A down payment, for the sword. In case this whole benefactor thing is a flop. I appreciate you being patient."

"It's nothing. I've got all the time in the world."

She leans closer and taps her knee against the dagger I'm wearing. "Is that another of yours?"

It's a slightly shorter replica of one I lost on the banks of the Yr long ago. I loved that knife. I draw the weapon and hand it to her, hilt first. Her hand grasps softly, like the knife is precious to her too, and I can't help thinking of Melly's words. A fragile gift should be looked after.

How many times have I cleaned and polished this blade?

"It's beautiful." Her fingers trace the decorative double twist of iron and copper. We sit together in the moonlight, all around soft motion of water running, night birds crossing from tree to meadow and back again. I am cooling like the rock which still has the lingering warmth of midday in its dark surface.

She returns the knife. "I'm glad Melly introduced us."

"Me too." I surprise myself. It's not a lie. I wish Melly wasn't involved, but it has been nice spending time with Ro. Nice being around someone who seems to be simply living their life, pursuing their own interests.

"How come you didn't say you knew how to sword fight?"

"I didn't think it mattered. You weren't looking for a sparring partner." I wonder why she got into this. If it's her fae blood or an ancestral call.

"Well, you're good. Why give it up?"

I haven't. But there's no easy way to say that either. "I'm getting too old for it."

She scoffs. "Didn't feel that way to me."

Maybe we do come back, as some religions insist. Perhaps she's been a knight before. I don't think I'll amount to anything but waste when the light finally shines on me.

It's just as well. I've been here far too long. I smile at the compliment. "Ah, you just didn't expect it. I'm stronger than I look."

"You can say that again. Well, I enjoyed having you kick my ass." Ro runs her hand over her bicep where a fresh bruise blooms.

Even with the armor, such as it is, those hits leave a mark. I try to stop myself from imagining the way I will need to mark her skin. I certainly don't think about all the ways I'd like to, and narrowly avoid a crude comment, asking instead, "Are you getting cold?"

"Only a little."

"Ok, let's head back."

For a moment, she looks like she wants to argue but relents. "Maybe my millionaire is waiting," she jokes and knocks her shoulder into mine as we walk toward the meadow.

WE HAVEN'T GONE FAR WHEN I WISH SHE HAD ARGUED. I wish she had been convincing in it, too. We should have stayed on the crag over the river, because the trail we came on no longer exists. This is another walk entirely. From the corner of my eye, I see Melly leaning against the trunk of a massive oak but when I turn my head she isn't there. The land seems to whisper. *Turn her.*

I'm contemplating how I might make Melly pay for this trickery when a loud crack, like a stone falling from a high place, splits the night. Before I can process my thoughts, I'm on the ground. Ro leans over me, her arm around my chest pulling me to her. She's maneuvered us behind a break in an old stone wall. The lichen, so close to my face, is bright in the moonlight. I feel Ro breathing hard against my back. Another crack and whizz. Bits of rock spray around us. An engine roars and rumbles, moving west, moving away. Slowly, the cicadas resume their song. She loosens her hold on me; her grip on her knife—a small but functional Norse-looking thing— remains white-knuckle tight.

"Are you alright?"

She wants to protect me. If I weren't who I am, I'd be flattered. I suppose some part of me still is, though a greater part reckons with the absurdity. *The absurdity!* But how did she manage to get me to the ground? How did she know before I did? "I'm fine."

There is no damage, but I feel myself shaking, I smell her blood and then feel a drip of it fall hot across my face. I'm too old to swoon or lose control, but I am tempted.

"You're hurt," she puts her hand on my cheek to swipe the blood away.

"It's not mine," I manage to reply, then turn my face toward the leaves and inhale hoping to mute the too vibrant aroma of honey poured over hot iron.

We lie side by side behind the wall staring at each other in a slash of milky moonlight. The cut on her face is small, but deep. The blood wells and drips from it.

Not thinking, I reach up and press my fingers to the cut. The feeling of her blood is dizzying. *Is this a trap? Will I die if I drink?* I take my finger back and taste her. My eyes close and are still closed when she seems to awaken from a daydream.

"You're cold. Are you sure you aren't hit?" She runs her hands around my arms, my legs, frantically searching for a wound. Looking for a reason I might be so cool and pale.

"I'm not hit. I'm not." I put my hands on her shoulders, grip them so she knows I am serious and sure of myself.

"Fucking poachers," she grumbles. I let her believe that. It's autumn in rural New Hampshire, why not? Maybe they were poachers who thought we were deer, or maybe bored teenagers not particularly aiming at anything. They weren't, but those are simpler explanations.

"How did you know to hit the ground? Did you see them?" I ask.

"No."

"How, then?" It comes out more intense than appropriate, but I need to know. Perhaps this is the key to it all.

In an instant, her eyes glisten with tears. I've seen a lot of weeping in my time. I've even done some, though it's been a while. I am, for the most part, immune to the pain of others and immune even to my own, but Ro alarms me all the same. Maybe it's her proximity, the scent of her blood, almost floral now, or maybe it's the very real possibility that she actually did pull me to safety. It's not like I would have died, but she doesn't know that. If I weren't already dead, she might have saved my life.

I lift my hand to her face. "You should put pressure on this." Her blood seeps hot between my fingers.

"You have it," she whispers.

I do have it. I don't bother denying myself. I keep my hand where it is and gently press, then ask again, more softly. "How did you know?"

"The trees told me." A few tears spill and one runs down my wrist. She doesn't know why, but she knows she is different. She's been hiding it.

I actually feel for her, a little. "Ok."

"Ok?"

"Yeah. Thanks for pulling me down." I don't need an

explanation and I can see she's powerless to give one. I know what she doesn't.

She smiles and sobs before covering it with a laugh. "Adrenaline," she mutters.

"I'll be your patron," I say, not wanting to listen to her cry. Besides, there's no time for it. We need a plan because things have gotten suddenly very complicated. We're so close, I feel her breath warm on my cheek. "There are stipulations, but—"

"Name them."

"A mark, to show we work together."

"Like a token?"

"Yes. And whoever Melly introduces you to, deny them."

Her face registers a mix of surprise and amusement. "Because I'm yours?"

"I didn't say—"

She nods and repeats the words. It is not a question this time. Ro bends forward and kisses me, her tongue softly tracing the curve of my lips. As moves go, it's not subtle, but it is effective. I take her face between my hands. I kiss the gash on her cheek. She moves closer to me, radiating heat. I could have her here. Drink from her as much or as little as I please. Sate every desire. And I want to. Every cell calls out for satisfaction. Instead, I trace my tongue along the cut. What small measure of closure had been forming undoes itself and she bleeds again into my waiting mouth.

I am nothing if not a master of my longings. I lick just enough to leave a trace of myself behind. I see it there, blazing and fresh. She kisses my mouth again, licks her own blood off my lips, and smiles.

"You ok?" I ask, because I don't think she's ever been

shot at before and I'm sympathetic to how unnerving that might be.

"Yeah."

"I can drive you home if you want." I don't know where she lives, but I'm sure there'll be enough time between now and sunrise. It's not even midnight.

"No, I should stay. I've got a contract. You can crash here if you want. My camp bed is really nice."

I shake my head.

"Your day job sucks."

"It does." We should go back. As much as I'm sure neither of us wants to. We dust the leaves and grit from our clothes. Small flecks of granite fall from Ro's hair. That explains the cut. A shard of stone. I think of ancient blades then and almost laugh. She leans close as we walk, her arm around me, and I let her, why not? I think of the many times I've emerged from a forest with a beloved comrade.

The trail is ordinary now, and I find our way with ease. Camp still sounds raucous. Fire dancers practice their talents. The fighters have turned to arm wrestling and some, judging by the snores, have already passed out in their tents.

Melly finds us. Her gaze smothers. A thick bed of duff in an ancient wood, leaves matted over me so damp that bluebells lift under my eyelids. I don't look back. My gaze is trained on the dancers beyond.

"I wondered where you two went," she says pleasantly.

"We took a walk in the woods," Ro replies.

"Well, I want you to meet someone," she beckons to a man in well-made woolen breeches and a comical codpiece. He hurries obediently to her side. His pores emanate the copper and iron tang of his last hasty meal. Trying to keep his hands warm, no doubt. "This is Micheal Williams, heir to the Williams and Bennet shipping empire. He's a great fan of your sport."

His eyes fix on Róisin and then on me. My would-be replacement is hardly up to the task. I feel his cold terror. He can't be more than a hundred years old. Hardly a match or a worthy sire. Ro leans closer, and puts her arm over my shoulder. She's trembling, I wonder if it's cold or shock or some sixth sense of danger. Melly's eyebrow twitches.

"A pleasure to meet you." Micheal extends a pallid hand.

I take it firmly, but not too harshly. There is no need for a macho display. He knows his place. "I'm Nik."

"Ro."

Another handshake. His eyes remain on Ro's face. He sees her as I do. Claimed, a mark bright as fresh smelted ore telling all of my kind to politely fuck off. Melly squints. I don't know what she sees. Perhaps just me and a still breathing halfling who has her arm slung over my shoulder.

"You are very fortunate to have such a skilled friend," Micheal says to Ro with a deferential smile in my direction.

"I am."

I have had more than enough games for the night. I tighten my grip around Ro just a bit. "Well, if you'll excuse us, we have things to do. Blades to forge, battles to win. Ro, walk me to the truck?"

Melly's gaze lingers on us as we depart. No doubt Micheal is explaining it all. She has my mark. None of my people, save for very few unspeakable elders, would dare touch her. If Melly wanted an alliance, she has it, but on my conditions.

In the dark of the parking lot, we say our goodbyes. I lean against my truck, wanting to drink, wanting her. These are both terrible ideas, so I undo my knife from my belt.

"Take this."

"As token?"

"Yes. Keep it close, and if someone tries to hurt you, put it in their fucking heart."

Her fingers close over the sheath and she draws my dagger almost tenderly to her chest.

"I'll see you tomorrow night." I lean up and kiss her cheek, blood and sap singing all around me.

About the Author

Forever feral, Jules Revel writes stories exploring courage, chance, and the magic in the mundane. Jules loves iced coffee, sharp things, and the women who wield them.

julesrevel.com

For Now and Always
Rose Goodwin

I HAVE TO STOP. I CAN'T DO THIS.

"No!" the voice shouts in my head. "You're nothing but what I've made you. Now kill her!"

I try to resist. I see the fear in her eyes. The woman I've fallen in love with is terrified of me.

Seven Years Ago

THE NIGHT WAS DARK. INTERMITTENT CLOUDS TOOK their turns obstructing the moonlight, making my journey through those mysterious woods all the more challenging. Escaping the temple had been easy. I'd been planning it for weeks: leave my bed in the dead of night, wait for the right opportunity during the hierophants' nightly patrols, sneak to the section of the outer walls currently under repair, and make my way to the woods beyond.

The only problem with my plan was that I had no idea what to do once I got to the forest. I knew that what I sought was out there, but where exactly and what awaited me was a total mystery. Nor did I plan for my courage to leave me the moment I reached those woods. It was as if it'd decided that it'd gone far enough and simply went back to my warm bed.

Not my desperation, though. No, that would never leave me.

A howl pierced the haunting silence of the night, jolting me and sending my already racing heart to a faster pace. I looked around, searching for its source. Looking for danger in the distance, I missed the danger in front of me. My foot caught on a root, causing me to tumble forward and down into a small ravine. Pain shot through every fiber of my body as I tried to pick myself up off my stomach.

It was then that I heard her, feet crunching the dead leaves with each step towards me.

"Are you lost, little one?" she said in a sweet voice.

I looked up at her. Tall with pale skin and raven black hair, eyes and clothes as pitch black as the night. At the base of her neck sat a purple stone on a black metal chain, pulled tight to her skin. She watched me, head tilting, waiting for my response.

"I...I am."

"And where exactly are you headed?" Her eyes bore into me, like she was trying to figure out everything there was to know about me.

"I heard tale of a wizard who might be able to help me. I'm an acolyte in the Temple of The Goddess, but I know that I don't belong there."

"And where, pray tell, do you belong?" She took a few steps closer to me then crouched down as if to examine me in more detail.

"Among the women of the Queen's Guard, protecting

the queendom from ruin." The truth I'd never told anyone, my dream that haunted me every night, poured out of me. I couldn't help it. This mysterious stranger was the first person who'd ever asked me what I wanted.

I fully expected her to scoff, to laugh, or something much worse. But she didn't. She simply smiled and asked, "But certainly, you must know that men are not allowed to be members of that elite group? Do you seek the wizard so that he may change the rules of the land? I'm afraid he may not be the best choice. For that, you'd need to see those hypocrites in the castle, and they will most likely be reluctant to help you."

"No. That isn't what I seek." My heart pounded in my chest, the full extent of my desire laid bare. For the first time ever, someone other than myself knew what I wanted more than anything in the world. The thought terrified me, but I had to say it.

Slowly, her face shifted as she understood what I wanted. "Ah, now I see. You wish to be made a woman, something you clearly are not?" She spoke a kind of truth, but it still felt like a dagger to my chest.

"But...but I am, though. I feel it, deep in my soul I feel it." Despite what everyone had ever called me, I knew my truth.

Clearly, the anger in my tone didn't affect her. She simply smiled and stood to her full height. "I see," she said before spreading her arms wide dramatically, "Well, luckily for you, I can also perform the type of magic you require. And I'm right here."

A sense of hope blossomed in my chest, taking some of the weight of my anger and fear with it. Not fully, though. A knot of suspicion remained in my gut. "And what would your price be?"

Sensing my unease, she smiled at me reassuringly. "Don't worry. I know you have nothing to offer me now. When the time comes, though, I expect repayment. So, do we have a deal?"

It took me only a moment to consider her offer. For years, I'd lived with this pain, this knowledge that I wasn't right. I'd experienced so many days of torment as everyone around me treated me as if I was something that I am not, leaving me a tattered and weeping mess with little hope that the next day would be any better. I couldn't live like that anymore, with my inner truth in a constant and futile war against a world that deemed me broken.

This witch wasn't who I set out to find, but here she was, offering me what I desperately wanted, a way out. A way to live a life in which my inner truth was also my outer truth. "Yes. We have a deal."

"Good." Her smile widened. "Now, hold still."

The interior of the crystal at her neck began to swirl and grow darker as she leaned down and extended her finger, the tip solid black, and touched my forehead. In an instant, everything went dark.

When I awoke, I was no longer in the forest. The dirt that was beneath me had been replaced by a warm bed. Slowly, I pulled back the silky sheets enough to sit up and take in my surroundings. Gone was my dirty and torn acolyte's robe. Instead, I wore a sleeping gown made of the softest linen I'd ever felt. I was no longer surrounded by tall trees but instead by solid grey stone walls. Mid-morning light streamed through the window on the opposite wall. Out the window, I saw a city stretch out before me, the red stone roofs of countless buildings going for what felt like miles. The sounds and smells of the city wafted into my room. Wherever I had been transported to, it was far from the dark woods or the temple from which I had escaped. This was somewhere new.

Looking down my body, I discovered that something else was different about my situation. Two mounds rose underneath my gown where my flat chest used to be. I lifted the neckline to look inside and there they were, a pair of small breasts. My pair of small breasts. Quickly I moved my hand to between my legs and found nothing laying there. I jumped from the bed and darted to the dingy mirror above the wash basin next to the window. Staring back at me was someone else. They looked just like me, but the features were softer. I brought my hand to my face and the stranger in the mirror did the same. No, not a stranger. Me. A smile slowly formed on my face as the realization struck me. The witch had done it. She'd brought my inner being to the light.

A knock at the door halted my moment of shocked elation. "Hello, stranger?" said the voice behind it.

Before they could knock again, I got back into bed and called out, "Come in!" in a voice like mine, but higher and more resonant. A sound that brought me a small tingling of joy deep in my chest.

The door swung open and in walked the most beautiful girl I'd ever seen. She was around my age, maybe older, and had golden blonde curls that fell just below her shoulders and blue eyes that drew me in. Her smile was soft and welcoming as she walked to the chair beside my bed and sat down. It took me a moment, but slowly I realized who she was. I'd met her before, when her mother had brought her on an official trip to the temple and I'd been caught staring too long, earning me a smack from one of the hierophants. The person sitting next to my bed was none other than Princess Amara, First of Her Name, Heir to the Throne of Lavandula.

She set the tray of food she was carrying on my bed. "Good morning! How are you feeling?" Her kind voice instantly sent a warming sensation through my chest.

I couldn't find my words at first. Here was the future queen of the entire realm, sitting next to me and asking me, a lowly acolyte of the temple, how I was doing. But that wasn't right either. I wasn't an acolyte anymore. I was someone completely different.

"I'm, I'm well, your grace," was all I could manage to say.

"That's good. We were all worried for you when we found you. But it seems like a very long sleep in a comfy bed did the trick."

"Yes, it did, your grace. If I may ask, though, how was it that you found me?"

At this, she giggled. "You really don't remember?" When I shook my head, she continued. "We found you outside the gates of the castle. You were wearing a tattered garment caked with dirt and blood. You looked like you hadn't eaten in days. So, we brought you here." At that, she took a roll from the tray of food and offered it to me, the sight of it awakening a powerful grumbling in my stomach. In all of my confusion at my surroundings and elation at the changes to my body, I hadn't sensed just how much I needed to eat. I took the roll from Amara's outstretched hand and devoured it. As if sensing my desperate need for food, Amara grabbed the other roll from the tray and offered it. I took it and, like the one before it, ate in just a few bites.

After finishing the second roll and taking a drink of water from the cup on the tray, I asked Amara, "And how long ago was that?"

"Two days ago. For a moment, our healers thought that

you wouldn't make it. But I prayed to the Goddess that you would."

My eyes widened. "You...you prayed for me?" No one had ever done that before, cared enough for me and my well-being to pray to the Goddess. The fact that Amara had done that for me without even knowing who I was amplified the warmth spreading through me. It was as if she was the morning sun and my chest was laid bare to her rays.

"Of course I did. "Why wouldn't I?" Her response was so matter of fact, as if the thought of not praying for me had never crossed her mind.

I was at a loss for words. What could I say? That I didn't deserve it? That I was too broken to be cared for? Did I believe that anymore now that I was in this body? There were too many questions that I was in no shape to answer at that moment. So, rather than go down that road, I simply replied, "Thank you. It looks like your prayers worked."

At this, she smiled back. "Yes, I guess they did. Now, can you tell me anything about yourself? Who are you? What brought you here? And why were you in such bad shape?"

I didn't know what to say. I couldn't tell her the whole truth, that I was a runaway acolyte from the temple who met a witch in the woods and was transformed into a girl. That would sound insane and probably end with me being sent to the dungeons. Or worse, back to the temple. If they would take me back, since no women outside of the queen and her court are allowed within its walls. The hierophants also don't take kindly to any magic that doesn't come from the Goddess.

No, I had to come up with a story. I settled for half-truths based on what little I knew of my life before being orphaned at the temple. "I come from a small village on the outskirts of the city." Not entirely false, but also not the entire picture. I know that I was born outside of the city walls. "I came all the way here because I want to be a member of the Queen's Guard." Truth.

Amara's head tilted at that. "And why do you want to do that? What was wrong with your life back home?"

More half-truths. I looked down at my lap. "It wasn't for me. My mother and father died when I was younger. I was left with some people who tried their best, but it wasn't what I wanted, what I needed. No matter how much I tried to make myself fit what was expected of me, I just couldn't." A tear dropped from my eyes to my lap.

"And why the Queen's Guard?"

"I saw them once when they visited my home. The way they stood, tall and powerful in their resplendent armor, left me in awe. Their strength and their dedication to helping others, to protecting those who can't help themselves, and," I gazed up at her, into those deep blue eyes, "to protect the heart of our realm. They're valiant, and that's what I want to be."

At this, she smiled, a smile I would come to adore. "Well, you just might get your wish. But first, you forgot to tell me one thing. Your name."

My name. I paused for a moment. My old one would never work. I'd always hated it, anyway. In all my planning for my escape, though, I'd never given much thought to a name. Maybe part of me never truly believed I'd be in this situation.

Yet, there I was. And she wanted to know what to call me.

I said the first thing that popped into my head, a name

that represented everything I wanted to be. "Uh, Val. It's Val."

Amara smiled at me. "Well, Val, it's very nice to meet you. My name is Princess Amara."

That's how our friendship began. For those first few weeks, Amara would visit me every day, coming either for lunch or dinner. I didn't have much to talk about, so I'd sit and listen and ask her questions about her life. Over time, I grew more and more comfortable in my new body and in this new life until I was ready to join the others training to become a member of the Queen's Guard.

Five Years Ago

I COULD FEEL THE DULL ACHE IN MY LEGS AS I KNELT IN the mud of the training ground. It was as if the muscle fibers had been pulled and stretched to their absolute limit and were begging me to stop, to stay here or collapse to the ground below. My body was covered in sweat, soaking my clothes and sticking them to my skin. My breath was heavy as my lungs ravenously pulled in oxygen. We'd been training for hours. Despite how much heavier it'd grown over that time and the cries of protestation from my shoulder and arm muscles, I shakily picked up my sword from where it laid on the ground and stood up once more.

"Are you ready to give up, Cadet?" Captain Mariette asked with a dubious expression. She stood tall and seemingly unaffected by our sparring matches. "I think I've beaten you enough today."

She wasn't entirely wrong. We'd been going at it for

close to an hour and she'd beaten me over and over again. I'd yet to lay my blunted sword on her, but the bruises that now dotted my body showed just how many times she'd gotten me. My sword arm. The backs of my legs. My back. My stomach. All carried painful marks from her prowess.

Normally, Captain Mariette and the other Queen's Guards officers who trained us would take it easy during combat drills, opting for light taps of the sword when making contact. Not with me, though. I'd told them from the very beginning to not hold back, to hurt me, and to make every single strike sting as much as it could. I needed to know true pain if I was to be able to push my body and mind to its absolute limits. This was the only way I could become the best Queen's Guard. Only then would I feel like I belonged.

As I lifted my head up to look at Captain Mariette, weighing whether my body was going to be able to go another round, I saw Princess Amara looking down at me from her usual perch on the walkway above the training grounds. It was always nice to see her there, a heartwarming reminder of our friendship in spite of the gradual distance that'd grown between us with her official duties and my preparation for a life of martial service.

I looked directly at Amara. The encouragement in her eyes eased my aches and pains. She mouthed, "You can do this."

Resolve coursing through my body, I stood up straight, lifted my sword into position, and said, "Yes. I am ready, Captain."

"Suit yourself." Captain Mariette lifted her sword to the starting position for a second. Then, she attacked.

As quickly as she had all day, she was on me, swinging

her sword with such speed and force that it took all my agility and strength to not get hit. Slash left. Slash right. Chop. The clanging sound of sword against sword filled the courtyard as over and over again she forced me to desperately block each of her strikes. The vibrations sent even more pain through my arms and shoulders. My footwork was slow and clumsy as I willed my weary legs to keep moving and not let her trap me against the sparring ground fence. In spite of it all, I had to keep going. Amara was watching; I wouldn't let her down.

Then, I saw it. A small opening in Mariette's attack pattern where, if I was quick enough, I could knock her off balance and take the upper hand.

My opportunity came. I summoned the last bit of energy I had to block her left slash and then parry her blade into the ground when she followed it up with a downward chop. Quickly, I spun to my right so that I was behind her and hit the back of her knee with my sword, knocking her to a kneeling position. I brought my sword to the back of her neck and let the blade rest there.

"I win," I huffed out.

At that, the captain dropped her sword, stood up, and turned to face me. Her expression gave nothing away, but I could tell that somewhere deep down, below the hurt ego at me besting her, there was pride. "So you did. Well done, Cadet."

I looked from her to gaze up at Amara. She beamed.

A few hours and one hot bath later, I was standing before the door of Captain Mariette's office. I took a breath and knocked.

She beckoned me in with a simple, "Come."

I opened the door and walked in, coming to stand at

attention right in front of her desk. "You wished to see me, Captain?"

Mariette was sitting at her desk, papers haphazardly splayed all over it. "Yes, I did. Great job out there today, even if it did take you half the day," she said with a smirk.

"Thank you, Captain." I nodded at her, feeling a little taller.

She looked at me for a moment as if she was measuring me up, then walked around her desk and to the door of her office. "Follow me," she said, opening the door and exiting into the hallway.

After a moment of stunned immobility, I did as she commanded and quickly followed, slowing my pace only after catching up to her.

We walked in silence as my mind raced in its attempt to figure out what was going on. The captain was leading me to a wing of the castle that I hadn't been to since I'd arrived. But we didn't head to that old room. We headed to the upper floors of the castle, to where the royal family resided.

The captain and I came to a stop in front of two wooden doors. Two fellow Queen's Guard were standing watch on either side. "Captain Mariette and Recruit Val to see the Queen." Realizing who I was about to see, my stomach sank.

The guards nodded to Captain Mariette and opened the doors. My mouth fell agape as we entered what was clearly Queen Lucinda's council room. It was spacious and well decorated with beautiful tapestries and paintings depicting pivotal moments in the queendom's history lining the walls. Three large windows let the remaining daylight flood the room with an orange glow. To one side of the room was a large table with three chairs on either side. At the head stood a larger chair with the royal symbol carved into its high back. Straight ahead was an imposing desk, much larger than Captain Mariette's own, with another high back chair with the royal symbol behind it and two smaller ones in front.

A sense of shock slowly crept through me, weighing me down. I was standing in the most important room in all the realm. In this room, the queen met with her councilors and made decisions that affected countless numbers of people. And here I stood, a former lowly acolyte turned hopeful member of the Queen's Guard. More than that, though, the queen had apparently summoned me to this most important room.

That thought filled me with cold dread. Why had the queen summoned me? What had I done wrong? Since arriving at the castle, I'd done everything I was told. As far as I was aware, I'd given no one any reason to punish me or wish me ill will. Had I upset Amara somehow? Worse, had someone from the temple come here, recognized me, and told the queen that I'd run away? It'd been two years since my escape and my facial features had changed, but what if they could still see through it all?

The opening of another door, this one in the far left corner of the room, broke me out of my spiral. In stepped the most powerful woman in all the land, Queen Lucinda. She was wearing a red dress that reached the floor with a tall collar that extended midway up the back of her head and long, wide sleeves. Her hands were interlaced in front of a broad belt that sat at her waist. She smiled at Captain Mariette as she remained at the door.

"Captain Mariette. It is good to see you again," her tone was cheery but did little to calm the unease in my stomach. "Is this Val?"

"Yes, ma'am, it is."

The queen's eyes fell on me, clearly inspecting me. "I heard she got the best of you today."

"It took her long enough, but yes, she did." The pride in the captain's voice was a calming balm that worked to settle my raging nerves.

"Good. Now, leave us. I wish to speak to her."

As soon as Captain Mariette left the room, the queen started walking towards the desk. She motioned to the chair in front of her desk and said, "Please, Val, sit."

I did as I was commanded and sat across from the queen. I tried to examine her posture and expression for any hint of what was going on but got very little. She sat straight in her chair, arms resting in front of her on the desk, her slight smile welcoming. I could tell that I wasn't in serious trouble, but beyond that, I still had no clue what was happening.

"How long have you been with us, Val?" Queen Lucinda asked me.

"Um, two years." I responded.

"And how long have you been training to be a Queen's Guard?"

My stomach fluttered. "Uh, just over 20 months," I replied, the tone in my voice making me sound uncertain of this fact.

"You've made a lot of progress over that time. It usually takes cadets years to finally best Captain Mariette. That's impressive." The queen's smile and kind voice letting me know that the compliment was a genuine one.

"Thank you, Your Highness."

"My daughter tells me that you've always wanted to be a queen's guard. She also tells me that is why you left your home and came to us."

My cheeks warmed at the thought of Amara talking to her mother about me. "That's right." I nodded.

"She speaks highly of you, you know. In fact, that's why I summoned you here. She has asked me to make you a member of the queen's guard. What's more, she has asked that you be assigned to be her personal guard."

My throat constricted at that, choking off my ability to say anything other than a "what?"

"Yes. She thinks you'd make a great bodyguard."

Coming down from the shock of this news, I asked, "And what do you think, Your Highness?" Part of me needed to know.

She sighed, then said, "I'm not sure." She stood from the desk and turned to look out the window. "You and my daughter are close. When you first arrived, she spent all of her free time with you. Even now, when she is not in her lessons or attending to her official duties as princess, she's watching you train." Queen Lucinda paused. "The way she talks about you makes me believe that there is more than simple friendship between you two."

The realization of what the queen was saying hit me. "I understand, my queen. Yes, Amara is my friend, the closest friend I've ever had. But, if you see fit, I will be a member of the Queen's Guard. My first and only duty is to protect her and keep her safe. I will not fail in that task."

"So you say, but let me ask you," she locked me in her gaze, "in your duty as her protector, you may be asked to do things you may not want to do. Your duty is to the princess of the realm, not your friend. Whatever is best for her and the realm goes before any personal wants. Many have tried to do this, to put the realm above their own heart's desire," she paused, a tiny expression of what seemed like hurt flashed across her face, "including some that meant the world to me, and failed. I won't allow this to happen to Amara or the realm."

I take a deep breath, then respond, "Queen Lucinda, Amara is the future queen of the realm and my friend. To me, my duty as a Queen's Guard is the same as my duty as her friend: to serve her, to make sure she is safe, and to do whatever she needs me to do for herself as well as the realm. In this, I will not fail."

She kept my gaze for a few moments, her steely expression revealing nothing. "Very well. Report to the Master of Arms to receive your armor and sword. Then, report to the princess's chambers afterwards. Dismissed."

"Yes, Your Highness." I stood and turned to leave.

"But Val," I turned back to face the queen, "remember what I told you."

I nodded, then walked out.

I made my way to the armory, a massive smile on my face and an extra spirited bounce in my stride. My dream of becoming a Queen's Guard had come true. Not only that, I was entrusted with one of the most important assignments: protecting the future Queen of Lavandula. And sure, Amara was stunning and summoned mad butterflies in my stomach by merely looking my way, but that was immaterial. The queen had made it abundantly clear: my sworn duty and my only concern was to keep Amara safe and to do whatever she asks of me. From here on out, I was to be her protector first, her sword second, and her friend third.

Wearing my new armor, I stood outside the Princess' door for what felt like forever but could've easily been just a few moments. I knocked and, upon hearing Amara tell me to come in, I opened the door and stepped inside.

Amara's bedchamber was massive. It was complete with a sitting room with a couple of couches and chairs in front of a fireplace. Across the room from that, another chair was placed directly below one of the windows next to a table, piled high with books. Amara's massive bed, nightstands, and a vanity were at the back of the room. A multitude of candles bathed the entire room in faint golden light. Amara was sitting at her vanity, which stood between two windows to the left of her bed. She wore a nightgown and had her hair up in a clip that, even from afar, looked as if it was barely containing her curls.

I remained near the door and stood at full attention. "Good evening, Princess. I was informed that I would be taking on the duties of being your personal bodyguard."

Amara turned her head to look my way, her unruly tresses bouncing about her head. The candle light glowed upon her porcelain skin. Her smile was warm and welcoming. "Well, look at you!" She stood from her chair and walked towards me. "You look so fancy in your armor. You really wear it well."

My cheeks heated at her compliment. "Thank you, Princess. It's an honor to wear the uniform of the Queen's Guard and to serve as your sworn protector."

"My protector, eh?" One side of her mouth ticked up in a smirk. "Well, as my sworn protector, can I ask you to do one thing?"

"What's that?" I asked.

"Can you stop with the formality? I may be the Princess of Lavandula, but I'm still just a person. Plus, we're almost the same age!"

Every single fiber of my being that absorbed the many lessons on formality and proper behavior for members of the Queen's Guard revolted. The queen's warning that she gave me just a couple of hours ago rang clear in my mind. No, I couldn't address Amara by her first name. I had to keep professional distance. "I'm sorry, Princess. I'm afraid that I can't. Custom dictates that I refer to you as Princess at all times."

"Ugh, custom." Amara plopped down onto her couch dramatically, emphasizing the groan to her voice. "Do you know why I picked you, Val? Why I asked for you specifically to be my personal bodyguard?"

I shook my head. "Um, no, Princess."

"Because I hoped that you'd treat me differently. That you'd see that I'm more than just some delicate princess that demands deference and protection. I spend my days being bowed to, being told how important I am, and of the responsibilities that I must eventually bear. I just," she let out an exhale and dropped her shoulders, then looked me in the eyes, "I just want a friend. And I've missed spending time with you like those first few months after you arrived. Can we have that again?"

Friendship. She missed our friendship. All the times I caught her watching me train, all the times our eyes met during feasts, they all made sense now. She wasn't just observing me to see how my training was going, whether I would make it or not. She was doing it all because she missed me.

Moments passed as I processed this information. Amara was the first person to see me as I truly am. She was the first person to accept me and enjoy my presence. Even before my arrival to the castle, I had no one. But now, apparently I had a friend in Amara.

"So, can you do that for me? Can you be my bodyguard and my friend?"

Despite the queen's warning, there was only one answer I could give. "Yes, I think I can...Amara."

Three Years Ago

"RACE YOU TO GODWICK'S THICKET!" AMARA declared right before urging her horse onwards in a speedy gallop, leaving me in the dust.

"Amara, not again!" I groaned as I tried to match speed on my heavier, slower horse.

Over the two years of being Amara's personal body-guard, I'd grown accustomed to her playful nature. It seemed like almost every ride through the Queen's Woods with her ended in some kind of race, as did almost every call to dinner. She routinely challenged me to archery contests, which I only occasionally let her win. While I had her in archery, she routinely beat me during our nightly games of chess or checkers. I could tell that she loved using these little games of ours to playfully tease me and, if I were asked by anyone besides Captain Mariette, I'd admit that I enjoyed it.

As I approached our usual meeting spot in Godwick's thicket, I saw no sign of Amara. I knew there was no way I had beaten her here. I had lost sight of her almost halfway to the thicket, my larger, slower horse unable to keep up with her nimbler one.

"Amara!" I called out as I made my way around the thicket, but no reply came. As I kept looking, I heard muffled voices. I got off my horse, tied her to the nearest tree, and began to walk towards them.

"Do you know who she is? She's the princess!" a gruff voice exclaimed.

"Oh, fuck! We can't keep her!" said another.

"Or, we keep her and ransom her off. I bet a princess will bring us some good coin!" said the third.

I entered a small clearing where I saw them, three men, all wearing the tell-tale cheap leather armor of brigands. One held Amara tight with a hand over her mouth while the other two faced him. Only the man holding Amara saw me, his eyes going wide.

"Let her go, now!" I commanded as I drew my sword.

The other two brigands turned to face me while the one holding Amara, clearly their ringleader, tilted his chin at me and drew a knife that he put at Amara's side. "And why should we? There are five of us and one of you, and by the look of you, you ain't much."

It was then that I noticed two more brigands step into the clearing behind me.

My nerves began to rattle. I'd never fought this many enemies at once before. They had me surrounded. Moreover, one of them had a knife pointed right at Amara's side. One wrong move and she would be dead, my duty failed, my best friend gone.

I looked Amara in her eyes, wide and filled with terror. My nervousness faded as pure rage began to boil inside my chest and course throughout my body. These people were trying to hurt the only person who ever truly cared about me, the first person to ever see the real me and accept me, the person who believed in me at every step of my journey. They would pay for what they were doing to her. I took a deep breath, funneling my anger into steely determination, and reminded myself of my training.

I kept one hand on the hilt of my sword as my other slowly moved downwards to hang near my left leg. "I will not tell you again. Let the princess go or this will end very badly for you."

"Fuck you," was the lead brigand's reply.

"So be it." I quickly grabbed the dagger from the sheath attached to my left leg and flung it at the brigand holding Amara. The dagger hit its mark, going through his left eye and embedding itself there. His body dropped to the ground. Before the brigand behind could bring his sword up, I quickly spun and sliced clean through his neck, separating his head from his body.

In an instant, I'd killed two of the five. On a lucky day, the other three would scurry away. Today, though, was not one of those days. All three pulled out their swords and made their way towards me. They'd completely forgotten about Amara. Good. Even if I didn't survive this, she could escape and live another day.

The first came towards me in a rage, his sword held high. Of course, that left his middle exposed, which I gladly took advantage of as I sliced through his abdomen, opening up his guts for the forest floor. The next two were not so easy. They'd had more training than the one before and instantly had me on the back foot, parrying and blocking as they kept coming. Still, I was a member of the Queen's Guard. I knew I could outlast them. I just had to wait for my moment.

The moment finally came. As I parried a strike from one of the brigands, I brought my elbow to his face and made contact with his nose, dropping him to the ground. Now with just one in the fight, I made quick work of him, plunging my sword into his chest after parrying his downward slice away from me. I watched him fall to the ground, dead, a lifeless expression on his face. It was over.

"Think you've won, eh?" I heard behind me. I turned around to see the brigand with the broken nose, the one I had left writhing in pain, standing next to Amara. His face was covered in blood. He had his arms around her and a dagger, my dagger, pointed at her. "You let me go, or the bitch gets it."

Fuck. I'd lost. I had gotten cocky, thinking that I'd beaten them all, when in fact I had failed.

Or so I thought. Amara flung a hand back, crushing his nose further and making him fall to the ground and drop the dagger. In a flash, Amara took it, jumped onto him, and began screaming hysterically as she plunged the dagger into the man over and over again. Blood spewed all over her as she brought the dagger down again and again.

"Amara, Amara," I called as I rushed to her to pull her back. I lifted her up off what used to be a human being and held her. "You're okay. You're okay. I've got you. I've got you." I repeated as I held her, her arms finally going limp and dropping the dagger. I fell to the ground with her in my arms, caressing her and holding her as she wept.

After a while like this, I let Amara go and let her sit next to a tree as I disposed of the bodies and wrangled our horses. From her blank facial expression, she was in shock. I couldn't blame her. I was trained for years to kill, she was not. Her hands and dress were covered in blood. There was no way she could've truly known how to handle this.

I picked Amara up and put her on my horse, then got on and drove us home. We barely said anything the entire way. When we arrived at the castle, I used one of the less populated entrances and used a back way to lead Amara to her chambers. Once inside her chambers, I led her to her bathtub. "Get undressed. I will call someone to draw you a bath."

"No. Please. Don't let anyone else see me like this." Her voice was so fragile it felt like it would break at any moment. I could see the tears in her eyes threatening to start again.

I nodded. "Yes. I'll be right back with some water." At that, I exited the room. I came back with the water a few minutes later. Amara had undressed and was sitting on her bed. She sat there, laid bare and covered blood, picking at her nails and inspecting her blood-soaked hands. The sight of her like that devastated me.

I brought her over to sit in the bathtub and went about helping her wash the blood off of her face, her hands, and all the places where it had soaked through her clothes onto her pale skin.

Once I washed off all the blood, I got her out of the bath and led her to the bed and helped her into a nightgown before laying her down. I picked up her blood-soaked clothes and told her, "I'll dispose of these."

"Please, come back. Don't leave me here."

I could feel my heart breaking for her. Amara had always appeared strong and capable, but in this moment, she appeared as brittle as fallen leaves.

I walked up to her, leaned down, and kissed the top of her head. "I'll be back. I promise."

I disposed of her dress in the most secret way possible and quickly returned to her chambers. "I'm back, Amara," I softly called out as I crossed the room towards her.

She turned her head to look at me. "Come here." Her voice was flat and listless. She was empty and exhausted. In that moment, my heart broke for her all over again.

I grabbed a chair and put it next to her bed and sat. I removed my gloves and took her hand in mine. Her eyes looked heavy as she looked at me, then down to her hand in mine. "Will you stay with me? Please?"

"Yes, Amara. I'll be here with you for as long as you need, for now and always."

At that, she drifted off to sleep. Soon, I joined her, never letting go of her hand.

Two Years Ago

THE EVENING WAS ALIVE WITH MERRIMENT. THE smell of roasted meat and wine and sounds of raucous music and conversation filled The Great Hall. Today was All Mother's Day, a day in which the entire queendom celebrated the birth of the first queen of Lavandula, Queen Amelia. The entire queendom was celebrating, with the epicenter of the celebration right here in front of me.

The Queen had retired after the massive feast, choosing instead to go to bed rather than continue the celebrations. She was beginning to show signs of slowing down in her old age, but we all still believed in her capability to lead our glorious queendom.

Amara had stayed. Amara, in her beautiful lilac ball gown and her hair down. Amara, looking resplendent as she laughed and danced with noblemen and women. It felt good, seeing her like this again.

For the first few weeks after the incident at Godwin's thicket, Amara had clearly been affected by what happened. She struggled to eat regularly, rarely spoke out in conversations or meetings, and was often distracted, as if she was replaying the events of that day in her head over and over again. I stayed by her side the entire time. When people tried to pry into the reasons for her changed demeanor, I kept her secret. When she needed someone to stay with her while she slept, I took my post in the chair beside her. When she finally needed to talk, to get out all of her trauma from that day, I listened and comforted her. I was there for her however she needed me.

As the song the band was playing came to an end, Amara walked towards me. "Hello brave knight," she said, the slight slur to her words indicating that she'd had a little to drink, "how are you this fine evening?"

I chuckled slightly and smiled. "I am well, Your Highness. I hope this evening has been good to you."

"It has, but do you know what would make it even better?" I could see on her face that there was mischief on her mind. "If you would dance with me."

My heart began to quicken its pace. As much as I wanted to dance with Amara, I couldn't let her know how terrible I was at it. I fell back on royal protocol. "Well, Amara, you know that as your personal guard my duty is to stand here and make sure no ill befalls you."

"Oh, don't give me that. It's a holiday! Everyone here loves my mom and the queendom. I'm perfectly safe. Now," she stood upright, adopting the regal stance I had caught her trying in front of the mirror over and over, "I command you, dance with me."

She had me. I had been bested in this joust of wits. Plus, there was something about her commanding me that made my heart skip a beat. I offered her my hand. "After you, Amara."

Wearing her best victory smile, the same lopsided mischievous grin that she'd worn every time she'd bested me, Amara took my hand and led me to the dance floor.

And so we danced for what felt like hours. Sometimes it was elegant, our movements matching the beat perfectly, and other times it was chaotic and wild. I didn't care, though. Here was this beautiful woman, her gorgeous golden locks twirled about, her porcelain skin soft to the touch, and her sapphire eyes upon me. Every detail of her being entranced me. I wanted this night to never end.

But the night, like all nights before it, did eventually come to a close. As the last note of the final song faded out, Amara looked at me, a sheen of sweat covering her skin and her breath heavy. "Well, Val, you have fulfilled your duty to dance with me. Care to escort me to my chambers?"

I snickered at her, amused at the playful way she asked me to do something I routinely did as her body guard, then offered my arm. "My lady."

As we reached the door to her chambers, I let her arm go. "Here you are, Amara. Sleep well and I will see you tomorrow." I turned and started to walk down the hall towards my bedroom.

"Wait," Amara called after me. "Val, could you stay with me?"

I turned back and stepped closer to her, curiosity crinkling my brows together. "Is something wrong? Are you afraid..."

Before I could finish that sentence, Amara had closed the distance between us, wrapped her arms around my neck, and brought her lips to mine in a slow and soft kiss that surprised me and lit a fire in my core.

"No," she said after pulling back, her thumb idly rubbing the back of my neck, "I'm not scared. Not with you. Please, stay with me tonight." She kissed me again, this one deeper and filled with a sense of need. "Will you stay?"

With each word filled with the longing that I'd carried for this woman, I said, "Yes, Amara, I will stay. I will always stay."

We spent the entire night making love, taking our turns worshiping every inch of each other's bodies until exhaustion took us. I cherished every single moment of it. Every single touch of skin on skin, every little movement of her body, every little noise she made as she came, all of it. In the moment, I had no idea if this would be just one night or the start of something more. Whichever the case, I wanted to make sure I remembered every detail for the rest of my life.

As the sun rose the next morning, I woke up to see Amara still sleeping, looking just as beautiful in her sleep as she did when awake. I shifted to lay on my side and watched her eyes flutter open. In that moment, my heart was full. I was in love with this woman.

"Good morning," she said sleepily, a smile on her face. She rolled onto her side to face me and leaned in for a kiss.

"Good morning," I replied and rested my hand on her hip. "How did you sleep?"

"Wonderfully. Thank you for a good night."

"You're welcome. And thank you, too." I smiled back. A moment passed between us as I thought of what to say next. I was sure what I wanted to say, but unsure how Amara would respond. She had initiated last night, but a confession of love after just one night may be a step too far.

I summoned my courage. "Amara, can I tell you something?"

"Sure."

"I," I paused and took a deep breath, "I love you, Amara. I've loved you since the day we met. And I know that I am your body guard and that you have so many more options than me, but—"

She stopped my rambling with a kiss, a long and deep kiss that told me everything I needed to know. "I know. And I don't care about those other options. I don't care that you're 'just a body guard'. You're so much more than that to me. I love you too, Val."

She kissed me again and pushed me onto my back. She

slid on top of me, the feel of her naked body reawakening my arousal. Her blonde hair curtained us. She looked deep into my eyes.

"Now, what do you say, we stay in bed all day?"

I leaned up to kiss her again, something I was beginning to get addicted to. "I love that idea."

And we did.

Last Night

THE QUEEN HAD DIED PEACEFULLY IN HER SLEEP. WE found out the next morning when one of my fellow Queen's Guard came knocking on Amara's chamber door. Normally, the news would come to me first and I'd be the one to break it to her. With our relationship now an open secret that even the queen seemed to be fine with, they knew not to go looking for me in my own chamber.

We'd known for some time that this was coming, that the Queen's last days were upon us. Recently, she'd been showing signs of declining health. She had attended fewer and fewer council meetings, instead asking Amara to take her place. At this, Amara had excelled, showing all the intelligence and grace that had made me fall in love with her.

Still, to lose your mother is no small thing. No matter how prepared you may feel, a loss like that still hurts. A world of new responsibilities will still feel impossible to bear. Even if I'd never know that loss, that weight, the expression on Amara's face that day told me everything I needed to know. That she was heartbroken and needed me.

During those hectic days between her mother's passing, the funeral, and preparation for her own coronation, I never left Amara's side. I rejected every offer of relief by my fellow Queen's Guard. At night, I stayed awake as long as I could, keeping silent watch over my new Queen, ready to comfort her in whatever capacity. Amara was my duty, my love. I would not abandon her.

The night before Amara's coronation, I was sitting in bed keeping watch over her as she slept when a voice I had not heard in years floated into my head.

"Hello, little one."

I stood from the bed and walked over to grab my sword. Drawing it from its scabbard, I slowly walked through the bedchamber, looking for the source of that voice.

"I'm outside. Come find me."

I stepped out of the bedchamber, closing the door quietly behind me. The two guards that were supposed to be keeping watch were sitting on the ground, fast asleep. There, at the other end of the hall, she stood. The witch of the woods.

"What do you want?" I asked, raising my sword as I approached her.

"Oh, please. Put the sword down. It wouldn't do anything anyway. And your friends are fine, just taking a little nap." She was right. As I got closer to her, I realized that she was merely an apparition, a ghostly projection of herself.

"I repeat: what do you want?" I kept my tone stern, not wanting to give an inch.

"Well, look at you, enjoying the fruits of my labor. You've grown to be quite the Queen's Guard. You've even bedded the future Queen herself. Certainly better than that scrawny and frightened little boy I found in the woods. You're welcome, by the way."

I felt my anger rising at the implication in her words.

"Your labor? I did this all on my own. I trained day after day to be the best Queen's Guard I can be. I killed those brigands who threatened to harm Amara. Queen Amara loves me for the woman I am and have always been and I love her. You had no hand in any of it."

She gave me an incredulous look and scoffed. "Remember, you only got to where you are because of me and my talents. You would've never even had the opportunity to be," she waved her hand up and down, "this if it wasn't for my generosity."

"Generosity? We made a deal."

"That's right. A deal that I'm now asking you to honor." A green octagonal stone attached to a necklace appeared in her ghostly hand. "Wear this under your armor tomorrow at the coronation. Make sure no one can see it." She stretched out her hand to offer me the necklace.

I examined the stone warily. It didn't look like anything remarkable, but my suspicion was still high. "Just this? What is so special about this? And more importantly, why should I?"

"Don't be so dramatic," the witch responded, "It's only a small favor. The late queen was an old friend of mine. I just want to watch her daughter's coronation."

Her answer did nothing to alleviate my suspicions. "If that's the case, certainly you could attend on your own without me wearing this thing. My answer is no."

Suddenly, a sharp pain flooded every part of my being, forcing me to my knees. It felt as if every muscle fiber was being ripped apart.

"Listen, boy," the witch spat back, another dagger to my chest, "what was given can be taken away, and we wouldn't want that now, would we? Wouldn't want the whole queendom to know about your little deception? Wouldn't want Amara to realize that her lover is nothing more than a liar who cheated his way into her bed, would you?"

"No...that's not..." I tried to respond, but found myself unable to. The pain was too much, flooding my senses and making it impossible for my brain to formulate an adequate response.

"That's not what, boy? The truth?"

The pain increased, every word another dagger to my chest.

"Say you'll wear it." she demanded.

"Yes, yes." I sputtered out.

Still, she did not let up. "Yes, what, boy?"

"Yes, I will wear it."

Instantly, the pain ceased and the witch's tone, once demanding, changed to pleasant. "Good! Glad to hear it!"

I looked up and she was gone. The necklace remained, lying on the floor, glinting up at me. A cold sweat washed over me, the witch's words still echoing in my brain. As I stared at the necklace, I hoped and prayed that my task would be simple. Wear it tomorrow, let the witch watch to her heart's content, and then toss the damn thing down the nearest well. After that, I would be free to live the life I had built for myself with the woman I love. And if the witch somehow found some useful information through viewing the coronation and caused trouble later, my fellow Queen's Guard and I would take care of her. She may have given me this body, but she has no idea what it is capable of now.

Today

Every important person in the realm stands in rows in the Great Hall, all waiting to see the coronation. I, along with the rest of the Queen's Guard, stand at attention along the main aisle, wearing our ceremonial armor and swords. Tucked beneath my armor is the necklace, the feel of its green stone against my chest causing my stomach to churn with foreboding anxiety. I want nothing more than to rip the damn thing off and toss it in the nearest river, but I made a deal.

We practiced the ceremony many times over the past month. Amara will walk down the center aisle of the hall, ascend the dais, sit upon the throne, and will be crowned Queen Amara of Lavandula, First of Her Name. I will then kneel before her and she, with her ceremonial sword, will bestow me the honor of being the head of her personal guard.

The crowd quiets as the massive doors to the Great Hall open. Everyone watches as Amara, wearing formal robes that look like they weigh as much as she does, slowly makes her way towards the dais. Behind her walks the Prime Hierophant, the leader of the Temple of the Goddess. I only saw him a few times before escaping the temple all those years ago. In his hands he carries the Crown of Lavandula on a pillow. He'll be the one to crown Amara, a sign that the Goddess herself chose Amara for the sacred task of leading her people.

As Amara approaches the dais, her eyes catch mine. She smiles and mouths, "Hey."

I reply with a "You look beautiful, my love." And she does. She's radiant, the perfect image of a queen.

Amara climbs the dais and sits on the throne. The Prime Hierophant stands before her and goes about his business, reciting lines about what makes a good queen and how a queen should be the embodiment of the Goddess. Truth be told, I'm not paying attention. I've heard it all before in rehearsal. No, I'm thinking about our life together, her on the throne and me as her protector. Mornings spent entwined with her under the covers. Days spent at her side, offering counsel and moments of reprieve from the stress of ruling. Nights spent dancing and making love. Day after day, lovers until the very end.

The hall erupts in cheers and celebration as the Prime Hierophant places the crown upon Amara's head and proclaims her Queen of Lavandula. A new era has begun. As soon as the crowd quiets down again, Amara stands and walks down the first two steps of the dais. A servant appears next to her side with her ceremonial sword.

She looks at me. "Val, please step forward and kneel."

I take a deep breath and do as she commands, kneeling before her.

"Are you ready to take your vow as the Queen's personal guardian?" She speaks with all the authority of her new title.

"I am, Your Highness," I say stoically, tamping down the guilt I feel at wearing the accursed jewelry under my armor.

Suddenly, the room grows dark and cold. I feel the necklace pulling me forward towards the ground. I grab the chain around my neck and rip it off, tossing it to the stones beneath me. A black and green smoke slowly begins to emerge from it and takes the form of a human. A human woman. Her.

"You." I try to stand and draw my sword, but find myself unable to, frozen to the spot. I look back to my fellow Queen's Guard for help. I see them and everyone else in the hall slump to the ground asleep.

"Yes, me. Now hush," the witch says to me before

turning to face Amara. "Well, hello Your Highness. Congratulations on your big day. Your mother was quite the woman." She gives an exaggerated, mocking bow.

Stunned, Amara steps back towards her throne. "Who... who are you?"

"Oh, did your mother not tell you about me? A pity. I am Giavana, and your mother and I were once very close before she decided that being queen was more important than being with me."

"What...what do you want?" Amara's face contorts in fear.

"What do I want? Well, it's simple really." She smiles a devilish smile. "Revenge. I want her offspring to suffer the same way she made me suffer. I want her daughter to feel the same sense of betrayal I felt when she banished me to those woods alone."

"How will you do that?"

"Easy." The witch walks over to me and touches me on the top of my head. "With her."

My field of vision begins to narrow until all I can see is Amara. The sounds of the room around me disappear. All I can hear is a voice. The witch's voice.

"Kill her. Kill the Queen."

I try to fight it, to resist. My hand reaches for the hilt of my blade and draws it from its scabbard as I stand.

No, stop. Don't do this. I try to tell myself. *It's Amara. Your queen. Your beloved.*

I take a step forward. My will screams at my body to stop, but to no avail.

"Kill her. Kill the Queen."

No, please Goddess, no. I respond in my head.

Another step. I see my arm raise my sword up, the tip of my blade pointed at Amara's neck, mere inches away. I can see the terror in her eyes. I can see the tears coming down her face. I can read her lips.

"Please, no. Don't do this. Val, I love you."

I have to stop. I think again. *I can't do this.*

I will myself to do anything else than what I am being told. Lower my blade. Drop it. Walk away. Anything and everything to end this nightmare.

I call on memories of Amara and I together. Afternoon picnics after riding all day. Evenings cuddled together in front of the fire. Her voice when she first told me she loved me. All reminders that that Amara is not my enemy. She is my beloved.

My arm begins to quiver. My vision begins to widen. Sounds begin to come back to me.

"No!" The witch's voice shouts in my head as she fights to maintain control. The borders of my vision quake. "Don't you get it? You are nothing but what I have made you. You are mine, my weapon of revenge to command. Without me, you're just a frightened little boy who can't accept his place in the world. Now, do your fucking job and kill her!"

"Mine. Boy. Kill her." The wrongness of those words reverberates through my head. I feel the spell shatter and fall away.

In an instant, I turn to face the witch and plunge my sword into her chest.

A shocked expression comes across her face as she looks down to see the protruding blade. I withdraw it and she collapses on the floor in front of me.

I look down at her as she struggles to breathe. "No. I am no boy, nor am I yours. I am a knight of the Queen's Guard. I swore an oath to protect the realm, her people, and most importantly," I turn to look at Amara, her face frozen in shock, "my queen." I look back and watch as life leaves the witch's body.

I drop my sword, turn towards Amara, and collapse to my knees in front of her, overcome with sorrow and regret.

The tears come hard and fast. "I'm so sorry, Amara. I lied to you. I lied to you and everyone here. I am not who I say I am."

I feel Amara's forehead on mine and her hands on my cheeks. "Val, it's okay, it's okay," she tries to console me.

"No, it's not. It's not. I lied. I made a deal with that witch and she almost made me kill you. I am so sorry." My words begin to fail me as my throat constricts. I can barely breathe, my breath hitching between deep painful sobs.

"Look at me," Amara replies, lifting my face so that our eyes meet. "You never lied to me nor failed me. You are a woman of the Queen's Guard."

"But I did!" I exclaim. No matter what Amara says, I know the horrible, shameful truth of what I've done, of my unworthiness.

"No, you didn't. Remember, you told me that you ran away from home. Isn't that true?"

"Y-yes." I admit. Despite the protestations of the shame that has gripped me, Amara's soft comforting tone brings some relief.

"Good. Did you lie to me when you swore your oath to protect me and my queendom?"

"N-no." My sobs begin to abate and my throat begins to loosen.

"And did you lie to me when you told me you would stay with me?"

"No." The sureness in my voice slowly returns as my mind begins to accept the truth of Amara's words. My breathing calms.

She smiled. "Last one. Did you lie to me when you told me you loved me?"

I shake my head firmly. "No. I love you, Amara. I will always love you," I say resolutely, needing her to know how much I mean each and every word.

She brings my mouth to hers and kisses me deeply. I taste the salt from our tears as we let the kiss linger, neither of us wanting to let it end.

"And I love you, Val. You've never lied to me. You've always been who you are. My friend. My protector. My lover. For now and always."

I kiss her again. "For now and always."

About the Author

Rose Goodwin (she/her) is a trans woman who lives in the South with her wife, daughter, and menagerie of animals. She loves stories about strong and chaotic women fighting for their happily ever after, be it in romance, fantasy, or science fiction. When she's not writing or reading, she enjoys spending time with family and friends, playing role-playing games, and cuddling her cats. You can find her on Instagram at @rosegoodwinwrites. This is her first published story.

Di-Caffeinated

Erin Branch

Awe

THE LYCAN GUARD AT THE DOOR GLARES DAGGERS AT me. His brown canine eyes narrow as they sweep down my frame. What in the astral plane did I do to piss off every being this side of the realms? But someone bothered to resurrect me a few weeks ago, and that's expensive, so I must have some decent qualities.

I give the guard my best sad eyes. "How is my official Lutist Consort seal not good enough? Wanna hear me sing to prove it? I really am part of the Luters."

I'm not, but he doesn't need to know that. At least I don't think I am. It's the biggest guild of bards, storytellers, and lute players across the realms and requires a hefty deposit to join. But my memories from the last year are shoddy at best. I can't even remember how I died.

Regardless of this asshole's opinion of me, I must get inside this tavern or whatever kind of shop this is. My Infinite Bag is here. I clench my thigh where I've checked my bag's tracking tattoo countless times today. If I can just get my hands on my instrument inside the bag, I know I'll be able to remember more about what happened to me. I'm sure I enchanted safeguard memory spells into it just for this situation.

I clench my woolen cloak tighter around me as sideways rain pelts my back, hitting me even under the alcove where I stand. Coastal weather makes for difficult travel.

The last few weeks have been awful—no memories, no money, no prospects, and having to rely on my music talents to beg for food.

Dying and resurrection are absolute demon balls.

I wave my forged Lutist Consort documents in front of the lupine guard again. My recall might be a bit fucked right now—okay, a lot fucked—but I have a sense I used to be better at buttering people up. I just need a few things to go right. Starting with getting my stuff back.

I catch a whiff of the guard's smell in this rain. Wet dog. Yuck. He crosses massive furry arms of corded muscle. "Knowledge of our grand opening is exclusive information, even to the Lutist Consorts. Only investors are allowed inside tonight."

News to me. "Of course I knew that!" I wave him off. "I mean, obviously, The Luters didn't send me—I only handed you my papers as proof of my craft and skills. It seems like you could use my help to entertain your investors. I wouldn't dare get out my instrument in this mess," I gesture backward to the gusting wind and rain, "but I'd gladly sing you a song to prove I'm a bard of high skill. What's your favorite song? Must be a boring night standing here in the rain." I flash him a wide smile.

Please, just let me sing one song... If he lets me, then I can weave some arcane into the vibrations, and I'll be going anywhere I want.

The guard's dark eyes lift quizzically. "Do you know "The Long Howl of My Heart?""

Sucker. I suppress a grin and open my mouth to begin.

It only takes a few verses of the song before he starts wagging his tail and escorts me inside.

A rich, nutty, earthy smell hits me as I step through the threshold. Wow, what a delicious scent. It has a sweetness in its roasted aroma.

The room is round and open, with a cluster of tables in the center near a hearth, a few more scattered chairs, and smaller tables along the sides, each with a candle on top. There's a long wooden bar with all sorts of steaming metal contraptions peeking from behind it, like some mad lich's chemistry room, only...not evil.

"*Who* was that singing?" A man, shorter than me by a head, walks to us from the bar. A dwarf, by the look of him, though instead of the usual long, thick beard that dominates their traditional style preference, he has his facial hair trimmed into lines framing his chin. He wears a slim tailored suit and jacket—also not typical dwarf fashion choices.

I have to hope he meant his question about my singing in a positive way. I grin and give a little bow. "Awe Danamark, bard and member of the Lutist Consort. I heard *this* is the place to be. Very exclusive."

The man laughs. "So exclusive, we aren't even open."

"Then who are all these people?" I cheat by saying it in a singsong voice, sneaking a trace of magic into the words, and then widening my grin. Sometimes, this trick gets me in deeper trouble rather than out of trouble. Here's hoping he's not a magic user.

He steps forward and pats me on the shoulder. "Awe, huh? I like you."

Thank the fucking Lady.

"Name's Zaci. Owner of Prestidigitation Perk." He gestures to the crowd of people gathered at small tables. "These are my investors. This shop is a new concept. Well, the whole town is. And all of it is based around my formula."

It looked like a regular, albeit small, seaside town. I'm a day from the capitol by foot—less by horse or cart. Of course it was raining when I arrived so I couldn't see the whole town.

I lean forward conspiratorially. "I'd love to hear more."

He points at me. "That's the reaction I'm hoping for. What brings you in? You a magic user that heard about the kaffe? Want a sample?"

Kaffe? Interesting name. Wonder what its link to magic is. "Oh, I'm just a simple musician. A low-ranked member of the Luters." Another lie. But I can't tell him, or else he could suspect what I've been doing to him—influencing his decision to let me in.

He laughs. "Better Luters than looters. Well, even if you can't understand the full effect of the kaffe, I've found that even non-magic users appreciate the boost." Zaci steps toward the large bar, and I follow. "Hunt, can you please fix one Kaffe? A single?" he calls to the bartender before turning to me and walking backward. "Hunt started working for me last month, and already, they're my best barista. See, *barista* is a new word for this region. Trust me, you haven't had anything like this drink before."

The bartender looks up and...*oh*. They're a tiefling, too. I touch my horns. Theirs are a deeper shade, contrasting with their brilliant teal hair. Hazel eyes meet mine across the bar.

"Um." They stare at me, tilting their head as we both lean forward. It's like I'm being drawn to them. "Who is...?"

Did we know each other? I desperately dig through my memories, but it's like I'm hitting a blank wall.

"Awe Danamark," Zaci answers their half-question. "Heck of a voice. And I think she's using a little magic, whether she realizes it or not. You know, I've been looking for a new bard since that good-for-nothing charlatan left us in the lurch." He almost spits the end of the sentence.

Hunt's eyes suddenly cut from mine. They turn back to the complicated set of what looks like lab equipment behind the bar. "Right. Let me get that drink for you, sir."

I know Hunt somehow from before I died. I have to. This magnetic pull between us...

Zaci is vibrating with excitement as the equipment hisses and gurgles. "Ooh, let me grab a few people to watch Awe drink the formula. Hunt, actually make it a double. And add some steamed milk."

After working for a few more moments, Hunt sets a beautiful bowl-shaped cup on the bar, filled to the brim with tan foamed milk in a heart pattern. I brush their fingertips with mine as I reach for it.

Without even blinking, I'm seeing a different place as if I were there now. Hunt and I walk through a market arm-in-arm and laughing. They whisper in my ear, teasing me about being too obvious. It tickles. Then they shove their body against mine, pinning me to a building, kissing me...

The image is gone as quick as it came—brief as the touch of Hunt's fingers on the hot mug. Holy shit. I must've known them!

I haven't regained memories like this so suddenly before. Maybe they could help me figure out how I died— and what I was doing.

Hunt could be why my Infinite Bag is in this bar! I take a deep breath. I need to calm down and ask in a coherent way.

I pick up the drink and take a long sip of the warm, foamy liquid. The sweet milk is nice on my tongue, contrasting with whatever infusion of roasted beans. It's slightly bitter but in a rich way that's not unpleasant. I swallow and look up to meet their eyes. "What was tha—"

"You need to leave. Now." Unmistakable fury covers their handsome features.

I recoil. "What? Why?" *Oh, shit.* What did I do? They must know me, and whatever happened, my prospects don't look good.

"I said you need to get out!"

Hunt

I unclench my hands again and smooth them on my apron. Everything's fine. She left.

"What was that?" Zaci combs fingers into his unkempt copper hair then swoops it to the left. "I was trying to book that bard for our opening. She's talented. Did you see how she convinced Fitz to let her inside? I want her working for me to convince these chumps—I mean, esteemed nobility—to invest."

"Yes." And that was the problem. Awe has a reputation, one Zaci can't possibly know as a newcomer to the area. Even though my memories are riddled with holes, I remember enough.

Zaci raises an eyebrow. "And?"

"I asked her to leave. She's a follower of the Lady of Deception."

He sighs and smooths the skin on his forehead. "Hunt. You know I love ya, but I simply *can't* with this paladin shit. I don't care if your deity hates hers, and it's on you to prove that you're worthy again to Ohmag or whatever."

"Oghma," I correct. Not that it matters. My attempts at restoration with Oghma have nothing to do with my asking Awe to leave.

"Whatever. If that bard comes back, tell her to come see me. I have a job for her."

I frown. I didn't explain myself well enough. Awe follows the Lady of Deception. That's not someone we want crawling around our shop, especially with a new formula as in-demand as Zaci's kaffe.

When I touched Awe's hand, I saw the moment of my death.

Her light brown eyes held mine as the world faded to black. I hadn't been able to remember that moment, and now I know it in my soul that she had something to do with it.

I shake myself and go back to my task of cleaning the kaffe equipment.

A smattering of Deepwater nobility is here, though the weather isn't helping Zaci's turnout. He's walking around, tending to them, showing them the process of growing and drying the kaffe beans. They're all staying in the cottages he and his guild set up by the sea. Over the next few days, we'll attempt to show them that our town can host them and keep them safe from bandits and rival guilds...and that's another reason Zaci hired me.

I fix at least six more kaffes, and my brain starts to zone out. Awe being here means something, and I'm not sure what. I shouldn't have sent her away so quickly. I need to know what happened to me—why I woke up last month with holes in my memory and no weapon. This bard could hold a clue to finding that information, and I'd messed up my chance of getting it by letting her spook me. I grab a broom and sweep up some of the grounds I dropped earlier. It feels like I should be holding something else—a weapon— but I can't see or picture what it used to look like.

Zaci is still talking to the nobles, but it's getting late. He bounces from table to table, just as animated as when this evening began hours ago. Probably from the kaffes he drank.

"Hunt." He beckons me over with a wave.

After wiping my hands and throwing a towel over my shoulder, I walk toward the table, but he meets me in the middle.

"Take this ring to the vault, please." He holds out a small fist, then drops a ring of cool metal into my hand. It's enchanted—the power sings through my palm immediately. "A donation from the elf behind me." He leans closer. "It'll cover commissioning a second machine. You can train someone else, and we'll double the production!"

I nod. He needs me to take it to the treasure room where no one can pick his pocket.

With a quick glance, I walk calmly back behind the bar and through the doorway that leads to the private rooms of the building. The treasure room is a nondescript door with an enchantment that leads people to ignore its existence. I look behind me again, then enter the code and touch my hand to the magical panel at the center.

When I step inside the small room, a handful of globes light up and float off the shelves, bathing the treasure room in warm light. The ring would sit nicely in the ring display box at the back, but as I take a step in that direction, the floating orbs suddenly flash red and start screeching. The alarm.

I whirl around and smack into something.

"Oof." A figure blinks, then comes entirely into view. It's Awe. Seriously?

"What in the nine hells are you doing in here?" I grab her upper arm so she can't run.

She puts up her empty hands spread in front of her, honey-brown eyes wide in the flashing red lights. "I'm sorry! I didn't mean to—I mean. I was trying to get to that!" She points at a shelf, where a small leather bag sits. It's an Infinite Bag with some sort of magical lock on it. I'd seen it in the treasury when doing bookkeeping with Zaci.

"Did you set off the alarm on accident, or—" Zaci rushes into the room, then scoots to a stop. "Oh. Hello." Zaci waves, and the orbs stop flashing red and go back to their usual soft glow.

Awe lets out a nervous laugh.

No way is she bluffing her way out of this one. I narrow my eyes at her, still gripping her arm tight enough that I hope she won't get any ideas about running. "I can only assume she followed me in here, invisible, in order to steal something."

"It's not stealing! I'm here for my Infinite Bag. It's right over there." She points again to the same spot. "I can prove it's mine. I have a magical tattoo. That's how I tracked it to this place. You see, I died recently. When I came to, I didn't have any of my stuff or even my memories of the past year. I don't know who resurrected me. If I had my bag, I know I could trigger some memories by playing my lute. Look, I'll show you and prove it. Can I have my arm back, please?"

I release her sleeve-covered arm. She died, too. Could it

be possible we died together? I want to ask, but not in front of Zaci.

"Okay, sorry to flash you or whatever. But here." She pulls her pants down, and I look away after seeing a flash of her underwear and the curve of her leg. She's a criminal, at the very least. I shouldn't be looking. "Right here." I can't help but glance when she points to the slightly glowing tattoo of a stringed instrument on her upper thigh. When she sweeps her other hand over it, the image changes to a map of the coast, with a softly glowing ping in the area where this shop is. My eye catches on the bag on the shelf again—it's glowing in time with the tattoo.

Zaci rubs his chin with his thumb. "Hm. I'm familiar with that enchantment. That spell does indeed prove the bag is hers. I have no problem returning it to her."

Okay, maybe she's not entirely a criminal.

"Where did we even get it?" I ask Zaci. My fingers hover over Awe's exposed thigh. I long to touch the enchantment on her skin and see if I can understand how the magic works. No other reason. Heat flushes my cheeks.

"That Infinite Bag was one of Bix's items, which he offered as collateral when we started this business. But it wasn't attuned to him, so he couldn't use it."

"Yeah, because it's mine!" Awe yanks her trousers up again, covering the tattoo. "Wait. By Bix, do you mean Bix Gemfinger? 'Cause I know that little shit. Called himself my rival when we were growing up." She makes a fist and scrunches her nose in a cute way. No, it's not cute. She was certainly involved in my death.

"Seriously, go ahead and take the bag. I'm not going to keep your items. That's not the kind of business I run," says Zaci.

"Thank you." She gives me a little squinty glare as she crosses the treasure room and gets the bag.

Zaci and I watch her open it and rummage around.

"Hold on." She sits on the tile floor and starts pulling things out. A leather drum, extra strings, a stool, rope, a repair kit, a...kazoo?

"I was never able to get any items out of it, though a magical appraisal said there were valuables inside," Zaci says as we watch her pull out item after item.

A steel long sword with a hilt shaped to look like wings clatters to the ground. "Ugh, where is it?" She piles more stuff around her. "Ignore this. Ugh, why isn't this working? What I need is supposed to come to me!"

I kneel beside her. "What is?" I squint at the sword. The weapon looks oddly familiar, but I can't place it.

"My golden lute! I know the key to unlocking my memories is playing that instrument. I wove protective and healing magic into its enchantments." She looks up at Zaci. "Did Bix take it?"

Zaci scratches his head. "Not that I know of. Like I said, we couldn't get any items out of it."

"Ugh. Fine. Maybe it's still in here." She reaches deeper, her entire arm and half her shoulders disappearing inside. She pulls out a second bag, then a third bag that looks on the outside to be identical to her Infinite Bag. "Be careful of that one. It's the Douche Bag."

"The what?" I ask.

"It's a cursed item that I call the Douche Bag," she continues as she rummages in the Infinite Bag. "It consumes people—oh, don't look at me like that, Hunt! It doesn't kill anyone. It just sucks them in and spits them out wherever their hometown is or near where they were born...and it spits them out naked. I use it on terrible men. Once, I used it to get rid of a demon. Sent him back to the nine hells, but I've also used it to get rid of regular douchebags at parties and shit."

I sense something magic about the other bag, too. "What's in this one, then?" As I pick it up, something rolls out.

"Um, nothing important!" Her cheeks flush, and she snatches up some cylindrical item. Was...that a sex toy? I avert my eyes as she shoves it back into its bag.

"Heh. It's supposed to be similar looking to a dragon's dick, but you know. Haven't seen one of those in person." She coughs. "Guess I had to take the vendor's word for it." She opens the bag wider, then leans her whole torso inside.

My heart lurches. What if she falls in and gets stuck? "Hey. Be careful. You're the only one who can use that! Don't get stuck inside." I grab hold of her waist. This feels so familiar. *She* feels so familiar. Something must've happened in our past. Maybe she was my enemy, and we grappled?

She rummages around a bit longer before pulling herself back out of the bag with a sigh. "It's really not here." Her pink hair is messy, and my hands itch to fix it.

Instead, I let go of her waist, stand, and step back.

Zaci clears his throat. "Awe, would you consider working for me? I can get the word out about the lute. Put up a good reward for it. In return, maybe you sing? I can get you a different instrument, anything you want."

This time I can't bite my tongue. "Seriously, Zaci? She broke into our treasury. Clearly, she's not trustworthy."

"Only to get something she already owned," Zaci says.

Awe stands, leaving the enchanted bag and all the random stuff on the ground. "Honestly, my magic hasn't been reliable lately. I haven't been able to cast Invisibility since I resurrected. I think it was that sip of your kaffe that let me cast it again." She turns those big eyes at me and blinks. "A longer drink of you could be what I need."

She had to have misspoke. "A longer drink *from* me. Um, like, a drink I make you." I just keep making it worse.

Awe smiles. "And like your boss said, I can convince even more people to come to the shop." She offers her hand. "Truce?"

I sigh. Why do I want to trust her so badly? That's a red flag in itself that she's using her magic to influence me. "Fine. But you can bet I'll be watching you closely." Very closely. I'm sure there are additional things about her I can't remember. Suspicious things.

She turns to Zaci. "A place to stay and some food is all I need. My lute is worth more than the rest of this treasure room. No offense."

Zaci shrugs.

"And once I have it again, I'll be able to perform anywhere. I won't be hurting for coin." She stretches her hand out closer to me. "Hunt, right? I'm sorry for sneaking in. In return for your boss's kindness, I'll help make sure the resort town's opening is a success. Okay?"

I take her hand and shake it firmly. Just like last time, something pulls me from the present moment. A memory? It's like I'm reliving that exact time again. Awe is looking up at me with those same faux-innocent eyes as I thread my hand in her soft, pink hair. Then I yank her mouth to mine greedily, tasting her sweet kiss. Our horns grind together, and even that sends pleasurable vibrations through my body. She wraps her leg around my waist and—

I'm back in the present moment, and I can't breathe. We weren't just enemies.

I loved this woman.

Awe chuckles and shakes Zaci's hand next, giving me a little glance before turning to my boss. "It'll be a pleasure to work with you."

Does she remember being with me?

It takes everything in me to not flee from her like she's a powerful infernal.

Awe

SEABIRDS SQUAWK AS I PUSH OPEN THE DOOR AND WALK outside the little cottage Zaci put me up in overnight. I rub my eyes and stretch out long in the early morning light. The sun is just peaking up over the ocean, glowing shades of blue and pink over the deep teal water. Damn, not bad for free digs. Not bad at all. And I'm so much more comfortable after getting my regular wardrobe out of my Infinite Bag. There are many of these tiny white wooden homes that dot the coastline—Zaci said something last night about how his guild rents them out. Trying to get rich folk from Deepwater to stay outside the city.

Why does Zaci want me working for him so badly? Right now, I don't have much better to do. I still have to figure out who has my lute, though I'd bet all my small amount of recovered coin on the thief being Bix. Why is it so easy to remember my childhood irritating nemesis, and yet I can't remember what I was doing last month? Or who I was doing, apparently.

That bartender, Hunt...I knew them before I died. Intimately. The first glimpse of our past was so freaking hot—passionately kissing against a wall at some market. But the second time I touched their hand last night, I saw the two of us fighting in a duel. I was using a giant hand spell to push them off a ledge. Maybe things went bad between us, and that's why they're so set against me? Ugh. I really want to be able to trust my own memories again.

I slide on the leather sandals Zaci gave me and walk the path over the sandy dunes toward the little seaside town. He said I could come by the shop for breakfast when the sun was up, and well, it's getting up. Maybe this can be the new me—up and ready to greet the day at dawn. I've never been an early riser, but I was tossing and turning this morning. Thinking about where my lute could be. And who Hunt is to me.

Following the seaside path, I pass some scrubby trees and dune plants, heading toward the town.

Wow, the outside of the kaffe shop is gorgeous. I couldn't see it in the rain last night. It's themed, similar to the white wooden vacation homes, but it has teal shutters and a metal roof. Fragrant white flowers grow up along the siding.

I try the front door, but it's locked. Guess I beat Zaci to his own shop. I wander around the side of the building and take a peek . There's a stone patio with more plants for shade growing over a pergola, and...someone is on the ground doing pushups.

It's Hunt. I swallow. Their arms are bare, and I can only glimpse the top of their short, teal hair, curved horns, and muscular shoulders, and...damn, they look good. I duck behind a thick post covered in more of the same white flowering vine to watch. After a dozen more of the exercise, they stand, grab a towel from a bench, and wipe off their brow.

"I can see you." Their tone is flat. I can't tell if they're annoyed or just stating a fact.

I step out from the post and give a little wave. "Um. Hi."

They nod at me in greeting, face serious. They're clad in soft pants that I've frequently seen on martial artists and no shirt—only some kind of wrap over their chest that binds their breasts. Damn. Is it rude of me to stare?

"Good morning. I think we got off on the wrong foot yesterday." I step closer, onto the patio under the shade of the vines.

They straighten, not backing away. "I have to confess. We were intimate before."

Damn my malfunctioning memory. For one, if I could truly remember all the details of how their body felt against mine, then I'm pretty sure that'd provide good fodder for self-pleasure for the rest of this life and the next. For another, it's freaking embarrassing to not be able to remember. Makes it look like I'm some sort of asshole who uses people and forgets them—the worst kind of bardic stereotype.

I laugh, but instead of it sounding chill and reassuring, it comes out as nervous. Which I am. Dammit. "I'm so sorry. I promise—I'm not the type that just forgets my former lovers, and I know I'd remember you if I could. Like I said yesterday, the problem is, I died. Not from being in bed with you. At least I don't think so."

Though looking at them and their toned shoulders in the morning light, that's as good a theory as any. I'd gladly accept that kind of fate. Seems a fitting end for a renowned bard.

Hunt uses the towel to wipe sweat and sand from their shoulders, turning to avoid eye contact with me. "I...died too. And just like you, someone brought me back, and I'm missing memories. There are many things I'm trying to regain."

"Oh?" This changes everything! Maybe we weren't

enemies and were instead in a traveling party or on a mission together when we lost our lives...though that wouldn't explain the flash I got last night of us fighting.

They nod. "Yes. I was rude to you because when I touched your hand the first time, I saw the moment of my death, which I hadn't been able to see before. I thought you'd been the one to cause it."

Did...*I* kill them? Doesn't seem like me. I've been the end of a few people, but not good people like Hunt. Though I could be assuming they're *"good."* Really, I don't know enough about them yet to know their alignment.

They sigh and wrap the towel over the back of their neck. "Like you, I'm missing essential chunks of my memories. I know I was once a paladin." They look at their hands. "But I must've done something wrong to where my deity revoked my magic."

I've never cared for the deities of this land. They're beings who were lucky enough to have more power than mortals. Why should we have to worship them?

"Deities can go suck a big one. You shouldn't have to place yourself under them."

They give me a half-smile. "You serve a goddess. That much I remember. The Lady of Deception, if I've heard right."

I grin and give a little bow. "The rumors are true. But that's only because she likes to fuck with the rest of the pantheon."

Hunt's hazel eyes look particularly gold in this early morning light as the sun rises. "Gods like Oghma keep the powerful in check and the world in balance."

I hope Hunt isn't one of those paladins that'll wax poetic about the virtues of their deity. Yuck. "On that, we're going to have to disagree."

But they just nod again. "I...saw something else the second time our hands touched. The time we shook hands in the treasury."

Is that a flush across their cheeks? It could just be from the exercise they did, but what if they remember something similar to what I saw?

I take a step closer, wishing I could take their arm here. "Was it a certain market trip that we took? 'Cause I saw that too. We were walking arm-in-arm. Then you whispered to me that we needed to be less obvious. Then you shoved me against a wall."

They blush brighter and cover half their face with their hand. "I saw something different. But yeah, along those lines."

I wish with everything in me that I could remember Hunt. Anything about them. "Do...you want to hold my hand and see if we get a memory of something else?"

Their gaze pierces me with an intensity that makes me want to squirm. It's like they're looking for something. "What if we try that and then find out that we killed each other?"

That's a good point. Do I want to know while I'm still working for Zaci and have to be around Hunt?

Yeah, I do. Otherwise, the curiosity would kill me.

I hold out my hand, palm out. "I guess we challenge each other to single combat out here behind the kaffe bar."

Horror flashes across their face. "What?"

"I'm joking!" I hold my hands up in surrender. "Look, let's just say that whatever happened to us in the past can stay in the past since we both died. We can take this as a fresh start. But I want to regain my memories." Suddenly, I'm aching for them to touch me, even just palm to palm. "Come on."

They reach out hesitantly until their palm meets mine. Our hands are about the same size. Theirs is warm and a little sweaty from exercise, but it feels nice.

Now, where's the flood of memories I was supposed to get?

"I don't see anything this time," I say with a frown.

Their face flushes again, and they yank their palm back, averting eye contact. "Mm."

"Wait, what did you see?" I have to know.

"Let's go inside." Hunt's voice squeaks a little. "I'll make you a kaffe. You use magic, so it might help you regain some of your spells or even remember something. And it's time to open the kaffe shop for the visiting nobles."

They're trying to change the subject on me. Well, it's not going to work. I follow them through the backdoor to the bar on my tiptoes. "Hunt, please! You have to tell me what you saw!" I use what I consider my cutest pleading voice.

It's cooler in the shop and out of the sun, and I think Zaci must have enchantments to keep the indoor temperature from creeping up.

After Hunt steps behind the bar, they toss the dirty towel in a basket, wash their face and hands in the sink, then pull out a clean shirt from under the bar and put it on. It's made of some sort of linen blend and hangs loose over their frame. I take a seat on one of the stools and cross my arms.

They lean on an elbow on the bar in front of me. A lock of teal hair falls over their horns and over one eye.

I sweep it to the side before I can stop myself. This motion feels so familiar. I want to remember why. "What did you see?" I ask again with a grin.

They take a slow breath and blow it out. "It was a strong memory. Involving your hands. And your...nimble fingers."

Ahhh, I knew it! Butterflies flutter in my chest, but I try to play it cool. "I'm a bard of great renown. Of course I'm good with my fingers." I reach out and touch the edge of their shirt, leaning closer over the bar.

They drift nearer to me, staring at my lips. "I thought we said whatever happened in the past stayed in the past."

I grin wider. "I might be changing my stance on that."

Only a few inches are left between us. Their intense hazel eyes meet mine. "We still don't know if we killed each other. This could end really badly."

"Some things are worth the risk," I murmur.

The front door bursts open, and we both jolt back.

"Hunt, why isn't the shop open yet?" Zaci strolls across the floor, and Hunt and I each take a step back from the bar. Did Zaci notice how close we were?

"I'm sorry about that. I'll get right on it," Hunt says, smoothing their shirt.

Zaci waves them off. "I'm just messing with ya. I know you deal with that whole can't tell time thing. We have another fifteen minutes before opening, but I could really use a double-strength kaffe after schmoozing with the investors most of last night."

"Of course." Hunt turns away from me, gathering supplies. I don't know how I'm supposed to go about the day without finding out more about what they saw. And what I was doing with my fingers, apparently.

"Awe, come join me at a table. I'd like to talk about our marketing plan..."

I follow Zaci, and he starts talking logistics on how he's going to get more investors, more visitors, and tourists to the town after grand opening. I suppose I should try to pay attention. He's giving me a place to stay, food, and a job.

While he's talking, I glance back at the bar. Hunt stares

at me, their eyes piercing into mine. I want to hear everything they remember about us and try to figure out what
that means for our future.

"Awe." Zaci waves a hand in front of my face. "Are you
hearing what I'm saying?" He sighs and shakes his head.
"Hunt, can you make that two doubles, please? Trust me,
it'll help."

"I'm sorry." I really need to focus. Zaci has been good to
me—he even returned my Infinite Bag.

He pats the back of my hand. "I understand. Bix doesn't
deserve our attention, but I wanted to adopt a similar
strategy to his marketing, as his concert happening this
weekend has already sold out, and in turn, the guild's inn is
completely booked."

Wait...Zaci was talking about Bix? That jerk is my best
lead as to what happened to my lute. "His what?"

"His concert. If I plan a concert with you, I think that
could fill all our cottages, and once people come stay, I know
they'll want to return."

"I need to go to Bix's concert—need to see if he's using
my instrument." *Focus.* "I mean—to see their marketing
strategy and be able to copy it. Where is it?"

Zaci scratches his head. "Eh, it's in the Deepwater City.
But the security on that event will be pretty tight. From Bix
and my...history, I'm already banned from attending any of
his guild's events."

Oh, I'm *so* going, no matter what it takes to get inside. I
need my instrument...and my memories. I'm not letting this
pompous jerk keep me from remembering my past.

Hunt

SOFT LUTE STRUMMING RISES FROM THE CORNER OF the shop. A soprano voice with a tone I'd imagine a celestial would have floats over the sounds of the stringed instrument. *Awe.* I sigh and try to focus on making the drink I'm working on. If she's truly my enemy, I'm such a goner—maybe for the second time. Zaci managed to procure her a lute from somewhere, though she says she sounds much better with her signature instrument. I can't imagine that.

She's sitting in a beam of light at the corner window next to a potted palm. Her pink hair—with extra waves and curls from the coastal humidity—cascades behind her shoulders. When she brushed my hair from my forehead earlier, I wanted to lean into her touch like a damn fool with no sense of self-preservation.

Milk splatters out of the foaming cup and all over the counter. Damn, I just forgot what I was doing. *Again.* That's the fourth mess I've made today. It's like I'm back to day one in my training. I shake myself and put the half-spilled cup aside, then grab a rag to clean up the mess.

She's doing this to me on purpose. Singing poetic lyrics of *one more kiss*, of being haunted by a past she can't touch.

It's late afternoon now, and both of us have been working all day. Zaci's nobles have come in and out through the day, and he fixed them a spread of fruit, meats, and crackers for lunch. Awe's music seems to be helping their mood, but not my focus.

Zaci walks behind the bar and snatches the rag from me. "Go take a break, kid. You seem distracted."

I turn away from Awe. Maybe he won't realize I was staring at her again. "Sorry."

He smirks at me, lifting an auburn eyebrow. "I thought you were morally opposed to that bard's presence."

My mind draws a complete blank on how to reply to that.

Zaci laughs. "It's time for her break too. Just sayin'. There's a quiche and some tea in the breakroom. Noor made it."

Our baker and other barista is amazing, and perhaps I'll be able to think clearer once I get some food. I nod and take my apron off, hanging it on its wall hook. "Thank you."

I wander across the shop and sit at an empty seat near Awe, watching her play. Her nimble artist fingers dance over the instrument's neck. She starts singing again after the instrumental break ends, poetic words flowing easily from her lips about the intersection of luck and fate.

She's singing directly to me now, but unlike me earlier, she doesn't get flustered or mess up what she's doing with her hands. After one final chord, she lowers the instrument and gives a little bow to the sprinkling of applause around the kaffe shop.

"Um. Zaci said we could take a break." I incline my head toward him, standing in the place I was behind the bar. "Says there's food for us in the breakroom."

"I get you alone? Mmm, deal. I wouldn't care if we're eating raw squid."

I chuckle. "You're not afraid of me? We might've fought to the death."

She sets the instrument down on her chair. "In the past. Plus, if it was *to* the death, that'd mean we're good now."

I saw us fighting the first time our hands brushed. But then the next two times...I'm not sure what to do with how different those sets of memories are.

"Come...chat with me while we eat." I need to get her to understand—it could be dangerous if we both remember that we were enemies.

We walk around the tables of the kaffe shop and through the short hall behind the bar to the breakroom, which also doubles as Zaci's office.

Next to his desk is a small table with the quiche he mentioned and a pot of tea, still hot.

I shut the door behind us. I should lock it—we're just in here to talk, and it's not like anything else will happen, but I don't want Zaci walking in on us if we're speaking about something personal. Turning the latch, I put effort into keeping my breathing even. Nothing wrong with needing some privacy. Doesn't matter that my body continues to have an embarrassingly horny reaction to this woman.

"Your technique on foaming that milk was interesting." Awe smirks to punctuate her tease.

Of course she saw me get flustered over her while I was working.

I open and close my mouth, unsure how to reply.

"So." She takes a step toward me. "I'm gonna need to hear what you saw this morning when our palms touched. You've made me wait all day." She drops her voice low and quirks an eyebrow on the last phrase.

I lift my chin. "You know what? No. You're doing this on purpose, and I'm not going to fall for it."

She blinks and scoffs, putting a hand to her chest in faux innocence. "I don't know what you're talking about."

I refuse to be the only one getting flustered. But I can't get the image out of my head of us intimate together. Her moaning my name.

I corner Awe against the door, invading her space until she backs up into it, then lean my palms on the door on either side of her face. "If you want to get your memories back, then you're going to have to see them for yourself. I'm not influencing what you remember."

Her grin grows big, one pink eyebrow lifting. "Oh, I'm getting my memories. That's why I'm going to go steal my lute back from Bix this weekend."

"What?" She can't mean infiltrating that concert. Security is much too high for it to be safe. And I wasn't even talking about that.

Suddenly, she grabs my shirt by the collar and yanks my lips to hers. It's so surprising I gasp aloud. So much for playing it cool.

"Mmm, Hunt," she groans the words into my mouth, and she sounds just like she did in my memory.

Awe's taste is utterly intoxicating. Her scent is familiar and comforting—lavender and lemon soap, the salt from the coastal air, and a unique-to-her smell I could never hope to describe. Her lips move so softly against mine. The kiss started out urgent, but now she's relaxed into it like she's savoring me.

I wrap my arms around her, one in her hair, and snake the other around her waist as I push her against the door and kiss her. She's shorter than me and softer in many lovely places. Arousal pulses through my body. *This.* I needed this. Since waking up from the resurrection, I've struggled with finding my purpose. I know I'd somehow lost my favor with Oghma but had no clue what to do next. While I appreciate all Zaci's kindness in teaching me his trade, I didn't know what I was missing.

But it was her. Awe.

We break for a breath, but I haven't had enough of her. I kiss her again, and this time, a memory pulls me in. Awe is lying across from me on two bedrolls that we've pushed together. Stars are above us as we make camp at the edge of a meadow. She kisses me then, too, and her horns and hair over me are suddenly all I see.

I draw back and cradle her face in my hands while her light brown eyes pierce into mine.

"I saw the end of the fight we had," she says.

Her words plunge me into cold water. I drop my hands and take a step back to give her some space. She can't want me close after seeing that.

She crosses her arms, still leaning on the door. "Good news. We didn't kill each other."

I blow out a breath of slow air. "That's a relief." When she doesn't offer more details, I have to ask, "Did you want to tell me what happened? Did you see how we died?"

A devilish grin crosses her cute face. "You'll have to come to my cabin after work to find out."

I scoff. "You'd make me wait? This is serious." My cheeks and ears feel like they're burning at the mention of visiting her cabin.

She pokes me in the chest. "You made *me* wait all day, you jerk, and you still haven't told me all the details of what you saw this morning."

"That's..." I hold up a finger, unbidden memories rising in my mind again of the two of us making love.

"Mmhm." She steps around me and plucks a slice of quiche from the plate. "Time to get back to work. You'll have to ask Zaci where my cabin is. Think of all the memories we could recover together." She unlocks the door and then blows me a kiss as she leaves.

Awe

Nervous energy buzzes through me as I lounge on a one-person hammock on the porch attached to my cottage, absently playing the borrowed lute as I watch the colors of the sunset. Was I too forward? Hunt certainly seemed to enjoy the kiss, coming back for more after we broke apart. Also, they freaking pinned my body to the breakroom door. That was...phew.

There's a figure jogging over the dunes toward my cabin. I smile. There's my hot barista.

I wave at Hunt as I stand from the hammock and put Zaci's lute in its case.

Hunt has changed out of their work clothes, wearing a nicer button-up linen shirt and black trousers. Their teal hair looks a bit damp, darkening its color. Hunt smiles and lifts a small tote bag. "Hi. I brought some of the extra fruit and bakery snacks that won't be fresh enough to serve tomorrow."

I'm not hungry, but I return their smile. "Thanks. Come sit with me."

I glance over my shoulder at the cabin. Where would be the best place to talk? The cabin is a small space—just big enough for one large bed, a small counter area with a tiny enchanted rune that can heat a teapot, and a small washroom with a shower. The double doors to the porch are open, though, making it possible to sit on the bed and look over the dunes and sea.

I'm sure, down to my bones, that I knew them intimately before we were reunited yesterday, but since we're both missing memories, it kinda feels like we just met. Guess I'll just have to wing it. Like usual.

I throw open both of the doors to the porch. "Come on in. Let's sit and talk."

We both kick off our sandals by the door and go inside, and Hunt sets their bag of snacks on the table near the teapot.

Their short hair was tussled by the walk through the evening sea breezes and going in a few directions. I want to run my hands through it.

"Something you said earlier is bothering me." Hunt looks me up and down.

"What's that?"

"You said you were intending to steal your lute back."

Is this some kind of paladin moral quandary? "Yeah, I am. But it was mine first, so it's not stealing. Obviously, Bix is the one who has it. He's not a good musician and an even worse storyteller, so if he's sold out a concert—and we know he was the one who had my bag before I got it back—then it must be because he has my instrument. I've been weaving spells into that lute for years."

Hunt shakes their head. "I know the instrument belongs to you. But you're going to get yourself killed if you try to infiltrate that guild's concert. They have some serious security, including a group of warlocks that can summon all kinds of nasty demons."

"I'm pretty good at getting out of things alive." I put on my best, most confident smile.

One of Hunt's eyebrows quirks up. "Are you, now?"

Such a low blow. I put a hand to my chest in faux indignation. "Ouch. Okay, fine. Most of the time, I am." I pat the spot on the bed next to me. "Come. Sit with me." My heart races faster as they move closer and sit on the soft quilt.

Hunt's hazel eyes meet mine. "Let's not rush into anything. How about we get the lute together at a different time when security isn't so high? Or better yet, wait until we have backup. We can hire some muscle if we need to. Also, even if we left right now, we'd barely have the time to comfortably travel to Deepwater City by tomorrow."

Seems it's not a good idea to share my travel plans with

them, then. I can tell I'm not going to get anywhere arguing, so I shrug. "Maybe."

There's no way I can let this chance go. Bix likes to travel, sometimes leaving on tours of over a year—what if this is the last chance I have to get my lute and memories back for a month or longer? I'm nothing without my magic, and it's infuriating to know that I was better at my arts in the past. Besides, I know the Deepwater stadium where the concert is, inside and out, which will help me remain undetected. I might not get another chance like this. In the night, I'll leave and make my way to Deepwater with haste. And once I get my lute, I'll be able to teleport right back here since I set up a teleportation circle. It'll be easier to ask forgiveness rather than permission.

Hunt cups my face, each touch of their hand sending a sizzle across my skin. "Well. How about this? Instead of going to get the lute right now, let's try a different way to regain your memories."

Oh. Now that I can't argue with.

They pull me into a kiss, searing all my senses with a blaze of desire. Hunt's temperature seems to run hot, like mine. Maybe it's a tiefling thing. I haven't been with another like myself, well, that I can remember. "Do you see anything new?" I murmur against their lips as our kiss breaks.

They lean back enough to run their gaze up and down my frame, stopping at my face and giving me a smile. "I see you. No new memories, though."

I kiss them again, my lips curling against theirs. "Not a lot of people get a second first time. Lucky us, I say." I touch the top of their linen shirt, fingering the first button.

"I'd thought my luck had run out. Then I found you."

I undo three buttons, aching to touch those muscular

shoulders, but before I can continue, they scoop me up and toss me gently to the center of the bed.

They climb on top of me, placing a knee between my legs, grinding down on the soft bedding while pinning both wrists over my head with one hand. I gasp and press up against them, seeking more pressure. The comfort of their weight on me is exquisite.

Hunt lowers their face to mine until our noses barely touch. "Earlier, you promised to give me information. How did we die?"

I groan, not wanting to think of that right now. "Your moves are good, but your pillow talk needs some work." The memory of our deaths is like a distant bad dream with Hunt's body over mine, their smell enveloping my senses.

Hunt strokes my cheek with their free hand, the other still pinning my hands. I love it. "Well, it's important 'cause it feels like I might immolate if you touch me. Burn us both down."

I take their lips with mine, pressing them open with my tongue. Immolate is right. I'm on fire with need for them.

Hunt breaks the kiss, then trails their lips down my jawbone. "Awe." They rub their thigh downward between my legs and even through clothing, I'm aching for more. "I'm not going to touch you or let you touch me until you tell me."

I huff. Damn them. We don't even have all our memories of our time together, and they already know how to push all my buttons. "Fine. We died side by side," I blurt out, really hoping this doesn't kill the mood.

Hunt pauses their movements, releasing my wrists and propping some of their weight on their other elbow.

I cringe, wishing I didn't have such a vivid imagination. "It was an eye monster's death ray. You shielded me with your body before falling first. Before this battle, you'd lost your favor with Oghma. I... think because you were helping me."

Hunt looks off into the distance, eyebrows knitting. "Why would Oghma fault me for helping another? They're a champion for knowledge and good."

I tuck an elbow behind my head. "That I can't answer for you. Maybe because the gods are just another set of petty assholes? Anyway, pretty sure we got disintegrated after that because my memory abruptly ends. Means our bodies were gone too, so somebody, somewhere, paid a pretty piece of gold to bring us back."

Hunt looks puzzled. "I have no idea who that would be."

"Me neither. But I intend to find out when I get my lute."

They shake their head. "Not tonight. Get it another time."

The gentle light of the evening shoreline through the window paints the angles of their face in exquisite beauty. "Not tonight," I agree with a small smile. It'll be early in the morning when I leave for Deepwater, and my summoned phantom unicorn can make the trip in half the time a normal horse could.

Hunt audibly sighs with relief, and I feel a little guilty. But they can't understand—I *need* my lute. Without it, I'm just regular me—a mediocre performer and magician. And I have bigger dreams than to settle for that.

Hunt

I REACH OVER TO PULL AWE BACK TO ME BUT FIND THE other side of the bed empty. Sitting up, I blink the sleep out of my eyes and look around the tiny, still-dark cottage.

"Awe?" I scramble around, feeling for the rune-powered light on the side table that Zaci set up in all of these cabins.

Soft, gold light bathes the room, but still, no sign of her. Is she really the type to ditch me after sharing what we did last night?

I glance at the chair in the corner. Her Infinite Bag is still draped across it, so she can't be that far. All her important stuff, sans the lute, is inside.

Maybe she went on a late-night beach walk? I dress quickly, then venture outside, taking along an apple and muffin for a snack and slinging Awe's bag over my shoulder. Since she can use her tattoo to find it, it'll be easy for her to find me.

An hour later, the sun is rising, but no Awe. I end my walk at the kaffe shop and knock on the door to Zaci's private quarters.

"Yeah?" He blinks blearily at me.

"Have you seen Awe?"

He presses his lips in a line as he squints. "Kid, I haven't seen the sun until now. Why?"

I frown. I don't want to have to explain that we were in bed and she snuck out without me. "I just...can't find her. She didn't say anything else to you about going to Deepwater today, did she?"

Zaci scratches his chin. "Dunno. She said something yesterday about wanting to go to Bix's concert, but I told her there's no point; it's sold out."

Dammit. Of course, the concert is where she went. I take Awe's Infinite Bag off my shoulder and hold it out. "She left her bag, though. Wouldn't she take that with her?"

Zaci lifts a brow as he regards it. "You sure it's the right bag? There's something off about it. She had another nearly identical one, remember?"

Oh, fuck. Zaci's right. Now that I'm looking at it, I feel like a fool. This isn't Awe's Infinite bag—it's The Douche Bag. I'm shit at identifying magic items now, and Awe knows it. This stand-in was probably a bag she left to throw me off the trail and stop me from going after her. I want to scream, then go tell her off for being so reckless.

"Can you and Noor cover the shop for me today?" I've never asked off of work before, and I know this is an important week for Zaci.

He crosses his arms. "Why?"

"I need to get our bard back before she gets herself killed. Again."

Zaci rakes a hand through his copper hair. "You're not going to make it all the way to Deepwater on foot or by horse before the concert tonight. Even if we assume that's where Awe went and that she has some way of traveling faster, it seems unlikely she'd make it either."

"I don't doubt Awe has many surprises up her ridiculous pink sleeves, including fast travel. She wants her lute. She'll be there." Which means I need to be there.

And, nine hells, I know exactly one way to make it on time.

Zaci shrugs. "Okay, kid. Good luck to you. Be back as soon as you can."

It's a terrible idea and will no doubt be horribly embarrassing. I'm about to jump into a cursed item that'll spit me out naked. But my hometown is Deepwater. And I have a bard to protect. Even if it means traveling by Douche Bag.

Awe

I jump up and down with the rest of the waiting crowd at the stadium gates, giving a whoop as I point at my sparkly shirt, showing the people around me.

After I arrived in Deepwater early this morning, it was a breeze to disguise myself as one of Bix Gemfinger's fans, as they stand out even in this city's colorful crowd, calling themselves "The Fingers" and wearing shirts that say their catchphrase: "Finger us, Bix!" Gross.

When I spotted a group of easy marks sitting by themselves—a gnome and a human that could barely be considered of legal age—I used a sleep spell to disable them and take their fan merch and tickets. Really, I'm doing them a favor by sparing their ears from listening to Bix's terrible squalling vocals and awful poetry.

The line into the stadium is taking forever. I want to get in, get my lute, and get out. Get back to that cottage. Back to Hunt. Hopefully, they won't be too pissed at me for leaving. I wrinkle my nose as the ripe smell of the "The Fingers" rides on the morning breeze. As much as I like playing for crowds, being *in* crowds is downright draining. We inch forward, and time seems to crawl.

At last, I'm at the front of the line, and the guard at the stadium scans my ticket over the runic device. It turns green. They nod and wave me in.

The crowds are almost as bad inside the stadium. They mill about, standing in more lines at tables of roasted nuts and terrible clothing choices. It's still a while until the concert begins, so I have plenty of time.

I walk down the stone steps like I'm headed toward the front standing area of the stadium. Two tall men dressed in the blue and purple of the Deepwater Noble Guards are posted at the doors that lead to the bottom hall under the stage, faces impassive as they look over the mass of people continuing to stream into the stadium. I whisper some magic, making it appear that one of the large batons strapped to their belts clatters to the ground. As they both bend over to pick it up, I slide behind them, quick and silent. I'm around the corner before they return to their posts. Perfect.

It's darker in here than human eyes would find comfortable, but I can see just fine. This corridor under the stadium leads to dressing rooms. I can't imagine that I'd be lucky enough to find the lute in Bix's room unattended. If only. But if I'm fast, I can probably rush his dressing room, knock Bix down, grab the lute, and hightail it out of there. After I nab my lute, I only need to escape and lose him for a minute so I can draw the circle that allows me to teleport back to my cottage.

I'm jogging down the hall toward the main act's dressing room, light on my feet, when strong arms wrap around me, yanking me back. What the hell? I squirm, bending myself forward, preparing to headbutt my assailant in the nose.

"Shh, it's me."

Hunt's voice!

When I stop fighting, they set me gently on my feet, and I turn around. "Heyyy... So, I can explain." I point at them with both hands like the fool I am. "I swear, I'm not one of those bards who just loves 'em and leaves 'em. Also, don't judge me for my shirt. It's a disguise."

"What?" they hiss. "That's not what I—you nearly got vaporized by a trap! What are you doing?"

"I'm fine. I've got this. This is the backway to the artists' rooms. I almost played here once. That's a memory I kept."

Why would there be traps during a concert? I squint at the floor.

"Almost?" They shake their head. "Never mind, tell me later. Look." Hunt points at a spot on the ground. "My magic detection isn't great, but I can sense that one. The evil radiating off it."

Interesting. "Is your deity coming around to liking you again, then?"

"Not at this rate." But the side of their mouth quirks up a bit.

I look them over. Somehow, they're in a Deepwater noble guard's deep blue and purple uniform with gold accents. "How'd you get in here? And how'd you get a guard's uniform?"

They glance around, leaning in to whisper closer. "I... had to call in a favor, okay?"

"I'm also really curious how you beat me to Deepwater." Even in this situation, I'm having a difficult time looking away from Hunt's lips. They look oh so kissable.

Hunt sighs, pinching the bridge of their nose. "I used the Douche Bag."

Wait. The seemingly practical, by-the-rules Hunt traveled by *Douche Bag*? I snort. "You jumped through a cursed item to come find me?" With only my word on what that bag did. I can't believe they'd show up for me like this—that anyone would.

Even in the near-dark, I can see the blush staining their cheeks. "I'll explain later. Just know that it's a good thing I did, or else you'd be dust on the floor."

"It's fine, I've got this." I wave them off. That trap couldn't have been *that* bad.

"We don't have the tools to continue this way without the key that turns off the traps. You need a new plan to get the lute back. Or, like, a new plan at a completely different time because the security here is insane. There are at least five traps that I can see, and I have no way to disarm them."

Well, crap. "We could go up the way I came, but then we'd end up stuck in the crowd. There's an exit toward the front of this hall, but it'll lead us to the back of the vendor stations outside."

"Then that's the path we need to take. Unless you have a spell prepared for a quick way out."

"Hunt, you don't understand! I *need* that lute. Most of my best spells are stored inside it. I can do little tricks and glamours, sure, but without more powerful magic, what use am I?"

They grab me by the shoulders, so close that the heat of their breath touches my lips. "You think I care about how good you are at music or magic? I need you alive."

In an instant, I'm plunged into a new memory. *"I came all this way because I wanted to save you! If you die, then you'd have been better off without me."*

The me in the past reached out and cupped Hunt's face. *"My darling. We're always better together. Promise."*

"Did you see that?" I ask Hunt now.

They make an annoyed noise instead of answering before hoisting me over their shoulders.

"Ahh, put me down! I haven't made a plan yet on how to get to Bix!" My words bounce along with my body as Hunt jogs with me across their shoulders. I hold onto their upper arms for stability. This isn't the time for me to be admiring their deltoid muscles, but I suppose that's the type of smitten I am now.

Hunt slows toward the front of the hall. "Which way did you say was the way to the vendors outside?"

"Um, try that way." I point to the path that leads to the

other side of backstage—the side the stadium usually uses for opening acts and lesser celebrities. Bix is the headliner, so he can't be there, but it's better than Hunt taking us completely out where the vendors are. Then I'd have to start all over again, and I'm not sure my ticket would get me back in to the event.

They gently set me on my feet. "You know, I came out the other side of that bag completely naked."

"Oh, I'm aware of how it works." Wish I could've been there.

"I had to sneak into my old school to grab something to wear..." They trail off, glancing around. "And this doesn't look like we're going outside. It seems like we went around the other side of the stadium."

"Seems so." I blink, giving my most angelic face.

Hunt glares back, then startles as a pack of footsteps coming from the other direction tromp toward us.

"In here!" I pull Hunt by the elbow into a dressing room, closing the door behind us.

The footfalls stop outside the door, and then someone bangs on the heavy wood. "Who's there? This space is supposed to be reserved for the opening band."

"But that's us!" I'll have to make a good illusion and quick. I take a deep breath and grab tight onto all the magic I can—really wish I had Zaci's kaffe boost about now—and channel it into making the most flamboyant outfits. Silky fabric wraps around my body, taking the form of a tight, sparkly dress. I direct the magic to do the same for Hunt, only in a suit of trousers and vest.

I burst out, striking a pose. Please, let this enchantment hold. "We're Darkvision," I infuse my words with magic, saying the made-up name in a sing-song tone, "and we got a late invite from Bix himself. I can show you my guild seal. We're super excited to get the crowd pumped up!"

The guard, one of the two from the door, looks me up and down. "I super don't care. The primary opener didn't show, so I was told to grab the understudy act. I wasn't expecting..." he blinks and shakes his head, "...this. Whatever. Not my show. Come. I'll escort you to the stage."

He actually bought my bluff. Phew. At least this'll get us closer to Bix. I pull Hunt from the line of costumes.

They're looking down at themself, shaking their head. "You have the ability to summon magical disguises. And *this* is what you choose to dress me in?"

Okay, maybe I went a little over the top. But they look hot. Somehow, I even enchanted make-up—black eyeliner around their eyes and a line of teal stars on their cheek. I go on my tiptoes and kiss right under the stars. "I think it could be your signature look."

Hunt

THIS WOMAN IS ABSURD. FRUSTRATING. UTTERLY enthralling. Awe dances across the stage, hyping up the crowd while strumming her lute up and down. The lights from the magical projector gleam off her early spring strawberry-colored hair. I'm waiting in the shadows for the main part of the song to begin, as she told me to.

Awe sings, and her voice floats as if carried by celestials, magically amplified around the stadium.

She better have really good enchantment spells lined up if she expects me to perform.

"Just sing from your heart—I'll take care of the rest,"

Awe whispered as we were about to walk on stage. Easy for her to say. I'm not used to singing, and showing my heart to a massive throng of Bix fans is the last thing I'd choose to do on any given day.

But if this is the way that we make it out of here safely, I'll do it. For her. And why shouldn't I have confidence in myself? I survived jumping through a cursed bag. I managed to save her from the traps under the stadium. We're making it out of this place alive, dammit.

A blue-green spotlight hits me, and I stride forward like I own the stage.

"We're going down, an inevitable fall, risking it all..." Somehow, the words flow, and miraculously, my voice sounds...good. Like, crazy good. It's not like I'm terrible at singing around the campfire or along with a group, but I've never sounded like this.

Awe effortlessly accompanies me on her lute and backup vocals. The people who appear to be the guild's band—a drummer, flute player, and two other stringed instrument players—pick up their instruments and join in.

Magic is everywhere on the stage. Does the crowd realize how much of this act is magic-enhanced?

Cheers echo around the stadium, bouncing off the tall walls behind the stage.

Awe pumps her fist in the air, yelling, "Bix, Bix, Bix!" as the song ends. Why is she cheering him on if she hates him?

Most of the crowd is into it, but some of them look confused. Bix isn't due on stage until a while—according to the guard, we're the first opening act of several.

"Come on out, Bix!" Awe calls, her voice amplified over the mass of people. "Join us for a little taste! My name is Awe Danamark, and I grew up with Bix! It's my dream to play on stage with him. If we call him, I bet he'll come out.

Surely, he's not scared we'll show him up before his main set even begins. Bix, Bix, Bix!"

The crowd joins in, chanting his name over and over.

"Where are you, Bix? Just one song! Give us a taste!"

A confused and obviously pissed-off gnome comes walking onto the stage, looking at Awe as if trying to size her up. Then he faces the crowd, waving with a wide smile across his face.

The audience loses it. People who were previously getting refreshments or merchandise are pushing their way into the stadium area, clambering for the best spot up front.

The house band breaks into a jaunty song I don't recognize. Not that I'm an expert.

Holding her lute, Awe curtsies. "Let's have an old-fashioned bardic play-off. Like when we were younger. I challenge you. Unless your fingers aren't as skilled as they say."

For as cute and unassuming as she often presents herself, I wouldn't want to fuck with Awe. I see what she's doing here—she's making him get the enchanted lute. If he's anything like she said, he probably doesn't have the performance skills to compare with her unless he uses the magical instrument.

The crowd shouts back, some cheering for Bix, others yelling, "Do it!"

Bix chuckles, then signals one of the stagehands to come to him, whispering in the man's ear.

Within seconds, another stagehand dressed in black is running a golden stringed instrument to Bix, who snatches it, shooting a disdainful look at the person before smiling at the crowd again.

The members of the band wink at each other and begin a new, jaunty song. It's like they're speaking a different language—music—and I can barely figure out what's happening. I clap along with the beat as I slowly back away from the crowd, hoping to blend into the back of the stage.

Awe steps forward, taking the first turn. She picks a melody on her instrument—does she know this song already?—and begins to embellish when the pattern repeats. The crowd claps along. Awe dances a circle around half of the stage, even going around me. After two more repeats of the musical pattern, Awe takes a bow, and the audience cheers. All the while, the song continues.

Bix saunters to the center stage, rubbing the golden lute with his sleeve before raising a hand in the air. That cheater. Even without knowledge of how this type of magic works, it's obvious that he activated something enchanted. His solo begins slow, weaving around the initial melody that Awe gave before picking up in speed and intensity. This is completely unfair—to the audience, it must look like he's the superior musician.

But Awe doesn't appear to be bothered, stomping one foot along with the rhythm that the band gives. Bix finishes with a flourish of fingers and strings, taking an ornate bow and sending the crowd into a frenzy.

"Now swap!" Awe yells and tosses her lute toward Bix. Time seems to slow, and my breath catches. I've never seen Awe be rough with any instrument, regardless of the quality. Now Bix will have to either dodge Awe's lute and hope he doesn't trip, let it hit him and the golden lute—possibly damaging it, or do the mid-air swap Awe is trying to get him to.

He tries to dodge, but his ornate shoe catches on the stage. In a flash, a stagehand rushes to him, catching Bix in one hand and the golden lute in another. Awe's lute clatters to the ground with a dissonant clang. The band winces as they continue to play, and some of the audience murmurs their disapproval. In one fluid motion, Awe sashays to the stagehand, whisking the golden lute from his grasp and picking up the melody again. What's her plan here? She can't hope to escape the stage with this instrument. There are too many stagehands and guards that'd stop her before she got halfway down the stairs.

"I concede to Bix's great talent," Awe sings as she finishes the pattern, coming to a stop next to me. And suddenly I see it. When she was playing her solo, she was walking a circle...and drawing a teleportation circle with her foot. "Catch you next time!" She waves goodbye to the crowd, grabs my arm, and the concert stage, band, and crowd around us winks out.

Awe

CRAP, CRAP, CRAP. I DIVE UNDER THE COTTAGE BED AND rub at the teleportation circle runes I'd previously drawn with my palm, hastily erasing them before anyone gets wise to what spell I did and comes through the one I made on the stage.

Exhaustion pounds through my body. I used so much magic in such a short amount of time. It'll take a while before I'll be up for casting again, even little things. Maybe I can bum some kaffe from Zaci and speed up my recovery time.

Hunt is still sitting on the bed where we landed. "You're absolutely diabolical. I can't believe I didn't notice you casting that circle."

I stand, a hand on my hip, feigning confidence. "Bix'll think twice about stealing from me again." The temporary enchantment I put on our clothing is gone—revealing the Deepwater guard uniform on Hunt and the unfortunate Bix fan wear on me.

"He could've bought it from someone that looted our bodies." Hunt holds up the golden lute, turning it around in their hands.

"It's still stealing." I huff.

"Did you remember anything when you touched it?" they ask, holding it out to me.

I take the instrument, running my fingers over the familiar fretboard, the round curve of the body, and the runes imbued on the back. Nothing out of the ordinary for this instrument. No memories flowing back. "I...there's nothing. Sure, I'd enchanted plenty of spells into this, where if you're used to this instrument, you can use them without tiring yourself, which is what Bix was doing with it. But I really thought I would've imbued my memories here."

Those moments before Hunt and I died... I'd known what was coming—what was about to happen. What steps would I have taken to preserve our memories and lives?

Resurrection is expensive but not unheard of. And I had rich friends. I'm sure I would've put enchantments on something to return to. But if not my lute, what?

Hunt puts a hand to their face and flops backward on the bed. "You risked your life for this instrument. More than once."

"It was worth a shot!"

Hunt sits up, their intense stare piercing me. "Was it? I don't have the money to resurrect you. It's so much that not even Zaci does. Plus, having someone bring you back again so quickly can have other consequences. You could lose more than memories."

"Doesn't matter. Without my abilities, I'm not worth having around." It was worth the risk. But now what?

"I'm missing my paladin abilities—seems I'd lost them before I died, too. Do you think I'm worthless?"

I recoil. "Of course not! That's different."

"Is it? Just like you, I don't have all my memories of before we died. But I'd rather have a future with you than know the exact events that happened our last few months."

"I want a future with you too." Guilt gnaws at my gut. While I didn't outright lie to Hunt, I acted deceitful when I snuck off. And turns out it was all for nothing but a pretty instrument.

"I asked you to stay with me. I promised you that we'd get the lute together when we had the resources ready. How was that not enough?"

"It is enough, I just thought..." That I could be in and out? That my luck would hold out? That my memories would be in this instrument? Arguing feels pointless. "...I'm sorry."

"I just wish you could see yourself the way I see you. You're amazing just as you are." Hunt stands, and I'm not sure what to say in response. "I have to go tell Zaci that we made it back safe and check on the shop. Well, after I change my clothes." They hold out their arm, pointing to their Deepwater guard uniform. A definite downgrade from what they normally wear. Too bad my stage enchantment didn't create real clothing. "Zaci would've already closed, but I need to make sure everything went okay today without me. We can talk later. Sound good?"

I nod. "I'll meet you there. Maybe if I keep messing with the lute, I'll get something magical to unlock."

Hunt looks like they want to say something else, but they close their mouth and sigh. "Okay."

I know that past me would've made a backup to my memories and spells, but this lute is my only clue. Hurting Hunt by rushing off to Deepwater, angering Bix and his guild...it can't all be for nothing.

A FEW HOURS LATER, WATER RUNS FROM THE SINK OF the shop, and dishes clang together as Noor and Zaci scrub them, their backs to me. Slouching in my usual corner chair, I put my forehead against the back of the lute, wishing I could transfer any information it holds directly to my brain. Why aren't my memories here?

We came back to a mess. Without Hunt running the kaffe bar, Noor and Zaci fell way behind on orders. To keep up with the work, they even moved Fitz inside from his usual guard duty to serve food and bus tables, and he, apparently, couldn't help himself from cleaning up the customers' leftovers...by eating them in plain view of everyone. Hunt is wiping down the counter at the kaffe bar, eyeing me as I repeatedly examine the lute. Three loud bangs sound through the locked front door.

Hunt starts to walk over to see who it is, but Zaci beats them to it. He pulls the door open, then jumps back. "What that—"

I stand from my chair, clutching my lute. Four Deepwater guards are on the other side of the door, flanking a human man in fine clothing who stands next to a familiar gnome. Well, fuck. They push their way inside, fanning out around Bix and the man—who, based on his clothing and guild crest adorning his sash, is probably Rodstun Thardd, Bix's guild leader. I don't see Fitz anywhere, and he should've been back at his front door post. My stomach drops. I'm not surprised someone from that guild came to find us. But on the same night? It's barely been a few hours since we escaped. Wasn't Bix going on stage after us for his full set? And Rodstun's presence at what should be a small matter is unexpected.

"This is private property," Zaci says, an unusually cold tone to his voice.

"Ah, Zaci." The human man smirks. "*This* is the new business which you left my protection to start? How...quaint."

"What do you want, Rodstun?"

Rodstun shrugs, glancing around the kaffe shop with obvious disdain. "If you were still operating under me, we'd be having an entirely different conversation, but since you've opted to divest, I have no choice but to demand repatriations for the financial loss I incurred today."

Zaci snorts. "Already sounds like bullshit but go ahead. I'm listening."

Hunt stands next to Zaci with a towel draped over their shoulders. They cross their arms, and I can feel the tension from across the room. I don't know if I should run away or put myself between Hunt and these intruders.

"The actions of one—" Rodstun pauses as Bix pulls his at sleeve and then whispers something in the man's ear. "Ahem, *two* of your employees at my concert today have caused egregious damages to both my reputations as host and benefactor." He lifts his eyes to glare directly at me. "Known charlatan and thief, Awe Danamark, blatantly and in the witness of thousands, stole a fine instrument belonging to my bard, Bix Gemfinger."

Bix puffs his chest. "And *I* claim separate damages and reparations for the loss of my artistic reputation."

It hits me what happened—Bix couldn't play the rest of

the concert without my lute. He'd probably been using the performance-enhancing spells in the instrument and hadn't prepared his own songs.

Rodstun's face returns to neutral as he regards Zaci again. "We're prepared to seize your assets—by force if necessary—until the debt of your employee is settled."

"No, wait." I rush across the room, holding a hand up in surrender and the lute out. "I'm sorry." I bow deeply to Rodstun, holding out the instrument. He takes it from my hands, and I remain in the supplicant position. I have to make this apology count. "I'm Awe Danamark. I'm a freelance musician with no ties to Zaci and his establishment other than his kindness. The actions I took were my own, not his, and not..." I shouldn't say Hunt's name aloud, just in case the guild hasn't figured out their identity yet. "...affiliated with any other employee here. If you have a forensic magician, they can look at the lute and trace the enchantments to me. I took such drastic measures to get my instrument back because I thought it had vital personal information stored inside it, and I didn't have the time to wait. Again, I deeply and humbly apologize for any inconveniences that might've occurred at the concert. I did, in fairness, trade instruments with Bix, so he could've used the instrument I left him for his set."

Bix snatches the lute out of the hands of his guild master. "There was a riot! The people wouldn't stand for it to have me play without my famous lute. Oh, my darling, I missed you so much." He starts dropping kisses onto the neck of the instrument like it's a lover, and suddenly, I regret not disinfecting it before touching it.

"Uh-huh. You mean that they started rioting after they realized that you couldn't actually play?"

Bix jerks his head up to glower at me. "Insolence!"

Zaci waves his hand in a 'let's get on with it' motion. "Okay. Your bard's instrument has been returned, and my bard apologized. Are we done here?"

"Sadly, no. Simply returning the instrument won't recoup the losses from today's concert. I'm afraid if you'd like to avoid seizure of your property and assets, then I'll have to ask Awe to come back to Deepwater with me. She can be my guest and work for me until the debt is repaid. We're not talking forever, just a few years."

Be his indentured servant, he means. He probably wants me to use my abilities to broker deals or influence others.

And other than Zaci, I don't think I've heard of anyone successfully leaving his guild, either. Once you're a part of that family, you remain in their clutches, or you disappear.

"You're not taking her." Hunt steps in between us, positioning themself between me and Rodstun.

"This is my bar, not yours, Rodstun. You and all your goons can leave," Zaci says.

"Oh, well. Suit yourselves." Rodstun turns to the guards. "Take the bard. Then trash the place."

Ah, shit. I'm still exhausted—I spent all my magic reserves on getting the lute back, and without it, I don't even have stored spells that I can use. It usually takes a full night's rest before I can cast again after exerting myself like that.

I should've had Hunt make me a cup of kaffe rather than trying to unlock the secrets of my lute. Its enchanter clearly had issues beyond memory loss.

"That's not happening!" Hunt moves quicker than the guards. They kick one in the gut as they shove another. The remaining two start toward me, and I scramble backward.

I have my Infinite Bag strapped to my belt—maybe

there's something inside that can help. Not as powerful as my lute, but something.

I reach inside, digging around and hoping what I need will come to me. The two guards moving toward me draw their short swords.

"Do you have a weapon?" Hunt calls.

A sword. I remove my hand from the bag, pulling a sword from inside. No, not *a* sword. *The* sword.

It's resplendent, even in the dim light of the closed kaffe shop. The wing-shaped hilt. The brilliant sheen of the steel. And there—I hadn't noticed before, but those runes, running along the base of the blade and around the pommel —those are enchantments in my own magical signature.

Back when I dug through my Infinite Bag in the treasure room, I cast this weapon aside because it wasn't something I could use. Now, even though I clearly enchanted it, I know the blade isn't mine. It's Hunt's.

It makes sense now: this is what I did in my last few moments. I imbued this sword and put my trust in Hunt, knowing that our fates are intertwined. I never needed the lute—all the abilities I need are within me.

"Hunt, catch!" With great effort, I squeeze the last bit of magic from my soul to throw the blade and guide it into their hands.

Hunt catches the sword, and the whole room is bathed in brilliant light.

Hunt

EVERYTHING COMES BACK IN A RUSH. I WANT TO slowly delve into all the memories, savoring the richness and depth of my love for this woman, but I must focus on both of us surviving first.

I swing my sword, connecting with the guard's blade in another flash of light. Even though he blocks, the force I send throws him back and over a table, smashing a wooden chair. Oops. I'll have to fix that later for Zaci.

This feeling is unmistakable. Not only do I remember everything, but my abilities are back—the ones I trained for years, and the ones blessed by Oghma themself.

The last guard is closing in on Awe, cornering her against the bar. I whisper a word and step through space and time, appearing in front of her to knock the man in the skull with the pommel of my sword. He crumples, so I kneel and touch his head, imbuing enough life to avoid any lasting damage but not enough to make him regain consciousness. I'll have to check the guard I sent over the table, too. I don't want to kill these people, but I won't let them take Awe back to Deepwater.

The first two guards I hit without a weapon are up again, swords in their hands.

A boom of thunder shakes the earth itself. I chuckle at our old inside joke and throw a glance at Awe. "That would be The Storm Lord."

She tilts her head. "What?" She still doesn't remember. There must be some way for me to transfer the memories she imbued in this sword to her.

Three more figures stride through the door. Our friends. I felt the magical signal go out when I touched the sword, showing our friends Awe and my location. Our cleric, Namfoodle, despite his diminutive gnomish stature, saunters in first.

Blue lightning crackles around him. His white hair, which only grows on the sides of his head, not the top, stands on end, and his forehead glows with the holy symbol of Procan. Solla looks amazing in her velvet robe, her long black curls floating around her shoulders and down her back. Her familiar, a black cat the color of the night sky with stars, chirps as it perches on her shoulder. And Croga, tapping her massive silver club against her green hand, winks at me from behind her monocle.

"I think we know them," Awe whispers.

The two still-conscious guards sheathe their swords as Fitz pokes his furry head inside the door behind our friends, looking sheepish.

This skirmish is over. Everything's okay. I smile as I lower my blade and put an arm around Awe's shoulders.

Namfoodle clears his throat. "This establishment is now under the protection of Procan, The Storm Lord. God of the wind and seas. The bringer of salt and justice. The mercurial hand of fate. Who's the fool that will answer for this attack?" Nam lifts his hammer, and more blue lightning crackles around the room.

"Ah, Mr. Ningle." Rodstrun, who'd previously slid back in the corner near the door, walks forward with his hands up and Bix peeking around him. "Of course, your reputation as Lich-Slayer of Deepwater proceeds you. I'm a big fan. But you see, this bard is—"

"Awe Danamark," Namfoodle answers. "One of my dearest friends."

Rodstrun glances around, clearly recalculating upon realizing the destructive potential of the three newcomers. "...which is why, as a thank you for your acts of service to Deepwater, I've decided to discharge the debt that she owes to myself and my organization."

Nam lowers his hammer. "I should hope so!"

"While it was a pleasure to meet you, my associates and

I must return to our business in Deepwater." Rodstrun dusts off his jacket and signals for Bix and the guards to follow him.

"What about your instrument?" I ask Awe. "Do I need to stop them and demand it back?"

She shakes her head. "If Bix needs it so bad, he can have it. It can't replace real talent. And all of Deepwater saw that today."

The guard that fell over the table stands, not unconscious after all, then moves to his fallen friend and hoists them over his shoulder.

Once they're all out the door, Solla squeals in delight, jumping up and down as she embraces Awe and me in a big hug. "We've been looking everywhere for you!"

"I knew the resurrections took," Nam says as he secures his hammer to his belt, "but we had no way of knowing where in the realms the two of you ended up. Also, Hunt, I had a word with my deity, who had a word with yours."

I look at my hand, feeling Oghma's power flowing through my fingertips. "And it seems they were waiting on Awe and me to trust fully each other again before deeming me worthy. I'm not held to an oath of vengeance anymore." It's devotion that guides me now. For Awe, for my friends, and for all good creatures.

Awe puts her hand in mine, squeezing it. "I still can't remember you all. Only flashes. I remember a little more of Solla, who I knew the longest."

"I think I can share those memories with you now," I tell her.

Her light brown eyes sparkle as they stare into mine. "How?"

I cup her cheek and kiss her with all the passion I have, pouring my entire soul into blessing her with the memories we'd lost. Our meeting in a rich man's study, when I thought I would have to kill her one day in an act of vengeance. Of fighting enemies of all kinds, side by side. Us laughing by the fireside late into the night. That first kiss when I pulled her to me after pushing a rude man away. They all rush through my being as my lips press to her soft mouth, my tongue teasing inside.

Croga lets out a "whoo-hoo" from somewhere behind me as we kiss longer than what would be socially appropriate.

Awe has tears in her eyes when we part. "Hunt…"

I press my forehead to hers. "We get a new chance now."

"Er, hi." Zaci waves, making his way to the center of the room where we all stand. "I'm glad for this reunion, but do I still have a barista?"

"Seems like this is a beautiful place to stay in between journeys," Awe says with a cute shrug. "I hear it's blessed by Procan."

"The Storm Lord," Solla and Croga fill in, followed by giggles.

"I have the space for all of you to have separate quarters. And if a famed lich-slaying party is interested in staying here from time to time, that increases security for all my guests."

"Yes," I tell Awe. Though I'd go anywhere with her.

Awe and me living and working by the sea, my friends close by…a home to stay in between our adventures. Nothing sounds more perfect.

About the Author

Erin Branch (she/they) is passionate about writing queer stories full of romance, comedy, and heart and often enjoys writing tales that explore what it's like to discover yourself later in life. Her debut novel, *Di-Curious,* is also available in audiobook and voiced by award-winning narrator, Lindsey Dorcas. Find Erin's latest updates at: beacons.ai/authorerinbranch

The Ice Princess and the Gladiator

Gwenhyver

A Jasyn and the Astronauts Story

Sword and Space

"Who in the Seven Heavens are you?"

Acasta struts down the steps of her chambers' grand entrance hall, her palm meeting the hilt of the ice-sword at her hip. As the air thickens, rolling into dark clouds that obscure the vaulted ceiling, she doesn't have to look at her sword to know there's a tangle of dark and light swirling within the blade. Moisture cools, meshing to form daggers hovering obediently ahead of her, awaiting permission to strike.

Beyond the therma-rock pit in the center of the hall, glowing blue and white with heat, the interloper looks up, sheathing the short-sword she'd been using to poke at the ice crystallized at the edges of Acasta's ornate entrance hall mirror.

"Princess." The interloper's gaze flits from the hovering

ice-daggers to Acasta's hand on the hilt of her sword. She doesn't look ruffled in the slightest.

Which is... a bit insulting, to be honest.

And Acasta could do without whatever this is right now. Spending the last hour roaring around a test track in her new ice-engine designs has made her thirsty. And finding someone in her chambers who shouldn't be there is always, frankly, bloody irritating.

But tempting as it is to keep the ice-daggers airborne, it's best not to toy with sharp edges too much. Acasta drops her hand from her sword's hilt, and the blades plummet like birds mid-flight: some smashing into icy shards across the floor, others sizzling into steam in the therma-pit.

The stranger idly observes the resultant mess.

"Yes. I know who I am." Acasta glowers from the foot of the entrance steps. "My question is, who are *you*? And why are you in my chambers?"

She already knows *who*, of course. The stranger's neon green hair, shaved at the sides, the rest falling in gravity-defying curls; the bronze glow of her skin; those sculpted muscles: Acasta's uninvited guest is none other than the gladiator, Herakles, renowned across Iolcus and the worlds beyond. But it's the prerogative of an Ice Royal to scour a judgmental gaze over whoever the fuck she wants. So she does.

If the gladiator is perturbed by Acasta's apparent lack of recognition, she doesn't show it. "I clearly have yet to make an impression." Herakles bows her head, holding eye contact through her mop of ridiculous hair. There's still no sign of fear or nerves, which is... odd. Her expression is impossible to place. "My name is Herakles. I'm here to train you."

Stars above. Why can't the worlds and the people in them just leave Acasta alone?

"Also, Princess, your door was open."

Fucksake. She's suspected for a while that one of her siblings must have a key. She'll need to check her chambers today. And she'll have to start icing her lock. Icing isn't the problem. It's the melting that's arduous.

She swallows, dryly. She could really do with some refreshment.

Instead, maintaining a safe distance from the gladiator, Acasta crosses to the floor-to-ceiling window that frames the Ice City—or rather, the handful of sky-rises high enough to break through the sea of snow clouds. But it's not the architecture Acasta is seeking. On Iolcus, it's always wise to keep an eye on the weather. Right now, dark clouds are swirling, painting over the evening's stars in aggressive strokes.

She eyes the gladiator in the window's reflection, letting the silence hang. The gladiator doesn't wither. She merely waits, looking far more relaxed than she has any right to be.

The gladiator could be telling the truth about why she's here. Since Acasta was a child, Father has insisted on sending her a string of instructors, none of whom he bothers to mention beforehand, and none of whom last long before running for the Unforgiving Mountains.

Acasta still isn't sure what his motivation is, considering half the assassins she finds in her chambers are also sent by him. To "test her", apparently. Over time, she's realized that while he doesn't care in the slightest about her safety or anyone else's, he does care about appearances. It wouldn't do to have his own daughter, the Ice Princess, embarrass him by losing control of her powers in public. Besides, who else is he going to get to spy on her when she's too stubborn to entertain personal servants?

The gladiator doesn't *look* like she's here to kill Acasta. If she were, she'd probably have tried by now. She probably wouldn't be loitering around Acasta's chambers in plain sight, either. But then again, the champion of a brutal weapons-based blood sport must be uniquely placed to be the perfect assassin.

"Herakles?" Acasta turns from the window, feigning having to place the name. "Daughter of Alcmene?" Discomfort flickers in the gladiator's amber eyes, blinked away in the same moment. "Captain of the Skies..." Acasta glances pointedly at the three staggered lines carved into the shaved sides of the gladiator's neon green hair, which everyone knows represent her rank from her sky voyaging days. "... *Oaf* of the Arena?"

The gladiator's mouth twitches, though with annoyance or amusement Acasta can't tell. "Don't forget Killer of Monsters."

Is that a veiled threat? Or mere fact?

Acasta narrows her eyes. Considering the gladiator's only worth these days is in entertaining the Iolcian masses, she certainly seems to have retained her elevated sense of station. Then again, when your mother is the formidable Alcmene, President of Zeus Industries, you probably can get away with more than most. Because no one sensible would invite the wrath of the woman with an intellect sharper than any blade and who controls the skies.

Then again, perhaps the gladiator's confidence is the result of her physical prowess. Or maybe she's simply taken one too many knocks to the head in the Arena and has forgotten basic survival skills, like respecting hierarchy and knowing when to hold her tongue.

According to her Games statistics (which Acasta will categorically *not* be admitting to having perused on occasion), the gladiator has thirty-two sun-orbits, which Acasta happens to remember purely because it's one more than her own. No other reason. Anyway, the point is that the gladiator is old enough to know better than to get playful with an Ice Royal. No matter how spectacular your muscles are, maintaining a healthy terror for those with the power of ice is just basic common sense. Acasta does, and she's one of them.

"What am I to do with you?" Acasta injects some petulance into her tone—because why not? —but keeps enough distance from the gladiator that she can draw her ice-sword if needed. "I'm not sure I need self-defense lessons from someone who bashes opponents with blunt objects." Not that the gladiator is carrying her famous Arena weapon currently.

"You're in luck, Princess. I can be just as oafish with a sword." To demonstrate, the gladiator casually unsheathes said sword, flipping it up in the air, over her head and behind her back as though the blade were no more dangerous than a filament-fruit. *Fucking hail.* It's a wonder she's still got all her digits.

"Well, I don't need an instructor. So..." Acasta gestures regally to the sweeping entrance steps.

Herakles resheathes her sword and strolls over to join Acasta at the vast window, thumbs hooked in the belt of her scabbard as she leans—fucking *nonchalantly*—against the glass. "I can't imagine that telling the Ice King you disagree with his assessment will go well for either of us."

Acasta's jaw clenches. For all her apparent indifference, the gladiator is clearly adept at navigating this world of egos and ice. The Ice King punishes servants and blood relatives alike for far lesser crimes than expressing a dissenting opinion.

She grits her teeth. "If my father wishes it, then I'm sure I'm thrilled."

Her ice-sword is crackling, echoing her disquiet. The gladiator eyes it coolly. "Very good, Princess. So long as we're both ecstatic to be here."

Her tone is flat, unreadable. Before Acasta can decipher it, Herakles—ignoring all royal protocol and basic common sense—pushes away from the window, turning her back on Acasta as she strides toward one of the two arched doorways leading off opposite sides of the hallway. "Let's not waste any more time, then."

"While I admire your enthusiasm, Gladiator... that is my bedchamber."

Herakles pauses with her hand on the doorhandle. Acasta buries her accidental smile. "Do you always show yourself into other people's chambers?"

The gladiator shoots a roguish smile over her shoulder. "Usually, Princess, I'm invited."

That's enough of that. Sculpted athletes and their unwieldy egos. Acasta nods at the doorway opposite. "The training sands are that way. However," she adds sharply, as Herakles changes course, "there's still the matter of your sword." Acasta's raised voice stops the gladiator short. "I don't allow weapons in my chambers. You'll leave it by the door and reclaim it when you leave."

Herakles turns an incredulous scowl on her. "Are you to be armed and I am not? In weapons training?"

"Do we have a problem, Gladiator?" Acasta sets her expression to utter frostbite.

The gladiator quirks an eyebrow at her. Holding Acasta's gaze, she unbuckles her scabbard, unashamedly making a show of complying and... Is she *flirting*?

What in the Seven Heavens is she playing at?

Acasta keeps her mask of frost unthawed as Herakles saunters back to the entrance steps and—with exaggerated care—places her sword by the doorway.

She's testing you. Don't look away.

"You should change, Princess." The gladiator looks Acasta up and down, her face impassive. "We don't want to dirty your fancy clothes, do we?"

Acasta raises her chin. Despite what Herakles obviously thinks, she doesn't need to waste time changing. Her garments might be adorned with intricate stitching, as befits an Ice Royal, but her outfit will serve her as well in a sparring match as it does on the ice-engine track. The layers of expensive fabric disguise an integrated armor-mesh, right down to her vest, while her breeches—stone-gray, today— are always selected for maximum maneuverability.

Unlike her siblings, who have a ridiculous entourage of servants to wrap them in whatever finery they choose, Acasta dresses herself because she has no inclination to look like a prize. She'd rather dress like a functioning individual, even if it is sometimes only an illusion.

Taking control of the situation, Acasta marches past the gladiator, leading the way to her entertainment and exercise chamber. "My fancy clothes can handle it."

Let's get this over and done with.

Silver Sands

ACASTA STRIDES INTO HER PRIVATE ENTERTAINMENT chamber, claiming a glass bottle of water from the ice-pit— fucking finally—as she sweeps an assessing gaze across the space. Everything looks as it should: comfortable seating arranged in front of the ice-wall and projector; Ace the palace cat luxuriating regally in front of the crackling blue heat of the therma-pit. Further into the chamber, past a circular training arena of silver sand, the floor-to-ceiling windows frame a churning snowstorm that whites out the lights of the city beyond. While Acasta crosses to the window, the gladiator loiters at the training sands. Her features, reflected in the glass, are impassive once again.

Acasta breaks the ice-seal on the water bottle and takes several glugs, eyeing Herakles's reflection the entire time. She can't see Ace from here, but she's sure he's watching the gladiator's movements as carefully as she is.

Thirst quenched, she reseals the lid with a touch of one hand to the hilt of her ice-sword and the other to the bottle top—something she'd learned to do when her siblings had first taken to slipping poison into her drinks. She sets the bottle down on the floor, throws open the chest that houses her training weapons, and pulls out two wooden swords that mimic the shape and weight of her own ice-sword. The real artifact she keeps holstered at her hip.

The gladiator is across the arena, scuffing the sand idly with the toe of her boot, hands in the pockets of her breeches. Acasta eyes her, weighing the wooden swords. *Let's see what this oaf can do.*

Without warning, she flings a wooden sword in the gladiator's direction. A confident hand lashes out and catches it by the hilt. Acasta buries her impressed eyebrow raise. *No need to bolster that ego.*

Herakles examines the training sword like it's offended her. "If you're already proficient with your sword, is there a reason we're using these wooden toys?" She flips the weapon experimentally, catching it, swiping with it. The bunch and flex of her muscles is impossible to ignore.

The gladiator isn't kitted out in her Games attire, nor smeared with war paint, but she's battle-ready nonetheless in an armor-mesh compression long-sleeve that leaves no contour to the imagination—plus, of course, that infuriating, untouchable attitude. Acasta's heart knocks louder against her ribs, which has absolutely nothing to do with the gladiator's display. Her body's just readying for battle, that's all—

"Oi. Princess."

A poke to her shoulder catapults her back to reality. Acasta bats aside the wooden sword to find unimpressed amber eyes zeroed in on her.

"What planet are you on? Or perhaps I should ask which of the Heavens you're in?"

Had the gladiator asked her a question? Apart from the daft ones, obviously. Well, either way, it's irrelevant. An Ice Princess doesn't have to answer anything if she doesn't want to.

Acasta transforms her lingering gaze to a withering assessment. It's a skill. "You're shorter than I thought you'd be." They're actually about the same height, but whatever. "The Games and ice-screen projectors must add a couple of inches."

"My height won't matter a jot when I've got your back to the sand, Princess."

Was that... a euphemism? Or is Acasta just flustered?

The gladiator's eyes linger on Acasta's ice-sword. "You're just going to keep that on, huh?"

Acasta's teeth grit. "You're just going to keep questioning everything, huh?"

The gladiator raises her hands. "Okay, but don't blame me when you land on your own fucking sword." And before Acasta can voice her ire, Herakles adds, "You should warm up."

Acasta bites down; her jaw is starting to ache. "I'm warmed."

With the heel of her combat boot, Herakles draws a line in the silver sand, delineating the center of their arena. Acasta tucks her quartz pendant safely beneath her vest and steps into play.

The gladiator throws three quick sword-jabs, each of which Acasta deflects with a satisfying *clack*. Ace the cat watches from the arena edge, tail swishing lazily, as Herakles advances. She's faster and nimbler than she appears in the Iolcian Games, each maneuver testing Acasta's co-ordination, her instinctive use of space—and, apparently, her resolve. Perhaps that whole oafish act in the Arena, all that parading around with that club, is exactly that: a performance, a tactic for the Games?

Stars above. When did breathing get so hard?

Herakles steps back, signaling for a time out. Thank the fucking heavens. Acasta's muscles are already burning.

The gladiator, meanwhile, hasn't even broken a sweat. "Need a rest, Princess?"

How is she not out of breath? "I'm—fine—"

"If you need some refreshment?" Herakles gestures to the water bottle by the weapons chest.

"I'm *fine*."

They circle each other.

"Why I'm here in the first place is a bit of a mystery, to be honest," Herakles says, and Acasta brightens. Perhaps the gladiator is actually impressed by her sword skills? Perhaps she's successfully hidden the fact that she's choking on her own lungs?

"I mean," Herakles continues, "someone with ice powers doesn't really need good technique, do they?"

"Excuse *me*?" Acasta is so astonished by the insubordination that she drops her sword arm without thinking. A mistake—Herakles claps her smartly on the knuckles with the flat of her wooden blade, and Acasta yelps as pain radiates all the way up her arm. Her sword slips from her hand, only for Herakles to snatch it out of midair and skip back a few steps, flipping the weapon nonchalantly

"I'm sure there was a lesson in there somewhere," the gladiator says, as Acasta clasps her throbbing knuckles. She casts the sword back to Acasta, who fumbles clumsily to catch it.

The gladiator's lucky they're using wooden swords, or there'd be a storm thrashing her right now. This impertinence will not do. But before Acasta can instigate a lesson of her own, Herakles darts behind her and smacks the length of her blade into the backs of Acasta's knees. Ace squints at her in withering, feline judgment as Acasta lands face down with a mouthful of silver sand.

The hilt of her ice-sword digs painfully against her hip. Ice needles beneath her skin, pestering to be used.

It's so tempting...

She leaps upright and launches at the gladiator, snarling. "How *dare* you? I'm your fucking princess."

The gladiator doesn't flinch. She just stands there, arms at her sides, eyeing Acasta with... what? Disappointment? Boredom? "Yes, Princess. And I'm your fucking instructor." Her voice is calm but steely. "Do you think an assassin will stand around and wait for you to pick up your blade? Let's try that again."

Again?

And just like that Acasta is sprawled on her back once more, a picture of sculpted, athletic smugness grinning down at her. "Do I seem taller now, Princess?"

Stars above. Acasta is starting to wonder whether her previous instructors might've, on occasion, let her win.

Ace licks his paw, swishes his tail, and saunters off. A fair response.

The gladiator offers Acasta her hand, but Acasta won't be fooled. She springs to her feet and reinstates the distance between them, her attention fixed on Herakles. She's not even touching her ice-sword, but its sharp whisper prickles under her skin. It's nauseating. She channels her discomfort into pacing the sands. Can't she nurse her wounded ego and be furious about all this in peace?

Yes. She can. She's an Ice Princess. She can do what she fucking wants.

"I'm tired," she announces, then regrets it immediately. Why did she have to admit weakness? She should have thrown some barbs; something that would get under the gladiator's skin and inspire her to never return.

"Do you think an assailant would care if you're tired?" Herakles sounds utterly bored now. Does she really think she can get away with this?

"Keep up that attitude and I'll have you exiled. Or worse."

"Worse? Has it occurred to you that perhaps I'd rather face death in orbit than waste my time training some brat princess?"

Acasta's mouth falls open. *No one* talks to her like that.

The gladiator is watching her, assessing her. Acasta glowers. The spurs of ice under her skin sharpen and intensify, urging her to reach for her blade. She clenches her fist against the impulse.

Herakles nods to herself as though deciding something. "Perhaps that's enough for today. Should I show myself out and return tomorrow? Or should I wait for the guards to get my exile underway?"

Acasta unclenches her fist, her tension dissipating just enough that the call of her sword quietens too. "Am I supposed to just... trust you, Gladiator?" She spits the words along with the sand between her teeth.

Herakles's eyes level with hers. "Don't trust me, Princess. Trust your instincts. Even if they're abhorrent, at least you'll have done right by yourself."

Trust her instincts? Her instincts are all in a tangle. They have her making false threats about exile and worse. They have her confronting the mortifying truth that she's not as competent in a skirmish as she'd thought. They have her respecting the subordinate who's brave or foolish enough to put her in her place.

But no fucking way is she telling Herakles any of that.

Taking her royal time, Acasta musters heroic levels of nonchalance to declare: "Come back tomorrow."

Hidden Depths

THE GLADIATOR WILL BE HERE SOON. EVEN ACE WON'T let her forget it, judging by his insistent mewing and sidling against her legs. Acasta has spent too long in her steam-shower, trying—unsuccessfully—to unknot the tension in her muscles and untangle her many thoughts and questions about Herakles and her own shameful performance yesterday.

The therma-pit in her entrance hall crackles with heat; a welcome white noise to distract her from her thoughts as she lingers by the mirror and tames her shoulder length white-blonde hair into a plait at the nape of her neck. Lightning forks beyond the expansive window, drawing her focus from her reflection to the unsettled horizon.

Ace darts off somewhere. Probably just as well. He's as much a people-cat as Acasta is a people-person.

Hair fastened, dressed for battle, Acasta tucks her quartz pendant beneath her vest, straightens her back, and sets her expression to her mask for survival. Cold, calculating, steely.

Just one more layer remains. Her most closely guarded secret.

The scar spans her entire face: rivulets of white tracking through shades of pink, as though her very features are a mask carved from rose quartz, or cracked ice tainted pink by blood. Ice or stone; nobody will ever know how fitting the Ice Princess's true face is.

After so many sun-orbits, it'll take only moments to blend the powder. Layer after layer, until the scar tissue is indistinguishable from pale skin.

But—

In the mirror's reflection, something moves: a flash of bright green. Acasta whips round to find Herakles frozen mid-step, staring at her from across the therma-pit. Her expression is a mixture of guilt, shock, and—worst of all—sympathy.

Nausea slinks through Acasta's veins like liquid ice. She never lets anyone see her like this. To see her without powder is to see her more naked than without a single thread upon her skin.

"Forgive me, Princess." The gladiator speaks fast, as if her life depends on it. "I wanted to see how close I could get. For your training—"

The sword at Acasta's hip hazes with ice. The temperature drops, freezing air hissing against the heat of the therma-pit. Acasta wrangles her breaths. *Keep it together.*

"Get. Out." Her voice comes out brittle as ice, so much like Father's it brings a shiver to even her own spine.

The gladiator must understand the severity of her situation, because she retreats without another word. And Acasta should let her leave. But instead, she rounds the therma-pit and catches up to Herakles at the foot of the entrance steps.

The gladiator swings to face her, hands raised in apology or surrender.

If it was fear, Acasta could forgive it. But sympathy?

Her hand twitches, vibrations under her skin imploring her to complete the connection, to claim her sword. She clenches her fist, denying it. The words she only means to think erupt in a shout: "You can fuck right off—"

She shoves Herakles, hard. And Herakles lets her, staggering backward to land on the steps, hands still raised. She could retaliate, could put Acasta firmly in her place, but she doesn't even try to defend herself.

"I was trying, Princess."

She *was* trying. And now here Acasta is, parading her true face to the gladiator because... she's angry that Herakles saw her face in the first place?

Acasta doesn't want to hurt her. She doesn't want to hurt anyone.

The gladiator's gaze flits upwards. "If you want to do me damage, Princess... might I suggest a different weapon?"

It's only then that Acasta realizes her arm is raised. And that the item she's brandishing is not in fact a weapon, but her powder sponge.

Fucking hail.

Hot embarrassment sluices through her body. With a

growl, she hurls the sponge across the hall. What a fucking stupid situation.

She stalks back to the mirror to smooth out the half-applied powder with her fingers, hiding her burning cheeks along with her scar. Behind her, Herakles climbs to her feet, lingering uncertainly on the steps. "I apologize."

So ego-personified knows how to apologize? That's... unexpected. Acasta looks up, temporarily distracted from the ice in her veins, the pressure on her chest: the storm inside her, demanding release.

"How did you get in?" She'd iced the lock, she's sure of it. And her mirror isn't far from the door. How had she not heard Herakles enter?

In the mirror's reflection, Herakles nods to a pile of belongings by the entrance: her sword in its scabbard—where Acasta had told her to put it yesterday—and a small pouch hazing with warmth against cool air.

"It's amazing how much ice just a few well-placed therma-stones can melt." The gladiator rubs the back of her neck. Is she nervous, or is she just showing off her arm muscles? "And it's, uh... possible I know a thing or two about lock mechanisms."

"Sky Captain. Gladiator. Monster Killer. Lockpick?" Acasta raises a questioning brow and Herakles simply shrugs. "Well, Gladiator, since there seems to be no end to your talents, perhaps you can demonstrate your proficiency at using a door."

Acasta returns to her face powder. But instead of leaving, the gladiator comes further into the entrance hall. She stays on the far side of the therma-pit, keeping her distance from Acasta, but—

Why in the actual fuck is she removing her shirt?

Herakles's shirt lands by the door beside her sword and

therma-stone pouch, leaving her standing in Acasta's entrance hall in a crop-vest that reveals the edges of dark tattoos. If the tight-fitting long-sleeve had left little to the imagination before, the spectacular definition of her unconstrained biceps and the ink in her skin is as awe-inspiring as Acasta is speechless.

She swings to face Herakles, only to discovers that the gladiator is... *unbuttoning her breeches?* "W-what are you doing?"

She tries to avert her gaze, only to find herself staring at vein-cabled forearms and defined abdominals, which by some science or sorcery send her pulse skyward. Apparently she's unable to control her bodily reactions in the face of Herakles, Captain of the Skies, Hero of the Arena, Sculpture of Physical Perfection.

She forces herself to tear her gaze away. *Get a grip. You're a terrifying Ice Princess, remember?*

She sharpens her voice, hoping to cover her fluster. "I think you've misunderstood your task here, Gladiator."

In response, Herakles drops her breeches. They pool on the entrance hall floor, leaving Herakles in only her crop-vest and neon green undershorts, and Acasta with scalding cheeks and no idea where to look.

Has the gladiator matched her undershorts to her hair color? Of course she has. Acasta shouldn't be surprised by this. She shouldn't be thinking about Herakles's underwear at all.

But it's difficult when it's *right there.*

Say something snarky. Scathing. Anything. But all Acasta can do is try to swallow.

"I invaded your privacy." Herakles's expression is startlingly earnest. "I think it only fair you have the chance to do the same." She pulls aside her vest strap, unveiling a dotted line perforation of scar tissue that stretches across her shoulder. "I got this on a lagoon planet from a creature with nine heads and a thousand teeth." She points to her left thigh, where a collection of unusual dents interrupts her otherwise smooth skin. "This one came from a lion with a bite so strong I feared I might lose my leg and my life."

Stars above. Acasta had been *trying* not to stare. At some point, her ice-hot rage appears to have dissolved into embarrassment and reluctant curiosity, mixed with something pulse-thumping she's not willing to acknowledge. And, yes, part of her wants to ask about Herakles's sky captain adventures, about all the worlds out there Acasta has never visited and will never be allowed to visit... but she doesn't dare. The skies aren't a sensible topic. And besides, what's the point when she's stuck here?

"I have no desire to see your flesh, Gladiator." Hail. She'd been aiming for lofty and dismissive, but for some reason the words burst out sounding distinctly flustered.

Herakles merely shrugs and pulls her breeches up. "Suit yourself."

Acasta straightens her back. "You've got a lot of old injuries for someone who's meant to be a proficient fighter." That's better: disguise fluster with being royally rude-as-fuck.

Herakles's eyes meet hers and Acasta daren't look away. Her breath squirms in her chest.

"Have you met anyone who's fought Nemean lions, Princess?" Herakles's tone is even, serious, and Acasta's about to answer, but— "No. You haven't. Because they got eaten."

Okay. The gladiator just managed to call her a brat *without calling her a brat.*

Herakles's demeanor shifts to something almost casual. "Which door shall I be going through now?"

Acasta narrows her eyes at her. "Since you're already here, and you didn't bother leaving the first three times I told you..." She motions toward the training sands. At least a bit of swordplay will help her burn off this antsy energy.

"You look like you'd enjoy throwing a few punches my way today." Herakles winks—fucking *winks*—at her. Acasta glowers back, but it's wasted. The gladiator, apparently blithely unaware of both Acasta's glare and her own missing shirt, is already sauntering toward the training chamber.

Gravity

"No weapons to start, so I can see what you've got." Gone is the gladiator's placation; that tone is all business.

"What I've got?" Distracted by shoulder muscles, tattoos and unveiled scars, Acasta is only half listening as she follows Herakles onto the training sands.

"How you carry yourself in a fight without weapons." Herakles turns and Acasta almost stumbles into her. Even worse, when she looks up, the gladiator is suppressing a knowing smile. She's got dimples *and* freckles. That should be illegal.

Shit. Say something. Anything.

"You don't cover them when you're training?" she blurts. And only when she voices it does she discover she's curious for the answer.

"My muscles or my scars, Princess?"

Ugh. Arrogance is so unappealing. And Acasta should know. She's got 'unappealing' down to a fine art.

"A good fighter uses any tactics at her disposal." Herakles smooths the shaved sides of her hair, ruffling the colorful curls on top. It's an unsubtle excuse to flex her biceps, and her barely stifled smile makes clear that she knows it. "Including distraction."

Acasta valiantly keeps her features impassive.

"As for my scars," continues the gladiator, "if they offend anyone, that's their problem, isn't it?" She draws a line in the sand with her heel. "The marks on my body are the map of my life. Of where I've been. Sounds pretentious, but it's true."

"Oh." That's all Acasta can think to say. She's spent so much of her life confined to this palace with its stalagmite spires, sharp and angular, and uncomfortably similar to the shape of her facial scar. So, in a way... the marks on her skin are the map of where she's been, too.

"What if you don't like where you've been?" The words escape before she can stop them. She shouldn't so much as hint at even the faintest discontent with her royal life, should she? Which must be why the gladiator is looking at her with a questioning curiosity.

"Lagoon monsters and lions are still part of the journey." Herakles's smile is gentle, and Acasta hasn't a fucking clue what to do with that. Nor does she know where to look as Herakles stretches each arm in turn across her chest, biceps and triceps on parade, with toned abdominals taking center stage. This gladiator is going to be the death of her. "I try to think of mine as medals to celebrate my survival."

Acasta's head snaps up. That tone... That fucking sympathetic brow... Both underscore that the gladiator isn't just referring to her own scars.

What is she meant to say to that? That the monster on Acasta's journey is Acasta herself? That this is what happens when an ice-sword is flung into your childhood with no fucking instructions? She can train with instructors all she or Father want, but if none of them understand her powers, what's the fucking point?

Her ice buzzes and prickles like needles under her skin. Calm. Control. *Breathe. Freefalling into an ice-hot panic doesn't help anyone.*

There are questions in the gladiator's eyes. Questions Acasta is unwilling to answer. *Give her something so she won't pry...*

"Steps in an ice kingdom are slippery," is what she says, at last, to put an end to the gladiator's curiosity and misplaced sympathy. It's not exactly a lie, but it's clear from the gladiator's frown that she knows it's not the truth, either. Whatever. Acasta raises her chin defiantly. It's not like she owes Herakles anything.

"I can't imagine you being outwitted by stairs, Princess."

"Not my fault you haven't got an imagination, Gladiator."

Herakles's mouth twitches. "Quite. I suppose even Ice Princesses aren't immune to gravity."

"If our session yesterday is anything to go by, obviously not." Acasta's smile is tight. She hadn't meant to be self-deprecating aloud.

The gladiator's responding half-smile is a puzzle. "Have you stretched?"

Of course I have. "I doubt an assassin would let me stretch before I fight them off."

"If you pull a muscle in training, you'll be making an assassin's job much easier."

"I'm ready." Acasta uses her *and that's that* tone.

Herakles shrugs in a *your life, your problem* manner. With an epic eye-roll, Acasta steps up to the line. The next second, pain explodes across her face.

She staggers backward with a cry, hands covering her nose and streaming eyes. When she glares at Herakles through her fingers, the gladiator's eyes are wide.

"You okay, Princess?"

"You fucking *punched* me?"

"As a training exercise! I thought you'd dodge." Herakles reaches toward her, then seems to think better of it. "Why didn't you step aside?"

"I wasn't ready!" It's so obvious now that her previous instructors were too easy on her. She doesn't have to look at her sword to know its surface is crackled with ice, straining to be let out.

Grimacing, she lifts her hand from her nose. No blood, at least. The cartilage smarts when she pokes gingerly at it, but nothing feels broken. Apart from her pride. "I could have you exiled for that, you know."

Herakles rolls her eyes.

"And that."

"You're fine. I pulled my punch at the last second. Don't be such a brat."

"*Excuse* me?" Does she have an actual death wish? Those muscles might look impressive, but they're no match for Iolcian Ice. Acasta wouldn't follow through on the threat, but the gladiator doesn't know that. The power is undeniably in Acasta's favor.

"Oh, my apologies. I meant to say: don't be such a brat, *your highness*." The glint in Herakles's eyes is as sharp as the ice prickling within Acasta's fingertips. "Look, if you're going to have me exiled, can you put us both out of our misery and get on with it? No wonder your technique's shit if you have your instructors banished every time they try to teach you something."

"You—" Acasta begins, but that's all she manages before Herakles swipes her legs from under her and she lands in the sand with a heavy thud that forces the air from her lungs.

Okay, maybe the power isn't *undeniably* in her favor.

Herakles stands over her, grinning. Evidently, flooring Acasta has made her feel a lot better.

Acasta heaves in a ragged breath. "You seem to be enjoying yourself enough."

Herakles shrugs. "I guess we have our moments."

Acasta lumbers to her feet and throws a punch. Herakles grabs her fist mid-swing, strong fingers holding her in place. "Nice try, Princess." Oddly, she sounds genuine.

As soon as the gladiator lets her go, Acasta channels her frustration into another punch. Herakles side-steps the blow neatly, retaliating with a series of much more controlled punches which Acasta manages to dodge. She still can't land her own, but at least she's finally got Herakles on the move.

"Yes! That's more like it." The gladiator has no business sounding this encouraging.

Acasta musters a solid swing, only for Herakles to casually step aside. Acasta's own momentum topples her face first into the sand.

"Good," Herakles says, from somewhere overhead.

Acasta can't see what's so 'good' about it. She glares up at Herakles, who responds by reaching down to offer Acasta her hand. Acasta eyes it with suspicion.

After a calculated moment, she accepts, trying not to notice the strength, the warmth as their hands entwine... Then she tugs, hard.

She means to bring Herakles down to land beside her, perfectly positioned for Acasta to pin her to the sand and show her who's in charge. Instead, she nearly yanks her own shoulder out of its socket.

Herakles, still solidly on her feet, peers down at Acasta with mild curiosity, muscles flexing as Acasta tries another doomed tug.

Acasta lets loose a growl of frustration. "Fuck!" She lurches to her feet and launches herself at Herakles's waist —but instead of tackling her to the ground, she simply smacks straight into the toned, solid wall of the gladiator's bare midriff. Herakles absorbs the impact with a single backward step, leaving Acasta struggling in a strange one-sided embrace, her legs paddling the sand. "An interesting move, Princess."

Acasta can't see her expression on account of her own face being buried against the gladiator's stomach, but she can *hear* Herakles gloating. They're close. Too close. And Herakles hasn't budged an inch. She's not even trying to grapple with Acasta. She's just *standing* there.

Channeling her unwieldy rage into a mighty shove, Acasta finds herself, yet again, slamming with an *oof!* into the sand.

Stars above. Which one of them is a ruthless Ice Royal again?

Once more, Herakles offers her hand. "Don't be gloomy, Princess. Progress takes time."

Acasta bats her hand away and scrambles to her feet. The only progress she cares about right now is getting to wipe that grin off the gladiator's face.

THE NEXT DAY, HERAKLES SOURCES TWO WOODEN swords from the weapons chest and casts one at Acasta. No sooner does she catch it than the gladiator is on her, raining a torrent of strikes that shudder through Acasta's whole body as she blocks them. Acasta is sweating within minutes, arms aching, heated breaths punching the frigid air. *"I could do this all day,"* is the level of snark she aspires to, but today she needs all her focus simply to catch her next breath.

When her next flailing stumble lands her in the sand, Herakles offers a smug outstretched hand. With a resigned huff, Acasta accepts. But as she lets Herakles haul her upright, she smacks the flat of her wooden sword against the back of the gladiator's knee and yanks down on her hand. And—

Yes! Herakles is falling—

But instead of watching triumphantly as she buckles, conveniently positioned for Acasta to pin her to the ground, Acasta finds herself the one pinned under the weight of an extremely solid gladiator. Pinned so thoroughly, in fact, she has to wonder whether Herakles had the upper hand all along.

Oh, heaven's hail.

Herakles's legs flank her thighs, her weight pinning Acasta's hips in place, her body pressing the length of Acasta's... And how in the heavens did she manage to pin Acasta's wrists above her head? Never mind that she has no fucking idea where her training sword landed.

Pressed between them, her ice-sword hilt digs into her hip. Even without touching it, Acasta can feel the ice straining within the metal. Fuck, fuck, fuck.

"Never thought you'd sweep me off my feet, Princess." Herakles smirks.

Empty threats of exile teeter on Acasta's tongue as she

attempts to get her hands free, but somehow having the full weight of Herakles pressed against her makes it very difficult to come up with a witty or scathing retort. Or any retort. She's about as useful right now as a pool of melted ice.

Only quickened breaths fill the silence. Her pulse pounds in her chest. And that's not the only place it's pounding. Acasta closes her eyes, hoping Herakles can't feel it too.

Her own ineptitude ignites a different heat in her veins. Her teeth grind, arms tensing. Not that it helps her any; the more she wriggles, the more Herakles's body is a solid wall of warmth against her.

Herakles's breaths meet Acasta's burning cheeks like a caress.

If she keeps her eyes closed, she can live in this moment; stretch it beyond the horizon. She can imagine how it would feel to let her fingers explore the smooth skin of Herakles's neck; to run them through that ridiculous neon hair. She can imagine how that smug mouth would feel against her lips. And how that insubordinate, infuriating tongue—

Herakles clears her throat and Acasta's eyes snap open like she's been doused with an ice-bucket. When she sees Herakles's expression, her stomach punches into her chest.

Herakles isn't gazing down at her longingly, studying Acasta's eyes or mouth with lingering curiosity. There's no teasing, no smug amusement. Only a furrowed brow, and a flicker of panic in her eyes as she angles away from Acasta.

Shit. Did Acasta just lean up toward Herakles's mouth when she was daydreaming about that kiss? What in all the Seven Heavens is wrong with her?

"I think that's enough for today," says Herakles as she lets loose Acasta's wrists and hops to her feet, somehow managing to set Acasta upright in the same single fluid motion.

As Herakles retreats, Acasta fights not to react to the disappointment lodging in her chest like a serrated blade. She'd like to exile herself into orbit right now. Instead, she brushes the sand off the back of her legs, trying not to care that Herakles is looking anywhere but at her.

Sand and Ice

"UNSETTLED SKIES ON THE HORIZON," CONCLUDES THE weather summary. Even the comfort of Acasta's entertainment chamber can't soften the fundamental message: that everything is bleak... bleak... *bleak* and not-so-bleak-but-still-quite-bleak. Nothing new there, then. There's not much more to Iolcus than ice and storm clouds.

Enduring a storm is bad enough, but having to live with its source is worse. Acasta could look out of any window in the palace and observe the miserable clouds smothering the city far below, but the info-blast summary tells her how far-reaching the tumultuous weather is, and that vital measure at least gives her a chance at anticipating Father's mood.

Iolcus is lucky Acasta doesn't have a remote link to her sword like he does with his ice, or after yesterday's abysmal training session she'd have been guilty of contributing a blizzard or two herself.

Yes. It would be fair to say Acasta is in a bad fucking mood.

Obligatory breakfast with her older siblings—Ice King's orders—never helps. The twins, Pelopia and Pisidice—still sore more than twenty sun-orbits after Father pitted them all against one another, only for Acasta to emerge victorious with the ice-sword—had complained about Father giving Acasta "all the toys", and then prattled on about Herakles's reputation for stamina beyond the Arena. Pelopia had been colorful in her description of how she wouldn't mind a "training session" herself.

And Acasta's hackles have been up ever since. She loathes the way her siblings talk about people as if they're nothing more than playthings, and she certainly doesn't need reminding that the gladiator reputed to have bedded a dozen women in a single night had recoiled from her like she'd been scalded by a therma-rock.

Herakles won't be returning today. Acasta is certain of it.

She flicks to a different projector-stream: a Games replay. Yes, that's what she needs. The sight of the gladiators all pummeling each other turns her stomach. A reminder of Herakles's oafish, bloody antics in the Arena will take the shine off.

But when familiar neon green hair swaggers into the on-screen Arena, there's no denying the chiseled athlete—a fan favorite, judging by the ice-devil roars of the crowds—moves with power and confidence, wielding her oversized club like it weighs nothing, and—

That's enough of that. Acasta swipes the projection away.

What had she been *thinking?* Who tries to kiss someone in the middle of a fight? Who tries to kiss someone who's given zero indication of being interested? Why would Herakles ever be interested in a brattish Ice Royal?

Such an idiot, Acasta.

Three loud knocks rattle through her chambers from the entrance door.

Shit. She hadn't been expecting anyone. Which is why she'd iced the door surrounds to seal her in. *Fucksake.* Acasta marches into the entrance hall and grabs the therma-pit tongs and a lump of therma-rock. At the top of the entrance steps, she skims the heated rock along the ice-seams. At least she hadn't iced the lock today.

She's about to call through the door, to demand who it is, but her heart is thumping. It won't be *her*. There's not a flame's chance in hail. It'll be Pelopia or Pisidice, or a servant, or a guard or—

Acasta heaves open the door with an iced crunch.

And—

Shit.

The gladiator's features are uncertain. Just a little; there's no sign of the outright panic that had flared in them at their last meeting. A thousand rehearsed apologies have swirled through Acasta's mind since, but now that Herakles is in front of her... she hasn't a clue what to say. She should apologize—

No. Ridiculous. Princesses don't apologize.

But she *should*...

"You're late." Or she could be an epic ass about it.

Herakles's eyes narrow as she unbuckles her scabbard and drops it by the door with a clunk. When she speaks, she sounds... detached. Like she really doesn't want to be here. Acasta can hardly blame her.

"Funnily enough, I do have a life beyond these walls."

That makes one of them.

And fuck you, Gladiator. As Acasta's jaw tightens, so too does Herakles's, like they're sizing each other up for real in the Arena instead of lingering on Acasta's entrance steps. Looks like Acasta's mood won't be shifting anytime soon.

Herakles steps carefully around her—*got enough*

distance, Gladiator? —and marches off toward the entertainment and exercise chamber. "Make yourself at home, why don't you?" Acasta mutters as she follows. She needs to take a damn breath.

As they approach the training sands, Acasta's palm brushes unthinkingly against the hilt of her sword. A whistle of blizzard swirls around them. She snatches her hand away, but it's too late: snow is already tumbling thickly through the air to settle on the silver sand.

Maybe Herakles won't notice?

No such luck. The snow has coated the back of her boots. But when Herakles stops to inspect them, she doesn't look horrified or disturbed. Just... curious.

The same curiosity she's directing at Acasta right now.

Acasta blusters past, turning her back on Herakles just to have a break from being watched. "Come on, Gladiator. We're not here to braid each other's hair."

She claims a bottle of water from the ice-pit in the entertainment lounge before heading to the training sands and dragging her heel to delineate the center line. *Let's get this over and done with.*

She can feel the gladiator's eyes still on her. Acasta breaks the water's ice-seal and swigs. She'll just pretend Herakles isn't there. That nothing else exist—

"You'll use your ice-sword today."

What? Acasta swings round, but the gladiator is crouched, apparently focused on fastening her boot laces. She doesn't look up.

Acasta sets her water bottle at the arena edge, taking a moment to reset and muster her iciest tone. "Excuse you?"

"Show me." Herakles nods at her ice-sword.

Acasta recoils. "No."

Herakles's blank expression suggests she's already had

enough of Acasta's shit today. Her attention returns to her boot laces. "We're not here to braid each other's hair, Princess."

An icy sweat prickles at the nape of Acasta's neck. She doesn't use the sword with her instructors. Not anymore. "It's dangerous."

Herakles finally looks up. "No? Really?" She stands, squaring up to Acasta, and though there's no difference in height, Acasta somehow feels more like a cornered vole-rat than an Ice Royal.

The shove Herakles plants beneath her shoulders is so sudden, so powerful, she's skittering ass-backward in the sand before she knows what's hit her. The landing jolts her spine, her ice-sword crackling its own protest.

"What the hail?" Acasta glares up at Herakles, who stands over her, stony and expressionless. There's no outstretched hand this time, no stifled, mischievous smile. Is Acasta being punished?

"You wield one of the most powerful weapons under the Seven Skies. Not knowing how to use it is both dangerous and stupid."

No fucking kidding.

"I practice in private," Acasta grits out. *Because I don't want to hurt anyone* are the words she's not allowed to say. The Ice King's daughter must never show weakness.

"*Practice in private* all you like. But if I'm to do my job, I need to understand your skills. Get up."

What is with *her today?* If Acasta weren't already halfway to her feet, she'd stay down just to show the gladiator she won't take her orders. Instead, she crosses her arms in a challenge. "You have extensive experience of ice-swords, then?"

The gladiator glowers, mirroring her pose. Of course she

doesn't. Only two people are known to wield Iolcian Ice: the Ice King, and Acasta herself.

"You're cranky today, Gladiator. Too much time spent on nocturnal activities, perhaps?" What is she *saying?* Like it's not bad enough getting floored by Herakles every time they meet, Acasta's just announced her own interest in the gladiator's bedroom activities.

Herakles stretches her arms over her head, biceps and triceps vying for supremacy through her tight armor-mesh. And there's no way Acasta can't look.

The gladiator's cheek twitches into a dimple. She knows exactly what she's doing.

"You spend a lot of time thinking about my nocturnal activities, Princess?" Her tone is so flat, Acasta hasn't a clue what to do with it.

Fuck this.

Fists clenched, Acasta steps into the gladiator's orbit. So swift, so close. Herakles's eyes flit to her mouth. She's not going to kiss Acasta, *obviously.* But tell Acasta's stuttering heart that.

"Hold your tongue, Gladiator," she growls.

"Your fascination with my tongue, Princess..." She's entirely deadpan, and it's as confusing as it is chilling. Acasta had never considered she might actually miss the gladiator's playful smugness.

You're the Ice Princess, for fucksake. Do something. Put her in her damn place. Or—something.

"You dare talk to me—"

But before she can finish her sentence, her world turns upside down. Herakles grasps her by the thigh and under one arm, lifts her expertly, and slams her onto her back in the sand.

Acasta stares up at the gladiator, her pulse roaring in her ears.

Don't lose your cool. Don't touch your sword.

No matter how tempting it might be.

"You have ice in your artillery." The gladiator looms over her, pacing like a caged mountain bear looking for a proper fight. "I need to know how you use it."

And Acasta finally gets it: what she's doing. Pushing her. Throwing her. Goading her to use her ice.

She takes her time before she replies: getting to her feet, straightening her clothes, realigning her storming heartbeat. Finally, she spits out a mouthful of silver sand and looks up.

"No."

To make a clear fucking point, she draws her sword and flings it across the arena. Even that brief contact is enough to set snow and hail whipping around them, as sharp and bitter as both their words, dying away as soon as the blade meets the sand.

Exasperation ripples through the gladiator's features. Her pacing steps up a gear. "You think I want to be here? You think this is how I like to spend my time?"

"What? Would you rather be practicing for the Games? Prancing around the Arena showing off your muscles to all of Iolcus? I suppose there's little other use for a sky captain these days."

Acasta might still not be able to land a physical punch on her, but she still knows how to hit where it hurts. The gladiator is suddenly in her space, snarling like she might actually bite. "Go fuck yourself, Princess."

If Acasta's jaw could drop to the sand, it would. If it could then up and leave, it would do that too.

"Why would I want to help make an Ice Royal more powerful? Haven't you done enough?" There's venom in the gladiator's words, and the fangs sink deep. Fuck, Acasta wishes she could make her understand.

"That's *enough*," she says instead, through gritted teeth. She steps right up to Herakles: close enough to feel her breath, to see the fire in her amber eyes. "What gives you the idea that I want you here?"

Herakles's face twists with contempt. "You seemed keen enough yesterday, Princess."

Blood thunders through Acasta's veins, liquid ice thrumming beneath her skin. Her sword strains for release even from across the sands.

Eyes locked. Breaths ragged. Every muscle taut. The moment stretches all the way to the weather-torn horizon.

Acasta's so preoccupied she barely registers the creeping shadow: the uninvited guest and the flash of their sword—

Frozen Inside

ACASTA'S HEART HUMS. TIME SLOWS AS THE SHADOW advances into focus, serrated sword angled, ready, and almost upon them.

Herakles's eyes widen, and Acasta understands that this isn't some test. It's real.

They both reach for their swords at the same moment, only to be met in unison with nothing but empty air. *Shit.*

Acasta steps in front of Herakles, sidestepping to draw the assassin and his blade away from her. It's the least she can do; it's her fault Herakles is unarmed. Her fault she's here in the first place.

She scours the arena for a weapon, but the chest of

training weapons is too far. The glass water bottle at the arena edge is closer. As she eyes it, the assassin lunges—

Acasta darts sideways, his blade swishing past her—

She dives for the water bottle, snatching it up and skidding on her heel to meet her attacker and his sword—

Not trusting a bottle to stop a blade, she thrusts it end-first toward him and slaps her palm solidly over its opening. Vacuum and pressure combine to blast the glass base into his face, showering him with liquid and shards. Enough to startle him, to cut him.

He stumbles backward, clutching at his face. Acasta's stomach tightens. *Don't vomit. Ice Princesses don't vomit at the sight of blood.*

She hurls herself past him to snatch up her ice-sword. Her ice-sword, which is currently sitting inert in Herakles's grip.

The gladiator's gaze flits from the broken bottle in Acasta's hand to the assassin clawing at his bloody face like she doesn't know whether to be shocked or impressed.

Why hasn't she run off with the ice-sword? Most people would have. If the assassin kills Acasta, Herakles could claim the weapon for herself.

But Herakles doesn't run. She looks right at Acasta. As their eyes connect, Herakles lobs the sword at her. Acasta plucks it from the air and the blade blooms immediately into blue ice, flickering like flame.

A gale whips around them, ruffling sand, clothes and hair. Overhead, the moisture in the air churns into dark, ominous storm clouds. The skies outside echo her internal weather, obscuring the daylight.

The chamber swirls with mist and shadow. Stinging ice shards whip around them. At the center of the storm,

Acasta breathes deep, balancing on that tightrope within her. Chaos versus control.

Breathe.

The bloody-faced assassin lumbers toward her. His confidence seems to be wavering; would-be assassins usually fall over their own feet once the sword is in her hand. Something about its reputation and her own combines to terrify any who stand within its orbit.

Which is probably why Herakles is nowhere to be seen.

Whatever. Acasta wanted her gone anyway. Even if it cuts like ice.

But lives are in the balance. Her life. His life.

With a single, purposeful thrust of her sword, ice spills from the blade, spreading slick beneath the assassin's feet and upending him.

"Who sent you?" Acasta raises her voice above the storm. "My father? My siblings?" She suspects one or both of the twins planned this. It's exactly the kind of thing they do.

As the intruder scrambles to his feet, there's movement at the edge of Acasta's vision. She risks a glance. Herakles stands framed in the doorway; sword raised. Something warms in Acasta's chest. *She didn't run.*

In any other skirmish, the gladiator would be the proficient one leading the battle, but right now, her presence is a distraction. The unpredictability of Iolcian Ice is a threat to all within its reach.

A single touch of the ice-sword to the silver sands, the blade angled just so, and ice spills like a river from the point of contact across the chamber's arched entrance, blocking the gladiator's path before she can do a damn thing about it.

"What the fuck—?" Herakles's words are muffled by the wall of clear ice. It's enough to keep her back. To keep her safe. Even if the thick-headed gladiator is already body-checking and hacking at the ice. Fucksake.

The assassin, meanwhile, is staring at the ice formation with horrified awe. "Tell me who sent you," Acasta calls, "and you can walk out of here."

His brows knit together as if he wishes he could dare believe her. And that flicker of desperation, it gnaws at her gut like a swallowed therma-stone, burning through her from the inside. He's on a mission, but there's someone in charge who's chosen it for him. Someone to whom *no* is never a viable response. Not without suffering the consequences.

"I have no wish to hurt you." Acasta's words are even and true. But the assassin launches as her, their blades clashing in a crackle of light.

One last try…

"Stop this," she pleads.

But he won't stop. He only strikes harder, faster, uncontrolled, desperate, fumbling uselessly to produce a second blade, a dagger. It won't help him; any skill has buckled under the weight of his terror. Sweat chills Acasta's brow and ice prickles from her blade like claws unsheathing, rebuilding itself in an instant even as splinters of ice fly like flint with every strike. She wishes she could continue like this until he's exhausted himself, but every shard feels like a part of herself is clipped away with it. It won't be long before she's exhausted too. And she's not willing to risk the sword and her life for his.

One strike. That's all it'll take.

His sword meets hers with a *clang*, and this time she keeps the contact, letting intention flow through her in an electric burst. As her frozen breath plumes, the assassin aims his dagger in a frantic swing toward her midriff.

Acasta doesn't want to watch this. He thinks he has the winning blow. He doesn't know it's already over.

When his dagger arm stops, confusion enters his eyes. And Acasta forces herself to watch. If she's choosing to take a life, she should at least have to witness it.

Her stomach knots as the panic in his eyes expands to dread. He's realized why his arm is frozen. He's painfully aware of the ice biting into him, a frostbite infection tracking from the contact of their crossed swords. He tries to wrestle free, but it's already too late. The fangs bite deeper. The ice is in his blood now, moving through him, freezing him from the inside. From what she's witnessed, from what she wishes she had never witnessed, it's an agonizing way to go.

Before he can scream, before he suffers too much, Acasta jerks her sword free from the congealing ice and spears it through his chest. Ice spikes out from the contact point in a dozen directions at once. His last gasp is nothing but a frozen plume.

In the silence, Acasta's own choked breaths splinter in the air. As she wrenches her sword from her attacker's chest, she doesn't notice the ice blockade crumbling. Or the familiar footsteps. She doesn't notice the ice that's slick beneath her feet.

She lands heavily, her sword clattering from her grasp, returned to its inert state.

The blizzard drops from the air and daylight unfurls beyond the window as silence, sharp and cold, buzzes in her ears. The statue of her attacker looms over her, weapons raised impotently, half-frozen blood spurting from his crystalline chest like some sick joke of a fountain.

Acasta tries to scramble away, but she slips again in the red slush, hot and cold coating her face, her neck. Her stomach twists, threatening to spew her own guts out. She clamps down on the bile burning her throat.

From behind, a forearm wraps tight across her shoulders. Acasta kicks and squirms, flailing for her sword as her attacker drags her away from it, ready to fight for her life all over again.

The arm gripping her loosens abruptly. On her knees, Acasta whips around, vibrating with sickening adrenaline, a feral cry erupting as she searches for this new assassin.

But... it's Herakles. She's beyond Acasta's reach, keeping her distance as though from some snarling, untamed creature, hands raised as if to appease her.

Not so quippy now, are you, Gladiator?

Whatever the fuck this is, Acasta doesn't want it. None of it. The chaos. The blood. The fighting for her life. And being witnessed through all of it.

"You're shaking, Princess."

Acasta's breath knots in her chest. *Don't cry. Don't let her see you break.*

The gladiator inches closer. "Here, let me—"

"Get out." Acasta's voice comes out quiet, brittle. "Get out and don't come back."

Herakles opens her mouth as if to argue. Of course she does. She's Herakles, Captain of the Skies, Hero of the Arena, Epic Pain in Acasta's Ass. But even she isn't that thick-headed. She must see something unforgivable and monstrous in Acasta's eyes, because she doesn't argue. She closes her mouth and retreats, exactly as Acasta demands.

Drowning

SINCE THE FIGHT YESTERDAY, EVERYTHING HURTS. Acasta's body, her thoughts, her *everything*. The bubbling of her chamber's therma-pool is doing little to soothe any of it. She must have over-stretched at some point, too, because a knot in her right calf throbs with a vengeance. She rolls her neck to loosen it, attempting to ward off a headache. That's where she holds her tension. Well, there and the rest of her body.

His agonized final gasp solidified with her ice... All that blood...

Who needs nightmares when this is her life?

She lets herself slip beneath the water, her quartz pendant swaying as she submerges. Her ice-blonde hair, freed from its ties, drapes and drifts. The hilt of the ice-sword, balanced within reach over the edge of the pool, blurs in the ripples as she sinks.

Three distant thuds echo down to her, and she dismisses them as the thump of her heartbeat in her water-logged ears. When had the attacker infiltrated her chambers? Had he been here yesterday morning, watching her from the shadows?

He couldn't have been in here overnight, or he'd have attacked sooner. He must have snuck in while she was with Herakles. Acasta had been too distracted by the grumpy gladiator to spend any time reinstating the door's ice-seal.

She'll need to do better to keep the sword out of her siblings' hands. To keep this world from becoming more broken than it already is.

The thud of her pulse grows more insistent. She's so *exhausted*. There must be more to life than just surviving; being constantly on edge, scouring the shadows. Her ice puts her next in line for the throne, but Father has never let her or the twins anywhere near the business of ruling.

They're not even allowed beyond the palace except for select, official, heavily guarded circumstances.

The Ice King never admits fear, but he doesn't have to. He doesn't keep his children contained to protect them, but because he's afraid that if they discover enough about this world and how it works, they'll one day be powerful enough to make a play for his throne. He can't fathom the truth: that Acasta has no interest in ruling any world.

Acasta squeezes her eyes shut, ignoring her aching lungs. This isn't what life should be. If she'd refused the ice-sword as a child, she wouldn't have had to live in fear ever since. Her siblings wouldn't have spent the last twenty sun-orbits resenting her. She wouldn't have to pretend to be everything she's not.

But if she hadn't accepted it... well... A kingdom in which Pelopia or Pisidice strut about, reveling in the omnipotence bestowed by their ice powers at others' expense... That's not a world Acasta would wish on anyone.

She breaks the surface to claim much-needed air. The water in her ears dulls everything but her own heartbeat. Gazing at the night sky framed by the vast window beside the pool, she lets herself drift back under the surface, the stars blinking down at her, undulating through the water like an ocean of possibilities.

Once upon a time, she could have explored them. When she was younger, she'd assumed the stars would still be there when she was ready. But Father changed all that.

It's been seven sun-orbits since he closed the skies. How must Herakles feel about the closure? Acasta cringes at herself, shame gripping her gut at the insults she'd hurled at the former sky captain.

How many worlds has Herakles explored? How many has she saved by vanquishing their monsters? And now that she's witnessed the devastation and bloodshed Acasta can create... does she see Acasta as just another monster?

Above her, a blurry neon blue blob flashes across her vision. Before Acasta can process what she's seeing, the blob lunges toward her with a *splash*.

Strong hands grip her shoulders. Acasta flails for her sword, but her fingers grasp only at water and empty air.

She expects to be shoved deeper under the water, to be pinned there. Instead, powerful arms lift her until her mouth and nose break the surface.

"Princess?"

Acasta gulps air. The grip on her shoulders tightens urgently. "Princess! Fuck. Are you okay?"

Acasta blinks water from her streaming eyes. The neon blur in front of her swims into focus to become Herakles, looking her up and down with wide, panicked eyes.

"*Gladiator?* What in the Seven Heavens are you doing?"

At her words, a different panic ignites in Herakles. The gladiator shoots backward across the therma-pool with startling speed and a sizable splash, retreating as far as possible from Acasta. Which, all things considered, isn't far at all.

"Sorry, Princess." Herakles's eyes fix intently on a portion of ceiling directly above her own head. Her freckled cheeks are crimson. Likely because Acasta—unlike the gladiator—is entirely naked.

"Have you taken a knock to the head since our last conversation about showing yourself into my chambers?"

"I knocked!" Herakles sloshes a sweeping gesture toward the entrance hall. She slicks her sopping hair back, her features tight, her eyes averted. "My apologies. It won't happen ag—"

"How did you get in? *Again?*" Exasperation strains

Acasta's voice. She'd been more thorough in icing the lock this time.

"I, uh…" The gladiator swallows, and Acasta's gaze draws to her throat. "…melted it. Again. I'm really good with locks." She shrugs. "But also—we really need to hone your door security."

An incredulous laugh escapes Acasta. "Was it strictly necessary to break into my chambers and jump into my therma-pool to make that point?"

"Uh—no." The gladiator's throat bobs again. "I, um… I knew you were in here because the door was iced. I knocked for ages, but you didn't answer. I… needed to make sure you… that no one had…" She clears her throat. "…And then I saw you in the water. You were so still. I…" She rubs the back of her neck. "I thought you were… I thought someone had hurt you."

Acasta stares at her, mouth half-open. Herakles has seen what she and her ice can do. And not only has she returned, but she also tried to *save* Acasta?

She didn't actually *need* saving, granted. But… still.

Herakles thinks her worth saving?

Acasta clears her throat and reaches for her towel-cape, wrapping it around herself as she climbs out of the pool. She ascends the steps, hiding her discomfort as her left calf protests at each movement.

Back straight. Shoulders square. She only half turns to Herakles. "I told you your services are not needed."

"You did."

Herakles lingers in the therma-pool, watching Acasta carefully. Her amber eyes are intense—they always are—but today, something in them is… different. Yesterday, when everything had gone so wrong, the heat in them had burned like wildfire. Now, when Acasta meets them, their glow is something soft and warming. Something safe. Something Acasta doesn't know what to do with.

She clears her throat. "Are you going to stay in there all day?"

"It *is* tempting..." Herakles's cheeks dimple, like she's considering adding another quip but then thinks better of it. Shame. It's not the worst thing when she gets playful. It's been a long time since anyone treated Acasta this way, or anything like it.

Herakles grips the edge of the pool and heaves herself smoothly out of the water, soaking fabric clinging to her every contour. Of course she's found a way to show off instead of simply using the steps.

And she's looking at Acasta. Shit. She should say something cutting before the gladiator realizes she was ogling her.

Acasta strides toward the floor vents, trying to walk off her limp. "I need to dry off." She raises a *What are you looking at?* eyebrow at Herakles, as if she'd been the one staring. It must work, because the gladiator turns away hurriedly.

The vent blasts her dry in seconds. Acasta stalks off across her bedchamber. "Get dried while I dress," she tells Herakles, pulling the curtains across one side of her four-poster bed as a privacy screen.

As she pulls a mesh-armor long-sleeve over her vest, the roar of the air-dry starts up again. Acasta peeks between the curtains to see Herakles standing barefoot but fully dressed atop the vents, boots placed on the grate beside her, clothes ruffling and hair on end. Her hands are held out either side of her, like she's balancing on a tightrope. In the admittedly powerful air-dry—more powerful than the tech in gladiator lodgings, probably—her face is the picture of guileless amusement.

Fuck, that's cute.

Get a grip, Acasta. Just because she's headstrong and heroic and has distracting dimples and cute-as-fuck freckles, that doesn't mean you should be swooning over her. Ruthless Ice Princess, remember?

Herakles pulls her shirt off over her head, presumably to dry it better. Acasta averts her gaze. She might still be in a crop-vest, but... *Don't be a creep.*

Quickly, not bothering with a mirror, Acasta plaits her hair and secures it at the nape of her neck. The air-dryer has fallen silent. Ready for battle, or something like it, Acasta throws back the curtain and marches out to demand an answer to the question on her tongue.

But Herakles must have decided she doesn't need her shirt today at all. Or her boots. She's barefoot, and on her top half she's wearing only her crop-vest. Which is... fine. No problem. Not distracting at all.

Stop staring. Acasta's eyes snap up and—

"Your hair is blue."

That's *not* a question, and not what she'd meant to say. Herakles smiles, as if she's fully aware of her power to muddle Acasta's thoughts. "It is. For now."

Be scathing. Quick.

"It's... fluffy."

Herakles smirks as she runs her fingers through said neon blue fluff until it springs into its usual gravity-defying curls. And Acasta has absolutely no interest in what it might feel like to run her own fingers through those curls. None.

Acasta narrows her eyes. "Why are you here?"

Finally. The question.

"To train you, Princess."

Acasta combines a huff and an eye-roll, because Herakles *knows* that's only a partial answer. "Were you born this frustrating?"

"No. It's a skill I've cultivated over many sun-orbits." The gladiator's playful smile is so disarming Acasta almost lets her own amusement show. But she buries it, because she still doesn't understand. Why in the heavens would Herakles choose to return here after what she witnessed yesterday?

"If you're worried my father will punish you for not training me... he doesn't need to know." Acasta nods to herself. It's the right thing to do. If the gladiator doesn't want to be here, she shouldn't have to be. Even if it's not the *worst* thing to have her around.

"That's not..." Herakles raises her eyebrows in... surprise? Confusion? She shakes her head. "I'm here because I want to be."

Really?

"Why would you want to help an Ice Royal be more powerful? Haven't we done enough to this world?" Acasta fires Herakles's own words back to her, their venom is still biting beneath her skin. Because Herakles wasn't wrong.

"It's possible" —Herakles's mouth forms a thin line— "that I might have a few things backward. About you. And your situation."

What in the Seven Heavens does *that* mean?

"You despise your sword and the position it puts you in. You fear the damage it can do. And you want to keep it out of dangerous hands."

Acasta keeps her expression impassive. *Cool, calm, collected.* But... Arena points to the gladiator.

"You're not the monster you pretend to be," Herakles continues, and Acasta's heart knocks against her ribs like it wants to be let out. "You're brave. You're a survivor. You're not what I expected. And I believe I can help you. If you'll let me?"

The question drifts in the air between them and suddenly Acasta hasn't a clue how to be. How to stand. Where to place her hands to exude a *fuck off* nonchalance.

Because she's spent most of her life building this fearless, cold-as-ice façade. And Herakles has dismantled it with a handful of kind words.

And for the first time in a long time, there's the possibility that Acasta is not alone in this.

Her breath stutters despite her efforts. She rubs her sternum, where a welcome warmth is taking root. But she can't admit that Herakles has put her finger on the pulse of truth. She'll need to concoct some other reason to agree...

"I suppose," she begins, reinstating her outward surety, "it would look bad for you if the princess you're training lost her life."

"I... suppose it... would?" Herakles says slowly, as if wondering where this is going.

"Well, we wouldn't want to tarnish your reputation, would we?"

Herakles's mouth twitches into a smile.

Fuck, those dimples are something else. Acasta looks away, her face warm—but then panic snatches her breath.

Her scar. The powder will have washed off in the therma-pool, and she's been too distracted by Herakles's splashing arrival to think of it. Touching her face, she lurches toward the nearest mirror—

"You don't have to do that for me." Herakles's words stop her in her tracks. Acasta fires a glare at her, but Herakles stands her ground, seemingly utterly relaxed. Like she hasn't just told Acasta to *be herself and not hide*, like that's *normal*.

She hates wearing the powder, it smothers her skin. But the thought of someone seeing her without it...

But Herakles has been looking at her true face this whole time, and Acasta hadn't even realized.

Cautiously, she returns the powder to its pot, then collects her ice-sword from beside the therma-pool and loops its belt about her waist. She never lets it out of reach; it's a habit for survival.

Except just now, that is. With Herakles.

Interesting.

"Something the matter, Princess?"

Before Acasta can respond, a flurry of white fur flies past her feet. Such sudden movement would ordinarily send her grasping for her sword, but she's used to Ace's fondness for dramatic arrivals.

Herakles crouches, reaching out a hand to him. "Who's this?"

"Oh. He hates people. He'll only—" But before Acasta can finish with *let me pat him* and *rip your face off*, the cat sidles over to Herakles and rubs the top of his head against her outstretched hand, flopping onto her still-bare feet. He even lets her scratch behind his ears.

Acasta's jaw drops at the inconceivable sight of such a pompous creature turned to total fluff under the gladiator's touch. Bloody traitor.

"He's your cat?" Herakles looks up at her.

"More of a palace cat. Pelopia tried to get rid of him once, to upset me. All she got to show for it was a scar on her chin. From him," she adds, hastily. "I call him Ace. Because of his markings and how he seems to think he's the highest ranking in the entire palace."

Hail. She closes her mouth and clears her throat. That's quite enough about a cat.

Herakles smiles. "Ace? I like that."

"If he was your cat, he'd be the Ace of Clubs," says Acasta. *Oh, stop talking.*

Herakles's laugh wraps around her like a hug. It's been so long since she's had one of those.

Acasta scowls, striding toward the exercise chamber. "Are we training, then, or what?"

Tension

"Come on, Gladiator." Wooden sword at the ready, Acasta rocks from foot to foot; partly to ease her tightened calf muscle, and partly to channel her nervous energy. "What's today's lesson?"

"How about *knowing your limits?*" Herakles, still barefoot, still in her base-layer crop-vest, follows her across the silver sands. "I saw you limping."

"It's fine." Acasta throws her a second training sword, which Herakles catches with irritating grace. Acasta's calf muscle twinges, and she yelps as pain shoots up her leg. "Aw, fuck!"

Herakles is by her side at once. Acasta flinches, but reluctantly lets Herakles help her sit in the sand, her back against the weapons chest. "I'm fine," she insists through gritted teeth, but even she knows her wince isn't convincing. "Go on. Say 'I told you so'."

But instead of gloating, Herakles gently unzips Acasta's boot and eases it off to inspect her lower leg. Acasta doesn't mean to flinch. Again. She doesn't mean for all her muscles to clench, radiating more pain from her calf. She's about ready to kick the gladiator away, but the kindness in Herakles's eyes holds her back.

"I think I've pulled every muscle at least once." Herakles's warm fingers are gentle against her injured leg. "Sometimes in places I didn't even think I had muscles."

Please stop talking about your muscles.

"You don't go through that without learning a thing or two about how to soothe pain." Herakles kneels in front of her, lifting Acasta's leg into her lap. Acasta grimaces.

"Princess. Tensing will not help you any."

She's *trying* to relax, but it's not the easiest with those careful hands moving up her leg, exploring, feeling for something. It's not usual for her to have anyone's hands on her, let alone those of someone she'd tried and failed to kiss all too recently.

The concern in Herakles's eyes turns more considered. Her fingers still. "You don't trust anyone to be close." Her tone is matter-of-fact, like she's piecing together a puzzle.

"Neither would you, if almost everyone who ever touched you was out to kill you." She hadn't meant to say that out loud. It's too much truth. She expects some quippy retort: *It must be your winning personality.* But when Herakles speaks next, her voice is soft.

"Do you think I'm here to hurt you, Princess?"

Her thumb swipes slowly up Acasta's knotted muscle. Acasta swallows a groan. *Oh, Seven Heavens.* The gladiator is going to be the death of her.

"Sending an assassin in the guise of a combat instructor is exactly the sort of game the Ice King and his offspring like to play. So forgive me if I didn't trust you as far as I could throw you."

As if completely unaware of the effect she's having,

Herakles continues working her injury, nodding thought-fully. "I'm sorry..." She frowns, and Acasta's half a second from throwing the unwanted sympathy back in her face. But then the corners of Herakles's mouth uptick mischievously. "...You think you can throw me?"

Acasta rolls her eyes. "I will admit... if you are an assas-sin, you're not a very good one."

Herakles's laugh is so sudden and so full it fills even Acasta's chest. "You're right." Her eyes are bright. "We've both made some assumptions. You're the ruthless Ice Princess, feared across the Seven Skies. I'm the club-wielding Games oaf. Perhaps we could both set rumors and reputations aside?"

The ruthless Ice Princess... "Are you afraid of me?"

Herakles's eyes connect with hers again. A jolt of fear runs through Acasta.

"Oh..." Herakles's cheeks dimple. "Terrified."

"Your questionable sense of humor is going to get you killed one day, Gladiator."

"You're not the first person to tell me that." Herakles's grin broadens. Is there *anything* about her that isn't annoy-ingly charming? "So, since we're getting to know each other —what would you like to know about me?"

She looks so at ease, like all of this is *normal*. Like she's completely forgotten that she's had her hands on Acasta this whole time, the pads of her thumbs pressing idly up the length of Acasta's tight calf. Acasta digs her fingers into the sand. *Don't gasp.* "Huh?" she manages.

"We don't know each other. So ask me anything. If I'm not comfortable answering, I'll say so."

What? Just... have a chat? Acasta blinks at her. She doesn't *get to know* people. Her only people skills are in keeping everyone at a distance and assessing their level of potential threat.

A question. Any question.

But all she comes up with is silence.

"Or... I could ask you?" Herakles's thumb digs deeper, triggering a pleasurable jolt. Acasta squirms, letting slip a strange, strangled sound. "Too much?" Herakles asks.

Acasta shakes her head, or nods. She's not sure which. Either way, Herakles must take it as permission to continue with both the question and the contact, her touch lighter than before. "You mentioned my, uh, reputation." Herakles's freckles are losing a battle to a blush, leaving no doubt as to which reputation she's referring. "Is that, um..." She clears her throat. "...Is that why you tried to kiss me?"

Discomfort slinks through Acasta. She could pull the *How dare you talk to your princess like that?* card. It would be so easy.

But she doesn't want to. Because if that's what Herakles thinks she was doing... that doesn't sit right.

"Because I hate to tell you, Princess, I doubt I live up to—"

Acasta gasps in mock disbelief. *Playful.* She can do playful. Maybe. "Are you saying the rumors are *exaggerated?*"

Amusement dances in Herakles's eyes. "Depends which rumors."

"Twelve a night, I heard." Acasta stifles her smile before Herakles sees it.

"Twelve?" Herakles whistles. "That sounds..."

"Exhausting?" Acasta raises an eyebrow, and Herakles's chuckle rumbles through the exercise chamber.

"I was going to say *complicated.*" Herakles's dimples re-emerge, and Acasta's urge to kiss them resurfaces with them. She closes her eyes, steeling herself. Because as much as this honesty, this sharing, makes her squirm... the least she owes Herakles is the truth.

"It's not why I tried to kiss you." Shame heats her cheeks, and Herakles looks like she has a thousand more questions. Questions Acasta isn't sure she can handle. Her —hopefully—final words on the topic rush out of her. "I shouldn't have done it. I didn't even mean to... I don't know what I was thinking. Anyway—I'm sorry I made you uncomfortable. It won't happen again."

Okay, those questions in Herakles's eyes are multiplying. Quick, change the subject—

"You have ink in your skin." *Great job, Acasta. State the obvious.* "Um... Are they all... part of the map? Like your scars?"

Herakles smiles. "I suppose, yes. The pretentious map of my life."

"I'm good with maps," Acasta blurts. "I mean... I study them." Does that make it sound like she wants to study Herakles? Her breath catches in her throat. "I mean—I enjoy working with them." *Is that better?* "In the palace library. Where the maps and blueprints are."

Her jaw is aching, either from clenching it or from the foot she seems to have wedged in it. What a fabulous time to discover that she has no natural skill whatsoever for normal conversation.

"Maps and blueprints?" Herakles might be smiling, but she's not poking fun. She looks... interested?

Acasta nods, not sure what else to say.

"What kind?" Herakles asks.

"Anything. Ice-engines. Ice-houses. Buildings. Cities. I like to understand how things fit together, how they work."

Herakles's thumbs press deeper into her calf. Acasta

sinks back against the weapons chest with a groan, her body finally relaxing. She's not sure whether it's the closeness, or Herakles's magic touch, or the sharing. But this feels... good?

She snaps her mouth shut. She hadn't meant to make those sounds. Herakles's eyes connect with hers like she's about to speak, but Acasta recoils, the fleeting warmth and calm replaced by an unsettled buzz beneath her skin.

Enough. She scrambles to her feet, unzips her other boot, and casts it to the arena edge, the silver sand cool and soothing against her toes. If Herakles is sparring barefoot today, then so is she. "It's time we actually do some training, don't you think?"

"Your move, Princess," says Herakles, a playful glint in her eyes. She towers over Acasta, wooden sword resting on her sculpted shoulder as Acasta scowls up at her from the sand.

Apparently, training still involves Acasta getting repeatedly floored. The only positive about her current position is the view. Does the gladiator know how hot she looks doing that?

Herakles grins, rolling her wrist and sweeping her blade fluidly past her own elbow. "Caught your breath yet?" She toe-kicks Acasta's wooden sword back to her, angling it so Acasta can catch it by the hilt. The hypnotic ripple of her abdominal muscles is giving Acasta ideas. Combat ideas, obviously. No other kind. And that smirk needs dealing with, too.

She looks up. "Gladiator?"

"Princess?"

"Can you please put your shirt back on?" She doesn't try to keep the exasperation from her tone.

Herakles looks down at herself as if to ask, *Why would I need to do that?* Acasta's eye twitches. Fucksake.

"It's..." Acasta smooths back her hair and gestures vaguely in Herakles's direction. "...distracting. You've got an unfair advantage."

Herakles smiles: a self-satisfied, infuriating, wonderful smile. "Fair, Princess? I never said our sparring would be *fair*. But if you need me to go a little easier on you...?"

Acasta rolls her eyes as Herakles reclaims her long-sleeve and saunters back to her, delivering some sort of lecture about focus and self-control as she pulls it over her head.

Game on.

Acasta strikes. A full-body tackle, knocking the gladiator clear off her feet and sending them both thudding to the sand, Herakles still wrestling her shirt. Acasta can't help her triumphant squeal of laughter as she finally pins Herakles beneath her.

"No fair." Herakles's voice is muffled as she tries to wriggle her arms free.

"Fair, Gladiator? I never said our sparring would be *fair*."

Herakles huffs, and Acasta's elated laughter fills the room, filling her chest with a pleasant, buzzing warmth, too.

Finally, Herakles emerges from her battle with her shirt. She casts it aside, grinning up at Acasta, and by the time Acasta notices the mischief in her eyes, strong hands are already grasping her hips, upending her and pinning her to the sand so firmly she can only gasp.

Floored, again. Herakles is so close Acasta can feel the heat of her. And there's nowhere she'd rather be.

No. She shouldn't be thinking that. Herakles isn't interested in her advances.

"Your move, Princess." The gladiator's voice is a whisper, a caress.

The air chills, highlighting the heat radiating from the press of their bodies. Acasta's mind is swimming, her body humming... and a gentle snowfall is swirling around them. Shit. She must have touched her ice-sword.

But Herakles isn't looking at the weather-based event. Their breaths are entwining in the whisper of space between them. And Herakles is watching her.

The perfect, gentle pressure of Herakles's hips between Acasta's legs steals the breath from her lungs. She didn't imagine that, did she? She bites her lip, willing herself to stay silent. But then Herakles rolls her hips again, and the gasp that escapes her echoes Acasta's own.

Surprise ignites in Herakles's eyes—

And morphs to panic just as abruptly. Herakles retreats, springing to her feet with—of course—impressive ease. She stands tall and mighty for a whole second, before both of them discover that Acasta has embarrassed herself by accidentally spilling ice across the sand.

Herakles's face-plant is so thorough and so graceless, a mournful groan is her only response.

Melting

ACASTA REACHES FOR HERAKLES SO INSTINCTIVELY SHE has to hold herself back. The gladiator is injured in the first place because she was trying to put distance between them.

Herakles must be a little dazed, because she takes a

moment to roll over and sit up on the iced sand. There's a bloody scrape on her jaw, but judging from the glance she darts at Acasta, her grimace is more from embarrassment than mortal injury.

"Don't move," Acasta instructs. Barefoot, she navigates past the ice spill and hurries back to her chamber to claim a clean cloth and medi-kit. She cleanses her hands before returning to Herakles's side.

"What are you doing?" asks Herakles, using the strap of her crop-vest to dab her bloodied jaw. Acasta pulls a cleaning swab from her pack, but Herakles waves her away. "It's fine. My ego is hurting far more than my face."

"Stop fussing. It needs cleaning."

Herakles opens her mouth, probably to argue. Definitely to argue. But maybe she's all out of bluster, because then her mouth snaps shut and she lets Acasta settle in beside her, nodding her permission when Acasta reaches out again with the swab.

Tilting Herakles's chin with one hand, Acasta cleans the wound with her other. Discomfort bristles through her as Herakles stifles her wince, but she can't help smiling a little too. "Such a brave gladiator."

Herakles scowls, but there's at least a touch of amusement in it. And if Acasta teases her, she doesn't have to think about how close they are, or how much she prefers this proximity to that of combat.

She squints to assess the wound. The bleeding has stopped. Some bruising is blooming, but the graze is already closing over.

"That was quite the fall." Acasta tidies away the swab. "It's starting to swell." This—this is something she knows how to deal with; she's tended enough of her own injuries.

But it means showing herself to Herakles in a way she's not sure the gladiator will be comfortable with.

Granted, she's already seen Acasta's ice: the chaos, the control, and the damage both can do. And she still came back. Now, though, when she's on the floor, bruised and unexpectedly vulnerable—she might not want to be near Acasta's specific set of skills.

Stars above. All this thinking is giving Acasta brain freeze. If Herakles doesn't want what she offers, she'll doubtless waste no time in making her feelings known.

She hovers her hand just above her ice-sword. "This, uh, might help...?"

When Herakles watches on with intrigue rather than trepidation, Acasta touches the hilt. Light swirls within the orb set within it as the blade blazes white and blue.

Acasta breathes deeply, carefully, to keep the sparks beneath her skin from transferring too readily along the weapon.

The air around them rolls into clouds. Amidst the electric tremors, wisps of snow curl. Acasta's explanation, her suggestion, is on the tip of her tongue. But Herakles reaches out and plucks an oversized snowflake from the air, and the look on her face could almost be... awe?

A distracting glow blossoms in Acasta's chest at Herakles's wonderstruck expression. The tumbling snowflakes turn to sleet, and... now they're both soaked in icy slush. That was not what she was going for.

And yet—when Herakles turns to her, the wonder still lingers in her eyes.

Acasta clears her throat. There was a point to all this. "There's, um... not much call for ice in a world that's entirely plagued with it." *That's the fucking truth.* It's a rare occasion that her ice can do good. Rarer still that she can admit to it. "But occasionally..." Keeping one hand on her sword, she lets the coolness travel through her until her other palm hazes and crackles with newly formed ice. "...I have my uses." She gestures to Herakles's cheek. "Um. May I?"

At Herakles's single nod, Acasta places her iced hand on her swollen jaw, forcing herself to focus on creating soothing ice and absolutely not on how warm Herakles's skin is, or the curiosity in her eyes, or the fact that she is literally caressing Herakles's face.

Acasta's careful breath swirls in the cool air. Herakles is tensing a little, biting her lip.

"Is this okay?" Acasta asks.

"Mmm. It's... yes... good." Her cheeks are tinted. Is that from heat or cold? Before Acasta can ask, Herakles clears her throat. "Can we pretend that me landing on my face has some sort of lesson behind it?"

Acasta smiles. "Can we pretend I put the ice there in the first place as a valuable learning opportunity?" She lifts her hand away to check on the bruise. The swelling is already receding. She returns her hand to Herakles's face, finding a gentle half-smile punctuated by adorable dimples.

"You know," Herakles says, "I'm tempted to accuse the terrifying Ice Princess of kindness."

"Nothing kind about it, Gladiator." Acasta brushes her thumb over Herakles's cheek to settle the coolness where it's needed. "I just don't want you bleeding all over my chambers. If you did, I'd have to have you—"

"Exiled or worse?" Herakles smirks. "Yeah, yeah."

There's that feeling again; that expansive warmth in her chest, ignited by playfulness. "Perhaps..." Acasta swallows. "Perhaps you can tell me about your sky adventures sometime?" She keeps her eyes trained on her task, but she can feel the heat of Herakles's smile, the way Herakles studies her as if searching for a clue to something.

"Perhaps we can go on some together, Princess."

Acasta looks up sharply. Herakles's words are... gentle; shy, almost. She would want Acasta along for a voyage? Does she mean that?

She wouldn't say it if she didn't mean it. Leaving the palace would be a logistical challenge, but right now Acasta doesn't care about logistics.

The warmth in her chest keeps expanding. Herakles's features settle into something reflective, sincere. Watching her, Acasta can well imagine why a skyship crew would choose to journey with her across the galaxies.

Herakles reaches for her, or toward her. Acasta has no idea, but she doesn't flinch as she normally does when anyone enters her orbit. She only holds her breath as Herakles lifts the white quartz pendant that's fallen from beneath Acasta's vest and examines it carefully.

"You know..." Herakles's cheek moves against Acasta's hand as she speaks. Her voice is quiet, as though she knows she could startle Acasta into flight at any moment. "... from afar, this looks like a skull?" She thumbs the quartz, her knuckles stroking the hollow of Acasta's throat.

"I'm sure that—does wonders—for my reputation." Acasta only just gets the words out.

"But up close, it's different." There's that glow in her eyes again. "Hidden depths... full of light..."

Acasta swallows. Is... is she still talking about the pendant...?

Herakles's amber eyes meet hers. "...Drawing me closer."

They're already close enough that Acasta can hear the

hitch in Herakles's breath; that Acasta's thumb smoothing against her jaw could be a caress.

Herakles's eyes search hers. "Maybe... we don't have to pretend, Princess?"

Pretend? That Herakles's sudden retreat, Acasta's over-spill of ice, had nothing to do with the two of them being pressed so close?

Herakles lifts one hand to cover Acasta's. Her other, meanwhile...

Acasta's eyes drop to her quartz pendant. Though Herakles is no longer inspecting the stone, her fingers hover at Acasta's breastbone, tracing her skin so gently Acasta's breath abandons her.

Oh. Acasta's heart double-steps. Herakles is leaning closer...

"Princess?" Herakles's voice is a whisper, as gentle as her touch, but full of mischief, too. Stars above, Acasta loves that tone. "If you wanted" —her gaze detours to Acasta's mouth— "you could try kissing me again?"

Their eyes connect, and it's *electric*. Static crackles in the air. The ice in Acasta's palm melts. She moves to pull away, so as not to rub melting slush into Herakles's face—but Herakles, her hand still covering Acasta's, only presses her closer, her smirk making clear she's fully aware that all Acasta wants to do is press her mouth to that infuriating grin.

But Acasta doesn't want to rush this. She strokes her thumb across Herakles's cheek, lingering on that distracting dimple before following the shaved line at Herakles's temple to tangle in her neon blue curls. They're even softer than she'd imagined.

Snow clouds roll around them, cocooning them, and yet it's not cold in the way her weather usually is. Something about the electricity fluttering like ribbons in the air is turning snow and ice to steam. Warmth hazes around them like the threshold where a therma-pool meets frozen air.

"Please, Princess…?" The need in Herakles's voice draws Acasta to her, electricity crackling and sparking around them, flooding Acasta's whole body as Herakles meets her kiss for kiss, her powerful arms and steady warmth a protective wall against the chaotic swirls of ice.

The snowfall pulses and thrums in time with Acasta's heartbeat. She feels Herakles smile against her mouth before her kisses divert to Acasta's jaw, her throat, hands exploring the shape of her, hinting at a yearning for more than kissing. Acasta can't help smiling too, her inner glee taking form as fluffy snowflakes at the sound of Herakles's ragged, quickening breaths. Because she, too, finally has something to be smug about.

Acasta's hand drifts from the hilt of her sword to stroke the shaved fuzz at the nape of Herakles's neck, grounding herself with the connection. And yet snow keeps drifting, kept aloft by the static in the air.

Acasta unfastens the belt of her scabbard and places her ice-sword in the silver sand. Herakles's hands grip her hips, lifting her into her lap with a surety that has Acasta gasping into their kiss and her fumbling hands tugging at Herakles's vest.

Herakles leans back to let Acasta lift the vest over her muscled shoulders. Normally, the knowing quirk of her mouth—that look that says she knows *exactly* what's fueling Acasta's racing pulse—would make Acasta want to throttle her, but right now that desire is diverting to other urges entirely. And either Herakles needs a moment to catch her breath, or—since that would be a first—she's laying out the ink and scars mapping her skin in an invitation for Acasta to look.

Well, it would be rude not to.

But maps are meant to be explored, not just looked at. Acasta's hands gravitate to the taut lines of Herakles's stomach, following the trail up through mysterious inked designs; numbers, notations and sky-maps, to the most prominent design, decorating her sternum. A playing card. An Ace of Clubs, no less. Acasta quirks an eyebrow at that, but Herakles only manages a lopsided smile.

The desire in Herakles's eyes fuels Acasta's exploration, inviting her to navigate the gentle swell of Herakles's breasts, lightly traveling the soft skin; marveling at Herakles's hitched breaths, the shape of her mouth when she's biting down on a moan. Acasta's fingers continue their journey, up to the contours of her shoulders and the divots of scars.

On a lagoon planet... a creature with nine heads and a thousand teeth. A life of adventure, of near misses and triumphs... and Acasta wants to know *everything*. Every scar, every point on Herakles's journey, everywhere she wants to go and hasn't yet been.

It's a lot. The kind of seismic, foundation-shaking discovery that should send Acasta running until she's gasping and choking for breath. Instead, with each gasp, her lungs are rejuvenated, like she's taken her first breath after being submerged for so long she thought she would drown.

Herakles's next kiss is gentle; reverent, almost, as she frees Acasta from her mesh-armor long-sleeve. Warm fingers trace up her spine, into her tied-back hair, pulling her closer, deepening their kiss. With a secure arm around her back, as if they were still sparring for points, Herakles plants her firmly back in the sand, her weight covering Acasta in a perfect full-body embrace.

Acasta raises an unimpressed eyebrow—*Really? Right now?*—and Herakles simply shrugs down at her in a maddening faux-apology. "Habit."

Upended in the sand *again*, this time with pleasure pulsing through her veins, Acasta is—willingly—at her mercy. But at least now she knows how to deal with that self-congratulatory smile.

With an exploring hand on the back of her neck, she draws Herakles down to meet her, kissing her slowly. This time, when Herakles rolls her hips purposefully against her, their moans mingle.

"You do seem taller, Gladiator," Acasta murmurs, and the rumble of Herakles's gentle laugh through Acasta's own chest is a balm.

Lifting herself off Acasta, settling on her knees and then back on her heels, Herakles unbuttons Acasta's breeches. As she hooks her thumbs beneath the waistband of her briefs, she pauses, a question in her eyes. An enthusiastic, gasping nod is all Acasta can manage in response.

Her pulse thunders in her ears. Her breath stumbles. And for the first time in a long time, it's all good sensations. She'd expected the creeping, uncomfortable grip of self-consciousness, but the way Herakles's appreciative gaze lingers, Acasta could believe *she's* the one whose physical form entices cheers from an entire stadium.

She stifles a smile. "So you *can* hold your tongue, Gladiator." She cuts off Herakles's retort with a gentle tug to her belt, her fingers making deft work of the buckle as she draws the gladiator back down on top of her.

"I can do much more with my tongue, Pr—"

Acasta slides her hand beneath the waistband of Herakles's undershorts to the irrefutable evidence of her desire, a new depth of delight flaring within her as Herakles's moans caress her cheeks. She could get used to feeling this smug.

"I welcome your instruction," she murmurs truthfully, as she explores. Fuck; just the sound of Herakles's pleasure makes her feel like she's the one being touched.

Herakles's half-lidded eyes sparkle. "Trust your instincts, Princess. I'll let you know if we need to adjust course—"

Acasta's fingers maintain their rhythm, to dizzying effect. Her eyes dart down to the place where her hand disappears beneath open breeches and neon blue undershorts. She smiles, nuzzling against the cropped hair at Herakles's temple that matches the fabric.

Herakles's mouth finds hers in an almost feral kiss, a deep groan escaping as her whole body bucks under Acasta's touch. Finally, her muscles uncoil with a long exhalation, her dimples deepening as a satisfied grin unfurls. But before Acasta can bask—again—in her newfound smugness—

Those dimples are on a journey. Herakles's tongue traces down Acasta's throat to her breasts, exploring her with hot and languorous kisses, mischief glinting in her eyes as Acasta's breath catches. Her tongue traces down the valley between Acasta's breasts, lower and lower, until—

Heavens above and below. Herakles's velvet tongue finds direction with each new stroke, sending Acasta's pulse skyrocketing. All she can do is grasp at the silver sand as she writhes beneath Herakles's touch, heat and glorious tension building inside her.

"Fuck... me..." she gasps. She'd had no idea her body was capable of such fire.

"Yes, your highness." The cheeky glimmer in Herakles's

eyes has Acasta surprising herself with a laugh, before the Hero of the Arena demonstrates her most effective distraction tactic yet: a masterful coordination of fingers and tongue, unfurling heat through Acasta until her senses sail skyward.

Stars above.

Acasta runs her hands through Herakles's neon hair, gently encouraging her back up to greet her satisfied smile with Acasta's own. Outside, hail rattles against the window, but in Herakles's arms, Acasta is cocooned in warmth, her every tension melted away.

"Okay, Gladiator..." she murmurs between kisses.

"Okay...?" Herakles squints lazily down at her.

Acasta presses closer. "...maybe it wouldn't be the worst thing to learn a thing or two from you."

If you enjoyed this dynamic, the Ice Princess and Herakles are part of the *Jasyn and the Astronauts* novel series. Their story will be explored more in *Jasyn and the Astronauts - Book 4 - The Ice Princess*, due to be released in 2026.

About the Author

Gwenhyver (she/her) is the author of the sapphic, swords & sorcery in space novel series Jasyn and the Astronauts and the upcoming, in-universe, Theseus and the Sky Labyrinth (releasing summer 2025). She loves writing adventures with fantastical elements and queer characters. She lives in a village on Dartmoor, England, with her wonderful wife, and when she's not happily hermit-ing in her writing den, she's exploring cycle trails wearing too much hi-vis! https://linktr. ee/gwenhyver

Sisters in Arms

Cassidy Percoco

THE DUELISTS WERE THE LEAST IMPORTANT BRANCH OF the military, Leonide was sure. "Branch of the military"—ha. They barely even *were* part of the military.

Technically, they were a sort of elite rank of the palace guard, but as best as she could tell, they didn't actually do anything. Like the guards, they accompanied the queen at all times while dressed in uniform, but unlike the guards, they didn't stand at attention, hold their weapons at the ready, or keep their eyes always moving to find threats. No, the duelists dawdled along in the queen's retinue, flimsy little rapiers very much sheathed. And they flirted. Flirted incessantly with the queen, courtiers, passing servants, even occasionally, the guards.

It was unseemly. It was *unprofessional*. And worst of all, nobody but Leo seemed to mind at all.

Leo stood as straight and stiff as the pike in her hand beside the queen's chair as the last of the day's petitioners bowed his way out of the hall. It'd been a long one, full of complicated cases of property rights and inheritance squabbles, and she thanked the gods she was nearly at the end of

242

her shift—although even when she was off-shift, she still seemed to spend all of her time preparing for her next one. Cleaning her armor, sharpening her weapons. Still, it would feel good to sit down and relax the part of her brain that was looking for possible threats.

And there, right on cue, the next shift marched in. Bediver led the squad, the silver braid embellishing his coat shining as though he'd polished it just before he put it on , which he probably had. If only everyone took their uniform as seriously. Once Leo made captain, nobody would ever see a speck of tarnish on hers. Bediver gave her an approving nod that reinforced her belief that that time would be sooner rather than later, and then they all began the elaborate routine of guard-changing, which made sure that there were always at least three individuals standing to attention and surveying the room. It was an accomplishment to do it all gracefully and in good time (Pol so often tripped herself up on her own feet, which was painful to witness), and the reward was a warm glow of satisfaction.

Meanwhile, the new shift of duelists sauntered in and greeted the two already there. There were jokes. There were winks. There was genial elbowing. As they took up their slouching positions in the corners of the room, one of the new pair caught Pol's eye and grinned, and when Leo glanced again at Pol, the guard was blushing.

Leo's guard shift and the duelists due to leave filed out, Leo at the end of a line walking in unison and the other pair, Vell and Dexamene, traipsing about in roughly the same direction. Dexamene's hair was impractically long, and she tossed it from side to side; Vell's was at least chin-length, but it was an eye-catching blonde that waved in a way Leo suspected was artificial. (Guard regulations mandated hair no longer than the jawline, and none of them styled it.) Feeling her eye caught, Leo blinked angrily.

Vell couldn't have noticed that, of course. Nobody could *feel* an angry blink. But all the same, she fell into step with Leo as Dexamene went on ahead, ambling with her hands behind her back in a way that threw her coat away to reveal her sword's filigree hilt.

"Lovely day, isn't it?"

Leo snorted, despite her intent not to make a sound until the squad was out of the presence chamber. "It's cloudy."

"But warm!" After that, Vell let her walk in merciful silence for the rest of the way out of the chamber.

It didn't last. "Do you know, I heard from the Countess di Barri that Count Femy is trying to buy up the entire market's worth of pearls to make into a strand hundreds of feet long? She said he wants to give it to the queen to entice her into—"

"You should spend less time gossiping with countesses and more time watching for threats to the queen." It came out harsher than she meant, and Leo winced internally—she didn't want to be cruel, just to make her priorities clear—but it didn't seem to faze Vell at all, somehow. She actually laughed.

"Count Femy having designs on influencing the queen with gifts *is* a threat, isn't it?"

The worst thing was that she was right. Leo was not about to admit that, though, and just sniffed.

Everyone relaxed once they were far enough from the queen's general area (apart from Leo, as a rule), and the guards fell out of formation. Pol wrapped her arms around two fellows' shoulders and proclaimed that it was time for a drink. Dexamene giggled and asked who was buying. The others were headed out to the market, and they peeled off as well. Somehow, despite all her inclinations, Leo was alone with Vell. This happened with a bizarre frequency when she thought about it.

"Not going off with the rest?"

"It's none of your business what I do when I'm off duty," Leo snapped.

Vell held up her hands with a smile. "Of course not." Then she leaned forward. "Or is it?"

"You're ridiculous."

"Maybe *we're* ridiculous."

"For all the gods' sake," Leo said, half-crazed with annoyance and turned the corner so recklessly that she almost ran headlong into a maidservant in a plain brown dress and a neat linen cap and apron. That made her even more irritated—look, Vell was a hazard to all the staff, not just her—which Leo knew was unfair, but Vell's behavior was always so confusing that it riled her up to an absurd degree.

"I am *so* sorry," Leo said, but before she could go on to explain to the maidservant that it was Vell's fault, something tickled her brain, throwing up a warning. Despite her irritation, she paid attention to that sort of thing and took a second look, which showed her ... soft hands. The wrong kind of shoes. And then as her eyes traveled suspiciously up to the maid's face, the woman's eyes narrowed and her stance shifted into one Leo recognized very well.

This wasn't a servant. It was an assassin.

The woman suddenly had a dagger in her hand, one of those thin stilettos that were made only to thrust between the ribs to the heart. That was good: those things didn't have much of an edge, being all *point*, which meant you could knock them aside pretty easily with an arm or a boot. But also, every assassin Leo had come across or heard about who worked with a stiletto also coated it in poison, one of the really bad ones, so it only took a nick to kill you or, at best, to result in the surgeons having to take off a limb to stop it from spreading.

Leo took a step forward and leveled the pike in her left hand, then drew her short sword with her right. Best try not to have to touch the dagger at all, then.

Vell drew her own whippy little rapier. "Get back," she said to Leo in a voice that was suddenly steel rather than velvet, and Leo risked a startled glance sideways.

"I'm a member of the queen's guard," Leo reminded her. "I'm supposed to—"

"This is exactly what *I'm* here for," Vell snapped, and darted forward to strike at the assassin, who was already diving away nimbly.

That would've been all to the good, except that then there was the *tap-tap-tap* of someone else running up in soft boots, and when Leo spun to tell whatever courtier she was assuming needed to be told to get the seven hells out of there, she found herself facing up with a second assassin, taller and broader, with his own stiletto.

It was a good thing, at least, that she and Vell were each busy with their own opponents. Leo would've been completely thrown off her rhythm if she'd been thinking that Vell was watching her, checking her form, noticing every flaw in her stance. As it was, the second assassin was taking all of her attention. By rights, she should've been able to cut him to ribbons—two blades versus one, big weapons versus tiny—but you didn't get hired to kill the queen with a little poisoned stiletto unless you were very, very good. He kept dodging, lithe body shifting and bouncing back and forth while testing her defenses with his dagger.

One nick. All it would take was one nick. One stab. One cut. That would be failure. Leo couldn't fail. She couldn't last through the siege only to fall in a back corridor to some stupid unfair poison trick.

There was a sound from behind her, a woman's whimper, and Leo couldn't stop herself from turning to make sure that Vell hadn't been hurt with the wicked little weapon, because—she couldn't—not again! But it was the assassin who was drawing back, blood on the arm holding the stiletto, and Vell was shaking her head exultantly to throw her hair back. A rush of relief went through Leo and she sagged, the point of her pike dropping involuntarily.

The male assassin saw his chance—stupid of her to give it to him—and rushed forward for a blow that would punch through her leather armor before she could lift either of her weapons again. He was fast, so fast, and Leo's blood was pumping so hot and loud in her ears—

And a silver rapier appeared between them, batting the stiletto aside and piercing the man's shoulder before pulling back. Vell caught Leo's eye and winked, and for the first time, Leo really *got* why everyone seemed to find the duelists so gods-damned attractive. Time hung still for a moment, the light from the window turning solid between them and the bead of blood on the point of Vell's rapier holding on ...

Then the man swore in Citralian and the blood dripped to the flagstones. The other assassin was darting toward them so quickly that Leo barely had time to swing her pike around to ward her away. But the battle was more than half done. The male assassin was flagging, with his wound (not a mortal one at all unless it got infected, but certainly hard to fight with), and the female one seemed to realize she wasn't going to get past Vell's flashy but deadly moves. Together, they started maneuvering to get Leo and Vell into the corner where the corridor bent at a right angle, made one last powerful push, and then turned and sprinted away in opposite directions. Leo met Vell's eyes again, and all it took was the glance for them both to know what was going on. They split and followed their quarry.

This was worse than the fight by yards. Leo wasn't a runner, she was built for stamina rather than speed, and she had to push herself beyond her limits to follow him. He was still wounded, though, and the pain had to be eating at him. What was she going to do when she caught him? He still had that bloody poisoned stiletto...

It turned out not to matter, because just as she was bearing down on him, he put out a hand and somehow—impossibly—flipped himself out a window. Leo skidded to a halt, chest heaving, and watched him run across the roofs. When he was far enough away that it was obvious she couldn't chase him, he turned back, raised a middle finger, and shouted some more Citralian oaths at her. She gave him a mock salute with the hand still clutching her sword, too exhausted to do anything else.

The only thing left to do was to go back to the queen and her on-duty guards and report it. They'd have to beef up security with rank-and-file soldiers, put the investigators onto rooting out more assassins, and all kinds of things that were fortunately well above Leo's pay grade. She ought to be thinking about what she was going to say as she legged it back toward the presence chamber—she'd be essentially reporting directly to the queen, for all the gods' sakes—but her thoughts turned relentlessly to Vell, and whether she'd caught her woman or if she'd gotten close to her again and then the woman had swiped out with that dagger and its poisoned tip and...and...

There was no point in thinking about it, but her thoughts wouldn't stop racing around and around even faster than her feet, her head swimming with the effort of keeping them going even while she knew her face was taking on that same impassive outlook she always wore.

It's the work, she reminded herself. This is what we do, this is what we're here for. Any of them could die at any time doing it. She knew that better than anybody.

When she reached the queen's presence chamber, though, Vell was jogging toward it from the other direction, and Leo's breath left her lungs in the loudest exhale she might've ever made. The duelist was mussed and sweaty and limping slightly but a very welcome sight.

"Oh, gods," said Vell. "I was—well, I know you're good, you're the best of the guard, but—"

Leo only had time to nod before they were admitted into the queen's presence, ushered through the heavy oaken door to stand before the court.

"Your majesty," Vell began as soon as they were announced, and Leo was grateful that all she had to do was stand there with her eyes semi-focused on the cloth of state while the matter was explained. Her hands would be shaking if she weren't clasping them so tightly behind her back, she knew, and the thought made her clasp them all the tighter. Assassins. Danger. Prevent. She understood the words that went flying past, but she didn't have to follow them entirely; she and Vell weren't on duty and weren't fresh enough to be useful anyway. The queen, brow furrowed, said something and Vell was bowing which meant Leo should also be bowing, so she bowed too, and then they were backing out of the chamber, thank the gods.

"I don't think either of us really needs medical attention," said Vell, "but when the queen orders it I suppose you'd better check in, hm? Oh, holy hells, are you all right?"

"I'm fine" came out of Leo's mouth by rote, but her knees were buckling, and she reached out behind her for the wall as she slid down to the floor. Oh, she wasn't fine.

"Right." Vell descended in a more careful fashion, brushing aside her coattails in order to sit right on her breeches. Immediately, she reached out for Leo's hands and started to check them over, then pushed up the sleeves of her coat to look at her wrists and forearms. "Did he get you? If the cut's small enough, there should still be time—you should've *said*—"

Not too roughly, Leo pushed her off. "No. I didn't get poisoned, it's nothing." It wasn't that, anyway. She concentrated on breathing normally while Vell looked at her and pretended that she was alone. It was stupid, it was so stupid, she was supposed to be *over* this...

She was aware of Vell continuing to stare, but there was nothing to be done about that. Well, Leo could walk away. She did a quick internal survey and decided that she might be able to get back to her feet. It took a lot of leaning against the wall with Vell hovering nearby, but she managed it. Right—they had to get to the guard physician to be looked over. Leo would've rather gone to her bed and slept for half a day, but it was an order, so she'd do it. What did she have apart from her job and her loyalty?

Unfortunately, Vell was going the same way for the same reason, so she couldn't be avoided even though she was staying suspiciously quiet. Leo kept her eyes front and concentrated on making her breaths steady and even, but before they'd even turned the next corner she felt herself trembling too hard to keep going and had to hold herself up with the wall and put her face against it, hidden between her arms.

"Oh, dragonsbreath," she heard Vell say behind her, and then those delicate duelist's hands were dancing over her shoulders and arms. This time, she didn't have the strength to put up a facade of untouchability and straighten herself up: she just exhaled a quiet sob into the wall.

Vell didn't say anything else, but Leo could feel her waiting. She was obviously not going to go anywhere until Leo was able to pull herself together and explain what was going on.

"It's," she started, her voice muffled by the stone, but she didn't know how to finish the sentence. "Fallorfell."

"What?"

Of course, that wasn't enough to make the problem plain. "When the queen was at the castle Fallorfell this spring," Leo managed to say, "on progress. And I was—there were—"

But that had been enough for Vell to understand, her mind as quick as her footwork. "Oh, gods," she breathed. "The tower."

When the queen was on progress, she sometimes stayed with nobles she liked, who had pleasing conversation and acceptable politics, who would be proud of the honor of hosting her, despite the massive expense and disruption. And sometimes she stayed with nobles she didn't like, who needed their coffers drained and a reminder that she was in charge. The baron of Fallorfell was one of the latter, a dissident who'd been sullen and irritating ever since her accession to the throne over his preferred candidate. Usually, a royal visit on progress was enough to bring his sort to heel, but the baron was made of different stuff than most—his family had lived out in the mountains for generations, and they were more willing to get their hands dirty.

The queen's guards had gotten her up into a crumbling tower at the center of Fallorfell, a more defensible place, and arrayed themselves at the bottom of the twisting stair to engage the baron's soldiers. It'd been the best and only strategy, and it'd worked: the baron hadn't gotten through to kill the queen by the time reinforcements arrived. But it'd left all the other guards dead or dying, and it'd been touch and go for Leo with her wound and then her fever. A month later, she'd insisted she was well enough to serve again, the baron already decisively set down and ready to be forgotten, and the world had moved on.

For everyone but Leo.

Most of the time, she was fine. A little self-serious, everyone knew; overly concerned with making sure every link in her chainmail was polished and every rivet solid. Nobody had forgotten about Fallorfell, they still referred to it when it was relevant or made dark jokes, but it wasn't *real* to them in the same way. They hadn't fought there in a tight stairwell, elbow to elbow with their fellows, watching them get cut and hit and stabbed and gutted, seen them bleed out or have their heads stoven in, hadn't been pierced through with a pike and been sure they were dying just like their friends who were already staring glassy-eyed at the wall.

Everyone knew the guard never saw much real action, apart from occasionally stopping someone recklessly charging through a crowd or taking care of bandits who didn't realize whose carriage they were chasing down—that was just how it was. If the queen's personal guard were in real combat, there was a bigger problem than just the danger they were in: something had failed, something was breaking down. You had to be *capable* of proper fighting, of course, and there was plenty of training and drilling for that eventuality, but it wasn't the same as being in the infantry. You didn't go into it with the same expectations.

Usually, she managed to be alone when the memory hit her. At night, in bed, before she drifted off to sleep, she was suddenly right back in Fallorfell and had to sit bolt upright, panting and gasping like she'd just run a mile in full armor. Something squeezed her heart and made her feel she was actually still lying there with a pike in her side and that everything since then had been a hallucination. Or, worse, she felt that the guards who'd died that day were reaching out to her, trying to grab her from beyond the living world to drag her down with them as she deserved, winding their fingers in her clothes and her hair to pull her to her own death.

Nothing like that day in Fallorfell, nothing where there was real danger of death, had happened again until this incident. Nothing where she might've died, and worse, where someone else might've died beside her.

"Are you breathing?" she vaguely heard Vell ask beside her. "You need to breathe, Leo. Come on, in, out..." At another time, that might have annoyed her, but following their side-by-side battle with the poisoned daggers, she didn't take it as a condescending imposition. Instead, she breathed.

After a moment, most of her dizziness fading away, she looked up. Vell had been disheveled after the fight and ensuing chase, but now her face was drawn in an entirely different way, with no traces of her usual mirth. "Let's go find a cloister to sit in for a bit."

"Not necessary," said Leo, trying to go rigid again and failing. "I'm fine now. The queen said—"

"The queen isn't going to behead you for waiting to get

checked out by the guard medic," Vell retorted and slipped her arm into Leo's, an intimacy she'd normally never allow. It felt nice, though, like an offer of support rather than a liberty.

The nearest courtyard was around a few corners, and by the time they reached it, Leo felt almost normal again. The fresh air was even more restorative than the walk had been, even though the open space was covered with paving stones rather than one of the gardens that were in the larger palace lacunae. It was quiet and empty, and Leo found the dusty smell to be calming, in a way. There was a half-wall separating the cloister from the open center, and Vell deposited her on it, then sat down herself without any of her usual grace. They each leaned back against a column, almost in unison, and stared at each other.

This wasn't the Vell she knew, who irritated Leo at every turn with her insouciance and unserious attitude. And she wasn't the Leo that presumably irritated Vell at every turn by being emotionless and uptight, she guessed. It was a bit funny, now that she was feeling things again, and she let herself crack a smile, which seemed to make Vell's posture relax.

Leo cleared her dry throat. "Thank you for...all this. I'll dedicate a gold cup in the temple of whichever deity you like best."

"Eh." Vell shrugged. "Don't worry about it. I don't mind. You really scared me, you know."

"With all of the...not breathing and that?"

"Sure—but mostly the having to fight someone with a knife that could kill you at first blood. That's my job, not yours, and I didn't know if you could handle it." That might've come off as dismissive from someone else, but Vell's frankness made it clear that she was more annoyed with herself than anything else. "You could, though, clearly. For what it's worth."

"You could've gotten me out of your hair for good," said Leo, trying for levity, and Vell did give her a tired smile in response.

"But then who would I flirt with?"

The balance Leo had found while they'd walked suddenly deserted her again, as though a carpet had been tugged from under her feet (although she always planted her feet very deliberately in such a way that anyone would find it very difficult to pull a carpet out from under them, so maybe it wasn't the right metaphor).

It might just be a joke—like it was funny for Vell to suggest she'd been flirting because it was so obvious that she hadn't, that she wouldn't, not with boring, staid Leo. Yes, that had to be it, because who would flirt with Leo? But Vell was giving her a look that, well, Leo wasn't the best at interpreting looks, but it seemed soft. Truthful.

She was waiting too long to respond, taking too long to think about this conundrum. Vell's gentle smile slowly shifted into a puzzled expression as Leo failed to say anything, her head tilting to one side and her eyebrows drawing together, but finally Leo found her voice.

"You...flirt with me?" That was meant to come out as a snappy, sarcastic comeback, but Leo could hear a kind of plaintive whine in it, her total lack of knowledge shining through.

"Yes," Vell admitted immediately, as though it were simple and obvious. "All the time. The others say I'm scaling a brick wall, but I told myself I'd wear you down and make you crack a smile one of these days." After she spoke, there was a hideous silence.

Leo didn't know how to respond to someone flirting

with her, or to the idea that someone had been flirting with her for quite some time. She didn't know how to handle any situation where she was wrong-footed other than turning to stone. But she didn't *want* to turn to stone! Not this time, at least. She didn't know what she actually wanted *to* do, so much, but she wanted something other than her usual limited social skillset.

Of course, it was left to Vell to fill the silence. "Sorry," she said, "really. You've just had—a whole thing. You don't need me and my nonsense." There was a bitter, self-reproachful twist to her mouth that Leo had never seen on her before. It was beginning to dawn on Leo that not only had Vell been flirting with her at all, but that flirtation was more than the playful, meaningless banter the duelists tended to keep up with the courtiers.

A slightly strangled sound came out of her throat, and Leo shook her head to clear it so she could try again. "No," she said. "I mean—I just didn't expect that."

Vell's eyebrows rose. "Really?"

"Maybe you should've been less subtle," Leo retorted, and when Vell tipped her head back to bubble over with laughter that echoed in the empty cloister, she found herself ready to laugh a little as well as she took in the pleasing sight of color coming back to Vell's cheeks.

"Nobody's ever accused me of subtlety, I assure you," Vell said once she'd come back to herself, though amusement still thrummed in her voice.

Leo shrugged. "Too subtle for me, anyway." She really was a brick wall, when you got down to it, and she felt a bit of heat go to her own cheeks.

When they sat quietly and regarded each other after that, there was a comfort in it instead of tension. Everything about Vell was the same as before, but somehow there was a difference to every quality: the smile was kind rather than mocking, the beauty a gift rather than a taunt. Leo had never managed to have such an understanding, such a rapport with anyone else. And it'd come so easily, once she'd let it. How could that have happened?

Vell reached out and took Leo's calloused hand with both of her own, treating it like a delicate piece of porcelain. When she bent to kiss the knuckles, she moved simply and without the smoldering look up to the owner that Leo had seen as part of that maneuver before, and then she ran her thumb over the spot she'd kissed as though she could impress it into the skin.

"My lady," she said. "Or—good sir? Both of them fit you, I think."

The warmth that filled Leo's chest at the simplicity of it put paid to any remaining heart-pounding from the fight or her memories of Fallorfell. Gods, she'd been misreading Vell for so long—but not any longer.

"You're ridiculous," said Leo, but with a fondness that had never filled those words from her lips before.

About the Author

Cassidy Percoco (she/her) is a writer and historian living in upstate New York. She has previously published a sapphic Cinderella retelling, "The Happy Secret of It All," and a non-fiction work, "Regency Women's Dress: Techniques and Patterns 1800-1830". You can find her newsletter at https://buttondown.com/cassidypercoco

Royals and Other Beasts
Selina Rossman

THE KNIGHT'S CHARRED CORPSE PLUMMETED TO THE ground. It landed on the jagged rocks at the tower's base with a percussive clatter. The man's armor split down the middle, spilling his roasted innards onto the surrounding boulders. Illuminated in moonlight, there was no denying what lay at Sage's feet.

Choking down a scream, Sage staggered back. Maybe this wasn't such a good idea after all. *No,* she thought, shaking her head adamantly and tightening her grip on the falchion at her side. She'd already come too far to turn back now.

Clad in her twin's modest, boiled leather armor, she'd fled their small town, taking his favorite blade, a small pack of provisions, and any chances of him becoming a knight. She was confident that he'd never speak to her again.

Despite being much older than the average page, Henry had sweet-talked a local knight into taking him under his wing. Most boys began their apprenticeship at the ripe old age of eight. He was eighteen, and it was no small miracle that the knight had said yes.

Sage's guts twisted guiltily at the thought of her brother's ruined ambitions, but she had dreams to chase, too, and they didn't include being forced to marry the town drunk. Swallowing down the burning bile, she forced herself to keep moving until she had left the knight's body behind.

The entrance to the tower stood ajar, pried open by one of the would-be heroes that had come before her.

Creeping inside, Sage huffed out a sigh of relief. Someone had lit the candles lining the stone walls. She wouldn't have to make her way in the dark. Pressing her lips into a determined line, she gathered up her shoulder-length, strawberry-blonde hair into a bun and stepped inside.

At her brother's insistence, she'd joined in during his early sword lessons, even if it *wasn't right* for a young maiden to swing a blade. She hadn't picked up a weapon since, at least, not until now. To survive, she'd have to be quick because her minimal training would be no match against the princess's captor. Tightly clutching her blade, she crept down the long corridor which ended in a steep, winding staircase.

Craning her neck with a hard swallow, she stared upward, searching for the top but finding only darkness. Frowning, she shifted uneasily from foot to foot and considered her options.

She knew from the king's decree that the princess was being held at the tower's highest point. What she didn't know was whether or not light would be her ally or her foe. Could dragons see in the dark? *Probably,* she concluded, backtracking and snatching up a candle before beginning her ascent.

Legs protesting as she traversed the endlessly twisting staircase, Sage focused on her goal. Save the princess. Get the gold. Buy freedom.

The mantra kept her going as she continued her march upward. The flickering light beat back the shadows until the spiral staircase gradually straightened.

Shit, she thought as she crested the final stairs and her candle burned out. Expecting to be thrown into total darkness, she tensed, but the first gentle rays of morning were already filtering into the tower. It had taken all night to make it this far.

Drawing her single-edged sword, she slunk forward, the blade trembling in her grasp as her heart galloped in her chest. Her blood pounded so loudly in her ears that she was sure it would give away her position.

A guttural moan pierced the silence. Pressing herself against the stairwell, Sage froze.

The harsh sound of metal clanging against stone made her wince. Something heavy struck the floor with a clatter. The stones beneath her shook and she tumbled to her knees. Biting her lip to keep quiet, she drew in a sharp breath. A final pained moan echoed through the air, then silence.

Sword clutched hard enough to make her knuckles blanch, Sage rose to her feet and crept along the remaining stairs on shaky legs. Her heart was still hammering in her chest, and her breath came in nervous little gasps. Swallowing hard, she threw back her shoulders and stepped off the staircase into an enormous but sparsely furnished room. The far corner contained a single bed and a small wardrobe.

No monsters occupied the space, only a nude woman kneeling beneath the window.

The woman sighed softly. "You should leave," she muttered without bothering to raise her gaze from the floor. "You will find only death here."

Wide-eyed, Sage examined the tall, willowy woman before her. Ruby-red waves cascaded down her shoulders, the bold color juxtaposed with the woman's alabaster skin and soft curves.

Frowning, Sage sheathed her weapon and took a step forward. This had to be the princess. Edging closer, she cleared her throat uncomfortably. "Princess," she said softly, "I'm here to save you."

The princess's head shot up, revealing wide reptilian eyes. A stark yellow had replaced the once renowned aquamarine irises and dark slitted pupils left no question that the woman was no longer human. "You're a woman!"

Startling, Sage stumbled backward, nearly tumbling back down the stairs. Catching herself before she could fall, she dropped to a knee and continued staring at the yellow-eyed woman. After a long moment, she remembered herself and averted her gaze.

"Aye." Sage swallowed hard. "My lady," she added hastily and quickly snapped her mouth shut as a low chuckle escaped the princess, quickly turning into a throaty laugh. Unused to conversing with royals, she wasn't sure what to expect but laughter hadn't been it.

Sage wearily eyed the now cackling princess as she rose and closed the distance between them.

"Come now," the royal said, clapping her hands together. "Off your knees."

"As your highness wishes," Sage murmured, climbing to her feet and keeping her eyes on the stone floor. *I still don't see what's so funny.*

Gentle but insistent fingers captured Sage's chin, forcing her to gaze into the princess's face. Bright eyes peered down at her as full lips quirked into an amused smirk.

Sage gulped. She'd grown up on tales of beautiful royals sequestered away in lavish castles, but now, face to face with the kingdom's heir, she knew they hadn't been exaggerating, and an emotion besides fear made her heart thunder.

"*Any man,*" the princess muttered, shaking her head and continuing to chuckle darkly. "That she-devil was being literal." Releasing Sage from her grip, she began to pace.

"My lady?" Sage squinted at the light glinting off the manacles clamped over the other woman's wrists and ankles as she struggled to figure out what the princess was talking about.

"Stop that," the princess said haughtily, stomping her foot and striking a defiant pose with her hands on her hips. "My name is Rosabelle, and I haven't been anyone's *lady* since I was cursed."

Cursed? Sage thought in confusion and crossed her arms over her chest as she watched Rosabelle pace. "You weren't captured by a dragon?"

Rosabelle barked out a harsh laugh. "Is that the story my father is spouting?"

Sage nodded slowly. "Representatives of the king have spoken of nothing else. They say a great-scaled beast snatched you off the castle walls in the dead of night."

"Lovely," Rosabelle huffed. "I suppose that sounds better than my father's only heir being cursed to turn into a beast every nightfall."

Worrying at her lower lip, Sage quietly digested the new information. *If she's the dragon, what am I supposed to do with that?*

"My lady–"

"Uh-uh," the Princess cut her off, waggling a finger at her, "it's Rosabelle."

Sage cleared her throat uncomfortably. "Rosabelle," she

murmured, feeling her cheeks heat at the familiarity of using a royal's first name. "Why were you cursed?"

"Some people just refuse to accept *no* as an answer," Rosabelle growled.

Sage eyed the princess curiously, head tilted to the side. "Meaning?"

"It means the witch didn't get her way and decided to take it out on me." Closing her eyes with a groan, Rosabelle rubbed her temples. "I blame my father."

"My la–" The title died on Sage's lips as Rosabelle's bright reptilian eyes flew open to glare at her. "Rosabelle," she corrected and cleared her throat uneasily. "So, you know who cursed you."

"I do," Rosabelle admitted, striding across the room to the small bed and throwing herself onto it. "And until I met you, I thought I understood how the curse worked," she grumbled, a beleaguered sigh escaping her.

Frowning, Sage slowly approached the bed. "What changed when you met me?"

Rosabelle gripped the bridge of her nose as if it pained her. "The Witch's exact words were," Rosabelle paused, scrunching her brows together, *"by daylight, your gaze shall bring only death. Any man unlucky enough to be caught within it shall perish. By nightfall, you shall be a beast of scale and fang as chains weigh you down."*

Rosabelle continued to scrunch her brows together in a way that Sage couldn't help finding adorable. *Cut it out!* Sage gave herself a mental kick. She was here to help the princess, not gawk longingly at her.

"But you," Rosabelle met her eyes thoughtfully, "are no man."

"I am no man," Sage agreed, still not completely under-standing but relieved that she wouldn't be expected to slay a dragon. The circumstances had changed, but her mission hadn't. She had to save the princess if she was to save herself.

"Can you control it?" Sage asked as her mind raced to come up with a new plan.

Rosabelle squinted up at her. "The curse?"

"No," Sage shook her head, "the dragon."

Pursing her lips, Rosabelle pushed herself into a seated position. "I can't stop the change, but I'm still me," she murmured, dropping her gaze to her lap.

"So," Sage drew in a steadying breath and continued, "you wanted to kill all those knights?"

"No!" Rosabelle snapped sharply, and Sage flinched back. "I was just defending myself." Scowling, she shook her head. "Before this damn curse, I'd never even been hunting."

Shit, I'm an ass, Sage thought, searching for the right words to make it better. Of course, the princess wasn't killing for sport. The whole situation must be utterly hellish for her. "Sorry," she mumbled, staring hard at the floor. "I shouldn't have said that."

"It's fine," Rosabelle said icily, tugging a heavy blanket over her bare shoulders and regarding Sage coldly. "How would you know?"

She scuffed her boot against the floor as a tense silence stretched between them. "I think I can help you," Sage finally said when the quiet became too uncomfortable and sat down on the edge of the bed.

Rosabelle eyed her warily. "I don't even know your name. Why should I trust you?" Shaking her head, she pulled the blanket more securely around her shoulders. "Not even five minutes ago, you were accusing me of being a murderer."

Sage winced. "You don't mince your words, do ya?"

Pressing her lips into a thin line, Rosabelle glared at her but said nothing.

"Well, the way I see it—" She hesitated. The princess wasn't going to like what she had to say. "I'm the only one to make it this far, which doesn't leave you with many options." Running her tongue over suddenly parched lips, she met the yellow eyes boring into her. "Oh," she mumbled and smacked herself. "My name is Sage."

Without a word, Rosabelle continued to glare at her.

Are all royals this moody, or just the cursed ones? Sage wondered, coolly returning Rosabelle's stare despite the goosebumps beginning to break out on her skin.

"Fine," Rosabelle grumbled after a long moment. "What is the plan?"

Nodding curtly, Sage slid closer to Rosabelle. "First, I need to understand what we're dealing with," she said with a confidence she didn't feel.

"It all started when the Witch of the Wilds demanded an audience with my father." Absentmindedly running a hand through her wavy red tresses, Rosabelle frowned. "Few know her real name."

Nodding, Sage waited patiently for her to continue.

"I happened to be entering the throne room just as the witch was storming out." Rosabelle raised a trembling hand to her throat, tracing the manacle and swallowing hard. "She grabbed me by the throat and slammed me into a wall before the king's guard could react, and by the time they pulled her off of me, it was too late." Curling her knees to her chest, Rosabelle rested her chin on them. "Do you want to know the cruelest part of all of this?"

Sage wasn't sure how it could get worse, but she waited patiently for the princess to tell her.

"No matter where I go, a key appears." Thrusting her hand beneath a pillow, Rosabelle snatched up a large pewter key and thrust it into the manacle's lock. She twisted the key. Nothing happened.

"Why won't it open?" Sage wondered out loud.

Yanking the key from the lock, Rosabelle tossed it to the floor. "That's just it. It won't open for anyone but her. When she cursed me, she said something about how *only her blood* could free me." Snatching up a pillow, Rosabelle crushed it against her chest. "If I look at a man, he dies. When I shift, I'm weighed down by chains so that I can't fly away and even though I should be able to free myself," she gestured towards the key on the floor, "I'm stuck."

Sage's stomach knotted uncomfortably. The witch had certainly been thorough.

"And how did you end up here?" Sage asked, motioning vaguely at their surroundings.

Rosabelle shrugged. "That was the easy part. My father's men blindfolded me and rode hard to make it here before nightfall."

"Alright, then." Sage stood. "We must find the witch and force her to free you."

Rosabelle barked out a bitter laugh. "You make it sound so easy."

"Maybe it can be." Sage offered her hand to the seated woman.

Rosabelle eyed her warily but allowed herself to be hauled to her feet. "Why are you so intent on helping me? It's not too late to turn back."

"Because I might be the only one who can," Sage said quietly, her stomach twisting guiltily.

After a long moment, Rosabelle silently nodded. She threw back her shoulders, letting the blanket and pillow slide away, and strode towards the small wardrobe on the other side of the bed.

Flushing at the supple skin suddenly on display, Sage forced herself to look away. The princess was beautiful but Sage was here to save her, not stare at her. Gathering her courage, Sage stole a glance in Rosabelle's direction and discovered with a mix of relief and disappointment that the other woman had donned a black satin gown.

"Okay." Rosabelle clapped her hands together and returned to her companion's side. "Where do we begin?"

I wish I knew, Sage thought, clamping her lower lip between her teeth. *She's too pretty and if I find it distracting, then other people will notice her when we try to leave. Wait! That's it!* Grinning ruefully, Sage drew her dagger. "You're too pretty."

"Uh, thank you?" Taking a cautious step backward, Rosabelle eyed the knife in Sage's hand. "I'd rather you not disfigure me, though."

Sage glanced from her blade to the princess and burst out laughing. "You misunderstand," she said, still grinning as she got hold of herself. "I mean to cut your hair, not your face."

"Oh," Rosabelle said softly, a pretty blush lighting up her cheeks.

Sage gestured for the other woman to sit back down on the bed. "If we want to get out of here without anyone noticing you, then we've got to change how you look," she explained, climbing onto the bed and positioning herself behind the princess.

When she'd finished Rosabelle's haircut, the other woman sported an ugly bowl cut and could more easily pass as a man.

"Now what?" Rosabelle ran a hand through her freshly shorn hair.

Great question. "Now, we have to dye your hair and change your outfit so that there is even less of a chance that you will be recognized," Sage explained with a confidence she still didn't feel. She was used to flying by the seat of her pants but this was a little extreme, even for her.

Frowning, Rosabelle glanced up at Sage. "But we don't have any supplies here."

"Right," Sage said thoughtfully. "I'll have to go into town to get what we need."

"Right now?" Rosabelle asked, her voice cracking.

Sage nodded. "No time like the present, aye?"

"I suppose," Rosabelle murmured.

"I shall return as soon as I am able," Sage promised and strode across the room to the stairs. With a beleaguered sigh, she made her way down the seemingly endless staircase.

Her trek to the town, the procurement of henna, men's clothing, and some fresh bread and meat took the better part of a day and a half, and when she finally returned to the castle and made it to the top, it was nearly sunset.

Entering the Princess' chamber, Sage caught sight of Rosabelle and her legs threatened to give out from something other than exhaustion.

With her back to the stairs, Rosabelle stood gazing out the window. Naked in preparation for her impending shift and illuminated in the sun's dying rays, her pale skin glowed ethereally, making Sage's breath catch.

"Your highness, I have returned," she announced, dropping to a knee and bowing her head.

Glancing over her shoulder, Rosabelle frowned. "Stop that," she huffed.

"Sorry," Sage muttered.

"It's fine," Rosabelle mumbled as her body began to tremble. Gripping the windowsill tightly, she stole another glance at Sage. "You look exhausted," she said with a sigh. "Take the bed."

Sage glanced between the nude woman before her and the twin-sized bed on the far side of the room. Her feet throbbed painfully from the endless walking, and it would be nice to sleep somewhere besides the hard floor, but in a royal's bed? There had to be a rule against that.

"Sage," Rosabelle called, drawing her attention. "I don't want you to get too close when I change." Still clinging to the windowsill, she stared down at her blanched knuckles. "I'd feel better knowing you are safe."

Sage hesitated. "You're sure?"

Rosabelle nodded.

"Alright, then," Sage said, allowing her tired shoulders to sag as she walked to the bed, dropped her pack beside it, and began to strip out of her leathers.

"Sage!" Rosabelle snapped. "What are you doing?"

Sage's hands froze on the last buckle of her leather jerkin as she turned to look at the princess, who was now openly staring at her. "What?" she asked, taking in Rosabelle's wide eyes and the crimson flush creeping up her chest and throat.

"Why are you stripping?" Rosabelle demanded.

"I don't want to dirty the bed with my gear," Sage explained but refrained from undressing further. *What? She's the only one that can be naked? Royals are strange.*

"Oh, right," Rosabelle mumbled and hastily turned back towards the window. "As you were."

Shaking her head, Sage stripped off the rest of her clothing and slid into the cushy bed, pulling the silky-soft covers up to her neck and settling down among the goose down pillows. The kingdom might have abandoned their heir but at least they'd left her with some comforts. Hell, this bed was nicer than anything Sage had owned. *Maybe once I've cured the princess, I'll be able to afford something better than straw-stuffed pillows,* she thought, and allowed her exhaustion to drag her eyes shut.

Something cracked loudly from across the room as a pained grunt echoed off the stone walls. Sage's eyes flew open and her stomach clenched nervously. She shoved herself up in time to see the gorgeous redhead's monstrous transformation. A heavy scent of sulfur filled the room, making Sage cough and her eyes water.

Quaking violently, Rosabelle hunched against the wall, using the windowsill to support herself as her spine length-ened and splintered outward. Jagged fins protruded from the nape of her neck and down the length of her back, split-ting the thin skin along her backside. Groaning in pain, she collapsed to the floor, writhing as scales the color of blood covered every inch of her flesh, and her face elongated outward into a reptilian snout.

Choking down a scream, Sage watched in horror as the princess doubled in size, sprouting enormous bat-like wings, horns, and a long tail. Unable to look away, Sage kept her eyes glued to the once beautiful woman as obsidian-colored talons curved out of her paws to click against the stone floors. Lengthening with her body's change, the manacles adorning her flesh remained clamped in place. Bulky silver chains budded off the restraints, dragging along the floor with a loud clatter as the great beast swished its tail and stood upright on all fours.

Sage scarcely dared to breathe as stark yellow eyes landed on her and slit nares flared, breathing her in. "Your highness–" she murmured, her lips trembling.

Baring fangs the length of her arm, the dragon snarled menacingly.

"Ro–Rosabelle?" Sage stuttered, clinging to the blanket as if it were a shield.

Cocking its head to the side, vertical slits bored into her before the dragon huffed out a sigh and turned away, curling into a tight ball at the far end of the room, lowering its head, and promptly shutting its eyes.

Sage watched the beast's breathing steady and deepen with sleep and continued to stare until her eyelids drooped once more with exhaustion. Releasing a shaky breath, she sank back among the pillows, breathing in the contrasting scent of campfire and sweet honey. She'd caught a whiff of it before while cutting the princess's hair.

A gentle presence caressed her cheek. With a contented sigh, she leaned into the touch and reached out, her fingers brushing against something soft as someone nearby murmured her name. "I had the strangest dream," she mumbled, running her thumb over the velvety material in her grasp and opened her eyes.

Blinking sleepily, she gazed up into the princess's flushed face. The other woman's eyes raked down her body and back again, lingering briefly on her lips, and finally meeting her gaze. "You must have been hot last night."

"Why would you say—" Pushing herself into a seated position, Sage glanced down and felt her cheeks heat. While sleeping, she had kicked off the covers and stripped out of her undergarments. To make matters worse, she clung to the hem of the princess's crushed velvet dress like a needy child. "S–sorry," she stuttered, snatching her hand back.

A slight smirk adorned the princess's full lips as she

turned away. "You should get dressed so we can get ready to leave."

"Right!" Sage sprang out of bed, quickly collecting her garments and thrusting them on. "I apologize, your highness! I didn't mean—"

Rosabelle whirled around, scowling with her hands on her hips. "How many times must I ask you to call me by my name?"

"Sorry," Sage murmured. "It's just..."

Rosabelle cut her off with a raised hand. "This has always been the problem," she grumbled, beginning to pace. "All anyone sees is what I'm supposed to be. No one sees me for me!" Hands curled into fists, she stopped abruptly. "I need a friend, not a servant."

I guess being a royal is lonelier than it looks, she thought with a frown. "I can do better." Sage shook her head. "No, I will do better," she vowed, motioning for Rosabelle to sit down on the bed and grabbing the bottle of henna she had bought.

Rosabelle stared straight ahead as Sage slathered her hair in henna. "What is the plan?"

Tension settled between her shoulders. Sage had known she would eventually have to share her plan but she still didn't feel ready. Would Rosabelle think she was an idiot? Would she refuse to go along with it? If she refused, they were both screwed.

Fuck it, she thought and launched into an explanation. "Our first step was to change how you look, and if you don't speak, I think you can pass as a man." When Rosabelle said nothing, she continued. "We will blindfold you so that you can't kill anyone on the road and camp out in the woods before nightfall so no one sees you change."

Rosabelle glanced up at her. "Don't you think people will ask why you are traveling with a deaf, blind mute?"

Sage nodded. "If we're stopped, I shall tell them that you are my deaf brother and that we must cover your eyes because the sun hurts them." Sage's heart rate sped up as she waited for Rosabelle's answer.

The other woman's shoulders sagged, and Sage inwardly cringed. *Shit, she hates it! What do I do now?*

"Sage," Rosabelle murmured, her lips quirking into a tentative smile as she turned to look at her. "It's brilliant," she complimented, grinning in earnest. "When do we leave?"

Traveling on foot, it would be days before they reached the kingdom, and Sage could only guess how long it would take them to find the witch. "As soon as your hair dries, we should go," she suggested while examining her work. The princess's brilliant red hair color had been replaced by a dark, muddy brown. This was going to work. It had to.

It'd taken Rosabelle's thick hair longer to dry than anticipated, and by the time they had eaten a quick breakfast and descended the winding staircase, it was nearing midday.

Hiding Rosabelle's eyes behind a faded strip of green fabric, Sage stepped back to admire the woman before her. Dressed in a baggy green tunic and brown linen pants, her outfit was completed by a pair of ugly cowskin slops. She was unrecognizable.

Rosabelle held out her hand. "You're going to have to guide me."

Capturing the offered hand in her own, she smiled as Rosabelle threaded their fingers together. Sage absentmindedly ran her thumb across the other woman's knuckles, marveling at how natural it felt to touch her when she realized what she was doing. Her eyes fell to the princess's slightly parted lips. *Would it feel as natural to kiss her?*

"Let's go." Rosabelle gave her hand a gentle squeeze.

Sighing softly, Sage shook her head and released Rosabelle's hand, shifting it until it rested lightly on her bicep. It would be easier to guide the blindfolded woman with her holding onto her arm. Leading the way, Sage kept watch for tripping hazards as she silently berated herself. She was being foolish and she knew it. The princess would never look at her like that. Not only was she a peasant, she was a *woman*. Even if they were able to break the curse, the most the king would offer her would be gold. There would be no titles, no land, and certainly no promise of the princess's hand in marriage. Those prizes were reserved for men and men alone.

After being on the road for a while, Rosabelle squeezed her arm gently. "Why are you helping me?"

A fresh pang of guilt twisted Sage's guts. "I already told you."

Rosabelle nudged her with her shoulder. "What is the real reason?"

Sage's shoulders sagged. "You won't like it."

"Tell me anyway," Rosabelle commanded, stopping short and withdrawing her hand when Sage didn't immediately reply.

Wrinkling her nose, Sage blurted out the truth. "Your father's decree stated that whoever rescues you will be rewarded with riches, land, and titles." She paused. "All things that I am in desperate need of."

Rosabelle nodded slowly. "Facing a dragon is not something one does out of the goodness of their heart." She sighed. "It makes sense."

Not knowing what else to say, Sage caught Rosabelle's

hand and rested it on her arm. They walked in silence as she led them deeper into the woods.

"Why?" Rosabelle murmured.

"Hmm?" Sage glanced at the blindfolded woman. "Why, what?"

"Why do you need them?"

Sage scoffed. "Not all of us are lucky enough to be born into royalty."

Rosabelle halted abruptly, dropping Sage's arm and yanking off her blindfold to glare at her. "Oh, yes! I forgot what a charmed life I lead!" she snapped, her hands curling into fists. "Because when my bloodline isn't getting me cursed, or I'm not being sequestered away like some valuable object, I get to be a prim and proper lady to make my father look good!"

Sage raised her hands in defeat. "I'm sorry. I didn't mean it like that."

"Then what did you mean?" Rosabelle growled, still glowering.

"You don't understand." Sage sighed, staring at the ground as she scuffed her boot against the dirt. "I'm trying to escape being sold like a prized cow to the highest bidder."

Closing the distance between them, Rosabelle tilted the shorter woman's face up until she had no choice but to look at her. "Until I was cursed, my father had every intention of finding a man to make me into the royal broodmare." She shook her head. "We are not so different."

"At least you will rule," Sage argued weakly.

"Only if my husband allows it."

Disgusted with herself, Sage pulled away. "I'm sorry, princ– Rosabelle." Glancing at the sky, she frowned. "We should probably set up camp for the night."

"Fine," Rosabelle said with a curt nod, replacing her blindfold and holding out her hand.

Sage guided them deeper into the woods, stopping only when the shadows grew long and she'd found a peaceful space next to the babbling brook.

Removing her blinder, Rosabelle ate her cheese and dried meats in silence. Sage could feel her eyes on her as she unrolled her sleeping pack on a bit of mossy ground.

"Won't you be cold?"

Glancing over her shoulder at the princess, she shrugged. *It's what I deserve.* "I'll be fine."

"What about making a fire?"

Sage shook her head. "We can't risk someone seeing the smoke."

"Fine," Rosabelle huffed. "Then I'll sleep next to you after I shift."

Sage stared at her wide-eyed. "Uh—I thought I couldn't be near you when you changed?"

"I wasn't sure how safe it would be but now I *know* I won't hurt you." Rosabelle blushed prettily.

"Wait... you weren't sure?" Sage squeaked.

"Pretty sure."

"Pretty sure?" Sage grunted.

Grinning sheepishly, Rosabelle shrugged.

Sage groaned into her hands. "Okay, fine. I'll sleep next to you—but just to stay warm!"

The sun sank lower, and Rosabelle began to strip.

I'm a total stranger, Sage thought with a shake of her head. *How is she so comfortable being naked in front of me?* Grimacing, she ignored the growing heat coiling low in her belly as she caught a glimpse of smooth, milky-white skin.

Sage cringed, averting her eyes as Rosabelle let out the first of many pained moans. The sickening crunch of bone and the squelch of shifting, tearing flesh was already too much; she couldn't bring herself to watch the beautiful woman transform. One viewing had been enough to give her nightmares for the rest of her life.

Facing away from Rosabelle's shifting body, she slid into her bedding. Squeezing her eyes shut and willing herself to sleep.

With a loud clatter of chains, the princess completed her shift and dropped to all fours. Flattening her enormous wings against her back, she padded over to Sage. Yawning widely, she stretched out behind Sage and curled her spiked tail around the much smaller woman.

The warmth of three roaring fires engulfed Sage's backside as the dragon settled beside her. Her reservations about the large beast's proximity quickly fled as she settled more comfortably into her bedding. Sage rolled onto her opposite side with a wide yawn, relishing in the warmth rolling over her front. *If I gotta sleep rough, this is the way to do it,* she thought, letting her tense muscles relax as she sank into sleep.

Breaking through the thick tree cover, the first rays of sunlight greeted Sage's sleeping form, kissing her eyelids and inviting her to join the waking world. Yawning, she rolled onto her back, opened her eyes, and froze. Rosabelle was snuggled against her with a bare leg thrown over her waist and a hand winding under the covers and beneath her shirt.

Sage's breath caught as the princess's soft fingers brushed against the underside of her breast, splaying out over her nipple. A needy ache settled low in her belly as she involuntarily arched into the princess's touch with a soft groan.

Shaking her head at her own stupidity, Sage gently

removed Rosabelle's hand from beneath her clothes, hoping that she hadn't disturbed the princess. She glanced over and found herself gazing into hungry yellow eyes.

Stuttering, Sage scrambled backward. "I'm sor—pray thee, forgive me—I wasn't trying to—"

Rosabelle gently placed a finger to her lips, effectively silencing her. "There are worse ways to greet the morning," Rosabelle murmured, sliding closer as her lips quirked into an amused smirk.

Smiling shyly in return, Sage allowed her gaze to linger on the royal's full, rose-shaped lips while moistening her own with her tongue.

Rosabelle's eyes followed the movement, and a full smile bloomed on her lips. "It's been too long," she sighed, gently stroking the still exposed skin at Sage's waist, "since I've been touched." Her fingers traced lower.

Sage's heart thundered as her nipples hardened into twin peaks. "I've never been touched," she admitted, feeling her cheeks flame.

Smirking wickedly, Rosabelle eyed her from beneath hooded lids. "Do you want to change that?"

"Aye," Sage breathed, "I'd like that."

"Good," Rosabelle purred, peeling back the remaining covers and straddling the smaller woman as she quickly removed the only thing separating them.

Laid bare beneath the princess, Sage shivered as Rosabelle's eyes roamed her body appreciatively, and Rosabelle licked her lips.

Sage gazed up into twinkling yellow eyes and shivered. She'd never thought that her first time would be with a cursed princess, let alone one as devastating as Rosabelle. Even the ugly bowl haircut she had given her failed to dim her beauty. If Sage was dreaming, she didn't want to wake up.

Rosabelle captured her lips in a searing kiss.

Arching into the kiss, Sage groaned softly, letting her hands wander as Rosabelle's tongue began to tease her own.

Without pulling away, Rosabelle shifted until her leg pressed against the aching spot between Sage's legs. Panting, Sage dug her fingers into Rosabelle's back as she slowly ground against her. Grinning mischievously, Rosabelle pulled back and ran the flat of her tongue along the swath of skin between Sage's throat and clavicle. Sage's soft gasps and moans littered the air as Rosabelle traveled lower.

Sage groaned loudly as hot lips encircled her nipple and sucked hard. Tangling her fingers in Rosabelle's unruly hair, she drew the woman closer. This was far better than anything she could've imagined. Heat pooled low in her belly as the other woman slid lower, raining heated kisses down on every inch of her exposed skin until Sage was sure she would combust.

Sage gasped as Rosabelle ensnared her leg and slid it over her shoulder.

"What are you—" Sage's question died on her lips as Rosabelle pressed her wet, throbbing pussy against her own, rocking her hips against her and quickly finding a rhythm that made them both moan. They came as one, limbs entangled and panting heavily.

Chest still heaving, Rosabelle collapsed beside Sage with a contented sigh, resting her head on Sage's shoulder. "Thank you," she murmured and shut her eyes.

Sage snuggled closer, enjoying the heat radiating off of her lover as the sensation of afterglow lulled her back to sleep.

"Shit," Rosabelle snapped nearby.

Heart pounding in her throat, Sage jerked awake. "What?"

"It's almost noon," Rosabelle grumbled, gazing at the sunlight filtering in through the tree canopy. "We're wasting daylight," she said decisively, standing and pulling on her dress.

"I wouldn't call it a waste," Sage murmured, offering a lopsided grin.

Smiling in return, Rosabelle stilled her frantic movements, coming over and squatting down beside her lover. Catching Sage's chin between her fingers, Rosabelle tilted her face upward, meeting her gaze and claiming her lips in a fierce kiss. "No, that most certainly wasn't a waste," she murmured and pulled away. Straightening to her full height, she rested her hands on her hips. "Come on, we need to go before we lose more daylight."

When they'd both dressed and Rosabelle's blindfold had been secured, they continued their journey toward home. The silence, although companionable, made Sage's skin itch. They'd slept together, and it'd been amazing, but what did it mean for their future? Even if they were able to break the witch's spell, would the king allow them to be together? Would Rosabelle even want more than a one-time tryst? Sage needed to know.

Steeling herself, Sage threw back her shoulders and brought them to a stop. As if sensing her trepidation, Rosabelle's fingers tightened around her bicep. Clearing her throat, Sage turned to face Rosabelle and froze.

Rosabelle's entire body had gone rigid.

Alarmed, Sage pulled back the blindfold, searching Rosabelle's eyes for any hint of what was happening. Panicked yellow eyes stared back at her.

"Rosabelle, what's h—" Before Sage got her question

out, something struck her side, sending her tumbling into a nearby tree. Winded by the impact, she gasped for air and frantically looked for what had attacked her, but beside Rosabelle's frozen form, nothing seemed out of the ordinary.

When at last she was able to draw in a proper breath, Sage scrambled to her feet. Scanning the trail for threats, she drew her sword and cautiously approached Rosabelle. "We need to go," she hissed through gritted teeth as her ribs throbbed painfully.

Rosabelle's gaze flicked between the surrounding wilderness and Sage. She blinked slowly but remained otherwise immobile.

Reaching out with her free hand, Sage shook her without success. "Rosabelle, come on!" What's happening?"

Again, an unseen force flung Sage into a tree and she felt something in her side snap. Her breath came in shallow gasps as she forced herself into a seated position. She tried to draw in a deep breath, but the sharp pain in her side stopped her. "Show yourself," she gasped.

A low rumble of laughter filled the air, building in intensity and evolving into a high-pitched cackle that made the small hairs on the nape of Sage's neck stand on end.

Materializing from the tree line, a tall, cloaked figure strode towards Rosabelle. Stopping in front of the frozen woman, they let their hood fall away, revealing shoulder-length black hair, high cheekbones, and gray eyes that sparkled with malice. Full lips pursed, the newcomer glared in Sage's direction. "Stay down!"

Sage's mouth went dry. Could this be the witch? She'd expected to encounter a gnarled crone, not this beautiful woman.

Still scowling, the witch returned her attention to

Rosabelle. "You surprised me," she murmured, reaching out and stroking the frozen woman's cheek. "I expected you to stay where *Daddy* put you." She shook her head at Rosabelle's widened eyes. "It was never a problem before," she commented dryly.

Too winded to stand, Sage had no choice but to sit and watch the exchange.

Rosabelle's lower lip trembled ever so slightly as the witch drew a silver key from beneath her cloak and waved it in front of Rosabelle's still face. "I bet you wish you'd chosen me over your gilded cage, now," she growled, taunting the princess with the key. "What should I do with you?" she murmured, circling the Princess and twisting the key between her fingers.

Chosen her? Sage's mind whirled. *Were they together?* Clamping down on her lower lip to keep quiet, she eyed Rosabelle and the woman circling her.

"You should've stayed in your tower!" the witch snapped, coming to a stop in front of Rosabelle. The witch's hand shot out, catching the princess's face in her hand as her long nails dug into soft skin. "Such a waste," she tutted. "If you weren't going to be mine, you could've at least rid the realm of a few dozen knights for me."

"Witch," Sage wheezed out, struggling to her feet. Her ribs throbbed painfully, and each breath brought a new pang of agony. She was sure she'd broken something, but that was a problem for later. She needed to save Rosabelle.

"Ah, yes. The would-be hero," the witch condescended. "What did she do to get you to do her bidding?" Sneering, she shook her head, "Let me guess, she promised love and riches?"

Sage's cheeks burned as she silently drew her sword. They'd only slept together once, but no promises had been made. Clenching her jaw against the pain, Sage raised her weapon and took a staggering step forward. "Get away from her," she demanded from between gritted teeth.

The witch's face split into a venomous smile. With a flick of her hand, Sage's sword tore itself free, launching into the air and burying itself to the hilt in the bark of a nearby tree.

The blood drained from Sage's face. How was she supposed to fight magic?

"Stop wasting my time!" the witch snapped. "This isn't about you," she growled, whirling back to the princess and turning her back on Sage.

Gritting her teeth until she was sure they'd crack, Sage drew her dagger and slowly advanced on the witch.

Either oblivious or indifferent to Sage, the witch kept her eyes trained on Rosabelle. "What do we think would send a clear message to the king?" she asked, tapping her chin. "Should I kill you and leave your body on the castle steps?" Shaking her head, she cradled Rosabelle's face in her hand. "I could keep you," she said thoughtfully, nearly whispering the last part, "chain you up until you love me."

If I make it out of this alive, Rosabelle has some explaining to do, Sage thought, steeling herself against the agony that was to come. Surging forward, she gathered what remained of her strength and plunged the knife into the witch's back.

The sharp blade sank into the woman's flesh, and unable to stop her forward momentum, Sage lost her balance, pulling her dagger free as she fell. Hitting the ground hard, she gasped in pain and rolled away. If her aim hadn't been true, she'd be a dead woman soon.

Bleeding profusely from the wound, the witch

screeched, thrashing and clawing at her back as bright red blood spurted onto the ground in sync with her heartbeat.

The witch stumbled towards the treeline, her movements quickly becoming too uncoordinated to escape. Taking a final, staggering step forward, she collapsed, chest heaving as the earth around her turned crimson and her breathing grew erratic. A wet gurgling sound filled the air as she weakly reached for her throat. After a long moment in which the woman trembled, her chest stilled, and her hand dropped to her side.

I did it, Sage thought, struggling to draw in a deep breath and rolling onto her back. The edges of her vision were growing hazy, and her head spun.

Rosabelle's manacles clattered loudly beside her. Jerking aside, Sage winced as sharp pain lanced up her side. Her vision continued to narrow until gentle hands encircled her face and the looming darkness receded enough for her to gaze into bright blue eyes.

Kneeling beside Sage, Rosabelle peered down at her. "You did it. You did it!"

"Told ya I would," Sage mumbled and promptly passed out.

When next she woke, Sage found her head pillowed on the princess's lap.

Rosabelle smiled warmly down at her. "Oh, good! I was wondering when you'd wake up."

Despite her body's protests, Sage sat up and drew an unsteady breath. "So," she said and offered the princess a lopsided grin. "You slept with a witch?"

Rosabelle's cheeks flushed brightly.

"You'll have to tell me all about it," Sage heaved herself to her feet, swaying unsteadily until Rosabelle rose and supported her. "On the way to the castle," she wheezed, still grinning.

"Of course, I owe you at least that much," Rosabelle murmured, a faint blush creeping up her neck as she cocked her head to the side and eyed Sage.

"What?" Sage asked curiously.

"I was just wondering," pausing, Rosabelle smirked. "If you'd ever considered marrying into royalty?"

Sage blanched, staring at Rosabelle like she had two heads. "It's not legal in this kingdom."

"Well, no. Not in this kingdom–" Rosabelle agreed, her eyes twinkling, "but if we go two kingdoms over, the laws are quite different."

Sage laughed softly. "After all that," she gestured behind them. "You just want to run away? What about the gold?"

Rosabelle cupped Sage's face, leaning in until they were a hair's breadth apart. "Am I not prize enough?"

Eyes lingering on Rosabelle's full lips, Sage nodded slowly. "You are."

"Then come away with me," Rosabelle murmured.

Grinning, Sage leaned into Rosabelle's touch. "It sounds like a fantasy come true."

"So is that a yes?"

"That's a yes." Closing the distance between them, Sage pulled her princess into a passionate kiss.

About the Author

Selina Rossman lives in New England with her wife and two cats. When she isn't working on the rig as a paramedic, she can be found writing something new, devouring a book or spending time in nature. Her debut novel, First On Scene A Howling Sirens Novel is now available everywhere books are sold! IG: @thewriterossman

Targeting the Heart
Erin Casey

Dragons, wizards, centaurs, and harpies. Siwani Bane had hunted a plethora of beings as a mercenary, but the latest target surprised her the most.

A bard.

She'd almost laughed when word reached her that the Mercenary Guild had their eyes on a little song bird. Bards weren't primarily high on their list. But her old mentor's inside information had brought her chuckles to a stuttering halt.

"They know 'bout her siren song," Merphy had told her. *"They think she can use et ta help 'em take down a dragon and steal its horde. Blundering idiots, the lot of them, but they're desperate and eager ta pay a handsome price."*

Siwani fingered the wanted poster in her hip pouch with a talon, expression grim.

A round of applause pulled Siwani's attention back to the tavern's stage. She sat in a corner, cloak draped around her body while she nursed a tankard of mead in one hand. Her cloak hid a pair of blue and violet wings folded down her back, as well as the numerous weapons strapped to her

290

body. No need to alarm the locals. She wasn't certain of their opinion of a Fenix like her. Some folks feared her since she bore wings that could burst into flames at will. How that was different from a wizard or sorcerer trained in fire magic, she didn't know, but she didn't feel like taking any chances or drawing unwanted attention to herself.

"That was a riveting performance," a man on stage said, waving off the last act. "And now, please welcome the musical, the magnificent, Malinga Vandala!"

The crowd erupted in cheers and thunked their tankards against the tables as a blur of gold, purple, and green ascended the stage. Malinga waved her hands in the air, one holding a pan flute with an emerald strap, the other a tambourine. Decorative orange, gold, and red clothing adorned her body, accented by rich purple trim. Her skirt opened at the front to another swath of cloth filled with purple and gold circles. Bright emerald boots and jewelry were a pleasant contrast. Her muscular arms moved freely, sun-kissed tan skin already glistening with sweat on such a warm summer night.

"Thank you, thank you, you're too kind!" Malinga said with a melodic cadence. She blew a kiss to the crowd and ran her fingers through her crimson and golden hair. "You can call me Linny. We're all friends here, after all! Now, where should I begin?"

"Ballad of the Princes!" someone shouted.

"Rapture Rivals!" came another cry.

Siwani smirked to herself as more beings made their favorite songs known. Her eyes roved over them then up to the stage. To her surprise, she found Malinga shooting a brief glance in her direction, a sly smile on the bard's face. Siwani froze. Those green eyes were piercing and full of life, both intoxicating and terrifying. A familiar tingle ran down her spine.

Malinga turned back to the crowd. "Wonderful suggestions, and I will get to them all tonight! But let's begin with Edgard's Talon!"

Most cheered while a few groaned that their song hadn't been chosen.

Siwani took a sip of her drink and scanned the room again. Everyone seemed to be enjoying themselves.

Well, almost everyone.

Two figures sat on the opposite end of the room from Siwani, watching Malinga not with excitement but with calculating eyes. The human man was dressed plainly, though his cloak hid most of his body. His companion, a woman halfling by her height, gobbled on a turkey leg, her gaze never once leaving Malinga.

Siwani narrowed her eyes.

Let them try something, she thought, as if willing them to sense the unspoken threat.

Malinga blew an introductive melody into her pan flute before launching into song.

"Way down the fallow road,
knave Edgard took to wing.
With sword and spear
and feathers bright,
he bore a mighty swing.

He traveled through the towns,
offering up his blade
to save the young,
to spare the old.
He rescued men and maids.

One fierce foe still lingered.
tormenting the crop fields.
A beast of wings
and scaly hide.
No knight could make him yield.

Knave Edgard took to flight.
His heart burned bright with rage.
He'd fight this beast
and save the lives
of those who feared rampage."

The music flowed into Siwani's ears, filling her with a wonderful warmth that eased some of the tension in her chest. Though she tried to keep her attention on the two beings, she found herself drawn back to Malinga. Between the verses, Malinga played the pan flute and danced around the stage in colorful swirls.

"Beware the dragon's strike,
a lesson Edgard learned.
He cleaved through horn
and dodged sharp claws,
but not without pained burns.

Smoke ignited feathers.
He tumbled to the floor.
His sword was thrown.
His fate unknown.
Terror trembled his core.

He crawled o'er to his blade.
He swore he'd give his life

to save their towns
and rescue them,
no matter pain and strife.

The dragon made to feast,
his vicious fangs drawn wide.
But then a light
with magic flare
glistened at Edgard's side."

Siwani swallowed hard as Malinga reached the edge of the stage closest to her. Their eyes met again. She tried to ignore the warmth flooding her cheeks and in her loins.

"Goddess of song and strength
blessed his talons with light
'Stand my dear brave
warrior, knight.
Now we shall win this fight.'

Edgard attacked the beast.
Talons tore through scaled hide.
The dragon roared.
The Goddess soared.
'Now strike his throat!' she cried.

Edgard obeyed her words.
He drove talons straight through
the dragon's neck.
The beast collapsed.
From his flesh, flowers grew.

Edgard bowed to his God.

'Goddess, why did you come?
I'm just a knave,
a lowly man,
unworthy of you, great one.'

The Goddess laughed and beamed.
'Dear boy, I choose my knights.
Your heart is true.
Your bravery known.
You've saved them from this plight.

You shall rise my champion
and use your talons' might
to save the land
and serve me well
'til your eyes hold no light.'

So it goes, Knight Edgard
fought bravely through the land.
He served his God
and townsfolk, both,
'til his flesh became sand."

As Malinga played the final verse, the crowd clapped and stomped their feet to the beat. Even Siwani felt her foot tapping under the table. Most of all, she couldn't tear her eyes away from Malinga.

It was no wonder clients had warned the Mercenary Guild of Malinga's gift.

She reminds me more of some sort of enchantress than a bard, Siwani mused.

Malinga put her tambourine away and pulled out a golden bell on her hip. "Now then, let's jump to Ballad of the Princes!" As another cheer went up, Malinga launched into the next song.

The mead flowed, beings dancing to Malinga's melodies. Siwani tried not to watch her, but it was hard to ignore the music circling the room, prowling like some sort of mystical predator ready to leap into her ears and enchant her mind. Siwani knew *some* spells to guard her thoughts, but she didn't think it would work against music.

Just another thing to add to her list of skills to learn.

Siwani nursed her mead, glancing periodically at the two figures more obviously watching Malinga. Hopefully, they were mere admirers and not something more like assassins. This was no place to start a scrap; the tavern keeper had been known to spill the guts of troublemakers.

When the next song came to a boisterous close, the tavern exploded in claps and some drunken cheers. Malinga spun and bowed, her skirts swishing around her like the petals of a closing rose.

"Thank you, thank you! You've been a great audience!"

"Encore, encore!" a few shouted.

Malinga laughed and hooked her bell onto her belt. "Alas, I'm parched, my friends. But rest assured, I will return. I've heard the pockets of Galena are generous and bountiful."

In response, coins cascaded around her in a glittering shower. Malinga bowed deeply and began gathering them up.

Siwani finished off her tankard and opened a pouch, grasping a coin. She looked over at Malinga and held it between two fingers. The gold glinted in the tavern light and caught Malinga's attention. The bard cocked her head. She grinned and made her way over.

"Generous, indeed!" Malinga said and offered a polite curtsey before taking the coin.

"You played well," Siwani replied in a low, gruff voice. "Haven't heard some of those songs in ages."

Malinga chuckled, fanning herself with her hand. "You're too kind. I noticed you watching. Another music lover, perhaps?"

"Just appreciative of good talent," Siwani said, her gaze sweeping up and down Malinga's plump, beautiful body.

"Uh huh." Malinga eyed the gold coin then winked. "Wait here."

Malinga swept through the room. The people parted for her easily, some praising her as she went. A few shot Siwani a dirty look, as if offended Malinga had spoken to her privately.

If only they knew.

"Just appreciative o' good talent, eh?" a deep, heavily accented voice mocked behind her.

Siwani jumped and shot a look over her shoulder. Unlike her, this Fenix wasn't hiding himself in a cloak. No, he stood proudly beside her table, all four feet of him, a pipe sticking out of the corner of his mouth. His bright red hair twisted atop his head, matching the color of his scraggly beard that had caught flames more than once. Most of his attire seemed normal with a mix of metal and leather armor, but he also wore a very distinct pink kilt, though Siwani thought it too short to be called that. Thank the Goddess he had on pants.

The most distinct thing about him was his pair of red and gold wings. Tiny flames flickered on the tips of his feathers at times but were at no risk of lighting up the place. Fenixes had far more control than that over their fire. Honestly, the most dangerous weapon on him was his sharp tongue followed swiftly by the skull-crushing hammer on his hip.

"Merphy?" she hissed. "What are you doing here?"

Merphy's red bird-like eyes glinted, a smirk quirking his lips. "Makin' sure ya get the job done, lass." He shifted and plucked the pipe from his mouth. "The Guild wanted ta make sure one o' us followed through." He wiggled his bushy eyebrow at her.

Siwani curled her lip. "This is my territory. Go find your own."

Merphy released a belly laugh that could've shaken the rafters. Heads whipped around to look at them, much to Siwani's chagrin.

"*Idiot, you're going to get us caught,*" she grouched at him in their tongue.

"*Who looks more suspicious? Me with all me fine features on display, or the mysterious cloaked figure with peepers practically popping out o' yer head?*"

Siwani scoffed. "*You have your methods, and I have mine. I'd like to think mine are far less obvious.*"

"*Keep tellin' yerself that, lass. Guess it's a race to see who saves the pretty damsel.*"

"Merphy—"

But Merphy was already winding away from her, the pipe stuck between his lips. He headed for the bar at the same time Malinga turned around with two tankards and a plate of meat and cheese. Siwani tensed as her fellow Fenix mercenary stepped in front of the bard. He gave a sweeping bow and beamed at her.

"Lovely voice, lass. Ya thawed me cold, cranky heart."

Malinga blushed, chuckling. "I must have the blessings of the Goddess to wield such magic, then." She offered him a cheeky smile which set off another booming laugh.

"I like ya, lass. Good evening ta ya." He bowed his head and spread his arm, letting her pass harmlessly by.

Siwani shot him a withering look until Malinga returned to the table. The bard placed the drinks and food down and sat in the chair opposite of her.

"Hope you don't mind," Malinga said, pushing an ale across the table toward Siwani's hand. "I haven't had supper, and I like dining with a crowd. And with good company."

Siwani cleared her throat and picked up the drink. She fingered the ring on a necklace hidden beneath her dark tunic. "I can promise I'm not as entertaining as you."

"Did I say I needed entertainment?" Malinga teased. She nudged the plate. "Have some."

Siwani eyed the food and shook her head. "Ale is enough, thank you." She raised the tankard then took a sip.

"Any signs of trouble?" Malinga whispered, catching Siwani off guard. She coughed on her drink and quickly set the tankard down. She gave Malinga a look.

"I'm afraid I don't know what you mean," Siwani remarked.

Malinga pressed her lips together and sighed dramatically. "*Fine, let's talk like this then,*" Malinga said, using the Fenix language. There were few around who knew it. As a bard, Malinga was trained in many tongues.

Siwani snorted and picked her tankard back up. "*You know, it's going to be hard to keep up the ruse that we don't know each other if we get familiar like this.*"

"*Considering it's my life in danger, and you're putting yourself between me and another mercenary's blade, I like to be in the know.*" Malinga held her drink between both hands. She glanced up beneath hooded eyelids. "*I'm worried about you.*"

"You're the one with the price on your head. I'll be fine so long as you're safe."

"Still charming me, my beloved," Malinga said with a sweet little giggle.

Siwani blushed. She tugged her hood down over her face. Yes, she was smitten, and had been for years. They'd met long ago while Siwani was on a mission. She'd heard Malinga's songs back then too and had been captivated by her magic. Nothing had changed about that ever since, other than they both wore wedding rings on chains around their necks.

The Mercenary Guild was going to pay for putting a bounty out on her wife.

"Well?" Malinga pressed.

"I saw a couple patrons watching you, and I didn't get the sense they were here for the show." Siwani took a drink and glanced in the far corner where the man and the halfling were. A third figure had joined them, and the mere sight of him made Siwani's feathers quiver with barely bridled rage. *"I think we have our culprits. I know the third one who joined the party."*

Malinga's bushy eyebrows rose. *"Who?"*

"Talon," Siwani all-but growled.

"Oh...oh no. Wasn't he the one who—"

"Yep, he left me for dead after a mission went south. Blamed the failure on me to our boss, Corvis, and nearly got me kicked out of the Mercenary Guild." Siwani wasn't one to forget a face, especially not the scarred visage of *that* backstabber. He had the same smarmy smirk. His right eyepatch was also a dead giveaway. If he was here, then that definitely meant Malinga was his target. He wouldn't pass up a job that paid that much money. *"So far, I count three.*

Merphy might've spotted others, but between the two of us, we'll keep you safe."

Malinga propped her head on her hand and smiled adoringly at Siwani. *"Beloved, I think you forget how many beings I can enchant with my song."*

Siwani felt a lurch in her stomach. While she knew Malinga was right, she couldn't bear the thought of losing her wife should something go wrong. *"If you don't struggle, there's less chance they'll hurt you."* Her brow knitted together. *"Please, Linny. Let me handle this. This is what I'm trained for."*

Malinga huffed a sigh. *"Very well, I'll play the damsel in distress."* She shot Siwani the stink eye. *"One of these days, I'll be the one saving you."*

Siwani fought back a grin. *"While I pray to the Goddess that day never comes, I know I'll be in good hands if it does."* Oh, how she wanted to leap across the table and sweep Malinga up in her arms and take her away from the threat. In truth, Siwani wanted to steal Malinga back to their bedroom so they could distract each other with something far more pleasant.

They shared a private look before Malinga closed her eyes. "It's been a delight speaking with you, friend," she said loud enough for others nearby to hear. "But I should retire for the evening."

"Do you have a room here?" Siwani asked.

"Tch! My, aren't you being forward?" Malinga said, teasing. "My traveling cart will do. May the Goddess shine her blessings on you." Malinga rose and bowed politely.

Siwani nodded in return, her eyes begging Malinga to be careful.

Malinga winked. She stepped away from the table, her

outfit jingling. The moment she reached the door, Talon and his crew exchanged glances and slid out of their chairs.

Siwani set a coin next to her drink. Like a whisper, she swept toward the opposite outside door, praying Malinga wouldn't do anything stupid before she got there.

MALINGA HUMMED TO HERSELF. THE COOL SUMMER night air brushed over her skin and flushed her cheeks. Moonlight illuminated her bangles and bell, making her a perfect target for mercenaries on the hunt. This wasn't the first time unsavory folks had come after her. Her gift was a special one, though she only used its full power when absolutely necessary. A song that could control someone's emotions and mind was far too dangerous under normal circumstances. She would've dealt with these fools without Siwani's help had she seen the poster before her wife. Alas, Siwani was in hero mode, and while Malinga didn't begrudge Siwani wanting to protect her life, sometimes she wished her beloved trusted her enough to take care of herself.

Then again, Siwani seemed to know these people, so perhaps they were far more dangerous than Malinga gave them credit for. She'd noticed their eyes on her during the performance. The energy rippling off of them (an energy she could sense through the vibrations of their voices) was dark, sinister. Nothing good would come from them especially if Malinga and Siwani weren't careful.

Malinga tossed her hair behind her shoulder and headed for the cart she'd taken with Siwani to the tavern. It was in a darker patch of land near the road, an enticing place for villains to snatch up their precious prey. Already, she'd heard the tavern door open and close behind her. Though their steps were quiet, Malinga could still hear them on her tail.

Give it a minute. Let them think they're safe. Malinga reached the back of her wagon and turned to open it. She jumped, pretending to just notice the movement from the corner of her eye. "Oh! Greetings, friends," she said cheerfully, her hand still on the wagon.

The trio stopped. While the human man kept a lookout, Talon and the woman stepped closer.

"That was a mighty lovely performance," Talon said with a grin that reminded Malinga of a rat's sneer. "We meant to toss some more coins up there, but you were already leaving. Here." He stuffed his hand into his pocket and held out a bright gold coin. "For your performance. Perhaps we could entice you to play for our master. He's having a great banquet, and we could really use a lovely musician like you to get the blood pumping." He leaned forward, winking. "We can make it worth your while."

Malinga sighed inwardly. It was a trap, obviously. Even if she hadn't known they were after her, Talon's sniveling voice would've driven her away. She knew she should accept the money and croon over the offer so Siwani could come in and save the day. But Talon's face was so punchable, and three people were hardly a challenge to take on, mercenary or not.

"You're quite kind, sir," she sang to him, directing her voice to Talon, the woman, and the lookout. "But I'm afraid I must decline. Your sweet words are poison, and you're no friend of mine."

Green magic swirled in front of her eyes as she wrapped them up in her song. She could march them off a cliff to their deaths were she so inclined. Or perhaps a jail cell would be more fitting. "Unsheathe your blades, and place them there," she gestured toward a spot near her wagon. "Then on your knees, you will–"

Something cracked across the back of Malinga's head. Blinding pain burst through her skull and sent her to the ground. Before she could gather her senses, a gag was shoved into her mouth and bound at the nape of her neck. Hands grappled with hers, twisting her wrists behind her and binding them with coarse rope. Malinga swore into the gag and looked up as Talon and his people shook their heads, coming out of their trance.

"I told you not to trust her, you idiots," a new man snarled behind her. He tangled his fingers into her hair and pulled, dragging her up to her feet.

Malinga cried out in pain.

"Sorry, sir," Talon growled. He fisted his hand. "Oh, wench, you're going to pay for that."

A hemp bag was yanked over her face, and for the first time, Malinga started to panic. There were more mercenaries than she and Siwani had thought! Had Siwani *and* Merphy both been snatched, too? Normally, Siwani would've done something by now! Sweat beaded Malinga's brow. Rough hands grabbed her arms and started to drag her away. She released muffled screams of fear.

A burst of blue light suddenly filled the air, the only thing Malinga could see through the hemp bag. Two people grunted and fell. The man holding her swore and pressed a cold, sharp blade against her throat.

"You take a step closer, and I'll give her another smile!" he shouted.

"No, you won't," Siwani said in an icy voice. "The poster says she's wanted alive. You'd forfeit your treasure.

Drop her, and I might consider letting you run away with both your legs."

The man swore and pressed the blade harder, causing it to cut into Malinga's flesh. She squeaked in alarm.

The blade was yanked away and the man fell backwards with a cry. His hand grasped at Malinga, but he only managed to grab and rip off the bag. It still caused her to stagger and fall to her side. As she suspected, the lookout and the woman were already dead on the ground with Siwani's daggers in their backs. Her beloved Fenix towered over them with her blue and violet wings spread out behind her, the feathers burning with fire (the light Malinga had seen through the bag).

Talon scrambled away from Siwani, keeping his sword protectively in front of himself. Malinga looked behind her shoulder and saw Merphy standing over the other man, a boot to his throat. Merphy balanced himself on his war hammer, which was firmly planted on the would-be mercenary's chest. He puffed on a cigar the entire time, a smirk on his rugged face.

"Seems ya picked the wrong treasure ta' steal, lad," Merphy snarked. "Now, how many more are ya?"

The man glared back at Merphy.

The Fenix gave a grave nod. "Ah, I see, me very presence must've made ya go mute. Well, we can get yer tongue waggin' again." He pushed down on the war hammer and slid the cigar from his mouth. He leaned over, putting the burning end near the man's face.

"Wait, wait!" the mercenary cried. "It's us! They told me to wait out here in case there was any funny business!"

Merphy paused then brought the cigar to his mouth. "Ya hear that, lass? Funny business, he calls et." He chuckled as he looked at Siwani. His head snapped around like a viper and zeroed in on the man. "Well, I don't think this lass," he nodded toward Malinga, "finds it very funny. Too bad. I hate dirtying me clothing." In one swift move, he snatched up the hammer, whirled it, and brought it down on the man's face with a loud crack and a squelch.

Malinga gagged at the sight and rolled away.

Siwani slammed Talon up against the side of the wagon, talons wrapped around his throat. "Is what he said true? Are there any more of you?"

Talon grappled with the talons pricking his skin. "Are you going to kill me too even if I tell you the truth?"

"Depends on how much you piss me off."

Talon glared into Siwani's eyes. "Not much incentive then." He choked as she tightened her hold. "It's just us!" he cried. "We only wanted the bard. We were going to let her go once it was all done!"

Siwani leaned in close. "I know your way, Talon. You forget, you betrayed *me* when times got hard. You really think I trust that for a second?" She flipped a blade up in her hand. "I'll make sure you don't come after us again."

As Siwani moved, Talon grasped something on his neck. He crushed it in his hand, releasing noxious purple fumes that sent Siwani reeling backwards. Malinga tried to roll away from it, but the smoke spread swiftly. It filled her eyes and nostrils, making them burn. She yelped and desperately tried to press her face into the grass to get it off.

Warm arms suddenly held her. Gusts of wind whipped around her, sending the smoke away. The moment the air cleared, Malinga gasped for breath. She looked up at Siwani who still had red-rimmed eyes, but otherwise looked no worse for wear. Siwani smiled sadly at her then reached behind Malinga's head to undo her gag.

"I'm sorry. Merphy and I were waiting to see if more would come out. I knew they wouldn't kill you."

"No, just try to split my skull open," Malinga complained, but she made sure to smile so Siwani didn't think she was angry. She rested in her wife's arms while Siwani supported her and untied her wrists. "I've got you." Siwani lifted her into her arms and wrapped her warm wings around Malinga.

Malinga glanced down at the dead bodies. A little bile jumped up her throat at the awful sight. "Where's Merphy?"

"He went to track down Talon," Siwani explained. She stepped over a dead body and carried Malinga toward the tavern. "Don't worry. Even if Merphy doesn't find him, Talon's boss will probably punish him for failing. They won't try this again." Siwani kissed her forehead sweetly. "For now, let's get you to our room so you can rest."

"The bodies?" Malinga asked, glancing back toward them. They quickly disappeared into the darkness.

"Merphy will take care of it. Now rest. I've got you, Linny."

Malinga smiled up at her wife. "I know."

Siwani sat in a wooden tub with Malinga resting against her bare chest. The coals burned beneath them, keeping the water nice and hot. Any time it grew cold, Siwani swept a wing toward the coals and reignited them. She'd intended to wash Malinga, but considering Siwani, too, now had blood on her, a joint bath made more sense.

It also meant she could hold her beautiful naked wife.

She nuzzled her face into Malinga's hair, breathing in

her scent. That whole plan could've gone a lot worse had there been more mercenaries. She and Merphy had been right to suspect backup, but it hadn't been easy watching Malinga be taken down, bound, and gagged. If Siwani could slit their throats again, she would.

"Your heart is pounding," Malinga said in a soft tone. She trailed her fingers up and down Siwani's bare arm soothingly.

Siwani sighed. She pulled Malinga's long hair to the side and kissed her warm neck. "I'm glad you're safe."

"Me too," Malinga whispered.

Siwani paused. She slid an arm around Malinga's waist and held her wife firmly against her body. "I wasn't going to let them take you, I swear it."

"It's not that." Malinga leaned her head back, her nose brushing Siwani's chin. "You and Merphy dispatched them so quickly. I didn't think we'd have to...kill them all."

Siwani frowned deeply. "They would've kept coming after you."

"Are you sure?" Malinga turned a little to look at her. "I caught them in my song. If you'd ungagged me, and I had sung to them again, maybe I could've sent them on their way; made them forget about me. About us."

A tightness settled in Siwani's chest. She had to remind herself that Malinga wasn't used to being on the battlefield. Sometimes death was inevitable. It was both the only and the kindest option. "They would've held you captive. Used up your magic. If we'd let them go, they would've come back with reinforcements. Or if not that, their master would've killed them anyway for their failure."

"You don't know that," Malinga argued.

"Linny..." Siwani slipped her finger beneath her wife's chin and lifted it. "I'm sorry, but I couldn't take the risk.

They knew what could happen. Every mercenary has to prepare themselves for death before they go on a mission. Talon's crew was cocky, thinking their only challenge would be taking a bard. They didn't account for how tough that particular bard was, and who she had watching over her." Siwani pressed her head against Malinga's, her breath catching in her throat. "Please don't hate me. You knew who I was when you married me," she said, slipping her fingers to the ring dangling from her necklace.

To Siwani's surprise, Malinga turned fully and pulled Siwani into a hug of her own. "Don't *ever* say that," Malinga said tearfully. "I could never hate you, Siwani. I love you. I —oh, never mind, it doesn't matter."

"No." Siwani kissed the top of her head. "No, this is important to you. I'm listening, Linny. I'm letting my own defensiveness come out. And I'm still learning. It's hard to let go of my old ways."

Malinga heaved a deep sigh and kissed Siwani sweetly on the neck. "I feel bad about their deaths. I've never had to kill anyone because my song has always been enough. And I don't use the darker songs that cause pain and death." She looked down at her hands, shivering. "I'd rather bring joy and happiness to the downtrodden than to use my song to take over their minds and force them to do...unspeakable things to themselves and others. Where there is life, there is also death. Balance. I've never had reason to use my music to cause harm, and I never want to. And yet..." Malinga shook her head. "Part of me feels like their blood is on my hands."

"You didn't deliver the death blow."

"No, I just led them into a trap," Malinga murmured.

Siwani hugged her tighter. "Linny, I think you have a big enough heart for both of us." She ran her fingers up and down Malinga's back before cradling her wife's head in her hand. "And I love you for that."

A little blush and a smile grew on Malinga's face. "I love you, too."

They gazed into each other's eyes, Malinga's emerald irises drawing Siwani in. She pulled Malinga into a deep kiss, which she returned eagerly. Two thick thighs slid around Siwani's waist. Warmth flooded through Siwani's nether regions, and it had nothing to do with the hot tub. Their hands explored each other's bodies, caressing, applying pressure that left the other moaning. Siwani slid her fingers down between their legs and—

The window blew open as a stout figure flew through and landed in a crouch feet away from the tub. Malinga screamed. Siwani nearly threw herself out of the tub to attack, damn her nakedness, until she spotted the culprit tugging a new cigar from his belt.

"Merphy!" she shouted, incredulous. Siwani swept her wings around herself and Malinga, covering her wife's modesty.

Merphy held the cigar out to one of his wings. A flame sparked and lit the tip of it. "Ach, no need ta hide. Not like I haven't seen a lass undressed before."

Malinga splashed water at him. "Merphy, get out!" She hid against Siwani, turning crimson.

Siwani glowered. "Why can't you come through the door like a normal person?"

"Gotta keep 'em guessing yer next move," Merphy replied with a wink. He leaned back against the wall and folded his arms and legs. "Talon gave me the slip. Followed that bastard as long as I could then, *pop*, he vanished. Probably a backup spell ta transport him away from danger.

Why the dullard didn't use that earlier, yer guess be as good as mine."

"Talon escaped," Siwani repeated.

"Aye, got soap in yer ears? That's what I said."

A slew of curses bubbled out of Siwani's mouth, most in the Fenix tongue. She looked down at Malinga who seemed far more relieved than Siwani expected. Then again, after their talk...Siwani bit back her better judgement and hugged her wife again. "Let it be, Merphy. He knows death awaits him if he pulls another stunt like that."

Merphy's eyebrows rose sharply. He looked ready to argue (after all, he'd been the one to teach her not to leave any loose ends), but then he must've caught sight of Malinga's expression. He held up his hands. "Fine, fine. I doubt we'll see him any time soon. Tavern should be safe tonight." He jerked his thumb toward their bedroom. "I'm in the room down the hall if ya need me."

"Good," Siwani said then pointed at the door. "Now, will you leave us alone so we can finish bathing, you old pervert?"

Merphy snorted loudly. "Keep yer window locked next time," he called over his shoulder as he slipped out of the bathing room.

Siwani ran a hand down her face. "That old idiot is lucky I adore him, otherwise I would've strangled him by now. Are you okay?" she asked, looking between her fingers at her wife.

Malinga was still scarlet, but mischief sparkled in her eyes. "That was quite thrilling, wasn't it? Getting caught like that?"

Siwani cocked her head. "I suppose?" Her eyes widened. "Wait, did that turn you—"

Before she could finish, Malinga giggled and threw

herself at Siwani, dunking them both beneath the water and into another delicious kiss.

MALINGA SNUGGLED AGAINST SIWANI IN BED, HER wife's arms wrapped tightly around her. She slept deeply, body and mind both comforted by their fun in the tub. While she expected to have nightmares, her mind was quiet and at peace.

At least until a loud crash jolted her awake.

Malinga and Siwani both jerked up in alarm. Someone had thrown open their bedroom door and smashed it into one of the windows. Glass tumbled to the floor and crunched under a heavy boot. Two figures sprang at them.

Siwani punched one full in the face before he could grab her. Malinga rolled out of bed and to the rug. A hand snatched her by her hair and jerked her back against the bed. He wrapped his arm around her throat, strangling her before she could utter a single note.

"Linny!" Siwani shouted.

The man holding Malinga suddenly screamed and dropped her. Malinga choked and scrambled backwards as Siwani threw him into a wall with talon marks gouged into his chest. Siwani went for her blades when four more people burst through the door, weapons drawn. Malinga tried to shout a warning, but her aching throat wouldn't allow it.

Siwani, dressed only in a simple long tunic, whirled with her wings spread and blades drawn. Fire flared on the tips of her feathers. Her eyes widened at the sight of their attackers. But instead of throwing herself at them, she looked sharply at Malinga. Siwani's fear wasn't for herself, it was for *Malinga.*

Don't do anything stupid! Malinga wanted to scream.

Siwani vaulted over the bed, putting herself between their attackers and her wife. She slapped her wings in front of herself and sent a wave of fire cascading toward the advancing figures. One ducked, while two cried out as their clothes were set aflame. They tossed their cloaks to the ground, not caring as the rug and curtains caught fire.

"Get out of here," Siwani hissed at Malinga, chin jerking toward the door.

Malinga shook her head stubbornly. She grabbed the closest thing that might be of use: a fire poker. As Siwani took on the next attacker, Malinga swung as hard as she could, cracking the front of it against a woman's face. The mercenary went down hard, clutching a broken jaw.

The rest set upon Siwani, sliding in to strike and stab her without actually killing her. Few had their attention on Malinga. She could only assume they were trying to subdue Siwani so they could get to *her.*

Malinga ground her teeth and struck someone else in the back with the poker as he was about to stab Siwani in the wing. He shouted in pain then turned, backhanding Malinga across her face. It knocked her into the wall, dazing her. She looked up as someone wrapped a collar with a chain lead around Siwani's throat. They yanked hard, taking her to the ground with a strangled gurgle. Her fire instantly fizzled out.

"No!" Malinga finally managed to cry. She sprang to her feet with the poker and rushed them. She wouldn't let them hurt Siwani! Her poker stabbed into a woman and then a man. As she raised her weapon above her head, she was struck from behind. Malinga fell. Her attacker grabbed her by the throat and hefted her up. In an instant, she recognized the enraged face. Talon!

"You're entirely too much trouble," he growled at her and dragged her to the window. "But thanks to you, now we have who we really want." He looked at Siwani viciously as she was beaten and bound.

Malinga's mouth dropped. They wanted Siwani? Had this all been a trap? She reached out for her wife, hand groping uselessly. If only she was strong enough to protect Siwani! Their eyes met for a split second; her wife's face twisted in horror as she realized what was about to happen. She tried to fight off her attackers again, but it was too late. With a sneer, Talon shoved Malinga out the window.

Malinga fell, hand still outstretched. She waited for the hard earth to greet her. It would be kinder than enduring the guilt ripping through her heart and soul. She'd failed Siwani. She'd let them—

Something hit her from the side. Suddenly she was no longer falling. Malinga yelped. She looked up and gaped at the familiar burnt beard above her head. Merphy!

"Hold on, lass," Merphy grunted, arms tightening around her.

"Bu-But, Siwani!" she choked out, struggling.

"Nothin' we can do fer her now. Just trust me." He looked at her, fire burning in his eyes. "We'll get her back, Linny."

Malinga wrapped her arms around his neck and looked back at the tavern. She watched the dark figures drag Siwani out as fire began to lick the roof of their room. With a sob, Malinga pressed her head to Merphy's chest and let him carry her far away from the fight and from Siwani.

They stopped sometime later south of the tavern. Merphy landed roughly, jostling Malinga without dropping her. Instead, he fell to his knee and set her back on her feet. Malinga rose quickly and turned, ready to demand what they were going to do next.

Blood stained Merphy's left leg.

"You're hurt!" Malinga cried, kneeling beside him.

"'Tis but a flesh wound," Merphy said with a smirk, but he couldn't hide the pain in his eyes.

"Sit down right now and let me look at it."

"We don't have time fer that, lass—" he started to argue.

Malinga shot him a fiery glare. "I said SIT! I've already lost one person I care about. I'm not about to lose another."

Merphy grumbled, but he did as she commanded. He leaned back with a groan and stretched his leg out. Malinga rolled up his pants and grimaced at the sight of the gash in his leg. It had to be from a blade, but at least it didn't look like it had cut him too deeply. She reached to her hip where she usually pocketed a healing kit, but her fingers brushed her cloth nightgown instead.

All her belongings were back at the tavern.

"No," she whispered.

"Oy," Merphy said and tossed her a bag. "Ya ain't the only one who keeps a kit on hand."

"You could've started with that," Malinga complained. She opened the satchel and pulled out a bone needle and thread. She did her best to clean up his wound and added a poultice over it to help numb his skin. "Talon was in the tavern," Malinga said between clenched teeth as she started weaving the needle and thread through his flesh.

Merphy barely batted an eye. "Aye. I saw him chuck ya from the window." He sighed heavily. "They came after me, too. Caught me while I was out takin' a piss. What sort o' bastard attacks another with his drawers down?" He snorted, offended. "Couldn't get ta ya both in time to warn ya. I'm sorry."

"You stopped me from breaking my neck," Malinga said and looked up at him. "I wouldn't have survived that fall without you." She swallowed a lump in her throat, an image of Siwani getting yanked down by the collared noose around her neck flashing in front of her eyes. "Who has Siwani? How are we supposed to get her back?"

"Corvis." Merphy said the name like a curse. "He once hired me and Siwani for a mission before we met ya. He wanted us ta do some dark things, be his enforcers when money was due. Never sat well with Siwani. He tried ta hire us full time, but Siwani refused. And then she turned the authorities on him, though she did it in such a way we didn't think he could prove it was her." Merphy winced as Malinga tied off the thread. "He's been after her fer awhile, now. Thought he was off our tail, especially with how Siwani was layin' low. But once he put that hit out on ya." He waved his hand. "We were duped. So now Talon's likely bringin' her back ta Corvis ta get his reward."

Malinga's shoulders fell. It sounded so hopeless. She'd barely survived facing only a couple of mercenaries, and Merphy had been wounded. How would they even find Siwani, much less save her?

No, you can't think like that, Malinga scolded herself. *Siwani would find you, come hell or high water. You can't abandon her. You still have your song, and Merphy still has his hammer and sass. You can't, no, won't leave her to Corvis.*

She took a deep, calming breath. "Okay. We know who has her and why. What are our next steps? How do we find and save her?"

A slow smile creased Merphy's grizzled face. "That's mah lass. Just so happens I managed ta hear where they were goin'. I know that hide out. We'll go get some supplies, weapons, and clothes first then go after Siwani. We'll be up against a motley crew, lass. But if we can get Siwani free, then the three o' us can take 'em down. Especially if you use that voice of yours."

"Oh, I'll do more than that," Malinga said coolly as she rocked back on her heels. Maybe before she would've shown them mercy and forced them to drop their blades. But now, she'd make them put those blades to much better use. She'd break her own promise to herself not to use the songs of destruction.

Soon, they'd learn how truly terrifying a little bard could be.

ICY WATER SPLASHED ACROSS SIWANI'S FACE, STARTLING her awake. She coughed and tried to wipe her eyes clear, but her wrists were chained above her head to a loop sticking out of a pole. Chains and leather straps tethered her wings to her back. Siwani shook her smarting head and took stock of her situation. Bound wrist to ankle. Wearing only a long tunic; her weapons were all missing. No wonder they'd been attacked while in bed. It made it less likely that Siwani would have her blades. And Malinga...

Siwani's eyes grew wide. Malinga! The last thing she remembered was Talon throwing Malinga out the window and then someone pulling a bag over her own head and knocking her unconscious. Gods, had they taken Malinga too? Or had they left her for dead?

She concentrated on her fire magic and tried to ignite her feathers to destroy the straps bound around her, but no flame came when called. Instead, she felt the collar around her neck heat up, as if absorbing her power. Not even her natural Fenix magic could save her; she'd been cut off.

A bucket clattered to the floor on Siwani's left. She turned her head and growled. "*You.*"

Talon smirked back at her. "Not so haughty now, are you?" He boldly strode up and grabbed her chin in a sharp grip. "If you're wondering where your bitch is, she's long de—owww!"

Siwani whipped her head around and sank her teeth into his hand. She bit as hard as she could, drawing blood, until two sharp jabs to her gut forced her to release him. Talon danced back, cradling his hand, a murderous gleam in his eye.

"You stupid bi—"

"Enough," a deep voice bellowed through the room.

Talon spun. "But sir! She—"

"You were foolish enough to antagonize her," the now familiar voice retorted. A man cloaked in crimson stepped forward and ran his fingers beneath his hood. Stark, white hair slid down his shoulders and brushed along the scars on his cheeks. "And we all know what happens when you cross paths with Siwani Bane."

"Corvis," Siwani hissed. She spit on the ground and looked around the room. More of his cohorts surrounded her, watching intently. Their smiles promised pain and suffering before Corvis ended her, because why else would she be there? "This is why you put the hit on Malinga. You wanted to draw me out."

"It was so easy, too," Corvis said, sauntering toward her. He unsheathed a dagger on his hip and ran the tip along her arm, adding enough pressure to split the skin. "You were very good at staying off my radar when I put a bid out for you, but of course I knew you wouldn't be able to stay hidden if your precious wife was in danger." He fingered the ring on her necklace. When she tried to pull away, he pressed the dagger to her throat, pinning her in place. "Do you have any idea what you've cost me with your betrayal?"

Siwani snorted. She leaned her head back, trying to give herself room to breathe. "How could I betray you when I never joined you in the first place? We had a contract, which ended with the mission."

Corvis's eyes burned with rage. He pressed the dagger harder, cutting skin again. "But you couldn't leave well enough alone, could you? You had to bring the authorities down on my head. So much for a mercenary's code."

It was getting harder to breathe, but Siwani wasn't about to let him think he'd won the conversation. "The code only goes...so far...until our morals...are questioned." Corvis loosened his hold slightly. "You had us torture people who owed you money, and deliver so-called elixirs that made folks sick so they would have to pay you for the remedy. You wanted to wipe out an entire town just to claim their goods and properties! How did you expect me to keep my mouth shut?"

Corvis sneered. Without warning, he struck her across the face, causing her lips to break and ooze blood. "They deserved it," he hissed. "The people of that village were liars and hypocrites, promising shelter to anyone but turning away a father and his ailing daughter. They were too afraid to risk spreading the sickness through their ranks."

Siwani shut her mouth, unable to argue against that. She didn't know a lot about Corvis, but she did remember a masked young girl who'd been by his side. Then one day, she was gone. Siwani hadn't thought much of it then, but now? "She had the plague," Siwani realized. By the grizzled state of Corvis, he must've barely survived it himself.

"Aye," Corvis hissed. "And they offered no help. Instead, they cast us out like vermin, left us to die. She fought until her last breath. I swore to her I'd make those wretches pay."

"By killing an entire town? Including more children?" Siwani retorted. "How does that fix anything? It doesn't bring her back!"

"No," Corvis agreed and slid something onto his hand. "But now they too will know my suffering." He slammed his fist into Siwani's stomach, causing her to cry out in pain. Blood dripped down her gut as she stared at the small blades glistening on his knuckles. "And so will you." He struck again, this time in her side.

Siwani shouted and arched her back. Goddess, it hurt! At least she could take comfort in knowing Malinga wasn't enduring the same pain. If she was even still alive. *Be strong. She's out there. They can't snuff out her life that easily.*

That didn't make the pain any better. Corvis struck her over and over, leaving shallow holes in her body that bled. He breathed heavily for his efforts, and when the ground was already slick with blood, he staggered back and fell into Talon's waiting arms.

"Don't worry," Corvis sneered. "That's only the beginning of your punishment." He looked around at his crew. "She gets no food, no water. And gag her. I don't want to hear her except for her whimpers of pain." He spit at Siwani's feet and allowed Talon to guide him to a door where two women collected him and brought him inside.

Siwani bowed her head, exhausted. This was it, then? He planned to beat her to death? Only he wasn't going to make it quick. Though the wounds hurt, they wouldn't kill her. Her body healed a bit too quickly for that.

Talon returned, swinging a strap with a bit on it from side to side. "I'm going to enjoy this," he grinned.

"So, am I the only reason he's pulled you all into this and out of hiding? To torture me?" Siwani asked then laughed darkly. "Pathetic. Why even follow him? What do you even get out of it if he destroys the village? Do you think the authorities will stand for it?"

"Shut up!" Talon slammed her head into the pole, sending stars bursting around her. She felt his hand twist into her hair and yank her head back. He shoved the bit gag into her mouth and buckled it to the last loop, leaving the straps to bite into her cheeks. He banged her head a second time for good measure. "You know, I wish I'd kept that bard alive so I could cut her up in front of you. Oh well, at least the wolves will make a nice meal out of her."

Siwani released a muffled shout of rage and tried to kick him, but chains around her ankles held her back.

Talon made a rude gesture and wrapped his hand tightly around her throat. "Corvis keeps his promises. Once that village is destroyed, we'll pillage it and live like kings and queens. Their treasury will sustain us, something you could've had too if you hadn't turned your back on us. Don't worry, though. I doubt you'll be alive long enough to see it happen. You won't last past sunrise, not with what he has planned for you."

Siwani choked as Talon squeezed her throat hard enough to steal her breath. He held her like that for a moment before dropping her and letting her dangle in her bonds. Siwani wheezed around the gag and closed her eyes.

Malinga, please, my love, be safe.

Siwani was left alone for hours. She felt the others

watching her, their eyes hungry for revenge and far more nefarious things. She half-expected one of them to try to lay a hand on her without Corvis's permission, but they kept to themselves and rested.

Sleep didn't come to her. Between the pain and her worry for Malinga and Merphy, Siwani dangled and endured her punishment. What she wouldn't give to be back in the tavern, listening to Malinga sing on stage, the entire crowd enraptured by her beauty and grace.

If she thought of it hard enough, she swore she could hear Malinga singing.

Siwani blinked.

Wait...no, it wasn't possible, was it? A faint melody flowed into the room, catching her ear. She looked around and saw others do the same. Their brows furrowed in confusion. Two of the mercenaries headed toward the door located a short distance behind Siwani. They slipped outside.

The crunch of metal on bone greeted them.

People shouted, springing to their feet with blades drawn.

"Corvis!" one roared before they bolted for the door to head off whatever was out there.

The door blew off its hinges, taking the man down with it. Suddenly, the song was much louder.

Siwani twisted in her bonds and looked urgently, praying this wasn't some sort of specter.

Malinga stepped into the building, her eyes glowing red. She held her hands out toward the mercenaries who froze mid-step, eyes wide in fright. The melody was harsh and commanding, like nothing Siwani had ever heard before. Each person who listened to her song and fixed eyes on her fell to their knees in abject terror, their irises taking on a similar red glow.

Siwani tensed, waiting for the siren song to take her too, but while it brushed her ears, it did nothing more.

Malinga closed her fist and brought it down, letting a long, glorious note ring through the room.

In unison, the mercenaries drew their blades, held them to their hearts, and plunged them into their bodies. They dropped, the life leaving their eyes in an instant.

The few mercenaries who were further back and hadn't fallen under Malinga's spell shoved cloth in their ears. They charged, blades raised to take her down.

Siwani tried to scream at Malinga to run, but it was no use.

Malinga blinked back her red eyes and dashed toward Siwani. At the same time, Merphy burst through the room and flew straight toward their attackers. His hammer made swift work of them, caving in the skull of one person and breaking the jaw of another. They fell like sacks of potatoes.

"Siwani!" Malinga cried. She ripped the gag off of Siwani's face and pulled out her dagger to free her bonds.

"Linny, thank the Goddess," Siwani gasped. "Merphy, you're safe!"

Merphy stepped in front of her and threw a salute with his hammer. "Couldn't leave mah student in enemies' hands, now could I?"

Siwani's smile lasted only a second before she looked around frantically. "Talon and Corvis. Merphy, they're still here. They're—"

An arrow whistled across the room from an open door and thudded into Merphy's back.

"Argh!" Merphy shouted, collapsing to the ground in a heap.

"Merphy!" Siwani screamed. "Linny, get him! Get him out of here!"

"Not without you!" Malinga broke through one of the chains around Siwani's wrists.

Siwani dropped to her knees, barely missing an arrow as it thudded into the pole where she'd been standing. She used talons to tear at the leather straps and chains, freeing her wings, which she draped protectively around Malinga and Merphy. "Just hold on," she told her mentor. She grabbed his hammer and held it in one hand, trying to make it act like a shield. With her ankle still tethered to the pole and the collar on, she couldn't fight.

Talon appeared with a bow drawn and ready to fire. Corvis followed, sword in hand. His eyes swept over his dead crew, his face turning scarlet with rage.

"I won't let you take this from me!" Corvis swore. "Kill them!"

Siwani braced for impact as Talon pointed the bow at them.

Malinga's voice bellowed through the bloodied room, reverberating off of the walls and consuming Corvis and Talon in her siren song. Talon staggered with a cry. Corvis grabbed onto the man to help steady himself. Try as they might, they couldn't escape, and they were forced to face each other.

Siwani glanced up at her wife, green glorious magic glowing around her frame, though Malinga's eyes burned red. Her hair lifted as if by an invisible wind. Siwani felt a sick sense of satisfaction that the two men would die by her wife's hand.

But then their talk in the tub came back to her. Malinga had been torn that they hadn't found another way to stop the mercenaries. Now Siwani was letting her wife fight her battle for her, forced to take their enemies' lives.

"Linny, you don't have to do this," Siwani said.

Malinga glanced back at her, hot tears rolling down her cheeks, and it was unclear if it was from grief or rage. "I won't let them hurt you again," she said, her voice echoing strangely. She turned and jerked her fingers together, her song cascading over the men.

Talon fired the bow and Corvis stabbed his sword, arrow and blade finding each other's chest. Talon stared down at the sword embedded in his body, mouth falling open. Corvis gasped, the arrow quivering in his heart. He wavered then crumbled, taking Talon down to the ground with him.

The eerie song faded, leaving the room quiet save for Merphy's ragged breathing. Siwani looked down at her mentor and held him gently. The arrow was deep and too close to Merphy's heart for Siwani's liking. She wrapped her hand around it to keep it steady in his back and met his eyes. "I don't know if I can remove it without killing you."

Merphy grimaced. He laid a hand on top of her leg and gave her a devil-may-care smirk. "Nah, lass, I wouldn't make ya decide that." He squeezed her hand, his breathing growing labored. "Always been a stubborn one, but yah were the best student I've had."

Siwani's eyes watered. "Don't you dare say goodbye, you old fool."

"Fool enough ta train ya," Merphy teased with a tired smile. He rolled his head toward Malinga as she rushed to their sides. He patted her arm gently. "Ya watch over this one for me, alright, lass?"

Malinga sniffed and held Merphy's hand between hers. "There has to be something we can do."

"Aye," Merphy nodded sagely. "And I'm gonna do et. Ya two take care o' each other." He glanced at Siwani. "See ya on the wind, lass."

He moved, shoving himself into the arrow Siwani held until it went in deeper and pierced his heart.

"No!" Siwani screamed.

Merphy's eyes rolled skyward and glazed, the little smile still on his face. He slumped down in her embrace, his hand falling to the ground.

Siwani clutched Merphy close and sobbed. For as much trouble as he'd caused her, she'd still adored him and looked up to him as both a mentor and a father.

Malinga wrapped her arms around her and held her close. "Siwani... I'm so sorry. If I'd—"

"No," Siwani said, shaking her head. "No, you did exactly what you needed to do. You saved me." Siwani reached up and cupped Malinga's cheek in her hand. "I'm alive because of you."

"But Merphy," Malinga whispered.

Siwani swallowed and stared at her mentor. There was a story amongst the Fenixes, that should one perish in flames, they could be reborn. It could take days, months, years, but the soul lingered in the ash until it was ready to resurface.

Siwani dried her eyes "Take off my collar," she told Malinga. Her wife's warm hands found the lock in the collar, broke it, and removed the hated metal from around Siwani's throat. Freed, Siwani rubbed her neck then held out her hand, pushing Malinga a little behind her.

"Stay there," she said. Siwani trailed her wings over Merphy, caressing his still form. Blue fire ignited on the tips and crawled over his body. She heard Malinga try to protest, but Siwani kept working until flames started to consume him. With Malinga's help, Siwani stood up and limped back, watching. Her fire snarled around his body and wings. It looked like any normal pyre.

Siwani's shoulders fell.

Until a red flame ignited on his wings. Blue and crimson flames danced around each other, a mix of Siwani's magic and Merphy's. They spiraled into the air then crashed back down on Merphy's body, blinding both Siwani and Malinga. Siwani wrapped her wing protectively around her wife and held her there until the roar of fire faded.

Siwani lowered her wing and stared at the spot where Merphy had been. All that remained were ashes, and a single red feather.

Malinga looked as well. "We didn't even get to hold a proper memorial for him," she whispered.

"We may not have to," Siwani said. "Give me a pouch." She took it and leaned forward, scooping the ash into the bag. She held the feather reverently and could feel the wisp of life still flowing through the crimson plumage. "Not all Fenixes can be reborn from the ashes, but some have the ability." She held out the feather to Malinga with a smile. "We'll hold onto that until he's ready to reform."

"You mean—"

"He's not gone," Siwani said softly. "He'll be back to irritate us again, one day."

Malinga's eyes flooded as she collapsed against Siwani with a sob. Siwani held her close and stroked her hair. Her heart pounded with warmth to know the lengths her wife had gone to save her. If it hadn't been for Malinga, she'd be dead, another victim of Corvis's mad quest for revenge.

Siwani ran her thumb gently along Malinga's cheek and lifted her head. "I love you," she whispered and pulled her wife into a deep kiss. Malinga clung to her and wove her fingers through Siwani's short hair.

"I love you, too."

MALINGA HEFTED A SLEEPING BAG INTO THE BACK OF their wagon. As Siwani dropped another sack beside hers, she smiled at her wife. Three weeks and a few visits to the local healer had helped mend Siwani's wounds. She was still ordered to take it slow, but neither Siwani nor Malinga thought a short journey on the road to the next town would cause much trouble. There were more songs to learn and sing and more wrongs to be made right.

Malinga reached down and lifted Merphy's hammer with a grunt, adding it to their supplies. "One of these days I'll be strong enough to wield that."

Siwani chuckled and shook her head. "You'll have to fight him for it. That's his favorite hammer. He doesn't let anyone use it."

Malinga looked at the red feather bound in Siwani's hair. With each passing day, she swore she felt his presence grow stronger in the feather. Before long, they'd have him snarking in their ears all over again.

"Well, he can reform and take it himself, then," Malinga said challengingly and tossed her hair.

Siwani laughed. She grasped Malinga's arm and pulled her against her chest in a warm, tight embrace. They looked off toward the rising sun, the sky a gorgeous mix of red, gold, and orange. Malinga rubbed Siwani's back lovingly and tilted her head up. With a smile, Siwani kissed her. Nothing needed to be said. They held one another, greeting a brand new day together.

About the Author

Erin Casey (she/her) is an urban fantasy writer and author of The Purple Door District series. The first completed trilogy follows the stories of parahumans (werebirds, vampires, werewolves, fae, witches, magi, etc.) living in safe havens called Purple Door Districts. She's a founder of The Writers' Rooms, a literary non-profit organization that focuses on providing a free, safe environment to all writers no matter their income, skillset, race, and gender. Within the organization, she leads a fantasy/sci-fi group called The Violet Realm which meets twice a month. An advocate for mental health, she openly talks about her struggles with depression/anxiety/ADHD/CPTSD/eating disorder on her social media platforms. She firmly believes in supporting fellow authors be it through offering writing lessons in the Violet Realm, literary tips in her blog and on social media, or providing encouragement to those seeking to find their creative voice. And, of course, she's a devoted bird mom to six feathered kids. To learn more about her, her books, and her organization, visit erincasey.org.

Kindness
Susanne Salehi

Present day

LEYR SWATTED AT THE WHINING INSECTS BUZZING around her, which did nothing to deter the frenzied swarm. She grimaced, regretting her decision to conserve her magewell. She wasn't heading toward the edge of the world, just a particularly prosperous outpost on the outer lowlands along the coast. There was a difference. Probably. Her sigh shifted into a coughing fit as a bug flew into her mouth.

Firouzeh!

Vivid, emerald light flared around her, incinerating the cloud of insects. So much for preserving her magewell. Hopefully she could replenish her magic later.

Leyr had done her damndest to stay ahead of the mage order's increasingly insistent inquiries about the powerful artifact that had blazed into their awareness only a few months ago—Meridian's cursed sword, Kindness—but Meridian had figured her out and bolted. Leyr made a face. She had been weeks on the road, chasing down her quarry.

There were few swordswomen that matched Meridian's

description—a frame that large was better suited to a brawler, and fewer still bore a whole mess of blood sigils— but every last one of them had traveled to every separate end of the continent. By necessity, Leyr had conducted her pursuit mostly on foot. Nasty work for a mage, but her scrying was indifferent at best. She had needed to stay close to Meridian's trail, once identified.

Leyr cracked her knuckles and picked up the pace. She had released her heron an hour ago. No doubt it was striding back to the stables she'd rented it from, feathers still quivering with indignation. Poor bird wasn't built for these broken-down roads, or the thick, soupy mud that oozed through the cracked surface.

Then again, neither was she.

Leyr grumbled. Her new boots would never recover. Hopefully, that wasn't an omen for her upcoming reunion with Meridian. Her cheeks flamed at the thought. She had a few ideas that had nothing to do with the mage order's demands and everything to do with the memory of the swordswoman's powerful, calloused hands.

Rounding the bend, the dense copse of thick, gnarled trees anchored in brackish water thinned out, giving way to a raised field of riotous wildflowers. The thickets of flowers stretched on and on, ending against a gated stone wall easily twice her height. Past that, Leyr spotted a towering ramble of a dwelling, half covered in vines.

Leyr slowed as she approached the meadow. Flowers of every color and description tumbled over one another, blooming with wild abandon. She stopped to admire a blush pink peony, rubbing its velvety soft petals between her fingers. She frowned. It was far too late in the season to be blooming and far outside of its usual growing range.

Cataloging the oddity for later, she continued toward

the closed gate, just wide enough for two wagons to squeeze through. It was unusual for an outpost's entrance to be barred at midday, but the last village had been abuzz with rumors about the reclusive Landed who had taken up residence there. She snorted. Isolated to damn near the ass end of the continent and still the door was closed.

Leyr squared her shoulders as the gatekeep called to her.

"Gardener looking for work!" she shouted to the slotted opening. She looked the part at this point, mud-splattered and travel-weary as she was.

"Wait there."

"Not like I've anything better to do," Leyr muttered, crossing her arms. She tapped her foot, looked up at the carved doors, and blew out a frustrated breath.

Shrugging out of her pack, Leyr sat on it and crossed her legs. She tried not to think of her failed attempt at retrieving the sword from Meridian. It'd started so promisingly. There was that little inn with its convenient single vacancy, spared from Halcyon's summer rush, priced above the common mercenary's budget but lacking the typical merchant's comforts. Tucked into a back alley, their room had been quiet, with finely woven bedding and painted stone walls, spelled to maintain a comfortable temperature.

Leyr was not thinking about Meridian stealing in at sunrise with Halcyon's famous crescent breads, still warm and redolent with the smell of cinnamon and vanilla, or her slightly hoarse voice, marking the first words of the day. Leyr was definitely not thinking of that soft, snug bed or the morning Meridian, half-asleep, had rolled over and...

Leyr gritted her teeth. Surely, it wouldn't hurt to go over what she'd gleaned about Kindness from the swordswoman. For the mage order's mission.

That was why she was here, after all.

One Month Ago

"Tell me about your sword. Why do you call it Kindness?" Leyr asked, staring up at the whitewashed rafters. The thin coverlet was pulled tight to her chin.

Meridian laughed. "Is that all you can think to ask? The sword behind the hired sword?"

Leyr risked a glance over at the swordswoman.

Dammit.

Meridian had her back to her, the soft flicker of candlelight illuminating her strong, capable body. Muscles bunched in her shoulders as she removed her breastplate and undershirt. Leyr tried to hold back her gasp at the sight of Meridian's scarred back, and the massive, blossoming blood sigils covering wide swaths of flesh. She knew Meridian had a few, but this... this was terrifying.

Meridian glanced at her. "The hazards of sword life." She gave a half-smile.

Leyr looked back at the ceiling. "Not too different from mage life. I don't name any of my backup weapons, though."

Meridian yawned. "Every sword I've ever owned has been called Kindness. It's just a bit of gallows humor to keep the long dark at bay. Seemed funnier when I was a bright young thing."

"There's something to be said for the benefit of experience," Leyr blurted.

Hells, she hadn't meant to say that.

"Is that so?" Meridian asked, quirking a brow at Leyr, with a crooked smile on her lips.

Leyr's chest tightened, and she couldn't reply even if she had wanted to.

The bed creaked as Meridian sat, clad only in a loose tunic. Leyr was positive the garment was for her sake. Meridian didn't stroke her as the kind of woman who wore anything to bed.

Didn't *strike* her, dammit. Leyr tried to sink through the mattress. She tried not to think about Meridian stroking... anything. Heat rose to her cheeks.

Meridian full-on grinned at her and Leyr felt it all the way down. Shit.

Leyr cleared her throat and fully turned to face Meridian. Bravery, mage. "This is your latest in a long line of Kindnesses?" At Meridian's nod, she continued, "What is this one's story?" Her deep green magelight sparked around her for a moment and then subsided.

Meridian slid underneath the covers. "You want a tale before you sleep?"

The room was very hot. Maybe the enchantment was stretched too thin. It was summer, after all. Leyr scooted to the very edge of her side of the bed. "I'm just curious," she said, adding, "It would be... a kindness."

Laughing, Meridian tucked her hands behind her head and settled in. "Very well. Storytime it is. It started with a Landed merchant, as most unfortunate events do, out on the coastal lowlands. He hired me for a short contract to protect a ship's crew from living cargo. The entire hold had been emptied, and the creature was chained inside. It paced and shrieked, snarled. Sometimes it spoke." Meridian's face shuttered and her voice went flat. "I didn't need to watch the being as much as I did, and yet... I could almost taste its fear. A sword jutted from its side, attaching it to the spelled tether. The blade was a thing of light."

Meridian glanced at Leyr then, lowering her voice. "Sometimes the creature held the shape of a person, but one with too many limbs and a face with only rows of vertical-pupiled eyes. At other times, it oozed the length of that shining chain, formless. It was beautiful and it seemed like it was dying, but I have no doubt if it hadn't been pierced, it could've taken the entire ship under."

Leyr stilled, furiously turning over the possibilities. She tried to recall the mage histories, and further back, the legends. This was a powerful artifact for a powerful creature, but not even a snippet from her tutelage rose to mind.

"Sound familiar, mage?" Meridian asked.

Leyr shook her head.

"In turn, its wails pierced us, set our bones vibrating. We'd wake up with blood crusted around our earholes."

Leyr's eyes widened. "And yet you survived, clearly."

Meridian smirked. "More than that. The Landed merchant was a real prick, wanted the creature so he could boast about it. I swear, when we docked, I wasn't going to do anything. But that damn chain kept glinting in the sun. Right in my eyes. The captain had both hands on it, so I shoved her off the ship."

"Pardon?" Leyr croaked.

Meridian shrugged. "Any seafarer's a swimmer. Anyhow, I tried to yank the sword out."

A strangled laugh burst from Leyr before she could stop it.

"I know," Meridian said. "But it... it asked for help, Leyr. Looking like a human except for all those extra limbs, all those eyes open, darkness pouring from them, voice like stones grinding against each other. Deeper than the hollows in the earth." She swallowed. "But it didn't work. The sword was stuck. Then it asked for my blood sigils."

Leyr didn't react. She'd seen them for herself. Forged in agony, blood sigils were magic woven into flesh and bone, blood bruises that often took the shape of unreadable runes. They were an ancient, unknowable magic, at least to her mage order.

"I knew it was idiocy, and part of me thought certain death, but I cut the ones on my arm wide open. I let them bleed out onto the chain."

"What in the eight hells happened, Meridian?"

"The spell broke and the chain sizzled and liquified. I took the sword," Meridian gestured out into the semi-dark of their shared room, where Kindness lay waiting, "and I ran. I obeyed the letter of the contract—crew arrived intact —but you can see why I might not want to run into Landed fancy britches anytime soon."

"Or the creature," Leyr added.

Meridian nodded, lapsing into the brooding silence she adopted sometimes.

Present Day

"Head Gardener says there's work aplenty. They'd welcome more hands."

Leyr jerked out of her reverie and scrambled up at the gatekeep's words. "Thank you," she called, hoisting her pack to her shoulders.

The carved wooden doors swung open to an exquisitely manicured garden radiating in every direction, crushed shell paths winding amongst hundreds on hundreds of roses in various hues and states of bloom. None of the village rumors had done it justice. The scent hit her then, heady and floral. She closed her eyes and inhaled deeply.

"It tends to have that effect."

Leyr jerked to face the low, rumbling voice. She hadn't even noticed the figure robed in layers of iridescent woven scale, glinting in the late afternoon sun. Their face, too, was heavily veiled in layers of the same priceless material. Leyr had never seen anything like the glow it cast, and she itched to examine it for magical properties.

More importantly, just a step behind the cloaked figure was Meridian, sleekly kitted out in iridescent segmented plate armor with that damn sword strapped to her side. She was blinding. She was glorious. She was—ridiculous. Looking every inch the proper Landed escort, stern and approachable. Leyr worried at her lip.

Leyr inclined her head. "Landed. It's an honor." She was assuming the title, but Meridian's protective posture implied as much.

"If memory serves, we have not had the pleasure of a visit from one of your mage order brethren in some time. We were not aware our gardens were so renowned."

Leyr grimaced. Her shields weren't as good as she thought. That, or Meridian had said something. "Nothing like that, your eminence. I'm not here on official business. In fact, this is a personal trip. With my magic, I thought time spent among plants would be just the thing to renew my magewell." She was definitely babbling.

The Landed nodded to Meridian, who stalked toward Leyr.

"Why are you here?"

Leyr almost didn't hear the harsh whisper. She licked her lips and stared straight ahead at Meridian's brilliantly gleaming chest plate. Meridian briskly ran her hands over

Leyr's clothing. She found the dagger tucked into the small of Leyr's back, but the veiled figure nodded and Meridian left it.

The Landed spoke once Meridian had returned to their side. "We have recently prevailed upon Meridian to protect us, and now a prospective gardener appears. Mage order trained. Traveling a long way through the lowlands to play in the dirt, smelling like our new personal guard." The air crackled with anticipatory magic.

The Landed had some amount of power. At least Meridian hadn't sold her out. Leyr took a gamble that the Landed wasn't aware of her search for Meridian or why she'd undertaken it. "It is true, your eminence. I do need some time away from my responsibilities. Meridian and I are previously acquainted—congratulations on the promotion, by the way—and she's always had excellent taste in lodgings." She smiled at Meridian, who broke impassivity to frown at her. Progress! The Landed was inscrutable as ever.

Taking the Landed's silence as tacit approval to continue, Leyr said, "Please pardon my unannounced arrival. I am Leyret, of the mage order, here to lend my skill and magecraft to your gardens, if you'll have me." A trickle of sweat beaded down Leyr's neck as she waited.

The silence stretched on. Even Meridian fidgeted.

"We welcome you, mage Leyret. You will report to the Head Gardener by first light tomorrow. Meridian accompanies us until the late afternoon repast. Afterwards, you may renew your acquaintance. Do not make us regret our decision." The Landed motioned behind them as an attendant appeared, dressed in muted shades of blue and green. "Please tend to our newest gardener. Place her in the wing closest to the greenhouse."

"Thank you, Landed. You are generous. Would you also share your name?" Leyr asked.

"You may call us Syriax," they called over their shoulder as they walked away, Meridian in step behind them.

The syllables had a familiar sound to them, but Leyr wanted to be clean more than she cared to identify a fleeting memory.

Syriax's attendant brought Leyr to her quarters in the almost entirely unoccupied wing nestled near the greenhouse. After setting her pack down, she was walked briskly toward the bathing chambers. The attendant merely pointed to her clothes in disgust and Leyr eagerly tossed them aside.

Leyr paused in the doorway. It was a lot of luxury to take in: the arches of dark marble veined in gold, the private cleansing areas, the cabinets brimming with neatly labeled vials of product, and the enormous burbling, steaming pool in the center of the echoing room. The only thing more decadent would be a tray of bonbons resting on a pedestal by the entrance, but Syriax didn't strike her as a bonbon type of person.

"Lady Firouzeh." Leyr's voice echoed in the grand space. She whirled, prepared to apologize for the mild blasphemy, but the attendant had left. She let out a quiet shriek of joy and catapulted herself into the nearest cleansing alcove. With the turn of a spigot, hot water sluiced from the ceiling. Leyr nearly wept. Modern amenities in a lowlands outpost! She lathered herself with rose scented soap until the water ran clear.

Leyr stepped out of the alcove, wrapping herself in a fluffy towel as she went. Freshly scrubbed, nothing could stop her descent into the sunken steaming bath. She dropped the towel by the edge and slid in, letting out a deep sigh as the tingling warmth spread through her limbs. She closed her eyes and tipped her head back, letting it rest on the cool stone ledge. Surely, this was close to divinity.

Now that Leyr had managed to wriggle her way into the employ of the same Landed employer as Meridian, she needed a plan to retrieve Kindness. The artifact, rather. Leyr doubted she could convince Meridian to let the sword go, so she needed to be smart about this. Before anything else, she needed to know more: where Meridian slept, when she might leave Kindness unattended...

Leyr yelped and bolted upright as water splashed into her, signaling someone else had entered the bubbling pool. Green magelight glittered warning just above her skin before she realized that someone was a very naked Meridian. She caught a glimpse of the rampant array of blood sigils blazing strong across Meridian's body, before valiantly trying to keep her eyes collarbone or higher. She traced the scar tissue with her gaze, wishing... Nothing. Leyr only wanted to snatch the sword and get the hells out of here. Deliver it to the mage order and never have to think about the easy-going, muscular, strangely tender swordswoman again.

Meridian's eyes bored into hers and Leyr swallowed. She was acutely aware of her heartbeat. "Hi," she said weakly. "Surprise! I don't suppose you believe I decided this would be the perfect place to refine my growth magic and refill my magewell somewhere peaceful? Catch up with you while I'm at it?"

Meridian crossed her arms.

Leyr tried a different tactic. "I think it's fun that we have the same boss. Are we coworkers?"

"You want my damn sword," Meridian growled.

"Of course not," Leyr lied.

Meridian rolled her eyes. "It's obvious. You all do. That's the mage order. More like magpie order, snatching up every magical artifact in sight. Why didn't you just nick it back in Halcyon when you had the chance?"

Leyr hung her head. It hadn't been for lack of trying, but Meridian was a *very* light sleeper. Not to mention, while the damnable blade might leap quick and light to Meridian's hand, Leyr could barely budge it. "Even if that were true, of course I'd regret taking a job like that. But I wouldn't regret meeting you. Have you thought that I might want to get to know you better?"

"Enough to track me through the entire length of the lowlands and tip off most of my network that a cute little mage was out looking for me?" Meridian asked.

Leyr wanted to sink until she merged into the pool. Unfortunately, her magical talents lay in other elemental spheres. "Well," she hedged, "you did vanish. The decent thing to do would've been to leave a note."

"I'm not a decent woman," Meridian bit out.

"Neither am I!" Leyr shouted. Taking a deep breath, she tried to calm her racing heart.

"Good to know. Tell me why that is, Leyret," Meridian said.

"Sorry," Leyr muttered. "For raising my voice."

Humming, Meridian leaned forward and reached for Leyr's hand. She rubbed a comforting circle with her thumb across Leyr's palm that sent a glimmer of green magelight twinkling across her fingertips. "Tell me why you're here," Meridian whispered, leaning in so close she nearly grazed Leyr's earlobe. "Please," she added, releasing Leyr's hand and moving back.

Leyr cleared her throat. "Does that work for you, generally?" The question came out several octaves higher than Leyr had intended.

Meeting her gaze directly, Meridian smiled slowly.

Leyr considered her dwindling options. "It might help if you knew that I was a ward of the mage order." She looked down. "I won't linger on it, just like you haven't mentioned how you came by your blood sigils. Just know they aren't the only wound in the room." She risked a glance to Meridian, whose gaze had turned stony.

"The mage order is a hard place," Leyr said. "Rising through their ranks has given me a measure of protection. Wouldn't you take a contract if it kept you safe?"

"Loyalty to tyranny cannot be considered a virtue," Meridian said.

Leyr scoffed. "Pretty words, but some of us aren't unstoppable swordswomen capable of standing against the mage order."

Meridian's voice softened. "You're not a child anymore. You're a powerful mage in your own right."

Leyr opened her mouth to deny the statement and paused. "I'm not saying the mage order tasked me with retrieving your sword, but if they had, would it count for something to know that I'd been stalling them?"

"Does that mean you'll cancel your contract?" Meridian asked.

Leyr blinked back sudden tears. "It's not that easy."

"It rarely is." Meridian regarded her steadily and leaned in again with deliberate restraint. "May I kiss you?"

Realizing Meridian was waiting for her reply, Leyr nodded and whispered, "Yes."

Meridian closed the remaining distance between them, brushing her lips against Leyr's in a gentle, exploratory kiss. Her lips were so soft. Leyr moaned as Meridian deepened the kiss. Leyr twined her arms around Meridian's neck, pulling her closer.

Meridian drew back, cupping a hand to Leyr's cheek. "Think about it," she said. She stepped out of the steaming pool and bent down to pick up her towel. She dried off and strode out of the room, whistling an insouciant tune.

Leyr could've screamed in frustration. She sprang out of the water, grabbed her sad, damp towel and fled. After a quick dash across the hall, Leyr barreled into her quarters, slamming the door behind her. A platter of assorted meats, fruits, and cheeses awaited her in front of a cheerfully crackling fire. She softened a little. At least this was right with the world.

After careful consideration, Leyr decided not to dramatically fling herself in front of the hearth, opting to enjoy her evening meal instead. She took a crisp bite of apple and tried to calm herself. The tart, sweet flavor awakened her hunger and she finished the rest of the spread quickly, impressed with the quality of the simple meal.

Leyr's thoughts quickly returned to a certain swordswoman. Tugging at her hair, she paced the room, sparks of magelight flinging from her fingertips. This feeling was intolerable, but it often accompanied her specialty: musclebound women with sharp weapons working in dangerous professions. They kept their options open and their boots always half-laced. Leyr was almost used to it by now. She groaned and gave in to the urge to fling herself onto the bed. Perhaps things would seem simpler in the morning light.

Leyr awoke, determined to make the most of her stay at this distant outpost. At least she could replenish her magewell, and she genuinely looked forward to working in the gardens. The grounds were well-tended and the designer had an eye for beauty, even if they were a tad obsessed with roses. Leyr couldn't wait to ask the Head Gardener about it. She dressed in haste, throwing on an old casting tunic and leggings, dragging a brush through her hair.

Leyr bounded out the door, nearly running into Meridian, who caught her at the last moment. "Oh hells—I mean, hello, Meridian. Morning." Leyr batted at Meridian's stupidly muscular arms.

Leyr wasn't sure if she imagined the slight squeeze, but Meridian released her, handing her a wrapped packet.

"Breakfast," Meridian said. "I'm to escort you to the Head Gardener."

Leyr nodded absently, already having torn into her breakfast. Eggs—sausage—some kind of pepper? Delight. She hummed, barely paying attention as they made their way out to the grounds. They exited somewhere near the kitchen, skirted past the herb garden, and stopped at the greenhouse, a massive glass structure.

It looked oversized for the outpost, like it belonged in some grand city. "How?" Leyr breathed.

"Thought you might like it." Meridian gave her an unreadable glance.

Leyr gritted her teeth. "Still annoyed with you," she said. "Kisses and leaves. Who does that?" She tried to hold onto her frustration, but kept thinking about how soft Meridian's lips had been instead.

Meridian strolled over to the other side of the greenhouse, where Syriax waited. The Landed was wearing another formless garment, this one russet, woven with shining threads.

Leyr followed. "Landed Syriax—"

"You may dispense with the title. It does not suit us when you have our name."

"Where is the Head Gardener?" Leyr asked.

The veils obscuring Syriax face's fluttered, as though the Landed had exhaled. "We are. We are lovers of beauty."

Leyr attempted stoicism. "Very well. What would you have me do today, Lan—Syriax?"

Syriax gestured at several tidy rows of balled-and-burlapped roses behind them. "We wish to observe your planting. The places have been marked and your tools are ready."

Leyr nodded, loading several roses into the wheelbarrow. She trudged to the planting site. Syriax moved so they appeared to be floating underneath their robes and Meridian moved with her usual predatory grace. How nice to have an audience.

Leyr removed the roses and grabbed the shovel at the bottom of the wheelbarrow. She narrated her process as she went. If Syriax truly was the architect behind the outpost's stunning gardens, they'd want every detail. Once she unwrapped a rose, she gently reached out with her magic. "Not sure if you've been mage-trained, Syriax," she said, "but if you've the sight, I've begun my work."

The Landed merely nodded.

Leyr teased out the roots of the rose, then sought signs of corruption. Wherever she found it, she walled it off and shriveled the part from the plant. Once done, she fed the rose, weaving growth and protection into it.

"Like a chain," Syriax spoke. "Your kind is fond of those."

Leyr bit her lip, concentrating. She nodded. "The mage order teaches us young that magic can best be tamed with basic links that build on one another, as in a chain."

Leyr continued with the other roses, head bent and sweating. When she looked up, both Syriax and Meridian had vanished. She shrugged. She had a lot to do if she wanted to finish.

It was after sundown when Leyr finished planting and tending to her section of roses. She swayed on her feet. She had blisters in several new places and she was most likely even dirtier than she'd been yesterday, but she was pleased with her progress.

After a short foray to the bathing area, which Leyr could not ever fathom getting used to, she made her way to the kitchen. It was far past the evening meal, so Leyr wasn't surprised to find the space empty. She walked further in, toward the storeroom, when she spotted candlelight around the corner, coming from the staff dining area. She rounded the corner, hoping to meet some of Syriax's other employees.

"You again?" Leyr exclaimed.

Meridian smiled. "Thought you might be hungry. It's not every day one of the mage order flexes their muscles."

Leyr bit her lip. "Thank you," she offered at last. She was ravenous, actually. She sat down with Meridian and dug into the root vegetable stew. After a few bites, she realized Meridian was eating too. "You waited for me?" She asked.

"I wanted to take the evening meal with you. How was your first day as a gardener?" Meridian asked, as though she hadn't set Leyr's world afire with a single kiss.

"It's a nice break," Leyr confessed.

"Oh, so you don't love being sent all over the continent on foot to try and find a charming swordswoman and her magic sword?" Meridian quirked a brow at her.

Leyr gasped. "That was you?" She thought longingly about flinging the rest of her soup at Meridian.

"I might have helped with some of the false leads," Meridian said. "Anyway, I know you've been busy considering my enticing proposition—"

"Not even a little—"

"—but there's something else you should know, first," Meridian finished, lacing her fingers together. She met Leyr's gaze squarely. "Your mage order wants Kindness back so bad because they forged it in the first place."

Leyr froze. It made a cruel kind of sense. She licked her lips. "What was it made for?" she asked.

"I think you're smart enough to guess," Meridian said.

This time Leyr put both her hands on the soup bowl before reconsidering. "Tell me," she said.

"I took it from Syriax," Meridian said evenly.

"Wait," Leyr breathed. "You mean..."

"Syriax is no Landed. Not even human. They're an old, old being," Meridian paused. "Breaking their chains with my blood sigils connected us. When they came to me with an offer, I took it. Kindness is the sword that bound them, but now I wield it in their service."

"The creature on the boat you told me of— that's the Landed, Syriax?" Leyr could barely get the words out.

Meridian nodded.

"And all of this?" Leyr gestured widely, encompassing the idyllic outpost.

"The Landed merchant I initially contracted with wanted to own an intelligent being. He had Syriax's young slaughtered and took them from their home. So they took his."

Leyr tried to find fault, but couldn't. She would have

done similar or worse. Still, her mind stuttered over the incomprehensible knowledge.

Meridian continued, "I hope that helps you decide if you want to continue your mad quest to steal a magic sword from a continental legend and her mythical employer."

Leyr knew there was no exaggeration in the statement. "This is unexpected," she said at last.

"There are worse things. Here, you could get out from under the mage order. You said you wanted to get to know me better. Stay and find out?" Meridian's voice softened. Leyr saw how much it cost her to ask.

Leyr shook her head. Seeing Meridian's face fall, she clarified, "I need more time." She gave Meridian a tentative smile and hoped she would understand.

The swordswoman and mage finished the meal in companionable silence, elbows nearly touching.

For a week, Leyr retreated into solitude. She continued the work Syriax had assigned her, planting new roses and tending to those on the existing acreage. Leyr refilled her magewell slowly, marveling at the health of the gardens surrounding the outpost. She spent hours in the vast library, skimming ancient tomes that inspired her to try new applications of her growth magic. Syriax kept their distance, but Leyr could see their love of the gardens in every meticulously kept plant, and she could not fear a being that loved their plants so much.

Meridian gave her space, too, so much that Leyr ached with it. She had time enough to consider her days with the mage order and how her future might look in their hands. Her days had softened into gentle routines, but her heart wound tighter and tighter around the time she had spent with Meridian. This quiet outpost felt like the edge of the world, and it could feel like peace—with Meridian by her side.

Decision crystallized, Leyr practically ran to Meridian's quarters. She pounded on the door until Meridian opened it.

"Yes?" Meridian asked.

Panting, Leyr said, "Fuck the mage order. I'm not going back. Would you have me?"

Meridian's head snapped up. "What?"

Leyr hesitated. "Fuck your magic sword, too. Keep it. I don't care. I just want you." Her chest loosened at the admission.

"Don't say it if you don't mean it," Meridian warned.

Leyr looked up at her and took a step closer. "I'll be clearer. I want to be with you. In every way."

Meridian straightened. "Then I'm your woman," she said and bent, scooping Leyr into her arms with ease.

"That's a promise?" Leyr purred, leaning against Meridian's chest as she stalked toward the bed.

"It's an unbreakable oath," Meridian said, gently tossing Leyr on the bed. Meridian stripped down to her tunic and joined Leyr on the bed, pinning her there.

Desire pierced Leyr and her breath hitched. Meridian trailed kisses down Leyr's neck and she barely held back the moan that surfaced. This was everything she'd wanted and more.

Meridian had the audacity to wink up at her before descending further.

It didn't take long for Leyr to lose her capacity for rational thought. There was the glorious press of body on body, raking her nails down Meridian's back, and her own incoherent cries of pleasure. Leyr reveled in reciprocating

the attentions that had brought her to *multiple* ecstasies...
The ferocity of her desire stunned her.

Afterwards, Leyr rolled onto her back, stretching her
arms above her head, little arcs of emerald green sparking
off her ample curves. Her lips were swollen and she tingled
pleasantly everywhere.

Meridian hummed and wrapped her arms around Leyr.
"Just think," Meridian said, "If not for the sword, we never
would've met."

Leyr met her gaze solemnly. "It is a kindness," she
murmured, before dissolving into laughter. Happiness filled
her and she beamed at Meridian, who met her gaze with an
earnest smile and a tender kiss on the cheek.

About the Author

Susanne Salehi (she/they) is a queer Iranian American writer and editor. Their partner and two cats are the loves of their life and they live in the South, which you can pry from their humid, sweaty hands (please don't). They're currently finishing their popular fiction writing MFA at Emerson College, along with their first novel. Other than writing, they adore gardening, reading, cross stitching, doing puzzles, collecting rocks, and accumulating silly tattoos—they're particularly proud of the screaming possum. This is their first anthology publication, though they're a regular reviewer over at The Lesbrary. Find them at www.susan nesalehi.com.

Her Fiancée's Favor
Alyssa Rae Jensen

CITRINNE SAW HOW ROSABELLE'S FOOTSTEPS SLOWED with each step on their way to the cave. The way her fiancée walked reminded Citrinne of a criminal sentenced to death, dragging her feet in a vain attempt to prolong her life as guards dragged her to the gallows. But Rosabelle wasn't the one who needed to die tonight. That honor belonged to someone else.

"You don't need to come with me," Citrinne said. "The cave might be pretty once we walk far enough, but getting a face full of dragon fire tends to kill the mood, so it's really not the best place for a couple's stroll." Not that she and her fiancée had done any sort of couple's stroll. Or kissed. Citrinne couldn't even hold Rosabelle's hand for longer than two seconds. She'd timed it. Citrinne could only steal two seconds of bliss before the guilt gutted her. It was a bit hard to enjoy time with her when her sister, Karalina—and Rosabelle's first betrothed—was gone.

Rosabelle's torch illuminated her face and her blue eyes, once distantly anxious, now tentatively bright. "Well," she said, "are you thinking of turning back?"

"I can't. You can, though. It'd be good for your dress if you did. I know how much you hate getting dirt on your clothes."

That tentative brightness dimmed. Rosabelle's smile weakened. "Worse things have happened."

That was a no, then. Shit. Citrinne forced her too-glib smile to stay on, even as her stomach dropped like an anchor into an ocean.

"Fine," she said. Citrinne didn't have any more time to convince Rosabelle to leave. Not if she wanted to meet Commander Emeraude Hervieux's demands. Citrinne had never liked Emeraude, not even back when Citrinne had known her as nothing more than Karalina's sister-in-arms, pretending she gave a single shit about her disappearance. After all, Citrinne wasn't in the business of making friends with cold religious zealots. But her dislike had sharpened into hatred and fear after Emeraude issued an ultimatum: lure the Crimson Spectre to her death, or she would kill Citrinne's older sister.

It was strange for Emeraude to jump through so many hoops, arranging the Crimson Spectre's death through Citrinne's connection to her. By definition, the Crimson Spectre was a criminal. She fought demons by injecting their black blood into her own veins, which was medically unwise, religiously blasphemous, and highly illegal. Emeraude possessed enough authority to simply arrest her. But when Citrinne had confronted Emeraude, she'd said she could only imprison the Crimson Spectre, not execute her. She would be breaking the law if she did.

"And," Emeraude had added, "the Spectre is proving too...popular. The people may admire her for protecting others from demons, but they forget she does so through unholy means. They must be taught that the method matters more than the result, and they must remember what grisly end awaits anyone who consorts with Agathe's creations."

Citrinne set aside that fun little memory. She pulled out one of her last three vials of Fleurine Rose ink from her satchel, as well as a fine paintbrush. Well over half of Citrinne's tattoos glowed: most of them white, a few of them a frosty blue. But she still needed to trace over the rest of her plain, charcoal-inked tattoos, which ran along her left arm and right shoulder. She would have to rush to fill them in as they walked along. "Just keep close. And—"

"Stay behind me," Rosabelle proclaimed, drawing her rapier with a flourish.

Citrinne's mouth dropped open. Before she could protest that was what *she* was about to say, Rosabelle marched into the cave, the point of her sword forward, the torch held above her head. It might not be such a good idea to let her take the lead. Citrinne had watched Rosabelle duel for sport among the court in Fleuret, and though she wasn't the worst, she hardly numbered among the best, either.

But the gesture left Citrinne's cheeks warm. Then she recovered her senses, following Rosabelle.

Down into the cave they went.

Letting Rosabelle lead the way gave Citrinne more time to mark herself with the Fleurine Rose ink. She relied on the torchlight as she painstakingly painted over a dagger she'd tattooed along her inner forearm, which, along with the rest of her arm, showed off a downright mess of tattoos. Some of them really weren't that special. Citrinne had tattooed shit like paintbrushes and mugs of ale on herself, and a bull resided at her shoulder for this very good reason: she felt like it. But other tattoos had more meaning, like the one along her forearm. She'd replicated Karalina's favorite dagger as best she could, carving her sister's memory into her skin after she'd gone missing.

As someone who'd been drawing since she could hold a pen, Citrinne prided herself on having a steady hand. But she struggled to trace the ink over her tattoo as she walked in the dark. Rosabelle paused her pace long enough to see Citrinne struggle and held the torchlight closer to her. "Oh! Would this make it better?"

It did. But it put Rosabelle at arm's length from Citrinne, and that alone made her heart pound. Hardly the most conducive for focus. "That's not necessary. I don't need a puny thing like light."

"But you look like you do—"

"Then you've misread me. Keep going."

Rosabelle winced. Then she sighed, walking ahead. Citrinne waited until Rosabelle was a good ten arm's lengths away from her. Only then did she start following.

Citrinne wished she hadn't needed to rebuff Rosabelle. They'd been friends, once. Rosabelle had admittedly caught her eye, even then. But with Rosabelle engaged to Karalina at the time, Citrinne couldn't act on her attraction, which had made their friendship easier. Then came their engagement, and their relationship became strained.

After all, Rosabelle only been engaged to Citrinne once Karalina was declared dead. In any other circumstance, Citrinne would have to be engaged to Rosabelle, but she couldn't exactly enjoy it now. Not without metaphorically taking a giant shit on her older sister's grave.

Now that Citrinne knew the truth—that Karalina wasn't dead, but abducted—she dreaded what would happen once she got her back. To Karalina, the engagement had been purely political. It was her hard work and militaristic prowess that allowed the Laurier family to climb the social ladder over the years, but they still weren't titled. Marrying a noble—even a minor, foreign one such as Rosabelle—fixed that, and Rosabelle's family didn't mind sending her away to secure some influence in Fleuret.

As to how Rosabelle felt about the engagement...well, she'd never said she *didn't* love Karalina. Anyone would pick Karalina over Citrinne. Why would Rosabelle be any different?

Citrinne finished overlaying the dagger tattoo with white Fleurine Rose ink. The once plain tattoo brimmed with unused magic, now more 'useful.' Citrinne grimaced.

She needed to draw quickly if she wanted to use all six of the Fleurine Rose ink vials that Emeraude belatedly sent her. But intentionality was key. Citrinne couldn't simply smear the ink all over her face and expect it to work. Even if she had the option to be so base, she refused to be. The absence of time threatened to squeeze the breath out of her, but she couldn't resist exchanging one paintbrush for a smaller one she kept in her satchel, fine-tuning the details as she painted over a snake curling around her finger.

Citrinne withdrew her second-to-last vial. She painted over the bull tattoo as she and Rosabelle walked. The deeper into the cave they got, the more red crystals sprouted from the walls. The cave slowly opened from a natural walkway into what was practically a whole-ass chamber. Red crystals dripped from the ceiling as stalactites, one falling so low that Citrinne ducked to avoid the tip. They circled around a small pond, which Rosabelle stared into.

Citrinne could see why. Rosabelle always liked pretty things, and the pond sure looked pretty. What should've been pristine blue water appeared violet among its surroundings, so gem-like in its color that Citrinne would've wanted to kneel by it to take a look if not for the deadline. Well, and if not for the crystals jutting out from the bottom of the pond like a pit of spikes. Rosabelle stared deep into the depths, distracted, and didn't seem to notice how the toes of her shoes flirted with the edge.

Citrinne pictured Rosabelle tumbling in and impaling herself, and suddenly, she ran to her side. Rosabelle startled, half-jumping out of her skin as Citrinne steered her as far from the lake as the cave would allow.

"Oh!" Rosabelle said. "Um, thanks."

"Just don't get distracted again." Shit, she still held Rosabelle's arm. Citrinne ripped her hand away and paced two steps back. "I did say that cave could be pretty, but I didn't think it would be *dangerously* pretty."

Rosabelle laughed nervously, rubbing the place where Citrinne had grabbed her. "Sure. It's the lake. That's what's distracting me."

Citrinne narrowed her eyes.

"And I...really don't want to face a dragon," Rosabelle admitted.

"Then don't. Leave. I'd be happier if you did."

Why did Rosabelle flinch? Why did she shake her head and proceed through the cave without another word?

As they left the pond behind them and the cave opened up, Citrinne's arms prickled. It was in this cave, fighting a dragon, that Karalina first went missing. When Citrinne had received the news of her sister's death, she'd refused to accept it. She'd ran to this place without a plan, and though she'd found Karalina's severed leg, she'd also found that dragon. It'd nearly been the death of her. It would have been, if not for...

Citrinne plucked that splinter of a thought out before it could dig any deeper.

The cave walls, more crystal than rock by this point, glowed inexplicably. Citrinne doubted she and Rosabelle needed that torch anymore. Not when red light washed over the pair as if they'd been doused in blood.

Citrinne watched Rosabelle's back. She turned her head over her shoulder, catching Citrinne looking. The light illuminated her eyes in a way that made them seem not blue, or even purple, but red.

As fast as a finger snapping, the sight thrust Citrinne back six months. To when she'd seen another pair of blood red eyes flash in the dark, the black veins of the demon-touched pulsing against a pair of white forearms. The rest of her savior's face had been obscured by her crimson cloak, and the haze that came with Citrinne losing consciousness. But the eyes burned bright enough to sear a place in her memory forever.

Citrinne's footsteps faltered. Call her crazy, but Rosabelle's eyes, under the blood red light, looked the same as the Crimson Spectre's.

Then Rosabelle walked underneath a shadow, and her eyes faded back to blue. Citrinne scratched her stubby fingers through her undercut and exhaled. She needed to do a better job of plucking those metaphorical splinters.

Citrinne tried to keep tracing her tattoo with the magical ink. But her gaze wandered up to one of the crystals growing out of the wall, larger than any mirror, yet equally as effective as one. Citrinne watched Rosabelle tread in front of her, with her short stature, her pink dress, those elbow-length gloves she always wore—Citrinne *never* saw Rosabelle without them—and a face full of carefully-applied makeup. She looked so ladylike that most people missed her lean, defined muscle, not as delicate as the rest of her. Then Citrinne dove into a staring contest with her own reflection's acerbic eyes, getting a good look at her warm brown skin with dark hair cut close to her head, and her green overalls, smudged with the occasional ink stain. She was scrawnier than Rosabelle, but at least she was taller.

Rosabelle watched her, too, and Citrinne realized just how long Rosabelle had been staring at her. She bit her lip and said, "You don't have to do this, you know."

"Oh," Citrinne said, too blithely, "I see you can also make jokes in the face of danger. We have something in common."

"I'm not joking! You and the Crimson Spectre are on the same side."

"Switch that 'are' to a past tense, and then you'll be correct."

"You don't know if your trap will even work!"

"I wrote to her. I told her exactly where I'm going, and when. She knows I'm here."

"She's also a demon-touched vigilante in Fleuret, of all places! Someone like her—I mean, she has to keep her guard up, even around people she writes to. Even around you. What if she knows *exactly* what you're trying to do?"

"I'm still putting myself in danger. She'll come for me."

"Even if she does, what if she isn't overwhelmed by the dragon? What if she doesn't die?"

"Then that's it for me and Karalina, I suppose."

"That's not true! If anything, defying Emeraude will save you. *Both* of you. Think, Citrinne. Emeraude gave you a ridiculous task. You asked her to use her access to Fleurine Rose ink, to give you enough resources to survive. She complied in the most malicious way possible. She didn't send you any ink until *today*, and only gave you time to inscribe temporary tattoos on your skin. Those are weaker than the permanent ones Fleuretian knights use, right? She knows if you succeed, and she lets Karalina go, there's nothing stopping either of you from telling the queen what happened. I don't think Emeraude has any intention of upholding her end of the bargain. I think she wants to kill you, the Crimson Spectre, and Karalina all at the same time, and make it look like she had nothing to do with it."

Citrinne clenched her teeth. "Do you think," she said, "that I haven't considered that angle?" Rosabelle made a noise, as if about to interrupt, but Citrinne didn't let her. "If I'd thought anything other than complete compliance could save her, then I would have pled my case to the Queen of Fleuret herself. She'd risk her own life and limb for Karalina. She wouldn't be subtle about it. But Emeraude would slit Karalina's throat the moment she suspected foul play. Seeing Emeraude arrested means nothing if Karalina dies. Her life is too much to trust to anyone, I can't even tell others—"

"You told me," Rosabelle said quietly.

Citrinne winced. It'd been a moment of weakness. She'd blubbered and said too much. Nothing she could say afterwards could stop Rosabelle from trying to help.

"I shouldn't have." Citrinne put her paintbrush back to work. "It put Karalina in danger. It puts *you* in danger."

"I can take care of myself. But I'd be happy to walk out of here, with you, and find a different way to save Karalina."

Rosabelle closed the distance between them and took Citrinne's unoccupied hand. A drop of ink rolled down from the stalled paintbrush as Citrinne's hand froze in place, along with her breath, her thoughts, her heart.

"I know you don't want to do this," Rosabelle murmured.

Citrinne forced herself to draw breath again. Now was not the time for selfishness.

"It doesn't matter what I want." She yanked her hand out of Rosabelle's grasp. She couldn't keep her hand steady as she drew along the bull tattoo, and what should've been a smooth line came out in jagged starts and stops. "Karalina, I'm sure, in her heart of hearts, would want to live. The queen would want her commander back, and my mothers would want to see their more successful daughter again." She tightened her grip, remembering each time she'd seen Rosabelle happily talking with Karalina throughout their courtship, the days Citrinne told herself that she shouldn't be pining from afar. "And I'm sure you'd want a better fiancée."

"That isn't..." Rosabelle shook her head. "That isn't the point! Can't you see I'm trying to help you?!"

"I do. But I never asked for your help!"

"So you'll kill someone instead? Someone who saved your life? Are you truly okay with that?"

Citrinne met Rosabelle's eyes. Something as thick and pitiless as blood pooled at the bottom of her stomach. "Yes."

Rosabelle reeled back as if Citrinne had slapped her. Her legs shook as she stumbled away, staring at Citrinne as if some monster had taken her place. That stare alone was enough to make Citrinne's gut drop and her eyes sting.

But she didn't cry. Citrinne didn't flinch or swallow any lump down her throat. She met Rosabelle's gaze evenly and pretended to be okay with that stare, because Citrinne would have to be. If her fiancée's favor was one more sacrifice she had to make for Karalina, then Citrinne would drive a knife into it. Even if it felt like gutting her own heart out of her chest.

She used the last of the blue Fleurine Rose ink and exchanged the empty vial for her last full one. "We should—"

Before Citrinne finished, a shriek ripped through the cave.

THE DRAGON DIDN'T NEED ITS FIRE. ITS SHRIEK ALONE terrified Citrinne. She bent down and clapped her hands over her ears as a massive shadow swept over them.

A ruby-red dragon, nearly the size of a cottage, soared along the cave ceiling, its black underbelly like a long spill of ink. It passed over them, and that, along with the refreshing lack of fire, made Citrinne hope that they'd been beneath the dragon's notice.

Then the dragon circled back around, its crimson eyes latching on to them. It opened its mouth.

Citrinne threw herself in front of Rosabelle. She quickly snatched the vial before sticking one hand out in front of her, touching the other hand to the white tattoo along the side of her throat. A barrier as pearlescent as an opal shone in front of them as a torrent of fire rained down.

It should be impossible to drown in fire. But this felt close, overwhelmed by flame and heat until Citrinne lost her senses and couldn't see or hear or feel anything else. The barrier held under the assault, but it siphoned the magic from the temporary tattoo even faster than Citrinne anticipated. The white ink drained from the tattoos around her neck, and then from her collarbone, leaving the regular black ink in its wake. Citrinne scrambled to keep the barrier up by reaching to her shoulder, draining the magic from that tattoo instead.

Rosabelle tugged on Citrinne's shirt. "This is bad! We need to go!"

The magic slipped out of her shoulder tattoo faster than

water through her fingers. Half of her white Fleurine Rose ink was gone, all in ten seconds. Citrinne was one singed hair away from agreeing.

Then the dragon's onslaught stopped, and Citrinne gasped a lungful of smoky air. She coughed as the dragon soared overhead, bitter tears stinging her eyes. "Not yet!"

"But—"

"The Crimson Spectre *will* show up to save us. If we leave now, this will all be for nothing!"

Rosabelle looked ready to scream. She might have, but she saw something Citrinne didn't. She yanked her close to the crystalline cave wall just as a stream of fire lashed out from the dragon's mouth, accompanied by an unholy screech.

"Ugh, fine!" She strained to hear Rosabelle over the chaos. "We'll stay until you're almost out of magic. But then we run!" Citrinne did not verbalize any agreement to that arrangement, but Rosabelle glanced at the dragon and went on as if she had. "Until then, you keep back. I'll fight it from up close."

Citrinne did not verbalize any agreement to that plan, either. Before she could object, Rosabelle flung the torch to the opposite side of the cave. The dragon raised its head like a dog following a ball, and incinerated the torch. Rosabelle charged towards the dragon, rapier in hand. It turned at the sound of her footsteps, and she hit one of its hind legs with the edge of her blade. The strike glanced off the beast's gleaming scales.

The dragon breathed fire at Rosabelle's face. Citrinne nullified the torrent by tapping her blue tattoos and interrupting it with her own sharp burst of frost. Rosabelle skittered out of the way, but the dragon wasn't done. It turned its head as it spewed flames, brandishing a scorchingly hot arc at them. Citrinne was too busy shielding her own damn self from the passing flames that she couldn't cover Rosabelle—

But Rosabelle didn't need as much help as Citrinne had thought. The dragon ceased its assault as Rosabelle kept going. She poked the dragon's front legs, then Citrinne blinked and Rosabelle was prodding its hind ones. Citrinne quickly put out a few leftover fires on the ground with sharp whips of frost, especially ones that seemed too close to Rosabelle.

The dragon raised a clawed hand towards Rosabelle. Citrinne said, "Look out!"

She never needed to. One distinct second before Citrinne shouted, Rosabelle had turned her head, as if a sixth sense of hers had beat Citrinne to the punch. She squeaked, but dove to the ground. The dragon's talons tore at the place where she'd once been. Rosabelle popped back up, her wide eyes full of fear, chest heaving as she gasped for breath. Then the fear steeled into resolve. She tossed her hair out of her sweat-slicked face, snarled, and raised her rapier back up at the dragon.

Citrinne couldn't stop staring at her.

And that nearly spelled the death of her. The dragon screeched, and Citrinne swore she could hear frustration in it. A stream of fire spewed from its mouth, and Citrinne, acting belatedly, barely managed to leap in front of Rosabelle. Citrinne flung up a barrier until the danger passed, coughed up smoke, and checked her tattoos.

The only tattoos still glowing with Fleurine Rose ink were the ones along her left wrist and hand. The rest of her tattoos had been depleted of magic, back to their charcoal selves. If she'd need the tattoos on her hand to cover her escape, then she was out of resources to stay any longer.

The Crimson Spectre still hadn't arrived to save her.

"Citrinne!" Rosabelle screamed. "We have to leave!"

Citrinne hesitated. She still had one unused vial of white Fleurine Rose ink. If she could buy herself enough time to ink herself, it could make a difference. "But—"

The dragon's tail whipped towards them. Rosabelle pushed Citrinne out of harm's way, only to get hit herself. She shrieked as the force sent her flying into the wall, her head cracking against the crystal. Her rapier clattered to the ground, and her body crumpled. Rosabelle lay as still as a perfect porcelain doll.

Suddenly, Citrinne didn't think of Fleurine Rose ink or the Crimson Spectre, or anything else at all.

"Rosabelle!" Citrinne scrambled to her fiancée's side and turned her over. Blood matted her golden hair, and her eyes fluttered open only to squeeze shut again.

At least she was alive. Thank Leontine, Rosabelle was alive.

But if Citrinne kept them there any longer, Rosabelle could die.

Heat flared behind her. Citrinne threw up a barrier, keeping the fire at bay as she hooked her arms under Rosabelle's armpits. The barrier lasted long enough for Citrinne to drag Rosabelle out of harm's way, and not a second more.

The last of the Fleurine Rose ink sapped out of her hand.

The fire stopped. Smoke curled around them. Citrinne stifled a cough, and she heard the dragon puff air through its nostrils. Rosabelle, while preparing for the trip and researching this particular dragon's behavior, had mentioned it possessed bad eyesight. Did the dragon fail to see them? Did it think it'd won?

Citrinne shook Rosabelle back to consciousness. Rosabelle's arm slowly moved towards a large, leather pouch strapped to her belt. She undid the clasp, shaped like a heart, and reached in for...something. Citrinne didn't have time for this; she reached underneath Rosabelle's knees and chest to spirit her away.

That was the plan, anyways.

Rosabelle's eyes widened, suddenly much more awake, but the warning came too late. The dragon's claws, each as thick and tall as her own body, wrapped around Citrinne's middle before scooping her high off the ground.

"Shit! No! Fuck!" Citrinne squirmed, pushed against one of the claws, and tried to wiggle out of its grasp. Never mind that the dragon had lifted her so high above the ground that just looking down made her head spin. It opened its mouth, and Citrinne already felt the heat gathering at the back of it, ready to roast its next meal now that it had her like a worm on a hook.

Citrinne prided herself on being a stubborn bitch. If she would die, then she could at least die a stubborn bitch. She kicked and squirmed, and, remembering Rosabelle's complaints about how it could genuinely hurt to break a nail, went for one of the dragon's claws. She put all of her weight into snapping it off—

A crack tore across the dragon's nail at the same time that it roared. It lowered its claw and flung Citrinne aside. She had enough sense to tuck her head as she crashed to the ground and rolled away. Citrinne tasted warm blood in her mouth and spat it out. Her body screamed as she tried to push herself upright, and it took her more than a few tries to succeed.

When she did, Citrinne realized she hadn't freed herself.

Upon the dragon's head, clinging to one of its curved horns, was Rosabelle, her rapier already speared down into one of the dragon's eyes.

Rosabelle left the blade in its eye, holding onto the dragon's spine for dear life with one hand. With the other, she injected a syringe—where had she gotten that, and how had she gotten up to the dragon's head so fast?—into one of her forearms. For the first time, Citrinne saw them, ungloved by their usual elbow-length pink silk.

Black veins spiderwebbed up her arms. Rosabelle tossed the syringe aside, throwing it on the ground to join another emptied syringe. She held tight to the dragon as it flew, trying to shake her off the way a human would an annoying gnat. Rosabelle pulled the rapier out from the dragon's eye in a spray of black blood.

She glanced down towards Citrinne, just long enough for her to see that Rosabelle's eyes had changed from blue to a vivid, unnatural red, set against a pair of now-black sclera. Citrinne recognized those as the eyes of demons. Or of humans who'd ingested enough demon blood to become demon-touched.

Citrinne *knew* those eyes.

She couldn't do anything but watch as the dragon flapped up to the ceiling of the cave and smashed its back— and Rosabelle—against it. Citrinne clapped a hand over her mouth, sure that she'd just seen it kill her. But as the dragon swooped back down, Rosabelle lifted her perfectly intact head. Even the gash at her skull slowly mended itself together, like a hydra regenerating one of its heads. Rosabelle belted out a sound similar to a war cry, so unexpected and arresting that even though Citrinne's head knew that now was not the time, her body did not get the same message, and a frankly embarrassing amount of heat pooled between her legs. Then Rosabelle raised her arm and stabbed mercilessly down into the dragon's other eye.

The dragon landed so forcefully that the ground shook. It shrieked, spewing fire in a panic. Though it didn't reach Citrinne, she still skittered away. Rosabelle maneuvered herself away from the eyes, slipped, and yelped as she dangled from the dragon's horn by one arm.

Or maybe 'slip' was the wrong word. Her free arm moved like a blur of pink and black lightning as she drove the rapier into the unprotected hollow of its throat. Then Rosabelle leapt to the ground, landing on her high-heeled feet with demonic agility.

Watching the dragon die felt like watching an empire fall. It didn't scream or rage—though that was probably more due to the hole in its throat than any dignity—but it didn't immediately accept its own death. It resisted collapse, even as its front and hind legs buckled. When its body at last hit the ground, Citrinne felt the ripples of its death like a shockwave.

Citrinne limped towards Rosabelle. "So, the Crimson Spectre did arrive to save me."

Rosabelle turned towards her. Black demon blood dripped from the tip of her sword. She didn't say anything.

"My fiancée's a vigilante who saves people from demons," Citrinne said, desperate to fill the silence. "And you killed a dragon! Honestly, that was...hot."

Citrinne hadn't meant to admit it. It just slipped out, because she was nervous, and she tried to be funny when she was nervous. And because...well, it was true.

Rosabelle closed her eyes. Her cheeks turned a vivid scarlet. Before Citrinne could take any satisfaction in making the Crimson Spectre herself flush, she noticed more black blood gush from the dragon's throat. It bloomed across the floor, seeping towards Rosabelle's heels.

Citrinne crossed the distance between them. She hesitated, then she reached for Rosabelle's ungloved hand. "Let's go. We shouldn't—"

Rosabelle scuttled away, put that distance right back where it'd been, and raised her rapier at Citrinne. The tip hovered near the hollow of Citrinne's throat. She flung her hands up, but Rosabelle kept that blade staunchly level, her lips twisted in a snarl, and Citrinne realized she had dramatically misread the situation. She hadn't made the Crimson Spectre flush. She had made Rosabelle *furious*.

"You see me now." Rosabelle tilted her head, her stare so unblinking and pitiless that she seemed more demon than woman. "Tell me: when did I see you? Was it every time you've cracked a joke, or made a tattoo? Was it when I found you in your estate, sobbing on the stairs after Emeraude gave her ultimatum? Or was it when you looked at me, dead in the eye, and said you were fine with luring me to my death?"

Citrinne winced. "I...didn't know it was you," she said, the delivery every bit as lame as the excuse. "If you'd told me...you should've told me." Then she demanded, "Why didn't you tell me?"

Behind the blade, Rosabelle's face softened. "I wanted to. At first, it was a matter of necessity. Then it was...then it was for necessary *and* personal reasons." She lowered her eyes, long enough that Citrinne could've stepped away from the rapier's tip. If she wanted to. "We used to be close. But after Karalina disappeared, you started drifting away from me. You can be casually flirty, sure, but you also seemed just...like that. I've always wanted you to notice me. I wrote letters to you as the Crimson Spectre because that seemed like the only way to get your attention."

That rendered Citrinne speechless, but only for a moment. "But why not come clean when I told you about Karalina?"

Rosabelle's eyes snapped back up. "Then," she said, "it became a matter of safety. *My* safety. For as long as you tried to lead me to my death, I thought that if I told you, you'd report me to Emeraude. Then she'd kill all three of us.

"But I also decided that if you defied Emeraude's orders and refused to kill the Crimson Spectre for her, then it would be safe to reveal myself. Even if it made you angry or hurt or confused, I'd do it. So, I've asked you several times over the past few days to drop this, to find a different way, to stop and listen! I tried to give you different options, but you kept choosing this one!"

"What other options? None of them were concrete! I can't jump off a sailboat in a storm if you don't show up with another sailboat." But even as she recognized the merit in her own logic, a suspicious heat gathered in Citrinne's eyes. Between being untrustworthy because of a failure to come up with an adequate plan, and being untrustworthy because someone felt unsafe around her, she knew which was worse.

"We could have fixed that, together! But you never trusted me, never *saw* me—"

"That's not true," Citrinne snapped. "You were once my sister's fiancée. Did it ever cross your mind that I felt awkward? If anything, I tried not to notice you because of that. But you—you made that impossible. Or maybe that was impossible from the start."

She felt exposed, as if she'd cast off a plate of armor through pure accident. Rosabelle leaned back, blinking in silent surprise.

370

Then she shook her head. "So what's your plan now? What would you do with me?"

"I'm not the one holding the blade, dearest."

"But if you *could*? What if the Crimson Spectre wasn't me?"

"I don't know! I don't know what I would've done if it hadn't been you. All I know is that you're right. It's shitty that it took the Crimson Spectre being you to get me to stop. It's just—it's my sister on the line—" After trying to lead Rosabelle to her death, Citrinne owed her more explanation. "Damn it, fine. It's more than that.

"I never told you. But the last time I saw Karalina...we fought about the stupid Fleurine Rose tattoos. She couldn't fathom why I'd want to make non-magical tattoos. To do art for art's sake, because tattoos don't have to be useful to be good. That's a concept Karalina never wrapped her head around. She went on and on about how I should apply my talents 'properly,' by working for Fleuret's army and tattooing Fleurine Rose ink on our soldiers. So they could fight better, shit like that. She said I could bring honor to our family, so why wouldn't I?

"I told her just because she had a complex about being a golden child and living up to unreasonable standards didn't mean I did. She called me arrogant, short-sighted, and...selfish. When Emeraude tried to exploit my connection to the Crims—to *you*...I never wanted to lure you to the dragon. Not Rosabelle Heartwood, and not the Crimson Spectre. But I thought it didn't matter what I wanted. This time, I needed to put family first."

"Were you putting family first? Or were you trying to prove to Karalina and yourself that you could?"

"No! I was..." Citrinne fought to keep her sharp tears back. "I don't know."

Rosabelle's hand shook, the blade wavering near Citrinne's throat badly enough that she feared Rosabelle might slice her throat open through sheer accident.

"I'm mad at you. I'm mad at you, I'm so mad at you..." Rosabelle bit her lip. "I should be mad, I should be mad, I should be..."

Rosabelle stepped away and lowered the rapier. She shriveled, hugging herself with her free arm, and whispered in a quiet, dead voice, "You were right earlier. I did want a better fiancée. But not because I ever loved Karalina. I hoped...I wished you would...it doesn't matter."

Citrinne's face crumpled. Had Rosabelle actually loved her?

If so, then Citrinne had fucked it up. Rosabelle had no reason to love her now. Maybe she'd fall back into an easier, political engagement with Karalina, simply because she'd never tried killing Rosabelle. If she did...Citrinne would have to make her peace with that.

Until then, she could at least give Rosabelle what she wanted. Citrinne would be a better fiancée, for whatever amount of time they had left. Even if that time ran short.

She rifled through her overalls and pulled out a pocket watch. 8:10. Less than three hours remained before she was due to meet Commander Emeraude Hervieux at the Garden of Fleurine, and bring the body of the Crimson Spectre in exchange for her sister. Except Citrinne couldn't do that anymore. She hadn't realized it then, but that plan had stopped being an option the moment she'd decided to stop waiting for the Crimson Spectre in favor of getting Rosabelle out of the cave.

Citrinne walked towards one of Rosabelle's discarded, empty syringes and scooped it up from the ground. "You don't need all of your syringes, do you?" Rosabelle shook her head. "I'll lie to Emeraude. I'll say I succeeded. The dragon proved too much for you, and you're dead." Citrinne waggled the syringe between her fingers. "This will be the proof."

"Her exact demand was the Crimson Spectre's body for Karalina. That's not what she wants."

"It *is* yours, though. I'll say I couldn't get to your body due to the dragon. If she wanted me to collect it, then she should've given me more Fleurine Rose ink. It's not that unbelievable of a story. Who knows? Maybe this will teach her to better equip her independent contractors."

Rosabelle bit her lip again. She made a nervous noise in her throat.

"It'll work," Citrinne insisted.

The nervous noise got louder.

Citrinne sighed. "It's the only plan I can think of on short notice. If you have a better idea, I'm all ears. But I'm not involving you."

She dropped the syringe into her satchel, next to her singular vial of Fleurine Rose ink. Citrinne nearly didn't do it. But in the end, she held Rosabelle by both shoulders. She waited until Rosabelle brought her eyes up to hers.

"Go home, Rosabelle," she said. "You've done enough. I swear on my sister's life that I will not tell Emeraude who you are."

"But you could die if you go alone."

"Well," Citrinne hedged, "maybe not." Rosabelle didn't buy it, so she sobered. "If she does kill me and Karalina, then it's even more important that you go. You're the only one who knows her treachery. Let me protect you this time, okay? And for what it's worth, I'm sorry."

Citrinne regretted never kissing her. She regretted never going beyond kissing or giving Rosabelle a proper engagement sword. But it was too late now, and she doubted Rosabelle wanted to hear anything else from her. So Citrinne stepped back, allowing herself one last look at Rosabelle. Then she turned around and began her trek out of the cave.

She couldn't even wallow before she heard a pair of heels running after her. "I'm coming with you!"

"What?" Citrinne turned around sharply. "Didn't you hear anything I said?"

"I did, but it's still a dumb decision, and no offense, but you've already made enough dumb decisions." Rosabelle probably didn't mean to sound chipper and breezy. Her voice was naturally high-pitched. But by Leontine, Rosabelle sounded that way. "And you said it yourself! I'm the one with the sword. Do you really think you can stop me from helping?"

Unable to counter that, Citrinne fumed. Rosabelle clapped her hands, and this time, her beaming did seem intentional. "Wonderful! Let me collect some dragon blood, and then we'll leave."

Rosabelle explained everything as she and Citrinne walked out of the cave. Citrinne barely interjected, not because she didn't have questions but because Rosabelle overexplained so much that she answered Citrinne's questions before she could even ask them.

One of Rosabelle's mothers had been killed by a demon when she was seventeen. Everyone coped with such losses in their own ways. Rosabelle's way, apparently, was to join a secret faction of demon-touched mercenaries, poisoning her own body with dubious substances and undergoing rigorous

374

combat training until she could not only carry the blood of demons, but fight like one, too. With any luck, Rosabelle had said, she could stop someone from losing family the way she did.

That was all well and noble, but Rosabelle arguably shouldn't have been saving Fleuretians willy-nilly. She'd been sent to Fleuret to act as a spy and informant, not to perform vigilante shit. But she couldn't stop sticking her nose in places where it didn't belong.

What Rosabelle told her after that made Citrinne's jaw drop. Her mouth stayed partway open as they emerged from the cave and into the night air.

"Emeraude," Citrinne said slowly, "is plotting treason? And you have evidence?"

"Shh!" Rosabelle looked around the forest, as if an eavesdropper would pop out from the trees and kill them. "Not so loud!"

Citrinne tried lowering her voice. "*That's* why she was so intent on finding you. I can't believe I didn't see it before. She's a zealot, but she isn't just acting out of hatred, she's too pragmatic to do that. You've been active for a year, and she's never been this emphatic about putting you down until recently. She doesn't want to kill you because you're demon-touched. Emeraude wants to kill you because you're demon-touched *and* because you have blackmail that can fuck her up!"

Rosabelle's head shrank down into her shoulders. "I don't know if I'd say that. She's still a powerful woman. Would it really be enough?"

"If not, she wouldn't have tried to arrange for your death. In fact..."

Not all ideas struck Citrinne like lightning. Most of the time, it was like finding a lost object, an unexpectedly pleasant surprise that she could put to use. But this one made her freeze. It demanded that she hold her breath. It walked a tightrope between insanity and genius, and only hindsight would tell which way it would fall.

Rosabelle paused halfway up the hill. She frowned. "Citrinne?"

"I have a plan to face Emeraude. A new plan."

Rosabelle perked up. "Really? What is it?"

"Duel her." The more she talked, the more animated she became, like a boulder gaining momentum as it rolled down a slope. She grabbed Rosabelle by both shoulders. "Challenge her! If she wins, she gets the evidence, but if you win—which you will—we get Karalina, and you get to live."

Rosabelle looked sick. She pulled herself away, clung to a nearby tree, and shook her head. "You-You don't know if I'll win."

"Well," Citrinne gestured to her scrawny, magicless, combat untrained self, "you stand a better chance than me."

"This isn't funny! We can't do that. Anything but that."

"I know it's a risk—"

"It's all or nothing! There's a reason why I haven't tried to use that blackmail against her! Because I've been looking for Karalina myself, and wanted to see if I could break her out without handing over the evidence, but also because it's with a contact of mine, and I don't want to endanger her!"

"Yes, that's why it's a risk! It's not an objectively good plan—"

"Then why are you suggesting it?"

"Because Emeraude would have to agree to it. Fleuretian honor demands it. If that's not enough, then she'll do it because we have something she wants. Even if it's not a good plan, it's still the *best* plan we have. Unless you have better?"

"Pretend to give me up? And then, um, you take Karalina, I break free, and then we run?"

Citrinne smiled ruefully. "That'll never work. Karalina's crippled now. We won't be able to run fast enough. And Emeraude will have guards there, you know that. You can't tell me that facing down several swordswomen at once is preferable to facing down *one* swordswoman."

Rosabelle laughed nervously. "It is if that one swordswoman is Emeraude Hervieux! Haven't you seen her duel at court? Fencing is like lightning-quick chess with swords. It's a mind game. And Emeraude is nothing if not good at mind games."

"You killed a dragon! How could Emeraude possibly be more threatening than a dragon?"

"That was only a minor dragon. I've met other demontouched who've killed more deadly dragons, so what I've done really isn't impressive compared to them—"

"Not impressive? It's still a dragon!"

"—besides, dragons don't see me at court every day and sneer at me. They don't assume I'm empty-headed, judge me for wearing something frilly or fancy or over-the-top, or think I'm so beneath them that I'm not even worth sparring with. Their eyes don't pass over me like I'm invisible, as if someone like me can't also be the Crimson Spectre. And I shouldn't complain. The invisibility protects me. But... sometimes I hate just how well it does its job."

Her eyes burned crimson, but Rosabelle lowered them. Black blood coursed through her veins, but Rosabelle rubbed her hand up and down her arm self-consciously. It didn't make sense. Here stood the infamous Crimson Spectre, and she was getting into her own head.

The red of Rosabelle's irises burned away, back into blue. The sclera followed suit, though the black color of her veins was slower to fade away. Rosabelle's eyelids drooped, and she held her head in her hands.

Citrinne frowned. "Are you okay?"

Rosabelle nodded. "It's the demon blood. It's wearing off."

"Already?"

"Well, I've injected so much demon blood over the years that I'm lucky if a shot lasts an hour. Sometimes it's as short as ten minutes. Depends on the blood."

"I see."

Citrinne pulled a paintbrush and the last vial of Fleurine rose ink from her satchel. She rotated the warm glass within the palm of her hand, and it shone like bottled moonlight. She uncorked it and dipped the paintbrush into it.

She carefully stepped towards Rosabelle. "Your hand, please."

Rosabelle hesitated only minimally. She didn't ask why Citrinne wanted it. She just stuck it out. Citrinne reached for it with her free hand. Also hesitated. She got over herself, turning her arm over to see the inner wrist. Citrinne stroked her thumb across it, venturing over a red dot over a vein. One of Rosabelle's frequent injection points, she was sure.

Citrinne looked at Rosabelle's ungloved hand. It was both what Citrinne had imagined it to look like, and the opposite. It was delicate, her nails polished, filed, and painted pink. But track marks crawled along her wrist, and two callouses ran along the sides of the index and middle fingers of her sword hand.

Citrinne pointed to one of the callouses. "Those are from fencing?"

"They are." Rosabelle squirmed. "But they're not a pretty sight. Neither are the track marks that linger after the demon blood runs its course."

"I don't care. They're still yours."

Then Citrinne remembered the ink. "You asked me to trust you." She wiped excess ink off the rim of the vial, determined not to waste a single drop, and set the paintbrush against Rosabelle's inner wrist. "This is it. This is me trusting you." She paused, her eyes flicking up to Rosabelle's. "Do *you* trust you?"

Rosabelle bit her lip. After an entire minute passed, Citrinne realized Rosabelle didn't know the answer.

"Or we could try my other plan," Citrinne added. "I still have that syringe."

Rosabelle blinked. "You're joking."

"I'm not. That is a real possibility. You can go."

"No I can't! I mean, I *could*, but I don't want to, and you shouldn't have to..." Rosabelle sighed. "I'll do it. I'll...I'll duel her."

Citrinne raised her eyebrows, asking if she was sure without actually saying it. Rosabelle nodded.

So Citrinne did what she did best, and she created something from nothing.

THE GARDEN OF FLEURINE WAS TOO PRETTY OF A place for a hostage negotiation.

Citrinne wasn't one for flowers or holy places. But even she couldn't help but stare as she walked through the garden alongside Rosabelle. Roses grew along the wide stone path they tread, so overgrown that they threatened to choke it. They crawled up the stone walls like moss, curling around pillars the way tattoos sprawled along Citrinne's arm, and her eyes watered at the thick, pungent smell. If Fleurine was real, then thank Leontine she had gifted the queendom of Fleuret with an open-air garden. Otherwise, the goddess of life would have, ironically, killed everyone who stepped foot in here through sheer smell alone.

Just as pungent was the magic. Citrinne's elbow accidentally brushed against a bush of blue Fleurine Roses, and a small, gentle spiderweb of frost covered it, only to vanish the instant she moved away. Citrinne almost thought to pluck that flower. But up ahead, along the path, a gardener clipped thorns with thick leather gloves, slowing pace to eye Citrinne and Rosabelle. Even if Citrinne wouldn't be tossed out of the garden for the slightest indiscretion, she lacked enough time to grind any of the petals into ink.

The Garden of Fleurine was such a sacred place that she and Rosabelle passed through stringent security to walk inside. Then they endured another, less official round of security when they encountered Emeraude's personal guard, clad in dark, Fleurentian green. They stood along an invisible perimeter, one of them discreetly redirecting a gardener and whispering that it was of critical importance that the commander have her moment alone at the shrine. Citrinne and Rosabelle approached a wide archway, and though the guards expected Citrinne, one tried to demand that Rosabelle stay behind. Citrinne smiled and said, "Actually, Emeraude wants her, too. Trust me."

The shrine was secluded, rosebushes carefully planted along the perimeter to allow for a room's worth of paved stone along the ground. A marble gazebo stood in the center, and in that gazebo was an old, stone statue of

Fleurine mothering the baby who would become Leontine. Agathe, the goddess of death, was conveniently left out of the picture. She had, after all, kidnapped Fleurine and forced her to marry her. Leontine had killed Agathe for that after she'd grown up...sort of. Agathe was still a goddess. Her blood had allegedly infected all living things close enough to corrupt, and out of that corruption, demons were born. The myth described them as mindless beasts, controlled by Agathe's bidding, intent on corrupting everything they touched.

In front of that statue knelt a woman with a long mane of icy blonde hair, regimented into a practical ponytail. A rapier hung from her hip, and the long sleeves of her decorated uniform were neatly rolled up to her elbow. Gold, green, and white tattoos glowed across her forearm in a series of sharp, diagonal lines with no further embellishment.

Even from behind, Citrinne knew this woman. Not only because of her rank, or because of her ultimatum, but because she'd trained and bled and fought alongside Karalina in the same cohort. Emeraude and Karalina, always sisters-in-arms. Every two weeks after Karalina's disappearance, at Citrinne's mothers' request, she'd stop by to dine and reminisce with the family and click her tongue and say what a tragedy it was that Karalina Laurier had been stolen from them.

All of that time, Emeraude had neglected to mention that she was the one who'd done the stealing.

Citrinne and Rosabelle stopped at the foot of the gazebo. Citrinne counted the guards—ten, all armed with swords—and nearly quipped about how she was the only woman in Fleuret who didn't carry a sword.

Then her heart rate spiked. Two of those guards held a

sagging woman between them. A sack covered her head, and her hands were bound behind her, but those precautions seemed unnecessary when the prisoner lacked a leg.

Citrinne's breath hitched. Rosabelle glanced between her and Emeraude, clearly concerned. She itched to fling herself towards her sister and rip her away from those guards.

Instead, Citrinne whispered, "Emeraude masked this person's face. For all we know, it could be someone else." To conveniently have another prisoner with a missing leg, though? Even Citrinne couldn't believe her own words.

But it helped to think about the situation logically. She reminded herself to breathe, and prepared herself to act like she had a heart of stone.

Citrinne addressed the kneeling Emeraude. "So, how much do you have to bribe the gardeners to look the other way when you're bringing a hostage with you? Or did you pull rank, or—oh, I get it now, you spouted bullshit about how it was Leontine's will, didn't you?"

The hooded figure snapped her head towards Citrinne. A few of the guards huffed like birds with ruffled feathers. But Emeraude didn't twitch. The literal statue held more life than her.

"I had a dream, two years ago." Emeraude murmured. "I stood here, in the Garden of Fleuret, standing over a crimson cloak. Demon blood stained my hands black. No matter how I tried to scrub my hands clean, I could not. Then I heard a voice, ironclad in nature, tell me that they were not meant to be clean. I alone was meant to sully my hands, so that her queendom might be clean. I woke up, and I did not understand." Emeraude stood, her movements mechanical, and turned a cold green eye on Citrinne. "Now I understand Leontine's will much more clearly. I am to stand over the demon-touched's body. And I am to do it here."

The dream sounded so ridiculous, Emeraude so arrogant, that Citrinne wanted to laugh. But underneath the stupidity laid a line of thinking that threatened to harm Rosabelle. So no, Citrinne didn't laugh. Her skin crawled.

Emeraude's gaze pierced Rosabelle next. "You were told to come alone."

Before Emeraude could do things like kill her sister for Citrinne's incompliance, she quickly said, "Actually, she's exactly what you want. Emeraude, meet the Crimson Spectre." Citrinne gestured to Rosabelle, whose hands shook as she tugged down her gloves, revealing the red track marks along her skin.

She waited for Rosabelle to take her cue, but she trembled like an actress on stage, all lines forgotten. So Citrinne puffed up her chest and said, "She's here to challenge you to a duel!"

From someone as outspoken against demon-touched as Emeraude, Citrinne had expected horror, or disgust. Instead, her eyes widened from shock, and with that, Emeraude expressed her first whole emotion of the day, or perhaps the year.

She sputtered, "Her? You mean to tell me that your frivolous, weak, and air-headed foreigner of a fiancée is..."

"Not as air-headed as you thought. Not if she fooled you."

In any other circumstance, Emeraude's sheer stupefaction would have made Citrinne laugh. More astoundingly, it rendered her human.

But it didn't help that Rosabelle kept staring at Emeraude like a rabbit caught in a fox's sights. Emeraude's lip curled. "My instructions were clear, Laurier. Bring me the body of the Crimson Spectre – even a part would have sufficed – and only then would I return your sister."

"I've done as you asked. You just never specified if you wanted a living body or a dead one—"

"Do not act the fool. You willfully misinterpret my instructions, and now you attempt to pass off your fiancée as the Crimson Spectre. But someone like her cannot possibly be that demon-touched."

That snapped Rosabelle out of her anxiety. She leaned back as if she'd been slapped. "Um, *excuse* me?!"

Emeraude didn't even look at her. "When I asked you about your associations with the Crimson Spectre, you obfuscated stupidity until I showed you the correspondence I'd obtained. You admired her, studied her, and protected her, even then—"

"I'm right here!"

"—Now, you mean to tell me that she is your fiancée, when that same fiancée cannot even challenge me herself? She plays her part poorly, and I see through your deception. You mean to double-cross me, and I will not stand for it."

As Emeraude spoke, Rosabelle silently fumed. Her hand plunged down the one place the guards at the garden gates wouldn't look—between her breasts—and plucked out the one vial of demon blood they could sneak inside. She loaded it into a syringe, and then she hammered the needle into one of her injection points. Emeraude recoiled as black blood surged up Rosabelle's veins, and the whites and blues of her eyes melted into black and red.

Smoke billowed from her nose. Wisps of flame flickered out of Rosabelle's mouth as she snarled, "See me."

For a moment, Citrinne thought Emeraude did.

Then she said, "If this is true, then it seems the Crimson Spectre is more pathetic than I imagined."

Rosabelle bristled. She unsheathed her rapier and pointed it in Emeraude's direction. At this, several of the guards also drew their blades. Emeraude held up a hand before it could dissolve into a bloodbath.

"I, Rosabelle Heartwood, challenge you, Emeraude Hervieux, to a duel." Neither her hand nor her voice wavered. In fact, Citrinne couldn't help but think of the story where Leontine challenged Agathe. Citrinne wanted to tell Emeraude that, just to see her have a conniption at the idea of taking Agathe's role this scenario, but she didn't interrupt. "If I win, then Karalina Laurier, Citrinne Laurier, and I all get to go free. If you win...then I'll tell you exactly where I'm keeping the evidence of your treason."

Nothing about Emeraude's face changed. But Citrinne somehow felt her attention sharpen.

Now, Citrinne did cut in. "She told me everything. The day you delivered news about Karalina's 'death,' Rosabelle overheard a conversation between you and one of your sergeants that suggested you kept a secret prisoner. The way you talked about her, she had a hunch that it was Karalina. But she didn't know for certain." That, Rosabelle had explained, was why she'd never told Citrinne. She didn't want to risk raising her hope for nothing.

"One day, she intercepted correspondence between you and another military officer, confirming her support for a coup against Queen Verene. Because apparently, her laws concerning demon-touched have been too relaxed for your tastes. You think demon-touched need to be annihilated, and meanwhile, here the queen is, softening punishments against them. She's the one who decreed that demon-touched should be imprisoned for their injections, not executed. It's blasphemy to you, isn't it? You can't fucking stand that, and now, Rosabelle here has evidence of your treason. The only thing that stopped her from exposing you was your hostage. But I'm curious – how did it feel knowing each night, as you tried to sleep, that the Crimson Spectre had what she needed to ruin everything you worked for?"

Emeraude didn't answer, but that wasn't what Citrinne wanted. She looked from guard to guard, hoping that all of these accusations would elicit some kind of response. If honor was so important in Fleuret, then maybe at least one of these guardswomen would have some. If Rosabelle dueled Emeraude and failed, then someone could report what they'd heard to the Queen.

That might've been too much to hope for. None of the swordswomen reacted. It could be militaristic discipline coming handy in a pinch...or they were all complicit in Emeraude's schemes.

"And what," Emeraude said, thoughtful, "is stopping me from simply raiding your home?"

"You can try," Rosabelle said. "But it's not there."

Emeraude narrowed her eyes. "A counteroffer, then."

She made a signal with her hand, too quick for Citrinne to catch. One of the prisoner's guards ripped the sack off her head, and Karalina Laurier squeezed her eyes shut at the sudden light. A strip of cloth ran between her teeth, and her cheeks were gaunter, her brown skin more ashen. The circles under her eyes were dark and potent, and all of the Fleurine Rose ink had long since sapped out of her sleeve of geometric tattoos. It was as if Emeraude had taken a chisel to her and carved out all of the stone strength that made her the bodyguard to Queen Verene. But she was unmistakably her sister.

Rosabelle's uncertainty returned with a vengeance. Citrinne's own heart stopped. Breathing got a lot harder, as Karalina caught her eyes and frantically jerked her head away from the Garden, urging Citrinne to get out. Thank Leontine, they'd discussed this possibility on the way to the garden. If they hadn't, Citrinne had a queasy feeling that she would've capitulated.

"Don't," she whispered to Rosabelle. Citrinne grabbed Rosabelle's shoulder, clenching it tight. "Remember, if you give Emeraude what she wants, she'll kill Karalina anyway. Hold your ground."

Rosabelle's hand still trembled. But she said, "I'll only give you the evidence if you agree to duel me. You can threaten her. You can threaten me and...and Citrinne." Her voice hardened. "But it won't work. You'll only ensure that I will never give you what you want. You'll get it if you accept my challenge and win. That's it."

"That is an impossibility, here in the garden. You have willingly taken Agathe's taint into yourself. Should I spill your blood here, it would defile this holy place."

"Forget defilement," Citrinne said. "You heard in that weird dream—"

"My vision."

"Whatever, that vision of yours. What was it that Leontine told you? That you must 'sully your hands?' It sounds like you're the one meant to kill the Crimson Spectre, here and now. Don't tell me you're about to defy her orders."

Emeraude pursed her lips. They became as thin as a knife's edge. Citrinne held her breath, silently praying to Leontine for the first time in years.

At last, Emeraude murmured, "Leontine will guide my hand." She raised her voice and declared, "Very well. I accept your challenge, Spectre. We fight to the death, with rapiers, immediately. I declare Pernella Allard," Emeraude gestured to the guard closest to her right, and a grim-faced woman with spectacles stepped forward, "to be my second. I will allow you to declare yours."

Rosabelle started, "I declare Cit—"

"No, Karalina," Citrinne said, an idea striking her. "Karalina Laurier will be her second."

"What?" Rosabelle's head snapped towards Citrinne, like she wanted to be angry, but could only manage terrified. "I want you!"

"Listen." Citrinne grabbed Rosabelle by both shoulders, leaned in, and whispered, "Karalina's sparred with Emeraude before. She told me that half the time, Emeraude wins, but the other half of the time, Karalina wins. Emeraude's not a dragon. She's human. That bitch has weaknesses, and if anyone knows them, it's Karalina. She can advise you better than I can, I promise you."

"You're doing this so she has a chance to get away if I die, aren't you?"

"You are not going to fucking die—"

"I expect your decision, Spectre." Emeraude's voice cut through like a knife. "Tell me who your second will be."

"I..." Rosabelle looked indecisive. Then she squeezed her eyes shut. "I declare Karalina Laurier as my second."

Emeraude's nostrils flared, and Citrinne knew she'd made the right choice. She instructed one of her guards, tightly, "Find a walking stick for Karalina Laurier and cut her loose. But in exchange, her sister takes her place."

"*No!*" Rosabelle snarled, so vehemently that a spurt of flame shot from her mouth. Citrinne put a hand on her shoulder to calm her down.

Then she turned back to Emeraude. Citrinne said, "Deal."

"No," Rosabelle said again. This time, she didn't breathe

fire, even as one of the guards stepped forward, wrapped a pair of strong hands around Citrinne's arms, and hauled her away from Rosabelle. "No, no, no, no, Citrinne—"

"Don't worry." Citrinne mustered the most confident smile she could. "You'll win."

While she said one thing, her racing heart said another. Citrinne fought—and failed—to keep her breathing even as another guard came by with a length of rope and looped it around her wrists. After they cinched the tie, Citrinne twisted her wrists without thinking, trying to find any give, only to get a kick to the back of her left knee, a sharp reminder rather than anything intended to hurt. Citrinne forced herself to be still.

At least Emeraude kept to her word. The moment Karalina's bonds were cut and her gag untied, she spat at Emeraude's feet. One of the guards returned with a thick stick, and Karalina took a few reluctant steps forward, her face pinched with pain, her free hand drifting to her ribs. Citrinne, after realizing why she was hurt, immediately wished she hadn't. If Karalina was the queen's bodyguard, and if Emeraude was plotting a coup, then surely she'd... wanted information.

Karalina limped toward Rosabelle but paused in front of Citrinne. Karalina's upturned eyes assessed Citrinne the way she'd assessed Karalina, checking for injuries. Then Karalina shook her head and blurted, "You shouldn't have come. I was already set to die. You didn't have to set yourself and Rosabelle to die, too—"

"Love the gratitude, sis—"

Karalina winced and held up a hand, interrupting her. "No, stop. I'm sorry. There's no time, I shouldn't have—" She sighed, recollecting herself. "I don't want my last words to you to be ones I regret. Not again. So, I've missed you. I love you."

Citrinne waited for the lump in her throat to pass. She said quietly, "I love you too."

The guard holding Citrinne barked, "Move." A moment of reluctance from Karalina, and then she did, hobbling the rest of the way to Rosabelle.

Emeraude gave herself and Rosabelle two minutes to confer with their seconds. Citrinne wished Rosabelle would fight for more time, but she only nodded. Emeraude acted as if she didn't need it, rolling up her sleeve and only checking her multi-colored tattoos once, shaking her head to something Allard whispered to her.

But Citrinne mostly watched Karalina and Rosabelle. Karalina stopped twenty feet away from Rosabelle, eyeing her with reluctance and disdain. Citrinne couldn't fathom how anyone could look at Rosabelle that way, until she remembered that Karalina numbered among the devout. Anytime someone mentioned the Crimson Spectre, Karalina had expressed admiration for her deeds, but that good faith had always warred with her disgust for demons, and her more understandable concern about the substances the Crimson Spectre shot up her veins.

But whatever misgivings Karalina might've had, she seemed to set them aside. She ventured within arm's length of Rosabelle, examining both her and Emeraude with a strategist's eye. Then she leaned forward, pointing to Emeraude as she spoke quietly to Rosabelle. Citrinne knew leaning in wouldn't let her hear, but she still couldn't resist trying.

Rosabelle bit her lip. Karalina kept talking, and Rosabelle kept nodding along, not volunteering much. Karalina stood right in front of Rosabelle, but her red eyes kept drifting to Citrinne. Any time Rosabelle's gaze flickered back to Karalina, she leaned back on her heels, as if she wanted to get away. Considering Karalina's opinions on the Crimson Spectre, had Rosabelle always been uncomfortable around Karalina, and been too polite to say it? How did Rosabelle feel more at ease with Citrinne, even after she'd tried to lure her into a trap? Shouldn't that have been enough to send Rosabelle's romantic interest in Citrinne tumbling down a fucking ravine?

In any other situation, Citrinne might've selfishly liked that her chances with Rosabelle weren't as dead as she'd thought. But now, all that did was foster a sense of helplessness, and it clawed at Citrinne's belly. Her heart beat furiously. If Rosabelle didn't trust Karalina as much as Citrinne, then what if she'd made the wrong choice on Rosabelle's second?

But Citrinne had given her last vial of Fleurine Rose ink to Rosabelle, and she'd left the situation in the hands of those who could handle it better than her. If Rosabelle trusted Citrinne, then she would trust her decision to make Karalina her second, and she would listen to whatever her sister had to say.

Emeraude called time. Karalina patted Rosabelle reluctantly on the shoulder before stepping away, letting Rosabelle move forward with her drawn rapier. She met Emeraude halfway down a pathway to the shrine, and though formalities demanded they raise their sword and bow to each other, both Rosabelle and Emeraude bowed so stiffly that Citrinne didn't think either should actually count. Then they both turned around, walking ten paces away from each other.

Emeraude's second, Allard, officiated. She stood to the side and said, ritually, "For valor."

Rosabelle and Emeraude settled into their stances, rapiers at the ready, front foot forwards. Rosabelle leaned forward a little more than Emeraude did. Her mouth twitched.

"For faith."

Even though Citrinne was bound, even though Karalina stood several feet away from her, Citrinne itched to reach for Karalina's hand. She settled for clenching both of her hands into fists.

"And for honor. Allez!"

Rosabelle opened her mouth, and out lunged a long torrent of fire, so wide that Allard scrambled out of its way, and so hot that Citrinne felt its heat on her face. She almost turned her eyes away from it.

But something within the flames caught her attention. Something pearly white, and charging towards Rosabelle, not unlike a soldier running through a hail of arrows with a massive shield.

Citrinne only managed to shout, "She's getting close to —" before her guard covered her mouth with a meaty hand and hissed at her to be quiet. Citrinne bristled, ready to chew off one of her fingers, but she restrained herself. For now.

Even if she could talk, Citrinne realized it might be better if she didn't. Though Rosabelle kept her face and flames pointed in Emeraude's direction, her eyes flicked to Citrinne for a split second—all the time Emeraude needed to finish bulldozing her way through the flames, entirely unharmed. She pivoted to Rosabelle's side and dispelled her barrier long enough to extend her rapier towards Rosabelle's hand. Emeraude punished her with a quick slice to the wrist, and Rosabelle's flames guttered out as she squeaked. The blade cut through her glove and drew a thin line of blood. Citrinne's breath hitched, but the cut must have been shallow, because Rosabelle kept her grip on her rapier.

But now that Emeraude had drawn first blood, she sniffed for more. She pressed her advantage, her sword moving so quickly that Citrinne's eyes struggled to follow. Rosabelle miraculously parried each thrust, and even found an opportunity to riposte. Emeraude turned her body just so, missing the strike.

Rosabelle put more distance between them and breathed fire again. But Emeraude's free hand always hovered close to the Fleurine Rose tattoos engraved on her arm. Her finger hardly needed to twitch before another barrier sprang to life.

A scraggly, thorny stick, as flexible as a vine, suddenly shot out from the closest rosebush and lassoed around Rosabelle's ankle. She yelped as it yanked her off her feet. She turned her fire to the stick holding her and burned it to a crisp. Without the fire assaulting Emeraude, Citrinne found not just one of her white tattoos glowing, but one of her green ones, too.

More sticks lunged from the rosebushes, attempting to surround Rosabelle. She incinerated those, too. She went so far as to unleash plumes of fire on the rosebushes themselves, burning any she could see. It forced most of the surrounding guards to scramble, shouting for water or dirt or anything else that could put out the flames. A few ran forward, tapped tattoos of a darker blue than what Citrinne had employed in the cave, and water sprang from their hands as if from a fountain.

Citrinne relished how Rosabelle had stripped Emeraude of her ammunition. But as Rosabelle spun and directed her fire back towards Emeraude, her own advantage guttered out. Her fire sputtered, whittling itself to a few meager wisps of flame. Rosabelle's eyes widened as her irises changed from red to blue, her sclera from black to white.

Citrinne stared, just as shocked. Rosabelle's injections could run their course quickly, but the dragon blood lost its effect this soon?

Emeraude didn't look surprised. She tapped one of her white tattoos again, dropping her barrier before one of her fingers twitched towards a golden tattoo. She only needed to briefly touch it before light shone from Emeraude's arm. When Rosabelle tried to look at Emeraude's sword, she yelped, closing her eyes against the light. Emeraude lunged so far forward that it looked like a small jump, and Rosabelle staggered backwards, barely able to parry the thrust to her chest in time.

"You struggled to hold your own against me before," Emeraude said. "Your attempts to do so will only be more pitiful now."

Rosabelle had mentioned while talking about her brutal training that she'd sometimes been forced to duel blind-folded. That might be the only thing saving her now. Emeraude walked forward as her rapier clashed with Rosabelle's, forcing her back, back, back. Her movements were slower, almost lazy, but that only made her more imposing, like a predator willing to take all of the time she needed to kill her prey. It didn't help that many of Emeraude's tattoos were loaded with Fleurine Rose ink, her permanent tattoos depleting much more slowly than Citrinne's temporary ones. Rosabelle, sluggish from withdrawal, lacking sight, fought purely defensively. She acted almost as clumsily as she'd been all those times Citrinne had seen her duel at court.

Citrinne thought back to all of those stories she'd heard

of heroes fighting dragons, fictional and non-fictional. Dragons brimmed with power and razed entire villages to the ground. But in the end, some hero always defeated them, as if dragons existed to be overcome by someone stronger. For one moment, Citrinne worried Emeraude could be the 'someone stronger.'

But Emeraude hadn't killed a dragon three hours ago. That honor belonged to Rosabelle. Emeraude clearly saw how Rosabelle's technique had regressed. But what Citrinne saw was, despite that, Rosabelle still fended off Emeraude.

Until she raised her arm, trying to blink past the light. Emeraude seized the opportunity and cut a thin line of blood along Rosabelle's raised forearm, as if to remind her she wasn't safe. She cried out, stumbled back, and her spine hit a pillar. She lowered her arm.

But as she did, Rosabelle subtly tugged on the rip across her glove on her sword hand, widening the tear until Citrinne glimpsed a white glow. Rosabelle had let herself be hit. By doing so, she had given herself access without making a show of rolling down her glove and flagging her next move to Emeraude.

Citrinne fought the urge to grin.

A small spot of green glowed at the end of one of Emeraude's tattooed lines, and she used the last of that line's magic to add insult to injury. She summoned a root deep from the earth, wrapped it around Rosabelle's sword arm, and pinned it to the pillar. Rosabelle squeaked, tugging desperately at her wrist, and Citrinne worried that her struggling was real.

Emeraude advanced, the tip of her rapier directed towards Rosabelle's heart. She drove it forward just as

Rosabelle tore her entire glove off and slid her finger underneath the root immobilizing her hand.

The rapier rammed against a white barrier.

Emeraude's eyes widened. Rosabelle twisted her wrist, roaring as she yanked it free from the root. Now, Citrinne did grin under the guard's hand, in utter satisfaction. Underneath the glove, she could see parts of the pattern she'd drawn on Rosabelle's wrist: a rose, with a long stem that made it bear more thorns than petals. The design, by Citrinne's standards, wasn't perfect. But it was good, and it got the job done, and that was what mattered.

Rosabelle took advantage of Emeraude's shock. She leaned forward, ramming the magical barrier against Emeraude's rapier, pushing it to the side and out of the way, enough to force Emeraude to lean back. Her tattoos still brimmed with magic, sure, plenty of gold and green and white lines unused. But Emeraude struggled to reach for any of them at such an angle. Rosabelle's barrier flickered out of existence, and just as she left herself open, Rosabelle tipped the point of her rapier down towards Emeraude's chest and sank it in to the hilt.

Emeraude dropped her sword. She staggered back, blood bubbling from her chest and her mouth, the sword in her chest upsetting her balance. She fell to her knees, catching herself on her palm before she toppled entirely. Blearily, she blinked up at Rosabelle, looking at her with something new in her eyes. Not respect. But maybe an overdue acknowledgment.

Then she raised those eyes up to the moon. "Leontine," Emeraude croaked. "Forgive me."

Emeraude swayed and hit the ground sideways. The scent of her blood cloyed with that of roses as she rasped one last breath. She did not breathe out.

And then—

Chaos.

Shouts erupted from the guards all around, two of them running to Emeraude's body. Another two were still occupied with the last of the burning rosebushes. Most of them fought amongst themselves, panicking, arguing whether to cover their tracks and kill the three of them, or whether to throw themselves at Queen Verene's mercy while they still could.

But the guard holding Citrinne didn't let her go. If anything, her grip tightened around Citrinne's face. Rosabelle blinked herself out of some weird daze. Then she turned and marched on Citrinne and her captor with her sword drawn. Fury lit her face ablaze, and she did not need a drop of demon blood to sound feral. "Let her go!"

As dashing as that display was, and as much as Citrinne wanted to know whether the guard would piss her pants, she couldn't count on that. Citrinne chomped down on one of the guard's fingers. Just when she thought she'd have to bite the finger clean off, the guard took the hint, screaming as she released her.

Citrinne ran to Rosabelle, and Rosabelle to her. She grabbed Citrinne's arm, turned her around, and set to work untying her.

"That's my fiancée!" Citrinne laughed, and despite the situation, her heart couldn't help but swell with pride. "You killed Emeraude!"

"Barely." Rosabelle half-laughed, half-sobbed. "In some ways, she was harder than the dragon, and, and—" She rambled so quickly that she bordered on incoherent. "And I realized halfway through the duel that I hadn't told you I forgive you yet—"

"Huh?"

"Back in the cave! You said you were sorry! But I didn't say I forgive you, so—I forgive you, okay? You were trying to protect Karalina, and it baffles me that she called you self-ish, because I think you're one of the most selfless people I've ever met."

Tears burned in Citrinne's eyes. She couldn't totally keep them back, or stop her voice from croaking. "Thanks."

Rosabelle finished untying her. The rope didn't even finish falling to the ground before Citrinne hugged her. She breathed in the scent of sweat and blood, but under-neath it all cloyed a strong perfume. Rosewater. She laughed quietly into her hair, because, of course, she would wear rosewater perfume into battle. Rosabelle also clung tightly to Citrinne, as if she alone kept her from falling.

Karalina shouted, "Citrinne! Rosabelle!"

Citrinne's head snapped up. Karalina had managed to take advantage of the fissure among Emeraude's ranks, stumbling away until she stood under the shrine's entrance. She jerked her head to the side.

Citrinne got the message and let Rosabelle go. She ran towards Karalina, and Rosabelle followed, rapier drawn, pointing it in the general direction of any guardswoman who threatened to get too close.

Even running for her life couldn't stop Citrinne from talking. "What did Karalina tell you about Emeraude? Did anything she say make a difference?"

Rosabelle nodded. "She told me Emeraude's weakness was that she only saw what she wanted to see. Karalina said I should take advantage of that, because she wouldn't see me, even if I wanted her to." She tried to laugh, but between the running and being short on breath, it flopped out as a wheeze. "But you do."

A WEEK PASSED IN THE BLINK OF AN EYE.

After Citrinne had thrown Karalina's arm over her shoulder and helped her out of the Garden, she'd reunited her with their mothers. They'd hired a doctor to help her cope with the loss of her leg and spoke about finding her a prosthetic. In the meantime, Citrinne spent all of the time she could with Karalina. For once, having a conversation with her wasn't so hard. Almost dying had a knack for bringing people together.

But her mind never strayed far from Rosabelle. The day after the duel, Karalina had scrutinized Citrinne from her bed and commented, so observationally as to flirt with dispassion, "You and Rosabelle prefer the new arrangement, don't you?"

Citrinne had startled in her chair. "Well…"

"There's no need to sugarcoat the truth. It's always been obvious, how much she likes you. Before, well, Emeraude happened, I'd planned to talk to her about it. Both for her sake, and for mine. I can help my family climb the social ladder with a fiancée who trusts me, and *won't* be pining for my sister, thank you kindly. And…" Karalina had taken a deep breath, "for your sake, too. I want you to be happy. You have my blessing."

Citrinne had the decency to wait one full day before she made herself scarce, collaborating on a project with a specialized blacksmith throughout the week. Because her fiancée's favor was not something she'd been prepared to lose after all, and she would do her damndest to get it back.

When Citrinne was ready to visit Rosabelle again, she entered Rosabelle's bedroom quietly and found her standing on a balcony overlooking a beach, facing away from Citrinne. Rosabelle tightened her grip on something, leaning forward on the railing and muttered to herself.

Citrinne knocked on the wall, holding her special project behind her back. Rosabelle jumped, turning around and stashing an object out of sight. "Uh, Citrinne! Hi! What's, uh—what's that you're holding?"

"I don't know. What are *you* hiding?"

Rosabelle bit her lip. Instead of demanding that Citrinne go first, she revealed a hand mirror. She wore no gloves.

"I'm practicing," she admitted. "What I might say to Karalina when I...um..." Rosabelle cleared her throat, "When I tell her I want you instead."

Citrinne's breath hitched.

"Neither Karalina nor I ever liked each other that way." Rosabelle dropped her eyes to the floor, cheeks pinkening. "So, I think it'll be fine. Unless you don't...oh no, I should have asked first. Do you still want to be engaged? I would like to—but no pressure if you—"

Citrinne cut her off, pulling out what she'd been hiding. "How's this for an answer?"

Rosabelle gasped, flinging her hands over her mouth. A flourishing basket hilt capped off the engagement sword, rings of gold swirling around a hilt crafted from rose quartz. Stamped on the blade was Citrinne's contribution: the same rose design she'd drawn on Rosabelle's wrist.

"I never expected you." Citrinne drew in a deep breath. "I love you, damn it. I'd like to prove it, and I'd like to keep proving it. I was about to ask if you'd let me do that, but it sounds like you will. Which is shocking. I know I'm not as easy to like as Karalina."

Citrinne didn't realize how far down her chin had

slumped until Rosabelle put two fingers underneath and lifted it.

"But you're easier to love," Rosabelle said.

She set the engagement sword aside before grabbing Citrinne's shirt and yanking her closer with an intensity that startled her. But once Rosabelle actually kissed her, she did it sweetly, caressing her jaw and tracing her thumb along Citrinne's cheek. Citrinne grabbed the railing behind Rosabelle, just as much to keep herself upright as it was to keep Rosabelle here, and tried to return the favor slowly. She'd waited so long, and reminded herself to savor it.

But she could also savor the moment in different ways. Citrinne hooked one of her arms around Rosabelle's waist, pulling her in closer. Instead of exploring Rosabelle's mouth, she chased after it, and Rosabelle hummed, melting into her.

Rosabelle pulled away, just long enough to say, "I do still want to marry you. And I love you too. In case that wasn't clear."

Citrinne laughed. "Oh, it's clear." Then she eyed the railing Rosabelle sat on. "As much as I love your tendency for living on the edge – or kissing on the edge, as it were – I can think of safer, more private places to keep doing this."

"Such as?"

The way Rosabelle said it, Citrinne almost thought she somehow didn't know what it meant. But then she batted her eyelashes far too innocently. Citrinne grinned, holding out a hand. Rosabelle slid her manicured hand into hers, and Citrinne tugged her away from the railing, reeling her across the balcony and back into her bedroom. Rosabelle closed the curtains on her way inside.

Citrinne settled onto Rosabelle's sprawling, pink-blanketed bed, and pulled her down on top of her. Rosabelle's long hair dangled between their faces and tickled Citrinne's nose. Rosabelle huffed, rolling her eyes as she tucked it back behind her ears.

She hadn't even finished doing that before Citrinne propped herself up on her elbows and pressed her lips to Rosabelle's lips. Then she pressed her chest to Rosabelle's chest, her hips to Rosabelle's hips, tangled her legs between Rosabelle's legs. Citrinne kept an arm around Rosabelle's waist, melding them so close together that she couldn't tell where she ended and Rosabelle began. Both of them melted and shared whispers and sighs, pleas and cries, exploring each part of the other and loving each crook of the neck, stroking each curve of the hip. She lost herself for hours, and by the end of the night, Citrinne understood what it meant to worship someone.

The only thing better than that was waking up next to Rosabelle the next morning, crooking a smile as Rosabelle softly snored with her face buried deep into a pillow. Because this would be Citrinne's new forever. How fantastic was that?

About the Author

Alyssa Rae Jensen writes about morally complicated women and queer love with an edge. When she's not working on her debut novel, she loves to play video games, spar with her pink longsword, and travel wherever her wanderlust takes her. She lives among the Utah mountains, along with her girlfriend and her family. "Her Fiancée's Favor" is her first publication.

Find out more at: https://beacons.ai/alyssaraejensen

The Sword's Soul

Evelyn Shine

A ROAR RIPS THROUGH THE SILENCE, FOLLOWED BY A feline shriek. Boudicca grasps my forearm, dragging me faster down a corridor so low she must stoop. Her broken wing folds awkwardly against her back, stone-like skin gleaming where fractured claw marks didn't mar her hide. She is indeed a magnificent gargoyle.

"Viola," she pants, "I need time to heal. Can you get a shield up?"

I give her a grim nod. Every portal we've crossed through in the bōc-hord has been safe, lulling me into a false complacency. With wall to ceiling books and endless rooms and corridors, I've treated this inter-dimensional space as no more dangerous than any other library. How could I be such a naïve idiot? I dare a glance over my shoulder and the regret of looking battles with panic. The feline-shaped monsters are closing in fast, moving at a pace we'll never beat. I count three. The rest, I only hear—roaring, racing closer. A face that's far too human for comfort snarls from the sable tangles of a lion-like mane. Spikes dripping with slimy green ichor fly pass the tip of my nose.

404

I may not be the muscle here, but I can't be completely useless. Panic rattles through my shaking limbs. Facing forward, I fumble with a metallic sphere cupped in my palm, clicking a third interlocking piece into place. This should create a shield strong enough to protect us. Sweat trickles down my forehead, plastering my hair to my fogging glasses. "I thought you said this place was safe?"

"Maker Xander cleared this portal world themself. Manticores weren't present." Boudicca flinches as a volley of spikes clanks off her stone-like skin. "Love, I need that shield." Her panting breaths paint my cheek. Deep rents mar her chest and shoulders. Her left arm hangs in tatters. Jagged crystalline formations line the grievous wounds in calcified drips.

Seeing her injuries, I stumble, and my creation comes apart in my hands. "I'm sorry. I'm trying. Xander just showed me how to build this last month. It might work if I can puzzle it all together. I don't know."

If only my mentor were here. Even after half a year of tutelage, I have doubts I'll ever be skilled at making magical items.

Another roar rips me out of my anxious haze. Cursing, I sort through my satchel. Moth wings to contact Xander, bits of springs and crystals, orbs containing different experiments. Long metallic feet scrape my wrist. Perfect. Whispering the activation key to bring my creations to life, I dump the contents of a bag to the floor and excited metal chittering fills the air.

"Spiders? How is that..." Boudicca trails off as the tiny mechanical creatures surge forward in a wave.

Steel threads shoot through the air to tangle with clawed paws. I pause for the briefest of moments to admire my work as my metal minions hoist the manticores upward, trapping them. Maybe I really am deserving of the Bichler name, one of the greatest maker families of artificer mages, and my grandmother's heir. As the spiders swarm over the manticores, the beasts spit curses and hisses.

"Not bad." I grin.

"It's perfect." Boudicca brushes a kiss across my forehead. She frowns at a monster already clawing its way free. "We should find safety before they get loose."

Even as the words leave her lips, stones pull from the wall where the webbing held. Dammit, I thought that would hold them longer.

A manticore crushes one of my spiders underfoot and snarls, "Your tiny toys can't hold us back."

Shock ripples over me. "Cripes, they talk?"

"They do have faces." Boudicca lifts me in her arms and charges away in an awkward crouch, flinching as my weight bounces against her torso. She always seemed so indestructible to me. Glancing down, I lock the sphere together, turning the intricate crystal lines back to a grid. That looks correct. I think. *I hope.* Gritting my teeth, I wish Xander were here to check my work.

Howls rip through the book-lined corridors of the bōchord, echoed by a wave of my fear. No time for that. Never in a million years did I think traveling through the passages of the secret magical wing of the Mazarine Library in Paris would end in being hunted by a pack of fantastical creatures.

Of course, I'm dating a fantastical creature, and I never thought that possible either.

"Viola, focus! You can do this."

I nod and point the sphere over her shoulder toward the beasts chomping my mechanical creations into smithereens.

Light flares sharp and bright, throwing the edge of

ancient books into stark contrast. A thin, glimmering shell grows until it spans the hall, separating the humanoid lions from us. They snarl and pace, tufted tails flicking and sharp teeth bared behind human-looking lips.

The magical shield flickers weakly. Hell, that's never going to hold long enough.

Boudicca grunts as she sets me down then tugs me around a corner. "We have to get back to the portal we came through. The gate will close in two days."

"How do we shake them?" I lift the hem of my dress higher, as if that will help me run faster. I should've worn pants today. My magical climbing slippers are beyond useless in a corridor this small. A shriek of triumph splits the air followed by more airborne spikes shredding the loose sleeve of my dress. A scream rises in my throat, but I stuff it down, needing the air to keep running.

"Stay close to me," Boudicca rasps. "One scrape of their spikes and you'll be poisoned. Your life is short enough without losing it to danger."

I frown but tuck myself closer to her as we slide on the marble tile. She likely didn't mean to remind me that she's near immortal and I'm just a frail human. Her claws dig furrows into the stone as she spins us left through a carved arch.

"We need to find somewhere to hole up. Maybe they'll get bored." Boudicca glances back with a wince. "I can't handle three in my current state."

Remembering the ambush earlier, I blink back the sting in my eyes. A pack of seven of the creatures descended on us while we were exploring a cavernous part of the bōc-hord. Boudicca threw me behind her and took out four of the beasts before we ran. By the ache in my thighs, that feels like years ago, not hours.

White doors line the hall ahead, their symmetry at odd with the rough-hewn stone walls. Stopping at the first door I grasp the doorknob, rattling it futilely. Locked.

"Love, please!" Panic dances in Boudicca's labradorite-colored eyes. The pounding of clawed paws announces our enemies closing in. "We need to keep moving."

"One of these might be open." I try another door, hissing as the heat from the brass knob sears my hand.

"Your flesh will be the most succulent I've had in a hundred years," roars the lead manticore.

Gross. So much for them getting bored. I jiggle another doorknob, being careful to check the temperature this time.

Boudicca lashes her thick, scaled tail as she moves in front of me. "I'll hold them off."

Racing to the next door, I wrench the knob. It swings open with a shriek. I let out a relieved sigh as I step forward.

To a cliff's edge over a star-studded endless space. "Gah!" My magical slippers stick fast to the ground even as I pinwheel my arms for balance on the sliver of rock.

"Any luck?" Boudicca grunts.

A feline squeal wrenches me back from the edge. "No. It's an abyss."

Boudicca's massive hand clutches the manticore by the scruff of its neck, and her injured arm wraps awkwardly around the creature's middle, keeping the sharp claws pointed away from her. Helplessness washes over me. All the knowledge in the world isn't going to keep us from becoming cat food.

"Try the next door." Boudicca growls as she twists.

A sickening crack fills the air. She flings the corpse into the void through the door then turns to meet the next crea-ture. I gulp and run for the next door. It takes a century to get there while yowls echo down the hall. More are coming.

I shake the doorknob. Locked. With trembling limbs, I shuffle across the hall to the next, and the next. A glance back at my lover leaves me shaken. Light reflects from the pool of black blood spilling from Boudicca's flesh, and the floor glistens slick with it. Dark crystals line the wounds, and her skin takes on the shine of polished obsidian. I'm not sure how much more damage Boudicca can take before she reverts to stone.

A star-shaped knob turns in my hand. The door pulls open hard, tossing me inside. I stumble forward a few steps into a small study lined with leather-bound books. A fire burns cheerfully in a grand stone hearth. Above the smooth, grey river stones hangs a leaf-bladed sword with an unadorned leather-wrapped grip. The area looks safe enough.

"Get in here, I think we can defend this room." Maybe hold it until the manticores give up. Or at least until Boudicca can use her stone form to rest and heal.

I fish another orb from my satchel and thumb it open to adjust the calculations. Perhaps the hall was too wide and that's why the magic failed. If I can just get the shield over the door, it might keep us safe long enough for those mangy felines to give up.

I duck into the hallway in time to see Boudicca hurl a manticore against the far wall. Four more turn the corner and charge toward her. "Run!"

She spares the barest of glances down the hall then sweeps us both into the room, shutting the heavy door behind her. My thumb aches as I mash the button on my creation, aiming it at the polished, dark wood door.

Loud thumps pound against the glowing wood, punctuated by frustrated howls.

Boudicca leans heavily against the door. Her torn wing

already has the shine of stone. She holds my gaze, and the pain in her eyes makes me quiver. "Stay here. I need to heal. I'll block the door while I sleep."

I glance around the room, but there's no way out, except maybe the chimney. Boudicca closes her hand around the doorknob as her skin shimmers to obsidian.

"Wait! Don't leave me alone until we know it's secure." My plea falls on stone ears. Looking at her wounds, it's a wonder she was able to hold out long enough to get to this room.

"You'll be fine." Her gravel-filled voice croaks through a hardening jaw.

"I can't do this alone," I plead as a lifetime of insecurities flood my being. "It's only recently that anyone believed in me. My family certainly never did."

Boudicca's eyes soften in her chiseled stone face. "Let go of that past and embrace who you are now."

The shine of stone dulls the affection in her eyes until only a carved statue stands before me.

My panting breath fills the silence of the small chamber. I slump against the muscled arm of my stone lover. This isn't fair. Earlier we were twined in each other's embrace, making love in the mossy bed of a beautiful garden and now...

I run cool fingertips over the rough warmth of her crystalline wounds. The cuts are already smoothing—unlike me, she'll live forever. Tears burn my eyes, and seeking comfort, I bury my face into her unmoving chest.

"Come back to me. I need you." My plea echoes off the high arched ceiling but is quickly muffled by the surrounding bookshelves crammed to overspilling with ancient tomes.

Blinking back tears, I crawl into Boudicca's hardened

arms, seeking the same comfort I had when I thought she was a lifeless statue. This is pathetic. Am I going to have a pity party for myself every time she reverts to stone? Forcibly stiffening my spine, I stand up to explore the cozy room. My vision blurs and my head aches as my world tilts to one side.

I slump into a leather chair near the stone fireplace and rub my aching legs. A delicately framed portrait of two women sits beside a pile of books on the table. I look it over, noting clothing at least a century out of date. Gold laces through the tightly coiled dark hair of the woman on the left, contrasting sharply with the icy blond on the right. Definitely not sisters—I note their interlaced fingers—or roommates.

A thump comes from the other side of the door, and I dig my slippers into the plush carpet, readying myself to spring away. Frozen in time, Boudicca holds the door firmly closed despite more bangs and scratching. They already got through my shield. I'll never be more than mediocre at magic. I should've stuck to research. A low yowl hums through the thick wood, tickling a shiver down my spine. Boudicca will need at least the night to sleep and heal. I hope those things hold off for that long. My hand throbs, reminding me of my earlier burn. I examine the pinked skin, brushing my thumb over the tender area.

A scratch along the wall rips my attention from my palm. The paint furrows in strips before disappearing behind a bookcase. Can the manticores come through the wall?

Dammit! I spring to my feet, searching for another way out but nothing is apparent. Using my magical slippers, I could climb the wall and cling to the ceiling, but I don't think that will get me out of their reach. And

Boudicca is helpless in her stone form. I can't let anything hurt her.

A low creak whines through the room as the shelf closest to the door tumbles with a thump to the thick rug. Yellow eyes peer through a hand-sized crack. Not good. My panic crescendos as a clawed paw swipes through the crack, ripping it wider. Visions of Boudicca waking to my eviscerated body leave me sickened.

Whispering the first spell my teacher Xander made me master, I rake the room for any signs of magical sparkle. Everything gleams. I reel with stupidity. Of course it gleams. I'm in a magical pocket dimension. Squinting at individual objects, I try to find something useful. A ring, a trinket, a secret door.

A sword.

The plain sword hanging above the mantel flares painfully bright. I could wield a sword against these creatures. Probably. Maybe. Well, I've read about it. I've read just about everything—it's the perk to being a librarian.

I pile some books up, and wincing, I lift a foot to step on them. Am I so desperate to climb on books as a ladder? The chair really isn't tall enough but maybe if I...

The yowling intensifies as a manticore shoves his ugly mug through the hole. "I'm going to eat you feet first so I can savor your fear."

Yep, books make a great ladder. I scamper up the stacked books. It's still a stretch to reach the sword, but my hand closes over it just as a crack splits the air.

A maker!

I turn at the foreign voice, nearly falling from the pile of books, and wrench the sword from the wall bracket as I do. Brandishing it before me, I realize just how heavy this sword is before using two hands to steady it.

"Get back!" I rush forward. Swinging with all my might, I manage to lodge the length of metal in the wall.

A great toothy maw splits into a laugh. "Look at this, boys. The puny one is trying to wield a sword. We've slaughtered greater warriors than you."

The beast pushes through the crack to its shoulders. I glance in vain at Boudicca but she's still solid. It's all on me. I can do this. I yank the sword from the wall.

Straighten your shoulders and bring your right foot forward.

Someone speaks directly in my ear. I jerk and spin, but the room remains empty. "Who?"

"Just you and me, girl," the manticore growls as it pulls the rest of its body through the hole. The two behind it try to enter at the same time, swiping and screaming at each other.

I slide my right foot in front of me and straighten my spine. "Don't come any closer."

The creature flicks its spiked tail menacingly. "Or what?"

Tightening my arm, I dart forward and slash down with all my might. The tip of the blade slides over the manticore's chest, leaving a thin red line in its wake. The sword keeps going to thump against the thick carpet. Damn, this thing is heavy. With as many books as I lift, I'd think this wouldn't be so cumbersome.

Not terrible. Try to use your core muscles instead of your arms to swing. It's the same voice, coming from everywhere and nowhere.

"If you think you can do better, go right ahead," I grit out as a clawed paw swipes at me. Scampering behind a leather chair, I use the antique furnishing as a shield.

Oh, I can! Let me take over.

"Take over? Who are you? Where are you?" Unsuccessfully, I stab the sword over the chair. I'm not even certain if this is the stabby type of sword. It could be the swooshy type. This would be easier if I had a moment to research weapons. The claws swipe past, narrowly missing my cheek. A few severed wisps of my hair float away.

You're going to get yourself killed if you keep leading with your head. Do it like this.

An odd sensation of otherness sweeps over my body, and I move like I never have before, expertly parrying the next strike and spinning to sever the creature's paw. Its eyes widen in shock and a howl reverberates around the room, echoed by the other two lodged in the nearby hole. Cracks around the hole grow wider. They'll be through soon. I can't handle one, let alone three. Hell, Boudicca got severely injured against three.

"Are you a demon?" I ask. It's pointless, really. If I don't accept the help, I'm going to die. I dodge as the manticore charges me and I duck behind the heavy chair again.

Don't be ridiculous. I'm a sword.

The voice's disdain burns my thoughts. A rain of wood shards heralds a bronze-furred body bursting through the wall. Three manticores snarl, prowling toward me. I'm out of time.

"Fine. Take over." This might be the foolhardiest thing I've done in my short, mortal life, but if all Boudicca finds is a smear of red giblets on the rug, at least she'll know that I tried.

The fiery tingle of magic flows through my veins, stronger than I've ever experienced, and my hand raises as if I'm merely a puppet. Cool violet fire burns from my fingertips as the sword swings, feeling strangely lighter now, into a guard position. My body settles into a grounded pose I've never taken before.

"Come beasts, my steel will be the last flavor your tongue will ever hold." What in the...that came out of my mouth but was definitely not my voice.

The presence shoves my consciousness backward. Peering through eyes that were mine but that I no longer control, I gape at the bloody scene. Muscles I didn't know I had flex in a dance I've never performed. My every step is utterly flawless. The first manticore leaps and my body rolls forward as effortlessly as if I were gliding through the air. The sword plunges into his sternum, slicing a bloody gouge all the way to his groin before she rolls away—I roll away. The sword has complete control of my body. Like I'm the weapon.

I gulp. At least it seems I still have control of my mouth. "I'm not certain how comfortable I am with this. Perhaps we could go back to you shouting suggestions in my head."

My shoulder rams under the jaw of the second manticore, snapping its teeth shut as the steel plunges straight between the beast's shoulder blades. A violet fireball launches from my other hand, hitting the third manticore between the eyes. How the hell did I cast that? Xander hasn't taught me any fire spells yet.

"I apologize for your discomfort," the sword's voice grunts out of my mouth with unexpected politeness. "It won't take me long to silence these kittens. Hold tight." That strange voice twists my tongue in a soft accent that definitely sounds Mediterranean.

Kittens. Boudicca was brutalized by these monsters and this woman—sword?—anyway, she treats it like it's another day, a simple task.

"I'm sure it looks that way to a baby mage," the sword says.

A baby? "Let's not be rude. I'm a librarian and an apprentice maker to one of the greatest artificer mages of this time. I've likely forgotten more information than you'll ever know."

A low chuckle echoes in my head. My irritation outweighs my fear as the final manticore prowls forward.

"Arezou would like you. She was haughty and always buried in books as well," the sword says.

I frown as my body jerks into a series of movements that becomes unnaturally fluid by the third step. "Who's Arezou?"

The blade slams down across the manticore's neck. With a thump, the head falls forward staining the carpet as it rolls away.

The voice pauses a beat, then sounds incredulous. "I— how did I forget her? She's my wife."

The sword drops from my nerveless fingers as I slump to the bloodied rug. Pants of air rush from my lungs, sounding hollow in the still room. Otherness slides from me, and my consciousness once again holds the reins of my weary limbs. Musky manticore blood hits my nose and its oily stench makes me gag.

"A sword has a wife?" I ask.

Only the cheerful pop of the fire answers as silence echoes heavy in my mind.

Eons pass before Boudicca stirs—at least it feels that way. It's hard to tell the passage of time with no windows to gauge the light. Her giant, bat-like wings flex first, and the tips brush the ceiling high above as a rain of small crystals fall, revealing her smooth, unblemished skin. The sword still lies silent on the carpet nearby. I didn't dare touch it again.

The dragon-like gargoyle twists to look at me then gives herself a hard shake, knocking the rest of the loose stone from her body. She takes in the bloodied carcasses on the floor and the crimson covered blade.

Boudicca's heavy brows draw together. "Are you injured?"

Muscles bunch as her arms surround me. Kneeling, Boudicca curls my body into her lap. That closeness, my skin to hers.

A small, relieved sob creeps out of my mouth. "I'm fine. I think. The sword took care of..." I gesture weakly at the mess surrounding us, more accustomed to reading about this type of adventure than being an active participant.

Still, a lot has changed in my life in the last few months when the magical world found me.

Boudicca stares hard at the blade.

"Can you see anything about the magical signature on it?" I ask.

"The vessel is older than me. But I don't recognize the maker. There's strong soul magic on it. Did it speak to you?"

Numbly, I nod, still unwilling to touch the blade. I would've died without its help, though.

Boudicca lifts the length of steel with ease then wipes the blade on the tawny fur of a nearby dead monster. Her pointed ear flicks, sending the tight coils of mane bouncing around it. "Hmmm, it's silent for me. It might take a maker like you, or at least a mage, to hear the soul bound in it."

She says it so casually, like souls are bound to objects every day.

"I'm not touching it again. The thing took over my whole body. Let's see if we can find another way out."

Firelight dances along Boudicca's unmarred skin, tracing every smooth line as her shoulder muscles bunch in a shrug. I flex my palm, still feeling the tight, sensitive burned skin and wishing I had a way to heal like gargoyles do. Gazing along the book titles, I see a few familiar ones, mostly old philosophy. There's another shelf full of culinary books. Curiously, I poke through them while Boudicca tugs at various hooks and statues along the wall. A low grinding fills the air as a wall behind a small alcove glides to one side.

"And there we are." Boudicca winks at me. "It looks like there's a stairway leading downward from here. I'm not seeing another passage out of the room beyond the way we entered."

She reaches for my hand as her thick tail thumps against the plush rug. I grasp her hand, feeling a measure of comfort in the steady heat her body always puts off. Her fanged grin sets me at ease, and I almost forget we were running for our lives a few hours ago. Almost.

"What if more of those things show up?" I ask.

With a gentle tug, Boudicca draws me closer. "There's a lever here inside the passage to close the door. They'll never know we're here."

The stairs smell of dust and disuse, spiraling down into a dark so thick it blunts the senses. I pull out a vial and give it a good shake to activate the bioluminescent contents, then raise it before me. Shadows splash along the walls as we move, revealing carved lines and whorls that seem to thrum hypnotically along the stone. The soft drag of Boudicca's clawed feet on the stairs draws me after her.

"This writing is ancient," she whispers, reverence in her voice, as she pauses to trace over the delicately carved swirls. "War mages of the Great Deserts far to the south used it over a thousand years ago."

I frown. "How do you know?"

Boudicca ruffles her leathery wings then folds them tight to her back. She tips her head to one side, and her black horns scrape lightly against the stone wall. "Maker Xander made all of us study the classical languages of magic. Even the ones like this that are no longer in use."

"Why isn't this one used anymore?"

Her hand drops from the wall. "Because all the war mages died out hundreds of years ago during the Storm War. The art of combat casting died with them, along with the use of their writing. Now only scholars peruse the artistic script."

"Oh." Sadness washes over me at the thought of a lost civilization and I make a mental note to research it later.

A flickering blue light illuminates the staircase as we turn the downward spiral and the wall to my left changes from rough stone to smooth translucent crystal. My breath fogs the surface as I press my face close to look at the workshop beyond.

"It's an alchemist's lab." Boudicca taps one black clawed finger against the crystal. "Is that a woman?"

I scan the area, lit with violet globes of mage lights, looking for someone moving about. Books and scrolls are strewn over a silver table and some sort of surgical instruments lay in a tray to one side. "Where?"

Boudicca points at a pale white pod propped against the far wall. Misted glass shows the rounded face of a sleeping woman. Her long blond hair lays limp against her broad shoulders. Glowing dials on the side of the case cast a myriad of sparkling lights against her pale cheek. I look away from the strange visage to the stairs below us.

"There must be a door into that lab along here somewhere," I say, descending the last few steps.

Boudicca slides her palm against mine, warm and secure. "And maybe a way out that doesn't involve us fighting felines."

"You did well enough." A grin tickles my lips.

She flexes at the praise. "So did you."

"Mmm, no, that was the soul of the sword." A long, leaf-shaped groove decorates the wall beside a rusted metal door. Gingerly, I touch the doorknob with my injured hand. Locked. My eyes pause on the thin, distinctly shaped indention in the wall.

"Oh no." I sigh. "We're going to need that sword again."

SUNKEN INTO THE THICK RUG, THE SWORD STILL gleams where I dropped it. Goosepimples prickle over my flesh upon remembering the loss of control over my body. The bite of my nails into my palm shakes me out of my indecision, and stooping, I wrap my hand around the hilt.

Oh, I'm so glad you picked me back up. Since you touched me, my consciousness is present again and things were pretty dull laying on the floor.

I suppress a groan as the chipper voice balloons into my thoughts. Of all the things to find here, why a chatty sword?

Boudicca raises one dark brow. "Is it talking to you?"

It? I'm a she, thank you very much. One of the most decorated war mages in the Empresses' legions. My name rang in the ballads of—

"Yes. She's incredibly chatty for a sword. What's your name?"

I... a wave of puzzlement entangles with my own exasperated but curious thoughts. *I don't remember.*

"Alright." The word draws out on a long sigh. I caress the simple leather of the hilt consolingly. "Do you know where we are?"

This is the place I shared with my wife. The voice sounds more hesitant this time. *But I died far from our home. How am I here?*

A weighty pause follows before horrified words shriek through my head. *I died! Seven hells, I remember. That sorceress bitch ripped my body apart with shearing wind.*

I flinch. Boudicca rests one smooth clawed hand on my shoulder and I press my now throbbing forehead against her chest, wishing for all the world we could return to the solace of this morning. "It's shouting."

She, the sword insists as if that's the last bit of identity she possesses.

Muscles tighten my jaw, grinding my teeth in frustration. "Look, there's a chamber below and it appears you're the key. Maybe we can jog the rest of your memory, and you can help us get back where we belong."

Sullen agreement washes over me.

"Do you want me to carry the sword?" Boudicca asks as her fingers comb through my loose hair, brushing it from my forehead with aching tenderness.

No! A gargoyle can't hear me. It takes a mage or maker. You need me.

"I'm going to drop you into the abyss next door if you don't stop shouting in my head," I growl.

Sorry. Look, it's been a really long time since anyone could hear me. Your hand is injured. Let me fix that.

Heat followed by cool tingles over my burned palm,

soothing the singed flesh. A sword that can heal...that's useful.

Boudicca's warm thumb strokes soothingly over my temple. "Come. We're wasting time. We need to find another way back to our portal before it closes, and I'd prefer not to fight our way through those beasts again. I can't risk losing you."

A sigh that I'm not entirely sure is my own slips from my lips as I follow her back down the dark winding staircase. My mortality will always be a hinderance to our relationship. One I don't know if there's a solution for, beyond enjoying the handful of decades we'll have together. And then Boudicca will be alone. I swallow hard, pushing that grim thought aside.

"If Xander missed the danger in this world, how do we know any of the bōc-hord's portals are safe to travel through?" I brush a hand along the cool stone wall to steady myself.

"They wouldn't have missed manticores." Boudicca's deep voice bounces off the walls, echoing back at us in an eerie whisper. "Those felines are mage-made. Maker Xander is far too thorough to miss something as dangerous as that. Besides, you handled yourself well, and you'll only get stronger as your apprenticeship continues."

She squeezes my hand, and her strong blunt fingers caress my wrist, sending a shiver of pleasure along my skin. Pulling me closer, Boudicca wraps first her arms and then her wings around us, cocooning us in her warmth.

"I love you," I whisper into her rounded shoulder. "I know we'll get through this together."

Her coiled mane tickles my cheek as she holds me tighter. "We will. This'll be another tale for you to spin one day."

I chuckle. "Who'd believe it?"

Ahem. As touching as this is, it's making me feel like a voyeur.

Rolling my eyes, I fit the blade into the slot beside the door. A bright blue light surrounds it, searing my vision in the dimness of the hall. A flare of red sparks off the door, and with a grinding groan of stone on stone, it begins to slide open.

With a tentative step, Boudicca moves forward. Her nostrils flare in the stale, dusty air. I grab the sword from the slot, my hand tensing on the leather wrapped hilt. It remains uncharacteristically silent, but a ripple of apprehension that isn't my own tickles over my nerves.

It's her! That's the bitch who trapped me in this sword!

My body jerks forward. I fight against the sword's influence as she drags me across the room to the crystalline pod leaning against the wall. "Hey! I didn't consent to you using me like a puppet."

My hand thumps against the clear shell covering the woman's form. Blunt bangs of icy blond cover her rounded pale face. Even her eyelashes are ivory wisps against paler skin. Ring decorated fingers lace together over her chest, covered by polished chain mail. I wrest control back over my body before the sword actually hurts me.

"I don't think she's alive." I study the pod. Colorful gem buttons line one edge, lighting up as I hover my fingers over them.

She is!

"She is." Boudicca taps a claw against the crystalline side. "There's some kind of temporal magic on the encasement. It preserved her body well enough that her heart still beats."

I listen for a moment but decide my lover must have far

superior hearing to mine. "I'll see if I can get this thing open if you'll look this place over for a way out."

Yes! Wake her and I'll have my revenge for encasing me in metal for eternity. I know how these work.

Jerkily, my hand shoots out and fingers tap on the jeweled buttons. I fight the unwanted possession, teeth clenched. "Keep it up and I'm dropping you down a hole where you'll never be touched again."

Roars echo down the stone stairwell along with a feline shriek. With a snap of her wings, Boudicca darts toward the open door, then pulls it shut with a grinding shriek. "They're hunting us like prey. I don't see an obvious way out. We'll be pinned here."

"Keep looking." I stumble away from the pod, my feet clinging to the floor like each one is weighted with lead. Smooth, metallic walls line the room with no signs of an opening. Despair rises, coating my tongue in acid. None of this looks good.

Claws scrape along the glass window facing the stairs, and a hissing shriek fills the air. "Sword, is there a way out of this room?"

That mage in stasis can portal and walk between worlds. At least she could when she breathed.

My slippers scuff against the rough stone floor as I hurry back to the prone figure in the pod. Boudicca crouches to study the gemmed buttons etched with lines before pressing the end one with a black clawed fingertip.

She shrugs. "It says open."

Time crawls, interspersed by threatening yowls and scratches across the window to the stairwell. I don't look. The last thing I need to see is those nightmarishly human faces baring their pointed teeth at me. Mist curls in the pod, setting tendrils of the woman's hair to dance in an unfelt breeze before obscuring her face.

Boudicca glances over her shoulder. "Maybe it's broken."

No, give it time. The voice in my head intones, the pitch anxious and strained.

"Didn't you say she's your enemy? That she killed you and put you in that sword?" Silence greets my question. How reliable a narrator is this thing anyway? We could be running from one danger right into—

With a hiss and a rush of steam, the bowed front flips open. Ozone and a sweet herbal scent drifts out on the cool damp cloud. The yowls outside the door come to an abrupt halt and claws scrabble up the stairs and away.

Boudicca whips around, toward the exit. "That can't be good."

Coughing comes from before us and the gargoyle's brawny arm wraps around my middle, hauling me back. Cool mist continues to bubble from the pod in frothy grey waves. A hand emerges, gripping the side of the vessel before the blonde leans over and splashes waxy vomit all over the floor. Wracking coughs spasm her body again.

Trap her before she's aware!

I flinch at the mental shout. In a blink, the blade rests against the woman's throat. Her glassy blue eyes widen. A thick, reptilian tail lashes downward, knocking the blade from my grip as Boudicca sweeps forward. Her hands close around my shoulders and her tail continues to flick in agitation. The sword bounces and rolls, chiming musically off the stone floor. The blonde's hand flies to her throat as her icy gaze slides from us to the blade nearby.

"You'd awaken me then try to slaughter me? Not wise,

mageling." She hauls herself from the opening, stumbling a bit as her boot-covered feet touch the floor. Wiping her mouth with the back of her hand, she frowns. "What year is it?"

I adjust the dial on the translation gem set on my ring to clarify her heavy accent. "1912."

"So long," she mutters.

Boudicca leans down, claiming the sword she knocked from my hands. It looks miniscule in her grasp, more a long dagger than a sword. "The sword that unlocked this room said you can travel between worlds with portal magic. We were cornered here and the doorway back to our world is closing soon. Can you help?"

Her eyes narrow on the blade. "Roya?"

The sword vibrates in Boudicca's hands. Reluctantly, she hands it to me. "Don't let it control you again."

As soon as my fingers caress the warmth of the blade, the sword's voice erupts through my mind. *She's a killer! Contain her now!*

A soft chuckle floats through the room and the woman touches the blade. "It is you. I'd recognize that suspicious tone anywhere, my love."

"Your love? You ripped apart my body and stuffed me into this hunk of metal."

As the disembodied voice roars into the room, Boudicca blinks in shock. My fingers tighten on the blade as the urge to stab forward overwhelms me. Fighting off the desire, sweat prickles my forehead, soaking my skin in a cool sheen.

"I didn't rip you apart. I saved you when your body was no longer viable." The woman frowns at the sword then looks at me. "I'm Warrior Mage Arezou, General of the Eastwing. Or at least I was. Does the Empress still hold the middle lands?"

Middle lands? Wait—Arezou. That sounds familiar.

"I'm Viola. I don't know anything called the middle lands or an empress so I'm going to say no."

"Well, it's been a few centuries, I suppose. Nothing lasts forever. Except us, right Roya?" Arezou caresses the sword like a lover. A haunted look fills her eyes.

"I wouldn't know, seeing as I'm lacking a body. And until this moment, a name. I don't suppose you have a spare flesh vehicle somewhere that you can stuff me into?" Sarcasm drips from the words, harsh enough that Boudicca flinches.

"You know I don't have the ability to do flesh magic," Arezou spits. "Have you forgotten everything?"

I squeeze the leather grip in my hand. "Earlier, you told me Arezou was the name of your wife."

A pregnant pause fills the room with a silence so heavy Arezou's eyes glass with tears. For once, the sword stays conspicuously silent. Claws slide against the stone floor as Boudicca uncomfortably shuffles from one foot to the other.

"Have you forgotten that you love me?" Arezou whispers. "Was it all in vain?"

The war mage's pale blue eyes rivet to the sword in my grasp. I move to hand it to her, but she shakes her head. A sadness that isn't my own seeps through my veins to my soul.

"I'm sorry. Eons crawled by while I lay dormant, passed from one ungifted hand to another. Shards of my life surface in my mind, disjointed and confusing. I'm not certain how I ended up back in our study."

"Roya, what do you mean by our study? This is a pocket dimension, far from our land." Arezou's voice caresses the spoken name as if she wills her love to remember them.

"I don't remember." If a sword could cry, those words

would judder out of her with the fiercest of tears. "I'm sorry. I'm so sorry. I'm a thing now, aren't I?"

Darkness pools across the room. Shadows flutter like living things. Arezou raises her glowing hands, spinning a ring of light between them. "Let me remind you."

The room around us grows misty and indistinct before turning dark. I grab for Boudicca's hand as a sensation of falling fills me, but the only thing my hand catches is air.

"You can't be here. If we get caught, a court marshaling is the least of our worries," hisses a dark-skinned woman from a raised wooden cot.

I jerk at the sudden change of scenery. Gone are the cool, austere halls of the lab or even the warm wood paneling of the study. In its place, sun-heated sand softens my stance. Light-colored fabric forms a cozy shade cover. Nearby, a stand holds a suit of scale and leather armor, burnished to gleaming. Boudicca crowds beside me, wings tucked tight to her strangely translucent form. I reach out to touch her, only to notice I can see through my arm. Are we ghosts?

Words spill out, unheard, from my lips. Boudicca shakes her head, gesturing toward the women before us. I instantly recognize Arezou. Dust streaks her white skin and her blond hair hangs in tight braids that loop over themselves at her nape before continuing down her mail-covered spine.

"I rode all night to see you." A teasing smile plays across the war mage's lips. "The least I could get from my wife is a hug."

Arezou kneels by the cot with a confidence that says she won't be denied. Her lips brush the other woman's cheek and then her mouth. Hands move upward, toying with dark locs box-braided and decorated with bands of gold.

"You should be leading your battalion toward the Scarlet Scourge's palace. What are you doing here? If you're caught, we'll both be whipped." The woman sits up, shaking off the blonde. I recognize her voice. She's the sword's soul.

Undeterred, Arezou curls into the woman's lap, lips nuzzling a trail over her throat. "You've never minded a little lash of leather."

The sight of her hands pushing aside clothing leaves me blushing. Why would the mage choose to share such an erotic scene with utter strangers? Do they even know we're here?

"You should return to your troops," the black-haired woman gasps as Arezou teases a dusky nipple pierced with a heavy gold ring.

"Roya, please. I haven't seen you in a moon cycle and the longing for your touch is crushing me. When I heard your legions were only half a day's ride away, how could I not steal away to see you? Give me a precious second of your attention. We could die tomorrow." Arezou sweeps a hand over the woman's cheek and is rewarded by being gathered into her arms.

"You always say that. And yet you still live," Roya teases. Her full lips press to Arezou's as she lifts the other woman and settles her on top. Limbs tangle in frantic need and suddenly, I realize this part of this magical flashback isn't for Boudicca and me. I tilt my head toward the tent flap. With two steps, we're out in blinding sunlight in the middle of a war camp. Boudicca tries to take my hand, but her long fingers slide through my palm. Ghosts. We're nothing but ghosts in this past vision.

Boudicca moves her mouth, but nothing comes out. Her

forehead wrinkles in frustration before she gestures toward the creamy swell of dunes in the distance. Wind ripples the sand into mesmerizing patterns against the white burn of the sky. A haze of heat muddles the view, painting the world in a dreamlike quality. Around us, soldiers walk around the huge encampment going about their day with an efficiency that bespeaks of years of discipline. Uniforms of white and gold shine immaculately in every direction. Behind us, soft moans come from the tent. I guess that's one way to jog Roya's memory.

Boudicca waves a hand before my face then points again. An angry slash of red cuts through the colorless sky. A sunspot? I squint as the camp around us springs into frantic action. A hazy ripple over the horizon clears and I choke down a bitter swell of fear. A dragon?

Sun gleams along the crimson scales tipped in amethyst that cover the creature's hide. A low roar seeps into my ears as time slows down. Flowers of gold bloom from the dragon's mouth, raining down on the far end of the camp. Their delicate petals shower down in glowing embers. No, not flowers—fire. The world crashes back into my consciousness, moving too fast as Arezou and Roya race past me, hastily donning their armor. Panic swells as screams rise around me. I'm going to burn. We're all going to die here. I turn to run.

A hand clenches firmly around mine. Clawed and warm, this time Boudicca's flesh doesn't pass through my sweat slick palm. "This has already happened. Focus on me to speak or touch. We're in a memory."

A golden shield domes around the encampment, springing from Arezou's upraised hands. "I'll hold them off. Get the dragon before it destroys the camp."

Roya brandishes a familiar sword, chanting as she raises

it before her. Blue light shines from the blade, even in the brightness of the day. She swings in a graceful arc. In the distance, the dragon howls as a bloody gash opens from its shoulder to its ribcage.

A host of small, winged creatures hit the shield and Arezou grunts as if she took the blow. "Get the neck! If we don't get her head off this whole place will be ash on sand."

"I'm working on it! Did you think that thing would fly in here unprotected?" Roya swings again. The dragon banks sharply to one side, her reptilian head swinging toward the pair. Eyes like flaming coals narrow and she roars a challenge that splits my ears.

"It's coming toward us!" I back up, tugging Boudicca along with me.

The beast inhales deeply and I squeeze my eyes shut tight as the petal-like licks of flame barrel down toward me.

"It's a vision. You're safe." Boudicca stops my retreat to watch the war mages with studious interest. "Roya has the blade spelled to be a ranged weapon. The enchantment is fascinating. I've never seen anything like it."

The blast of fire washes over us, passing unfelt through our incorporeal bodies. The soldiers in this nightmare from the past aren't so lucky. I'm glad scent and feel isn't accompanying this horrific battle.

The blade shines like a shooting star as Roya raises it above her head and brings it down. In a splay of lurid blood, the dragon's wing spirals free from its massive body and the creature plummets toward the sand.

"That's not the thrice cursed head, love!" Arezou calls over her shoulder.

Roya wipes soot across her sweat soaked forehead. "You're welcome to go on the offense if you think you can do better."

"You seemed to like the way I took charge earlier." Arezou grins at her partner, like they aren't about to be eaten by a mountain-sized lizard.

Fire engulfs the cloth tents around us. Clashing metal blends with shouted commands and cries of agony that rise to an unholy wail. The dragon lunges forward, closing the distance between us one thunderous step at a time. Arezou casts again, adjusting a tight sphere of light around her and Roya. Whipping its bloodied head, the beast snaps at the mages, snagging Roya's shoulder. It tosses her like a doll to a nearby dune.

"Roya! No!" A beam of blue frost streaks from Arezou's fingertips, striking the large glassy orb of the beast's eye. Ice crackles over the eye until a thick opaque film covers it. Arezou chants something I can't quite hear, and a golden spear appears in her hand.

Sadness rests heavy on my chest. This must be how Roya died.

"You think I couldn't feel the filth of your presence. You can't hide behind your overgrown tadpole. Come down and fight me!" Arezou shouts then hurls the spear toward the encapsulated eye. It shatters, and globs of ooze splash to sizzle on the sand as Arezou's spear explodes out the back of the dragon's skull. Sagging, the beast nearly falls on top of me with an earth-trembling thump. Boudicca stands unflinching, her ghostly form in the dead beast's gaping maw. Slimy teeth longer than my gargoyle's arm clench once, then relax forever.

A ripple of tension shivers through Boudicca's shoulders, fluttering the dark leather of her wings as she moves closer to me, guiding me away from the body. Her whisper of denial reaches my ears. "Roya...No. This can't be how it happened."

"Tch." She clicks her tongue, clearly unimpressed. "And here I thought the two of you would be a challenge." A slight woman with fiery red hair slides down the shoulder of her fallen mount.

"It looks like you're one dragon short, Sinder." Arezou smirks.

Sinder dusts off a revealing silky dress, straightening it as if she were arriving from some grand ball. "I heard you were the best the Empress's legions had to offer."

An ornate ivory mask, carved and set with deep emerald lenses, covers half the woman's face as she tilts her head. Jewelry drips from her throat, her wrists, and her fingers in a multitude of colors and gemstones. Even her ankles are adorned in delicate chains and bells, which trail down to ringed cuffs on her bare toes. I wrinkle my nose. How ostentatious and gaudy compared to the sparse simplicity of the military camp and the unadorned chain and leather armor on the mages.

"Leave it to you to break the treaty your queen made," Roya says as she stands.

I gasp and squeeze Boudicca's arm in excitement. "She's alive!"

Roya grabs her cast-off helm from the sand and jams it over her springy coils of hair. The T-bar nearly covers her broad, wrinkled nose as she snarls, baring gleaming white teeth. "I relish the thought of taking down an honorless upstart traitor like you."

The wind kicks up, blowing sand around us. Pulling a cloth over her lower face, Arezou runs to her lover, bringing her shield so close it twines around their bodies, moving in the breeze like a clutch of snakes.

Lips the color of dried blood pull up in a humorless

smile. "Yes, well. What the child queen doesn't know won't hurt her."

Roya casually ties back her waist length braids before unsheathing her sword once more. "Oh, I'll be sure to get the missive to her. I'll send it with your head."

Roya's sword moves in a destructive dance. As she aggressively charges the interloper, the blade flares with the light of a burning star. Sinder blocks each blow with the ornate bronze vambraces protecting her forearms. Sparks fly, sizzling so hot the sands below melt into puddles of glass.

Arezou moves with her partner, like a shadow made of golden light. Sinder lashes out. Wind whips harder, yanking the cover from Arezou's face and abrading her skin with sand. Blood trails down her cheek, dripping from her chin to stain her battle-worn leathers.

My whole world narrows to this moment. This fight. Even though I think I know the end. Sinder blurs to crimson, slashing forward with fingers of wickedly sharp blades. She gestures and the wind hoists Arezou into the air, spinning her until her magic shield shreds and her screams rip across the camp.

Roya slams her blade down across Sinder's back, cutting a brutal wound. Ribs snap and the wind dies to a whisper as the woman crumples to one knee. Her red gown tears, exposing one breast and the sharp curve of her hip. Blood trickles from her nose.

Sinder drags the back of her hand over her nose, then with a hacking cough, spits viscous blood into the white sand. "Good hit."

Roya flips Sinder's wild red hair back then lays her blade across her bare neck. My breath stills in my throat. Arezou drops out of the sky to land with a grunt beside us.

"Anything you'd like to confess to your queen? I'll be sure to let her know at least your death was honorable." Roya presses the steel down, dimpling Sinder's white skin.

Sinder coughs a splatter of blood onto the sand. She smiles with pink tinged teeth then grabs the blade in her hand. The gold claws of her gloves tap menacingly along the steel. My heart sinks as I realize what this memory is.

My fingers dig into Boudicca's forearm. "Please, there's got to be some way to stop this."

"It already happened," Boudicca whispers. Her arms fold around my shoulders. "Turn away if you must."

"Such the good general. The perfect weapon." Sinder chokes again and spits. Tendrils of sparking red magic twine up the blade to the hilt, covering Roya's hand.

"Roya, move away!" Arezou stumbles.

A sudden gale of wind nearly knocks the blond mage flat. Sand twists through the air, spinning faster until it forms a twister-like tunnel. Blades of glass whip from inside the funnel of wind. Immediately, Roya's armor shreds, coming off in great hunks. Shards pierce her exposed skin like a hundred daggers.

"You bitch," Roya grunts as she first tries to tug the blade away and then presses it harder against Sinder's neck.

"Call off the wind and we'll see you have a fair trial." Arezou rises to her knees. She begins chanting but chokes as sand fills her lungs.

Amazed, I watch the wind driven sand curl around Sinder's flesh like armor. Roya snarls as the skin on her torso shreds off in slivers and hunks to spray across the ground. The white bones of her ribs flash in the sunlight. Her jaw clenches as she slowly eases the sword away from the woman's neck and positions the tip to the soft spot on Sinder's lower back, still bare of the hardened sand.

"You never had a chance." Sinder's cruel laugh cuts over the howling wind.

"I'll take you to hell with me." Roya grunts as she uses her weight to thrust the sword through Sinder, pinning her to the ground. Her face is now little more than a lipless skull. I flinch at the sight but resist burying my face in Boudicca's chest. Arezou wanted us to know what happened. It's only fair I bear this out to its conclusion. The wind continues to churn, leaving Roya's body as little more than a smear against the ground. The silence is deafening as the wind drops. I glance past the blood to the fire raging beyond. No one moves. Not a single soldier is in sight.

"Heh." Sinder kneels. Then she reaches over one shoulder to yank the blade out of her body and toss it to the side. A faint breeze stirs and sand whips around her, sealing the wound. "I thought you'd last a little longer. This was barely entertaining."

I blink. That should've been a mortal wound.

"I'll show you entertaining, you over glorified windbag." Arezou's hands clap together, and an explosion radiates outward, blinding me. I fling my arm over my eyes, once again forgetting this is a memory.

Sinder screams. I squint, but the light is far too bright to see anything. Boudicca's black wings draw over us both, partially blocking the blinding spell.

"It's almost over. Are you alright?" Her palm cups my cheek.

I nod, then rest my cheek to her chest. After what feels like a millennium, soft sobbing breaks the silence. I peek past Boudicca's wing to see the ghostly form of Roya standing over the bloody tatters of her body.

"I can fix this—just hold on." With jerky frantic movements, Arezou clutches the sword to her chest. "I can fix this."

Ghost Roya kneels. One hand palms her lover's cheek, a translucent thumb wipes at Arezou's tears. My heart wrenches at the sorrow in her deep brown eyes.

"I've almost figured out how to build the crystalla. I can put your soul in one. Just hold on."

Turning her head, Roya gazes off into the distance, past the slowly dying flames, past the horizon where the sun rises even higher into the sky. She takes a step forward, reaching for something unseen.

"I've got you," Arezou says as she finishes casting. A glittering yellow light surrounds what I can only guess is Roya's soul. It melts and shrinks until she's nothing more than a ball of light. Then Arezou gestures with her free hand and the soul sucks into the sword. "I'll keep you safe until I find a way for us to be together again."

BREATHING FILLS MY CONSCIOUSNESS, FAST AND frantic like the beating wings of a tiny bird before slowing to a low, unsteady rush. My tingling fingers grip the sword's pommel.

"What happened afterward?" Roya's voice is as numb as my hand.

"I tried for decades to transfer your soul into one of the crystalla bodies...but I'm no maker and it always failed. The war dragged on. Your legion was crushed that day, and mine shortly afterward. The Scourge hunted mages, and I went into hiding. Few of us were left." Arezou shrugs. "Sinder rose to power as did the puppet queen she manipulated.

Later she found me, holed up in my workshop at our home. We fought. I don't remember anything else until you freed me from that pod."

"What are crystalla?" Boudicca asks.

"Bodies made of living stone taken from deep within the singing mountains. Originally, I was creating them to be the ultimate armor for war mages—something we could put our consciousnesses into to fight without the risk of our actual bodies being harmed—but I never designed them to hold a soul. Every time I transferred Roya from the sword to the crystalla her soul returned to the sword within minutes." Arezou pauses, tilting her head. "Was there anyone else in your group?"

"No," I answer. Melodious, soft bells chime from the stairs outside, ringing at each step someone takes. "It can't be her, can it?"

Boudicca places herself between me and the doorway, flaring her great leathery wings wide. I swallow hard. My sweaty palms slicken the leather grip of the sword. A thread of confusion still swirls through my mind, seeking a sense of self.

Ting, chang, ting. The footsteps pause just before the glass window.

"Gargoyle, did you lock that door when you entered?" Arezou gropes over her shoulder, nose wrinkling before she gives up and pulls a dagger from the top of her thigh length boot.

Boudicca shakes her head. "Manticores don't have thumbs."

The three of us stare at the window, breaths stilled. None of us could reach that door before whoever—or whatever—is in the hall can burst through.

"Is there a way out of this room other than the door?" I whisper.

"It's going to take me time to conjure a portal, unless you can?" Arezou moves in some complicated dance, tracing the floor with azure glowing lines.

"Me? I make things. I don't know anything about casting portal magic." I drag my eyes from the mage and squint at the door, willing whatever it is outside to show itself.

"It's beyond dangerous to wander between the worlds and not know how to cast portals. What if you got stuck?" asks Arezou.

"We're about to get stuck if our portal closes," Boudicca mutters. "We came through the library in Paris."

"Ah, the hub of the bōc-hord. That makes sense." Arezou nods to herself, eyes riveted on the glass separating the room from the stairwell. "This isn't your fight. I'll distract her and you should leave through the door as quickly as possible."

A stinging sense of shame prickles my skin. Of course, she's some decorated war mage and I'm just a child playing at adventure. "I'm sorry. I got caught up in the thrill of discovery and I shouldn't expect someone else to bail me out of my thoughtlessness. We'll leave you be. Here's your sword, er wife, whatever. We'll find our own way out." When Arezou doesn't accept the sword, I place it on the ground nearby.

Boudicca glances back at me with concern for the barest of moments. A flash of crimson in the window catches my attention before a hooded figure crosses to the door. The knob turns.

"She's here." The mage stumbles and the blue glow

surrounding her diminishes. She draws a second dagger, longer than the first, and moves into a defensive stance.

"Pick me up!" the sword says, each word echoes as if dropped over a cliff.

I move away from both the sword and the war mage. I'm uncertain who the sword wants, but it's certainly not me. My shoulder bumps against Boudicca's side.

Her wing curls protectively around me. "I'll get us out of this."

Creaking fills the room as the door opens and a slim figure steps through. The stranger lowers her hood. Flowing loose tresses of red hair fall over her shoulders to her waist. A pair of crimson-lensed goggles with small levers on the left side rests over her eyes. It's the woman from the vision. Is she a maker like me?

She looks at a leather cuff covering most of her forearm then presses a few buttons on it. "Arezou, darling, it's been a while. How was your little nap?"

The woman smiles and my soul recoils from the very wrongness in the expression. I can't see her eyes through the goggle lenses, and it makes trying to read her impossible.

"Viola, pick me up!" Roya's panicked shriek cuts through the room.

"Hmph," Sinder rolls her eyes, "she's pushy as ever. I was alerted as soon as your stasis ended. How delightful to see you brought more friends for me to play with."

Arezou glares at Sinder. "Let them go. Your grudge is with me and mine."

Sinder flicks the barest of glances at Boudicca then pauses to study me. "No. I don't think I will."

"You broke our world a thousand years ago," Arezou snarls. "I'll be damned if I let you cross boundaries to break another." She side-eyes me. "Mageling, you're our weakest, wield Roya and we might have a chance."

"Viola, join with me again," Roya pleads.

Rude. I might be the youngest here but that doesn't mean I'm worthless. Remembering the loss of control and her dubious memory I frown. "I can handle myself."

Boudicca's claws scrape the hard stone and her wings flex high enough to brush the ceiling. Eyeing our petite adversary, I'm certain she's no match against the brute strength of a gargoyle, especially since in the past she used wind magic and we're indoors.

But then, wind tickles around the room and doubt gnaws at me. Wind inside?

I reach a hand into my shoulder satchel, feeling through my small collection of mechanical creatures. I already used all my spiders. I don't have anything left except some messenger hawk moths.

Why haven't I created something useful? Even my spiders didn't hold back the manticores for long. Eyeing the sword, I reach toward it. Roya can handle this better than me. Arezou said it herself: I'm the weakest link.

As my hand closes over the hilt, Roya's consciousness flows into me. I relax, trying to settle into the alien feel without flinching away. She didn't hurt me before. This time shouldn't be any worse.

Papers rustle, spilling from a counter. Glass tubes rattle on a metal rack sitting on a nearby table. I brace my feet, enacting my magic slippers to root me firmly to the floor. It's just a little breeze, and there's no sand here. What could she possibly do? The sword raises into a defensive position, moving my body into a stance I've never taken on my own before today.

"Why keep me here all this time?" Arezou circles Sinder, her daggers pointed toward the other woman.

"It amused me to know the two of you were so close but would never be together again. It was a skilled trick, putting Roya's soul in a sword. I'm sure you meant that to be a temporary vessel. Only a monster would put a living, breathing being inside a hunk of steel. Such a greedy little move."

"Shut up," Arezou growls.

"Think of the centuries she spent, slowly going mad, not able to see or hear without using a host. Losing her memories and sense of self until there was nothing left. Like some shadowy parasite, she waited for an unsuspecting fool to pick her up."

"That's enough. It wasn't like that," Roya roars through my mouth.

Sinder shrugs. "Wasn't it? But no matter, if you wish to be together forever, I can arrange that."

Wind blows my hair back as I race toward Sinder at blinding speed. The scent of blood hits the air before I've even registered that I've hit her. Another slash. Sinder parries it with the same bronze vambraces I saw in the vision. The sword skips off the metal and slides up her biceps, cleaving open the skin. Boudicca leaps forward, blocking the slash of Sinder's clawed gauntlets. My body spins, sending a spout of nausea up my throat. The sword twists in my grasp and plunges downward, burying itself in Sinder's thigh.

Sinder's howls reverberate off the low ceiling. Raising one hand, she encapsulates us in a wall of wind. Boudicca grunts in surprise as her movement slows to almost nothing. Her wings fold tight to her torso and her eyes narrow against the onslaught.

Brutal wind pushes me back. One by one, my fingers slip from the blade imbedded in Sinder's flesh. Roya groans in frustration. Even with her help, I'm not built for this. I'm not strong enough. I strain, joints stretching beyond their capabilities before the wind tosses me away like nothing more than a leaf. Boudicca leaps, putting herself between me and the wall to cradle my landing.

I land against her as her wings instantly rise to block the wind. A bright light flashes, and I peek under the thick leathery wing to see Arezou and Sinder locked in combat. With a grimace, Sinder yanks the sword from her thigh. Blood splashes the floor for only a breath before the wound seals.

Arezou's daggers flash with the fury of centuries of entrapment. Sinder snarls as she uses the sword to block the vicious blows, and I wonder if Roya is screaming in her head. That would be some small justice.

Small cuts and larger gashes pepper Sinder's skin but Arezou seems almost untouched. Even the wind isn't getting past her bubble-like shield this time. Arezou stabs one dagger through Sinder's shoulder, using it to drive her to her knee. The winds die down and I sigh with relief as Boudicca sags against the wall with me.

Sinder swipes the blood from her cheek, laughing in her twisted, dark way that makes my skin crawl. "This has been interesting, but it's time for you to join your lover."

Arezou's eyes widen as Sinder jerks forward, sinking Roya's sword deep into Arezou's abdomen. Red flames lick up the blade. Sinder's eyes gleam crimson.

"No! They can't both survive in the sword." Boudicca lunges, knocking the blade from Sinder's hand. Like a statue of ash, Arezou's body crumbles, tiny flecks of it floating away before she tumbles into a heap of dust on the floor.

I race to comprehend what just happened, but Sinder's smug smile says it all.

"You killed her," I whisper.

"Not exactly." Sinder tilts her head up to eye Boudicca warily. "They both live inside the sword now. Well, whichever one has the stronger resolve to survive will live in the sword. The other will fade in time, never to live again. And with the cycle broken, they can't even hope for reincarnation. I really wish I could hear it all. All that blubbering self-sacrifice as they decide who will die for the other. Ah, sweet love."

Boudicca hoists the woman by the neck, slamming her to a nearby wall. Boudicca's skin shines hard like stone as she shifts her form closer to her natural gargoyle state. Black claws dig into the woman's throat as the winds whistle higher.

"Put me down." Sinder grits out.

"Release the mage," Boudicca growls.

"Into what? That pile of ash?" Her maniacal grin doesn't erase the creeping fear in her eyes. She thrashes, kicking at Boudicca's thighs. "Call off your stone minion."

"She's not anyone's to command," I say.

The wind rises to a furious gale, pushing me backward, but Boudicca stands firm. I tumble to the wall, enacting my magical climbing slippers just to hold on.

"Wind doesn't move rock." Boudicca closes her fist around Sinder's neck.

She makes a distressed gurgling noise and then all the wind is focused on me. A flutter of papers hits me first, then a book. I dodge as a rack full of glass tubes smashes against the wall beside me. Ducking behind the table, I reach into my satchel again. The messenger moths! It might work. I pull them out. A dozen. I still have a dozen of the palm-sized mechanical creatures. Normally, I'd only use them to carry a message, but with a little retooling they should do the trick.

When I look up, horror coats me. Red shimmering light covers Boudicca's stone flesh. Her lower body has already reverted to rock.

"How is she hurting you?" I shout over the roaring gale. The master key twists into the body of the moth I hold, locking the commands in place.

"My soul, Viola, she's pulling out my soul."

Her soul. The very essence that Boudicca so recently gained. I won't allow it. I twist the master key into the last moth. Gathering them into my arms, I fling them into the wind. The moths swirl aimlessly, their grey wings fluttering as the wind twirls them relentlessly through the air. Then a soft green light emits from each one. Hope blooms in my heart. The fluttering wings steady and the moths ride the breeze as if they command it. A dozen metal clicks sound as wings beat up and down, channeling the wind to obey a different master. Me. They gather, and the first one lands on Sinder as she struggles free of Boudicca's hardening grasp.

"Hawk moths? Mechanical toys? Is that all you have against me? Me? The destroyer of the empire. Me, a goddess of wind." Sinder snorts.

She tries to flick the moth away, but another lands on her, then another. They lock around her mouth, followed by her hands. The moths still her movements, and with each new insect that lands, the wind dies a little more. The virulent glow on Boudicca begins to fade and her chest rises.

"That's how it is. Where one alone isn't strong enough, many banded together are. It's hard to cast without your voice or your hands, isn't it?" I say.

Another moth lands, this one over the lens covering her

left eye. Sinder shrieks but it's muffled under the soft metallic chirping of my moths.

"Are you ok?" I study Boudicca.

She rubs her thighs and then gives herself a shake that sends her mane tumbling around her shoulders. "Good enough."

"Let's take her and the sword back to Xander. Maybe they can help sort this out. They made the gargoyles after all."

Sinder trembles as the moth closes itself tighter to her mouth and nose. Suddenly, she starts struggling violently again and manages to spit the moth away. "I won't go."

Boudicca swipes at Sinder as she chants out a few harsh sounding words. The air rents besides her and she falls into it.

I blink. "Was that a portal? Did she somehow make a portal?"

Boudicca's warm palm slides against mine. She gives my hand a soft squeeze. "It seemed to be. We don't have a way to follow her. Let's bring the sword and head home before our portal closes. We don't have much time."

I pick up the sword, expecting two voices to fill my head. But the silence sounds like a death toll.

BOUDICCA STANDS PANTING BEFORE THE ARCH OF twining morning glories. She's passed through this gate numerous times with no success. The portal back to our home world has closed, and now all that remains is an arch of pretty flowers.

The delicate magenta and purple blooms sway with

Boudicca's next passing. Her muscles strain against her skin. "We can't get back this way."

I frown. We have no way to contact Xander. I used every messenger moth to silence Sinder from casting. "Maybe there's another portal in this garden if we search?"

Her mane tousles as she shakes her head. "I could see them if they were there. None are nearby. Is the sword still silent?"

I grip the hilt a little tighter. The wrapped leather presses warm to my flesh. "Roya, can you hear us? We really need some help."

The faintest stir, like a ripple in a river eddy tickles over my thoughts. Her voice echoes as if from the bottom of a deep well.

It hurts.

I tremble. "I can hear Roya."

There's not enough room in here and she's in so much pain. Can you get me out? Or can your teacher? We can't last long in here together.

I gnaw my lip, desperation growing. Xander taught me how to breathe life into a created creature. I've made small animals, but they all have programmed tasks. Instincts. None have shown the ability to think on their own like Xander's gargoyles do.

"Can she help?" Boudicca asks.

"They're dying, and in pain. She's asking me to move her soul. Can you do that?" But even as I ask, I know Boudicca can't. She's a warrior. Her elder sister gargoyle is the only one I've seen wield magic. But despair makes fools of us all.

"No," she says thoughtfully. "But if we found a proper vessel, you could try. From how Xander explained my creation, it's not so very different. We need to find an object created with love and attention. Something someone poured their heart into."

I gnaw my lip. "I don't know how."

I can help you, mageling, Arezou's weak voice threads through my mind. *The ability is locked within you. But you've already started to tease that magic open with your mechanical beings. You're greater than you give yourself credit for. Will you let me work through you?*

I swallow hard. It was one thing to swing a sword, but to have another being channel power through me is a little terrifying. All she needs is a body. What if they decide mine is roomy enough for two?

"She's asking to cast through you?" Boudicca closes her arms around me, and I rest my cheek on her comforting breast as I have so many times in my life. "That's dangerous. We can wander until we find a way back."

"I know." I nuzzle deeper into her chest, breathing her warm, earthy scent. "But we can't leave them like this, to fade into nothing with no way for their souls to move on."

"I'll support any decision you make. But in my heart, your life comes first. I'll break that sword before I let it hurt you." Her rumbling little growl makes me smile. She's warning the mages. I know Boudicca would go to the ends of the earth for me.

I direct my thoughts to the sword. "Arezou, what do you need me to do?"

I only have enough strength to portal us to my home. My true home not that illusionary jail Sinder left us in. There's enough information in my study for you to learn from there.

"Can't you open a portal to my world? I'm certain Xander could help you better than I can. I'm only an apprentice. My creations are insignificant." I hate the whine in my voice, the pleading. But it's uncontrollably there.

Nonsense. They knew what they were doing when they chose you as an apprentice. I need an anchor to where I can portal. So unfortunately, I can't travel to your home.

"She's taking us back to her home." I report to Boudicca.

Boudicca's lips pull so tight the spikes on her jaw flex. "I see. Well, then let's get to it."

Just relax.

Sword in one hand and my gargoyle's warm palm in the other, I take a deep breath and close my eyes. A brief discordance sweeps over me as the two souls trapped in the sword seem to struggle—or argue. Roya presses against my thoughts, the solid, stern presence unrelenting in my mind. She wants vengeance. The feeling begins to dissipate as Arezou's magic flows through my veins.

No. Not Arezou's. Mine. She's directing what's already inside me. Opening doors within me for which I don't yet have the key. I marvel at the tingling, glowing feel of magic running through my veins. Visions of home—her home— flash through my mind, but the feeling attached to it reminds me of my beloved Tower of Wind, my home.

With her guiding me, I raise my hands and trace symbols in the air. The space before us trembles like a heat wave on a summer road before tearing open to show a room much like the one where we first found Arezou. This one is larger, though, and with more clutter. Pale pink orbs sit on pedestals inset into one wall. Scrolls and books sprawl across a long desk tucked against the far wall. Racks of glass tubes line the table. Unlike the illusionary room, this one has great arching windows along one wall which overlook dunes of white sand. Roya's sigh of contentment at seeing her homeland again fills me.

Stop gawking and step through. I can't hold this open long, Arezou strains.

I tug Boudicca with me as I step through the wavering portal. She ducks, tucking her wings tight to her back. With a snap of light, the portal closes, leaving us standing in the mage's study. It's hot, and the dry air swirling in from the arched windows does little to cool the room.

"What now?" I ask.

My workshop is through the bronze door. The suite I shared with Roya is down the stairs to your left. The pink orbs are knowledge stones. Rest your hand on one to peruse it. It's like a library.

Boudicca moves ahead of me, looking for danger. She opens one door, and through it, a bed draped in translucent white cloth sits. A curved wall of open arches leads to a garden set with smooth stepping stones.

I move toward the bronze door, but she brushes past me, her thick tail rasping against the polished marble floor. "Allow me. Just in case there is something unsavory."

I nod. I've seen enough blood today to last the rest of my life.

The door swings open on silent hinges. Boudicca pauses, her large frame completely filling the doorway so I can't see past.

She gasps, and I'm uncertain if it's in wonder or horror. "It looks like an army of stone."

I peek around Boudicca's side. At first, it appears the workshop is littered with multicolored, carved chunks of crystals. A dizzying array of amethyst, rose quartz, chalcedony, and gypsum shine in the low light of violet mage globes. Looking closer, I realize most of these are carved body parts. Legs, arms, heads—even wings—lie on tables. Full mannequin-like bodies lean along the wall three-deep in some places. The sight is both wondrous and creepy. I understand Boudicca's gasp.

"Did this experiment work?" I ask.

No. None of the war mages involved with the experiment were ever able to project themselves into the constructs for more than a few minutes. And now, I'm the only one left.

I walk to the main table and mutter the spell Xander taught me to see threads of magic so I can examine how Arezou made the pieces. Some of them are rough-hewn, looking like the stone golems of fairy tales. Others are long-legged and slim crystalline creatures resembling the fey. As I move across the room, the crystalline bodies become finer and more precise. Instead of smooth orbs, lifelike features are carved onto the heads.

I got close a few times. The body in the case at the far end of the room was meant to be my crystalla. But an hour was the longest I was ever able to inhabit it before the pain grew so great that I was tossed back into my body.

"Your body?" I ask as I move to the case. Inside, rests a crystal warrior—its gleaming face carved in a mirror image of Arezou. Light refracts through the body, creating tiny, scattered rainbows along the wall. I open the case door and touch the creation. Arezou carved it every bit as beautifully as one of Xander's gargoyles, and with as much care.

When Roya died, I tried to transfer her soul into the crystalla but none of these accepted her. I was in the process of making one in her image when Sinder's minions attacked. I don't recall anything else until you woke me.

"Where's the one you intended for Roya?"

The table to your left, but she's incomplete.

A head carved of sardonyx gemstone rests atop a completed torso. One orange and rust striped arm cradles the head while the other lies unattached on the ground beside the table. I pick it up, examining how carefully she carved the fingers, right down to the lines of the palm.

It's me. Roya speaks for the first time in hours, her voice distant and soft. *She even carved the callouses left by my sword.*

How could I not? I missed you intensely. Arezou's voice is much stronger but still strained. *Hang on, love. Don't fade. We can beat this together.*

"Boudicca, can you help me with this?" I run my hand over the black striped legs laying near the torso. They appear to have a ball joint carving to fit into the hips.

She looks at the legs then lifts one heavy stone piece and fits it into the body. With utmost care, she does the same with the next. "This is lovely carving. You did a beautiful sculpture of her, Arezou."

The praise brings a warm flutter to my chest that I'm certain belongs to the mage. I line up the joint on an arm the press it into the socket.

"This isn't so very different from breathing purpose into your created creatures," Boudicca says as she studies the magic which hovers just under the surface of the stone. "It's worth a try."

I straighten the arm and frown. "If I screw this up, they'll end up as ghosts. Or disintegrate completely."

We'll perish if you don't do anything. It'll just be a different kind of death, Roya says.

Arezou's wispy voice adds, *Maybe you'll succeed where I failed.*

I straighten my shoulders. "Let's begin, then."

SWEAT ROLLS DOWN MY FOREHEAD AS I TEASE THE magic encapsulating Roya's soul away from its steel casing. She insisted on going first so I would "have some experience" when I worked on Arezou. It's been hours and there's not been much Boudicca could do. She found fresh water and some apples from the garden, which I was more than grateful for.

The last thread of Roya's soul releases from the sword. Carefully, I cradle the substance in my magic then feed it into the open mouth of the crystalla. Boudicca hovers over the worktable, watching intently. Nothing of the construct moves and I'm unsure if I need to somehow root the soul within or say some sort of spell. With the creatures I've made, I've simply breathed a part of myself into it.

That's a good thought. Let me kiss her, Arezou says.

"This isn't a fairy tale." The idea is preposterous, especially since she'll be using my lips.

I'm serious. You're right, thinking the creator needs to give something of themselves to the created. Let it be me.

Boudicca eyes me.

"This is about to get weird." I lean over the stone construct even as Arezou's magic flows through my veins.

"Even time cannot hold us apart, my love," Arezou says before she presses her lips on Roya's cool stone ones.

Light spreads through crystalline body. Limbs twitch and her chest rises. I watch as the striped stone shimmers to life and the crystalla that holds Roya's soul sits on the table.

Roya looks at me with night-dark eyes. "I remember it all." She looks at the crystalla on the next table. "Please get my wife out of my sword."

AREZOU RAISES ONE HAND NEAR THE ARCH OF MORNING glories and the portal to Boudicca and my home reopens. Moonlight shines through Arezou's transparent body,

453

refracting tiny rainbows of light around us. Beside her, Roya leans against a marble column. Her black and rust striped skin is covered now with bronze armor. Her wife told her they no longer had need of such things, but the war mage insisted that old habits die hard and she wasn't about to galivant about naked.

"There you are. That portal should take you back to your world," Arezou says.

"Are you certain you don't want to come with us?" I look between the two mages. There's so much I could learn from them, and I'm certain Xander would find it all absolutely fascinating.

"You'd fit in at the Tower of Wind," Boudicca teases. "Most of its residents are made of stone."

"As kind as your offer is, we have a criminal to track down." Roya traces a thumb over her sword's pommel. "You did well, Viola. I'd be proud to call you sister."

Warmth spreads through me. "Thank you."

"Take this token. If you need us, call our names into it with intent and we'll be able to use it as a focus and find your world." Arezou hands me a small silver coin.

"Thank you," I say again, stepping one foot through the portal. Boudicca is already through standing amongst the grape trellises looking impatient. "Will we see you again?"

"You can be sure of it." Roya's cocksure grin is the last thing I see as the portal closes.

We stand on the stone balcony connected to a second story office above the Mazarine Library. I take a deep breath and hearing the normal evening noises of Paris below, my shoulders unglue themselves from my ears.

Boudicca takes me into her arms and launches herself into the sky toward our home. "There were a few times I thought I'd lose you during that adventure."

Wisps of clouds race by us and I laugh. "Well, now I know how to move my soul to a stone body when I die, so I guess you're stuck with me."

"Hmpf. I like you soft. Let's keep you that way as long as we can."

I snuggle into her chest as the stars shine above in the night sky. I'm learning so much so fast. There's plenty of time to plan for forever with Boudicca. "Deal."

About the Author

Evelyn Shine (she/her) is a queer author of fantasy romance books for readers who enjoy steamy myths and swoony fairy tales infused with adventure. Her sapphic debut novel, *The Librarian's Gargoyle,* is a finalist for the GCLS Goldie Awards and was recognized by The Lesbian Review as one of their top books in 2024. Evelyn's stories all share common threads of magic, love, heart, and action. Find her updates at: beacons.ai/evelynshine

The Heart is an Inferno
Anna Burke

I ROLLED INTO THE SETTLEMENT ON THE TWENTY-seventh of Draconia, the month of dragons. It was the last place I wanted to be, but my mother had made it very clear that *all* her children were expected to return for the celebration of her matriarchy and the passing of my grandmother, so there I was, standing outside the bunker I'd once called home, the shifting ash fields blowing in my face past the plex of my helmet, hating the gray horizon.

This place sucked. Always had. Why anyone would live here instead of a green planet or, hell, even a space station, was beyond me. I'd gotten out of here as fast as I could, and as far as I could tell, not a single soul missed me. Not even my mother. That didn't mean I was exempt from paying my dues. I'd come to kiss the ring, and I'd be on my way as fast as the Drakkan winds allowed.

Drak, homeworld of my people, offered little in the way of hospitality. I stood in the security alcove outside the front door—an obscenely thick sheet of metal covered in studs—watching the sky and waiting for someone to buzz me into the damn complex. The security alcove wouldn't protect me if trouble came sniffing. Shifting clouds of ash obscured everything more than a hundred feet away, but I could feel them. I'd always been able to feel them, there at the edges, riding the Drakkan currents with their fiberglass-light bones and rippling wings: dragons.

I pressed the button again. Like hell was I going to be a snack.

The door hatch swung open into the airlock and I stumbled inside, hauling my things with me. I didn't have much —just a bag with some clothes and supplies. And my sword. Real Drakkan steel with a diamond edge the width of an atom, capable of cleaving through just about anything, even a dragon. Three feet of rippling beauty. I may have been off Drak for ten years, but I still had my sword.

I chose not to think about why.

Seeing my mother was going to be...fun. I was looking forward to it the way I looked forward to a lungful of ash, or maybe cancer.

The only person I wanted to see less than my mother was the woman standing on the other side of the door. A sneer decorated her devastating face.

"Linna." Her name wasn't the first word I wanted leaving my lips as I pulled off my helmet, ash settling down around my feet in eddies and whirls as the vents sucked the air clean, so I added, "Fuck."

"Makesha." Her sneer deepened into a malign smile. I catalogued the changes since I'd last seen her, looking for something new to hate. Her black hair still fell around her face in a straight curtain, dyed here and there with strands of gold, as was the Drakkan style. The gold flecks brought out the hazel of her eyes, and the warmth of her light brown skin contrasted with the charcoal of her long bangs. They fell a little over her eyes. My fingers twitched. Once upon a time, I'd tucked those strands behind her ears, smoothing away the errant whisps.

That was before I left, fucking everything up.

"The prodigal daughter returns," said Linna. "Your mother will be thrilled."

"My mother can choke on an egg."

"You're late, did you know?" She tilted her head, causing her hair to fall in a lush wave. Stars below, though, she was gorgeous. Regret wasn't something I could afford to feel, however, so I focused on the memory of her scathing rejection. It helped.

"I don't control the shuttle schedule."

"You waited till the last possible shuttle."

"I'd love to get out of my suit, don't suppose you could move?" I put as much scorn into my voice as I could, and she slammed her hand against the airlock door, granting us access to the suit locker. "Why are you here, anyway? This is a family affair."

Her smile cut sharper than my sword. "Didn't you know? I'm marrying Nikki."

It felt like the full brunt of a Drakkan gale hitting me in the chest, and I hid my hiss of breath beneath a curse as I fumbled with the straps of my suit. Linna watched me struggle.

"Nikki's a dick." And my brother.

"Nikki *stayed*."

I deserved that, but wasn't about to let her know. The buckle on my chest was plugged with ash and grease and my fingers stumbled over the familiar steps. With a curse of her own, Linna stepped forward and did the work for me. I contemplated immolation. Of all the things that could have gone wrong with a visit home, this was by far the worst. I hadn't expected to see Linna. *Not* seeing Linna was, in fact, a condition of my return, and now she was marrying my brother.

I'd be nursing this new wound for years. Fucking Drakka. I should have stayed away and burned all family ties, or begged off on the grounds of a mortal injury of some sort. I'd have gladly given myself one. Anything to avoid this.

The smell of her washed over me as she undid the buckles of my suit, standing close enough for the scent of marrekan blossoms and honey to suffuse my senses. I closed my eyes and allowed myself one moment to imagine a different kind of homecoming, then snapped them open to find Linna staring at me with a cruel and knowing look in her hazel eyes. I deserved that, too.

"Where's my mother?"

"In the hall. I'll take you."

"I can escort myself."

"Your mother asked me to, so, no." She spun on her heel, dressed in the stiff black jacket and formfitting pants I would also be expected to change into for the ceremony.

That had been my plan: arrive just in time for my mother's ascension and leave again as soon as I could, barring shuttle cancelations, which I'd forgotten happened with startling regularity. So far so good, minus the Linna of it all.

We fell into step as we walked down a dark hallway lit with sputtering electric sconces. My eyes traced the pipes on the ceiling like they'd done when I was younger, hating the monochrome palette of the place. Blacks and grays and golds. Off-world, people occasionally mimicked the Drakkan aesthetic. I'd seen it in high fashion publications once or twice, and it always made me shudder. Linna, of course, pulled it off. I looked like a sallow idiot with my fairer skin and white blond hair.

"Walk faster, Makesha."

Mother sat in state in the great hall with its gray walls and black and gold banners. The walk down the aisle to pay my respects was lined with the milling crowd of my relatives, all of whom looked at me coldly. My siblings stood closer to the dais, no doubt angling for succession now that Grandmother was dead. I hated them all.

Off-worlders were often confused about why we didn't hold funerals for dead matriarchs or patriarchs. The answer was complicated, but it boiled down to practicality; on Drak, someone needed to hold the reins of power tightly at all times. There were too many winged predators for political indecision.

"Mother," I said, kneeling with my sword scraping the cold concrete in its sheath on my back.

"Makesha. You're late."

"So I've been informed." I sensed rather than heard Linna's satisfied amusement and almost risked a glance to where she stood, wishing I couldn't still see her clear as a green planet's day in my mind's eye.

"Change and attend."

"Yes, mother."

I rose and descended the steps, meeting eyes with who else but Nikki, my eldest brother and possible future patriarch. Wet, hot hatred boiled up my throat. Nikki was the perfect son, steadfast, attentive to his mother's whims, and more than willing to rat on his younger siblings or deliver a punitive blow on mother's behalf. He'd never liked me, and I'd always despised him. That was all before I'd found out he was to marry Linna. Now, uncharitably, I wanted him dead. His smile suggested he was well aware of this, and he held out his arm in greeting. I clasped it too tightly. He squeezed back, and we took each other's measure in bruises.

"Funny what happens when you fuck off for a decade," he said.

"Enjoy my sloppy seconds, Nik." No point beating around the drakka bush. "You'll never satisfy her."

"Sounds like you didn't either, or she would have left with you."

"Fuck you know about it."

"I know more than you think, Makesha. You've been gone a long time."

"Not long enough."

Linna took her place by his side just then, shooting what was probably supposed to be a quelling look in my direction, but I was anything but quelled. Fuck them both. I shrugged as if none of this bothered me and started for the bathroom, where I could change into the dress clothes I'd had shipped to me rather than risk returning home early for a fitting, and didn't let my guard down till that door was shut behind me.

The gray walls and long mirror mocked me as I leaned against the sink, glaring at my reflection.

Fuck.

I fought a sudden and humiliating urge to cry. I would not cry over Linna. Not again. She'd made her feelings clear to me when I'd begged her to leave this shithole and she'd chosen her family over me, which I wouldn't have faulted her for if her family wasn't as shitty as mine—shittier, really. Maybe she'd felt like she didn't deserve to get away. Obviously some part of her thought she deserved shit. She was marrying Nikki.

Unless, of course, she'd chosen him to spite me? No.

Not even I was that egotistical. Just because nobody would have hurt more didn't mean it was calculated. Maybe Nikki had depths he'd never showed me.

I doubted it.

I pulled my clothes out of my bag, grateful for the magnetic tech that prevented wrinkles, and stripped out of my travel wear and into the dress uniform of my house. It was just as uncomfortable as I remembered and gave my lanky frame a boxy look I hated. At least my boots were still tough Drakkan boots, and I'd even managed to polish out most of the scuffs. Dragonhide made the toughest leather in the galaxy.

I combed back my short hair, lined my eyes with ashy kohl, as was required, and, sword on my back as a reminder to my house that I could still kick their asses, left my satchel in a corner and slammed the door behind me.

Linna waited on the other side.

"You following me?"

She pushed me up against the door with her hands on my shoulders and glared. Nobody could see us, here. The bathroom was in the entranceway outside the great hall, and the doors to that hallowed chamber had slammed shut behind me. My heartbeat stuttered.

"What did you say to Nikki?"

"I think you heard me."

"You had no right. No fucking right." Her eyes blazed a deep hazel-green.

"Not wrong, though."

"When did you become such an asshole, Kesha?"

"When you fucking left me." *Shit.* Wrong thing to say, but her use of my old nickname twisted like a knife in the ribs.

"When *I* left *you*?" Her voice rose incredulously. "No,

you know what? I'm not doing this with you. *You* left Drak. *You* left *me*. *You* have no idea what satisfies me. Not anymore."

My eyes slid to her lips and color flushed her cheeks.

"Don't, Kesha. Just—Don't."

"Okay." My voice softened despite my best efforts. There was real pain in her voice, and that I couldn't bear.

"Good."

Her hands remained on my shoulders. They were still there when the alarm blared and the firewall doors to the great hall slammed shut, trapping us on the other side. We froze instinctively. Only one thing triggered the firewalls on Drak.

Dragons.

THE EMERGENCY LIGHTS TURNED THE HALLWAY A sickly orange. I pushed Linna behind me slowly, wary of sudden movements, and drew my sword.

"Which entrance do you think it broke through?" I whispered.

"There are only three options."

"Well," I said, pressing her back against the wall for safety while orange light glittered like fire along the edge of my blade, "seeing as we're in one, I don't love those odds."

Nothing stood between us and the airlock except the suit locker and a conventional door, and that wasn't going to last long against dragonfire.

"We need to find you something to fight with."

"Did you bring anything?"

"I—shit, yes, actually. In the bathroom." I edged us along the wall until my hand hit the handle for the bathroom door. As it clicked, something bellowed close by and the sound of wrenching metal rent the air. We ducked inside and I dove for my satchel, fishing inside for the long, light ceremonial dancing knives I carried with me everywhere. "You've used these before, right?"

She narrowed her eyes and snatched them out of my hands, drawing the blades and discarding the battered sheaths. They looked as natural in her hands as ever.

"Stop it."

"Stop what?" What had I done now?

"You don't get to look at me like that."

"Like what?"

"Like you care."

"Fine," I snapped, looking around the bathroom. This wasn't where we wanted to make our last stand. "There's three hundred feet of hallway between us and the suit locker, which the fucker is currently shredding. We have no way to reinforce this door and it's a dead end. One breath of fire—"

"There's no cover outside."

"True, but—"

"We could catch it by surprise if it pokes its head in here." She pointed at my longsword with her knife meaningfully. Decapitating the creature before it could fry us wasn't a bad idea. I still didn't love the risk of ending my life in a fiery ball of death, with Linna of all people.

On the other hand, things with her had already ended in a fiery ball of death once, at least emotionally. Maybe this was what I got for coming home.

"We need to switch places, then."

She crossed quickly in front of the door to my side, eyes darting at the gap between floor and door as if smoke might curl underneath it at any moment.

"Linna." I clasped her arm before making the opposite journey. "If anything happens to me, get—"

"What are you trying to do, play hero?" She snatched her arm away. "Heroes don't fuck off for ten years without a word."

"You said you didn't *want* to hear from me."

"Stars below, you're such an idiot."

I crossed the door and glared at her. Maybe I was an idiot, but she had no right to point it out.

"I asked you to come." Probably the wrong thing to point out, too.

"Like hell you—"

She cut herself off and I immediately understood why. Something clinked outside the door. Dragon scales. An organic, heat resistant crystal that always gave away their presence. Of course, if you were close enough to hear them, you were already dead. We held our breaths in unison, eyes locked together. The tension radiating between us was different than the sort characterizing our argument. This was preparation.

Once, another lifetime ago, Linna and I danced the drakka every year at the tournaments. My muscles remembered the moves my mother drilled into all her children from the time they could walk. The drakka was a ceremonial dance, yes, but a necessary one; the leading cause of death on Drak was dragons. If we could still move together we stood a chance.

A shadow slid in front of the door, eclipsing the strip of light at the bottom. My hands tensed on the hilt of my sword and I eased deeper into a crouch. There was no way it couldn't smell us this close. Linna knew it too. Her jaw set. I could see the muscles twitching in my peripheral vision, but I didn't break her gaze. There were worse last things to see before I died.

Her words tumbled in my head like riverstones. *Like hell you*—Like hell I what? I'd asked her to come with me. I'd begged her on my fucking knees to come, and she'd said no. She'd been crying when she said it, but she'd still said it, and so I left. Alone. These were facts.

I mouthed, *I did ask you* while we waited for death.

I was pretty sure the response I got was *Shut up*, but lipreading was difficult in dim lighting.

Something slammed into the door with a whipcrack and a sound like shattering glass. The bathroom door swung inward, and Linna only barely leapt back in time to avoid getting crushed.

The motherfucker had used its tail. Now its head whipped round, but instead of poking it inside to investigate, it reared back, long sinuous body filling the hallway, wings pressed tightly to its sides, and waited.

None of us moved. The door swung on bent hinges, stuck open. At least it shielded Linna. If the dragon suspected something was in here, though, it might torch the place. Dragons cooked their food. Easier to pick snacks out of the ashes than to chase down living prey. There was an enzyme component, too, but that never interested me as much as the practical aspects of survival. I hoped I gave it indigestion.

Low booms sounded from the dragon's chest.

Fuck.

It *was* going to torch the place. We were dead. *Linna* was dead.

I dove forward into a roll out the door, leaping to my feet and thrusting with my blade at the finish. The dragon flinched back just in time, and, just like that, I'd lost the element of surprise.

"Makesha!"

Linna. The dragon's head snapped away from me and back toward the open doorway, where Linna crouched with her knives—the ones I'd stolen from her bedside ten years ago, unable to leave without some part of her, and had carried with me every day since.

"Jump," I shouted as the dragon lunged forward. She leapt back behind the door. All I saw of her was the slash of her knives as the dragon pushed its jaws in for the kill. It recoiled, and by then I had lunged myself, driving the blade into—

Air. I'd forgotten how fast they could move.

Scales glinted in the horrible orange glow. I couldn't tell what was fire flushing and what was the reflection of the damn emergency lights, which was a serious security flaw.

"Your right," shouted Linna. I ducked a glancing blow from the tail, avoiding death for the small price of a sliced deltoid.

"I know I'm right." I twisted her words deliberately.

"What?"

"I asked you."

"Makesha," she said, waiting for the dragon to test the entrance again, "you said you were leaving *with or without me.*"

I dealt a glancing blow of my own to the creature's shoulder. It shrieked and pressed back into the hallway, coiling in on itself. Our backs were now to the airlock. Stars below, I hoped there was just the one.

"That's asking!"

Linna edged around the doorframe and stood on the

opposite side of the hallway. "It's a shitty way of doing it, then!"

"I was dying here."

"You were just bored, Kesha."

We sprang forward together as the dragon surged forward, taking advantage of its miscalculation to slash at its neck. It slammed its head into the ceiling, raining down crystal scales, and recoiled with a snarl.

"*Bored?* My family hated me."

She huffed. "Because you hate it here."

"What's to like?" I said, staring at the dragon. It stared back out of glittering azure eyes.

"You could have tried. For my sake."

"That's rich." The dragon snapped at Linna, who deflected it with her knives. "I did try. I tried for years."

"Picking fights with everyone who loves you isn't trying! Fuck! Run!"

She was right. The booms started up again.

"Airlock." I raced toward it, grabbing her arm. "And you didn't have to marry my brother."

"We're not married. Yet."

"Oh good, there's still time for my invitation to arrive, then."

"Fuck you."

Our feet pounded down the hallway. The airlock was too far. We wouldn't make it. I leapt over the debris of the suit locker and flung myself against the wall. Linna did the same.

"Anyone but him."

Flames roared past us, deafening, and I prayed it had drowned out my words. Those couldn't be the last I said to her. In the ensuing silence, the sound of suits crackling and melting punctuated Linna's next words.

"You weren't willing to wait."

Wait?

"Wait for what? Things weren't going to change," I said, listening for the sound of the dragon's approach. Ahead lay the airlock—open and undamaged. Some fucktwat hadn't shut it. Protocol drilled and drilled the importance of security. No Drakkan in their right mind would leave a door unlocked.

Shit.

We'd been the last ones to use it. I'd been too surprised to think about protocol at the time. Linna, though, was usually meticulous. What had she been thinking?

Oh.

She was right—I was such an idiot. She'd been just as shaken to see me, even with the advantage of foresight, as I'd been to see her. I still messed her up.

"We need to get—" I began, but Linna was already running, this time grabbing me. I sprinted after and we threw ourselves into the airlock just in time to slam the door shut and lock it. The inside door wouldn't hold forever, but it bought us time.

"What do you mean I wasn't willing to wait?"

She laughed. "You left that same night. You gave me no time to think about anything, which I guess I should thank you for."

"Why's that?"

"For showing me how easy I was for you to leave behind."

I lowered my blade and gaped at her. "Easy? You broke my fucking heart."

Her eyes were glued to the door, but at that they slid to me, narrowed and dangerous. I didn't dare blink.

"Then you broke it yourself."

A heavy thud shook the airlock. I felt a similar kick against my breastbone. "We need a plan."

I hadn't had a plan, ten years ago. I'd waited until it felt like if I didn't leave home that very second I would crawl out of my skin, claw out my eyes and shred my scalp. It felt like dying. I'd tried to fight it for so long that when I snapped, I knew I had to leave immediately or it would end me in some way I couldn't yet see. I'd wanted Linna to come with me, too, but no—I hadn't waited. I couldn't.

"Fourth movement of the dragon empress's ballet," said Linna. "Do you remember?"

Like breathing.

I nodded. It could work.

The metal before us glowed with heat. Linna pressed *open* on the outside hatch door, then realized it was jammed half-shut and warped beyond repair. Flames would get out, though, instead of filling the space to incinerate us. It would do. We stepped back in unison—the first steps of the drakka.

She was gorgeous at my side. The emergency glow caught in the gold of her hair, which was lit, too, by the gray skies of the surface beyond. She looked like she wore a veil of flame.

A gust of ash blew in as the door exploded. Hot metal beaded on my clothing, burning through to the skin beneath in more places than anything made on Drak should allow. That's what I got for ordering off world. Linna flinched, too, but she'd shielded her face in time, as had I, and wasn't doubled over in mortal agony. Anything less was survivable—unlike the dragon.

It shot forward, and we spun, my sword audibly cutting the air in time to the swish of her knives, and raked long gouges down the dragon's neck. It screamed. We leapt. When it snapped its head around, the jaws closed on nothing but air. To move as one, synchronous, as aware of Linna as I was of my own body—nothing the dragon could do to me could take that away, even death.

Linna.

Linna, who'd wanted me to wait.

I dove for its belly; Linna moved to hamstring it, nearly succeeding before the wings flexed, missing me by millimeters, and threw her against the wall. Every vital organ in my body flew with her.

"Linna!"

I saw the tail flashing toward me but couldn't move. I'd just realized what Linna had been telling me.

"Don't, Kesha. Just don't."

"You don't get to look at me like that."

She was right. I was such an idiot.

I slid beneath the dragon, snaking my blade along its belly as the tail smashed into my leg, rearranging my knee. Scales hit the ground in a scatter of plinks along with the unmistakable hiss of dragon blood boiling on concrete. We'd be engulfed in flames any minute now.

Linna lay stunned, her knives scattered, blood dripping from a wound on her head.

"Linna, stars, Linna stay with me." I gathered her into my arms and smoothed her bangs back from her forehead to get a better view of the wound. Shallow, thank the stars, but she probably had a concussion.

"I'm fine." Her voice had never sounded so beautiful.

"You are not fine. None of this is fine. Lin, I—"

Instinctively I looked up to make sure the dragon wasn't about to toast us. It had crawled back into the tunnel, nursing its wound. I hoped the wound was deep. Fatal. I hoped it was as scared as I felt right now, looking down at the only good thing to come out of Drak, the only thing that had ever really mattered to me.

I stood, helping her to her feet and using my sword as a crutch. I needed to get her under some kind of cover, and the only thing available was the slim bit of wall between the airlock door. I rested her against it, pressing myself close out of necessity and the fear, irrational and all-encompassing, that she'd somehow vanish from my arms.

She looked up at me with those gold flecked eyes, a perfect child of Drak, and the pain I saw there looked a hell of a lot like the nightmares that had plagued me since leaving.

"Don't marry Nikki," I said, voice breaking.

"He loves me."

The dragon whined and thrashed.

"Dammit, Linna, not as much as I do."

"Don't say that to me." Blood dripped down her cheek. I wiped it away. "Don't say it unless you mean it."

My hand, red with her blood, traced her cheek. She leaned into the touch with a quiet desperation.

There was nothing for it. I tilted her chin up to my lips and kissed her, blood in my mouth, the taste of her the only thing that had ever felt like home. She whimpered, her hands fisting in my jacket and pulling me closer, closer, closer—

"I'll stay, if that's what you want," I panted when we broke apart to breathe the ashy air. "Whatever you want, Linna."

"Ten years. You didn't write me for ten years." Tears streamed down her face and her eyes were green, now, changeable as an ash storm.

"And it's the worst thing I've ever done."

Her laughter hiccupped, and I kissed her again.

"There's been no one else," I confessed. "No one like you. Please, Linna."

I wanted to say her name until it ceased to sound like words, the way the Drakkan wind howled until one forgot the sound of silence.

"Nikki—"

"I don't care. He'll live. I won't."

A small smile edged its way onto her perfect mouth. "Always so dramatic."

"Marry me instead."

She raised an eyebrow, but her cheeks flushed even in the orange light. "I barely know you anymore."

"Then date me. Anything. I can't—Linna, I'm so fucking sorry for leaving."

Her whole face changed. I'd finally said the right words, ten years too late, and I prayed to the stars it was enough.

"We're probably going to die anyway."

"Not yet." I kissed her forehead, her cheeks, her eyelids. "Please. My knee is maybe broken, else I'd kneel—"

"You don't have to kneel, asshole."

"I want to."

"Would you really stay?"

I thought about this because I owed her that much; I couldn't make her a false promise. Staying on Drak would test my fortitude in ways I wasn't sure I could bear, but if I had Linna... I was older now. I could survive my family.

"I would."

"Then ask me to come with you."

A hope so bright and bitter it soured my mouth rose from my chest to choke me. I couldn't speak. The dragon screamed again. Maybe it was really dying. I'd have to find out, soon, but not yet.

"Come with me. Come to a green world, get out of this

ash. I want to see you beneath a blue sky, Linna. There's so much I could show you, that we could explore together. But we can come back here whenever you want, I—"

"Fuck this place," she said fiercely, taking my jaw in her hand and pulling my mouth to hers. I slammed into her, kissing her like I'd failed to do before, kissing her like she deserved to be kissed: with everything I had.

"You'll come?" I had to be sure.

She smiled her dark, brilliant smile. "I'll come, Makesha."

"Good." My hand had found her hip and I stroked the curve of bone. "Stay here."

"What? I just said— Where are you going?"

I stepped back from her and adjusted my grip on my sword, testing my knee.

"To kill a dragon for you."

"Wait."

I waited, gesturing at the glowing remains of the door and the menace beyond. Linna reached up and slammed a lever, springing free the emergency suits hanging behind a gray panel. I'd forgotten about those entirely.

"What are you—"

"Put this on." She tossed one at me. "And leave the dragon for your mother. Let's get the hell off this fucking world."

About the Author

Anna Burke (she/her) lives in Massachusetts with her wife and their assorted animal friends. She is the award-winning author of the Compass Rose series, the Seal Cove Romance series, and several fairy tale retellings. Her most recent work is In the Roses of Pieria. When she isn't writing, she can usually be found walking in the woods, teaching creative writing, or drinking too much tea, which she prefers hot and strong—just like her protagonists.

www.ingramcontent.com/pod-product-compliance
Lightning Source LLC
Chambersburg PA
CBHW030918120726
47906CB00002B/390